CONTAMINATION

A NOVEL

CONTAMINATION

A NOVEL

CHAPMAN PINCHER

SIDGWICK & JACKSON

LONDON

First published in Great Britain in 1989 by
Sidgwick & Jackson Limited

Copyright © Chapman Pincher 1989

ISBN 0–283–99945–4

Typeset by Rowland Phototypesetting Limited
Bury St Edmunds, Suffolk
Printed in Great Britain by
Billing and Sons Limited, Worcester
for Sidgwick & Jackson Limited
1 Tavistock Chambers, Bloomsbury Way
London WC1A 2SG

A 'willie' is someone who carries out an intelligence task without being aware of it.

A 'dangle' is the presentation of a tempting opportunity to an adversary intelligence service in such a way that it will be accepted, to the adversary's detriment and without his being aware that the offer is deliberate.

CIA tradecraft definitions.

To Peter and Ann Hutley for so many years of warm
friendship

Acknowledgements

For assisting me in making this work of fiction as true to life as possible, I have to record my debt to senior officials, past and present, in the Secret Intelligence Service (MI6), the Security Service (MI5), Defence Intelligence, the Foreign Office, the US Central Intelligence Agency, the Federal Bureau of Investigation, the Pentagon and to certain former members of the Soviet Intelligence services, the KGB and the GRU. I am also indebted to certain former Ministers of the Crown and to former senior members of the Civil Service.

Chapter One

Lacerated by guilt, embittered by injustice and in no mood to continue with her research that day, or maybe on any other, Dr Wendy Payne needed to distance herself from her laboratory at Porton and its high-security confines. An autumnal mist, beginning to rise from Salisbury Plain, offered her an excuse to leave early for her little, rented flat in Salisbury city but, conscientious as always, she felt the need to deal with some correspondence first.

After collecting a beaker of coffee from the vending machine she repaired to a small room which she used as an office. She picked up a letter from an American scientist, unknown to her, and typed on headed paper from Stanford University, at Palo Alto in California. As was common practice, the writer congratulated her on several AIDS research papers which she had published in scientific journals, and requested copies, of which she had a substantial supply. She inscribed and signed the papers and put them in the three large, stamped and addressed manila envelopes which the sender had provided, licking the flaps, sealing them down and placing them in her out-tray for posting. The adhesive was not unpleasant to the tongue but she took a sip of coffee to remove it. Whoever the American was he had been unusually thoughtful in securing British stamps, which Wendy felt more foreigners should do, now that the postage of weighty packages was so expensive.

She read a few more letters and wrote brief replies but began to feel increasingly weak and dizzy. Weaving as she went, she managed to walk out of the room to seek help. By the time she found it she was in obvious breathing difficulties and was rushed to the Odstock hospital in Salisbury. While remaining mentally alert, she could offer no reason for her alarming symptoms, which had spread to eyelid droop, visual disturbance and severe general distress.

She was put to bed to be kept under observation, as she was, at intervals, throughout the night. By the morning she was dead.

It did not take long for the news to reach the media. Barrie Gordon, an unscrupulous journalist who specialized in disclosures from secret Government departments, had the advantage of being able to claim that he had known the deceased. It was by no means the first time he had written about her. His thick black headline read 'MYSTERY DEATH SHOCK':

Dr Wendy Payne, the brilliant young bacteriologist who has been hounded by MI5 and the CIA, died in mysterious circumstances after being taken ill in her secret laboratory at Porton Down yesterday.

Doctors suspect that she died from some kind of poisoning. The Porton establishment is involved in defence work on various highly dangerous toxins and the theory that Dr Payne may have been accidentally killed by one of them is being considered.

She is the eleventh scientist involved in defence work to die mysteriously in recent years. Several of the others proved to have committed suicide and this may have been the case with Dr Payne, though it is considered unlikely. The possibility that she had some secret fear connected with her work is being investigated.

For several weeks she had been under repeated and hostile interrogation by MI5 counter-espionage officers, concerning some top secret aspect of her research, which was mainly about AIDS.

Doctors have ruled out the possibility that Dr Payne's death was in any way connected with the AIDS virus or any mutant form of it.

Dr Adrian Allen, the distinguished scientist who heads the Chemical Defence Establishment where Dr Payne was working temporarily was unavailable for comment last night.

Inquiries by the police and MI5 are continuing and a post-mortem examination is to be carried out.

The rest of the story, which was accompanied by a photograph of Wendy and Adrian Allen together, taken at a scientific conference, was padded out by Gordon's imagination.

The local journalist serving Gordon's newspaper quickly secured the results of the autopsy from the police. The pathologists were agreed, from the symptoms and rapidity of death, that Wendy had died of botulism, a dangerous condition usually resulting from eating food infected by *Bacillus botulinus*. There was an immediate search of Wendy's flat and her rubbish bin by the police for signs of any processed food which she might have eaten, particularly tinned meat or fish as they were the usual sources of the infection. There was nothing of relevance.

Finding himself emotionally frailer than he had imagined, Adrian Allen, who had recently indulged in a torrid sexual affair with Wendy Payne, was shattered by her death. It was his unpleasant duty to telephone her parents and deal with her effects, including her working notes, which he locked away in his safe for security reasons. He was the first to think of an alternative solution to the mystery.

The toxin extracted from *Bacillus botulinus*, which was highly stable and storable for long periods, was the most poisonous substance known, the lethal dose being only about one-seven-hundredth of a milligram. It had long been recognized as a possible weapon of war and Adrian recalled how some idiot pacifist had solemnly announced that an ounce of it could wipe out millions, though without indicating how it could be administered. Supplies of it were always kept in Adrian's department at Porton for work on antidotes, which could be effective but only if applied quickly. The problem with botulinus toxin, which improved its potential value as a weapon, was the difficulty of diagnosing the symptoms early enough for the antidote to be employed.

In some agitation, Adrian checked on Porton's supplies, which were always locked under high security when not being used. Nobody, least of all Wendy, had drawn any for research in recent weeks. There was no record of her ever having access to the toxin because she had never worked in that field. However, to protect the department, and himself, he drew the police's attention to the possibility. On examination of the establishment and its records they agreed that Wendy could not possibly have secured any toxin from that source. After tests on what remained of Wendy's coffee proved negative, the police seemed convinced that she must have eaten contaminated food. They seemed unimpressed by the pathologist's failure to find any botulinus bacteria in her body.

For these and personal reasons, Adrian found himself unable to talk to his wife, Gillian, about anything else. As a scientist driven by curiosity, he was impelled to solve the mystery of Wendy's death, if he could, but his wife perceived that he was also desperate to convince himself that he had not been in any way to blame for it. She knew that it was her husband who had dragged Wendy into the world of official secrets, much against her will, and that this had led to a traumatic conflict of conscience for her. She also knew of his affair with Wendy and had forgiven him.

'You don't think it could have been suicide?' he asked Gillian. 'Like that fellow suggested in the newspaper? I suppose she could have been at the end of her tether, after all that turmoil with the security people and the press. She seemed very depressed and terribly upset, guilty in fact.'

'You mean because she had inadvertently discovered a new weapon?'

'Yes. Being such an ardent pacifist, it crucified her, especially when she found out that the Americans had instituted a crash programme to exploit its potential.'

Gillian's elegant features puckered in doubt. 'I wouldn't think, from what you've told me about her, that she would take her own life under any circumstances,' she replied, quietly, as she worked at her embroidery.

Adrian was not so sure. 'She was deeply ashamed at having acted against her conscience. In agreeing to work in secret, I mean, when it was so much against her principles. She told me, several times, that she felt unclean, contaminated. Silly, I suppose, but that was how she put it. For all her avant-gardeism, Wendy was really a religious girl at heart.'

'Look, darling,' Gillian said, with a note of impatience, 'you've said yourself that the cause of death is certain and there was no way she could have got hold of that poison, even if she had wanted to use it to kill herself. The idea is grotesque. Forget it. There is no way that you could possibly be to blame, if that is what you're thinking.'

Adrian was grateful for the reassurance. 'You don't think she could have been murdered, do you?' he asked, giving tongue for the first time to a possibility which had been niggling him.

'Murdered! Good grief! By whom?'

'I have no idea. The Russians, perhaps. You know there was a theory that Hugh Gaitskell, the Labour Party chap, was murdered by the KGB with something administered in his coffee. It was taken quite seriously, because Porton was involved in the inquiries.'

'I can see why the Russians might want to murder a senior politician but why would they want to bother with a young woman like Wendy Payne?'

'She had been accused of giving information about her discovery to the KGB through an old Polish professor she knew. But that couldn't provide any possible motive for killing her, if indeed they still do that sort of thing.'

'Sounds altogether too melodramatic to me, darling. Surely, if she was a source of information, the KGB would want to keep her alive.'

Adrian continued to think aloud. 'MI5 had been very interested in her. They had kept her under surveillance. But we can rule them out.'

'Are you sure that you can rule them out?' Gillian asked. 'Not from what I've read. They seem to be up to all sorts of skulduggery.'

'Don't believe everything you read, dear. The British authorities wouldn't be party to anything like that.'

'So that leaves you with the CIA.'

'It's vaguely possible, I suppose. But how could they have administered the toxin? It acts very quickly. There was, of course, that visit by Julian Flickinger,' he added, referring to Wendy Payne's American collaborator. 'He could have access to botulinus toxin and he spent some time alone with her, but it doesn't add up.'

'I should think not,' Gillian responded, assertively. In times past Flickinger had visited their home and she had found him charming.

'Well, you can't be certain. He could be mixed up with the CIA and strange things happen in the secrets world. But what motive could the CIA have? I suppose they might have feared that Wendy would spill the whole beans to everybody, the Libyans included. She was certainly threatening to go public.'

Gillian felt it was time he took his mind off the subject. 'Why not apply that scientific principle you are always on about – the simplest solution is usually the correct one?'

'Yes. You're absolutely right. Murder's a crazy idea. Forget I ever suggested it!'

'Best to forget the whole thing, darling.'

'Yes, but I'll have to go to the funeral,' he said. 'In my capacity as Acting Director,' he added, hastily.

Adrian was to remain as mystified as everybody else, save for those involved in sending the manila envelopes to their intended victim.

13

There was no way he could have examined the adhesive on the flaps, had it occurred to him to do so. The envelopes were already in the post to an American scientist who, had any inquiry been made, would have proved fictitious. The letter from Stanford University accompanying the envelopes occasioned no interest and had the original envelope containing it been available, instead of being already in the Porton refuse, the postmark on it would have read, quite properly, 'Palo Alto'.

Like so many seminal events which change the course of history, the secret discovery, which had cost Wendy her life, had been the result of an accident. She had never expected to be involved in anything of greater political significance than an anti-nuclear demo but, while innocently pursuing her humanitarian research, she had been dragged into the turmoil of the ceaseless intelligence war. She had become a prime target for assassination because the clandestine conflict which her chance discovery had detonated was raging at levels, in Washington and Moscow, beyond her comprehension. With unprecedented ingenuity, a few men of immense power were exploiting the situation she had created for personal political advantages which would affect millions on both sides of the East–West divide.

Chapter Two

When Wendy had arrived at Porton on the warm, late July morning of her fateful discovery, a date of deep significance in the secret history of the world which remains hidden from most people, she was of no great distinction. At thirty-two, she had a PhD in bacteriology and sound experience in that discipline but her research for the Public Health Laboratory Centre there was essentially routine. Though dull in name, the Centre was magnificently equipped because, a few years previously, it had been the Government's chief establishment for research on what the media called 'germ warfare'. Under the pressure of worldwide moral objections, but mainly because bacteria were not reliably effective as weapons, the whole establishment had been turned over to medical research. Of course, work on defences against bacterial attack by some less moral adversary had to continue and that responsibility had been conveniently transferred just a few hundred yards down a private road, to the Chemical Defence Establishment, which then quietly set up its own Defence Microbiology Division. The indignation of the vocal minority had been assuaged by these motions but most of the work went on as before, to the satisfaction of the silent majority.

Porton Down had been originally selected for such work because the Government owned the land for various military purposes and the laboratories could be cut off from the public, with plenty of room for dangerous experiments. The entire area was surrounded by a high-security fence and could be sealed off by gates. Such isolation suited Wendy, because her work, though completely non-military, involved the genetic manipulation of micro-organisms. Under agreed international rules, arising out of public concern about the possible danger of such gross interference with nature, this had to be carried out in closed laboratories, under such secure conditions that no mutant germs could possibly escape.

As a sideline to her routine research, which was concerned with AIDS disease, and to assist a project undertaken for the Department of Trade and Industry, Wendy had been working with a strain of iron bacteria: strange, naturally occurring organisms which had long been known to have the remarkable facility to feed on iron. A recently discovered variant had the power to produce an enzyme which corroded iron pipes, and the mutant strain on which she was working was especially voracious.

Her techniques were ingenious but laborious: teasing out the DNA from the central part of the bacterial cell, 'chopping' it with enzymes, 'splicing' genes and culturing the resulting 'clone' in glass dishes or conical flasks. In the process she was creating something which had never existed before, a living organism with unique characteristics. 'Playing God' was how she jokingly referred to it. Every stage of the process was recorded in a notebook in her neat, rounded handwriting, a discipline which had been instilled into her during her biological training at Durham University.

There was no foreseeable danger in her work with iron bacteria but, as a general precaution for her AIDS research, Wendy's small laboratory was of the type called Category 2, meaning that it was locked and under negative pressure, with an air-conditioning system keeping the air pressure inside slightly lower than the atmospheric pressure outside so that any leaks would be into the room and not out. It involved other minor inconveniences, such as the wearing of special clothing and the sterilization of all waste leaving the laboratory. Events were to show that they were more than justified.

With scientific research tending to be a lonely business demanding personal concentration, like composing and writing, and because of the inconvenient sterility requirements, colleagues rarely dropped in for conversation. Once installed at her bench, Wendy was alone until lunch.

She collected a glass conical flask, stoppered with cotton wool and labelled 'Clone Fe 113', from an incubating cabinet and was startled by something she had never seen before. Held up to the light, the flask looked as though the inside of it was etched, which it had not been when she had put it away on the previous evening. She examined it through a hand lens and found that the glass was indeed etched, and quite severely. Closer inspection of other cultures under a microscope showed that, without doubt, Clone Fe 113, which was supposed to be limited to attacking iron, was devouring the glass, in parts deeply.

16

She had never heard of anything like it and felt the heady thrill of a possible prime discovery.

To private comments of 'Incredible!' 'I just don't believe it!' 'How extraordinary!' Wendy spent a fascinating hour with fragments of a sacrificed flask mounted on a low-power microscope, watching the etching spread until she was in no doubt that the engineered bacterium was producing an enzyme with the capability to derive energy and sustenance from consuming glass. The oil industry had spent a great deal of money searching for a bacterium that could consume polluting oil, spilled from tankers; she had produced a glass-eater and it might be the world's first. She could not wait to get to the Centre's library of bacteriological books and journals to conduct a search of the literature for any previous mention of such a phenomenon.

Scanning every index, Wendy found no signs of any relevant record but deferred a conclusion until she had consulted the more specialized library 'down the road', at the Chemical Defence Establishment.

There was regular collaboration between the two Government departments, both professionally and socially, but it was particularly close in Wendy's case. She had a special relationship with the head of the Defence Microbiology Division, Dr Adrian Allen FRS, who was quite the most knowledgeable and academically distinguished microbiologist at either of the Porton establishments. Wendy and her yellow Mini were well known to the Ministry of Defence police who manned the security checkpoint which separated the two establishments, with its vehicle examination area and bold signs declaring that those let through were entering a prohibited area governed by the Official Secrets Act. The policeman passed her through with a bow and an exaggerated wave.

Again, she could find nothing relevant in even the most specialized literature but felt that it would be wise to take the opportunity to ask Adrian if he had heard of the phenomenon and called at his office. He was holding an administrative meeting; he was deputizing for the Director of the Chemical Defence Establishment during a lengthy absence owing to serious illness. Through his secretary he asked Wendy to wait and, as she did so, she was already composing the brief letter to the scientific journal, *Nature*, which had international circulation and would establish her claim to her discovery. She was as hungry as any other scientist for academic acclaim.

She enjoyed anticipating the special satisfaction she would derive from sharing her excitement with Adrian. Though he had never said so bluntly, she knew that, with his flair for making scientific success seem so easy, he regarded her as no more than a plodder, one of the necessary infantry of research but who was never likely to be much more than an NCO. He was a Cambridge man and, though he had never passed any remarks about her provincial university, she knew that he thought it much inferior.

It was common gossip at Porton, and in academic circles elsewhere, that Wendy and Adrian had indulged in a long, desultory affair, which had started when they were attending an international conference on microbiology in Geneva. Adrian, who had always been a sexual opportunist, was attracted by Wendy's natural aura of feminity – what he came to call her 'effulgence of sex' – which, through no conscious effort on her part, could cause stirrings in the private parts of men across the proverbial crowded room.

What Wendy might lack in facial beauty was more than compensated for, in Adrian's lustful eyes, by her good legs, which in his view were too often concealed in jeans, while her firm breasts, with their upturn which so excited him, tended to be lost in the too ample folds of 'sloppy Joe' turtle-neck sweaters.

He had sidled up to her at the bar of the hotel where they both were staying, commenting favourably on a scientific paper she had delivered at a morning session which he had chaired. Sitting on a stool, in a shortish skirt on that occasion, her legs dangling and her naturally blonde hair down to her shoulders, she was irresistible to such a catch-as-catch-can philanderer.

It was far from being the first time that a pass had been made at Wendy by a senior scientist away from his wife, hoping to take advantage of his position and prestige. She had become used to the brash ways of what, to her, were old codgers pulling their rank with all the finesse of a Hollywood director nodding towards the casting couch. But she had been flattered by the attention of such a scientist as Allen, who was not only distinguished academically, but seemed to have been unfairly endowed with Nature's assets, being tall, dark with temple greyness, attractively aquiline and, in his mid-forties, retaining much of the athleticism which had earned him a running blue. His interest in her work sounded genuinely more than a gambit leading to her eventual invitation to his room, which she had no intention of resisting.

Initially she had found sex with him passionately ecstatic, affording release on a scale she had not experienced, but, as familiarity eroded novelty, he had required increasingly peculiar deviations. These had been exciting at first but, perhaps because of her prim upbringing as an only child in a Methodist household, she had become shocked and sometimes rather frightened as the months passed. Adrian could be crudely verbal and even sadistic when 'body took over', a phrase he used when half-apologizing for his behaviour. His tutelage had banished her prudish shame about her nakedness but some words still made her wince.

With his habit of comparing people with his favourite animal, he described himself as 'a tabby tom-cat driven by desire' while he classified Wendy as 'an eminently pettable Persian'. She could be seen to have feline features, when these were pointed out.

The affair had also become unsatisfactory to Wendy's rather intense temperament because there was insufficient opportunity to develop what she called 'the dynamics of the man–woman relationship'. Adrian was a quickie man, always anxious to get back home or to his laboratory, once his demands were temporarily satisfied.

'Dr Allen will see you now, Miss Payne,' his secretary said, as his office emptied.

'Now what's all the excitement about?' Adrian asked, in the resonant voice which made him such a popular speaker.

Wendy explained, in as cold and matter-of-fact a way as she could, and Allen was immediately impressed. 'Let's duck lunch. I'd like to see this phenomenon right away. Let's go! We'll use your car.'

Once inside Wendy's locked laboratory he peered down the microscope at the preparation she had mounted on a glass slide. 'My God, it's eating the slide! And the cover slip! This clone reproduces at a rate like anthrax. Thank the Lord it's not pathogenic. At least I hope it's not.'

'I can't think why it should be, except to anybody with a glass eye,' Wendy quipped.

Adrian continued to watch as the bacteria etched their way out of the field of vision, like frost spreading over a windowpane, 'This will certainly cause an international stir. I suppose I should congratulate you on quite a discovery, Wendy. Who have you told about it?'

'Only you, so far. I was going to wait until I got a letter published in *Nature*.'

'That's wise,' Adrian remarked, plagiarism and jumped claims being all too common in the world of science, where professional recognition was the key to fellowships, grants, awards and academic appointments.

'I suppose, out of courtesy, I should tell Julian Flickinger,' she added. 'I might have to delay my work with him for a bit.'

For the moment Adrian did not comment. Flickinger, a specialist on the enzymes produced by bacteria, worked at Fort Detrick, formerly the US Army's biological warfare centre in Maryland, which had also been turned over mainly to medical work, and had visited Porton on several occasions, once serving there as resident liaison officer with Fort Detrick. Adrian had been mildly jealous of the warmly pleasant and able young American, for whom Wendy had considerable affection.

'I think that Flick-Finger will have to wait,' he said. 'And so will you. We could have quite a problem if this becomes public.'

'Are you thinking of the glass industry? I don't suppose they'll be very pleased.'

'It certainly won't do my Pilkington shares much good but I was really thinking about this place. If news of this leaks out, the media could concoct all kinds of science fiction and we could have demos at Porton claiming all sorts of nonsense. I can just see the hairy, rent-a-crowd layabouts waving their wretched placards at the TV cameras: "CLOSE DOWN PORTON DOWN", "SMASH THE MAD MEDDLERS", "FRENETIC ENGINEERING!" The wrong kind of publicity could not only damage the reputation of Porton but genetic engineering generally. That's the last thing I want while I'm in charge here. And I'm sure it's the last thing you want.'

Adrian looked at Wendy for support. With her strong feminist feelings and militant attitude to issues like nuclear weapons, he was not sure he would get it.

For her part, Wendy thought it typical of Adrian to be primarily concerned with his own position but, as she knew, he had a telling point. There was a strong possibility that the Director might have to retire through ill health and she was aware, from their pillow-talk, that as the senior divisional chief, Adrian had his eye on the post. He was very ambitious and a few years as Director, with a probable

20

knighthood because of his academic distinction, could lead to his heart's desire – a chair at a Cambridge college and eventually a Mastership. He had a special love and affinity for Cambridge. He had made his name there and had married the daughter of the professor holding the prestigious post which he coveted and which would not be available for several more years.

'Good grief!' Wendy exclaimed as she picked up her hand lens from the bench. 'Look at this.'

There was no doubt about it. A trace of Clone Fe 113, which she must have transferred by accident, was attacking the lens.

'If we're not careful it will be having a go at the windows,' Adrian observed. 'You realize that you won't be able to continue research with this in a C2 laboratory?' he said. 'You'll have to move to a C4.'

Wendy groaned. A C4 laboratory, originally developed for biological warfare experiments, involved complex precautions, like air locks, glove cabinets and much more stringent and time-consuming steriliz-ation procedures.

'We haven't got a C4 to spare,' she said, with relief. 'They are all taken up with the AIDS research and nothing will be allowed to interfere with that.'

'Then you'll have to transfer the work to my place. I have a C4 that's not in use.'

'Oh, I don't fancy working under tight security. It's against my principles. I've always been told that secrecy is a cesspool and that if I'm sucked into it I'll never get out.'

'That's a ridiculous exaggeration,' Adrian said, dismissively.

'Well, I don't think it is. I've given it a lot of thought. Down the ages, secrecy has been associated with everything that's evil. Conspiracy, plots, stealth, deceit, duplicity, cover-up, lies, treachery . . .' She ticked them off on her fingers. 'Secrecy contami-nates everyone and everything it touches.'

'In an imperfect world some evils are necessary.'

'That may be, but I want no part of them.'

'Even so, you have to face the fact that you have no alternative if you want to go on working with this little brute,' Adrian said, with some impatience. 'God knows what it is capable of! You'll have to do your cultures in plastic containers and keep them away from any form of glass. You'll have to use plastic slides. We have the facilities.'

Wendy looked dismayed but suddenly resigned. It did not occur

21

to either of them to solve the problem by destroying all the cultures without delay. That would have been scientific sacrilege.

'I'll see George right away,' Adrian said, referring to the rather timid chief of the Centre where Wendy worked. He was almost a caricature of the absent-minded professor, who would always defer to Adrian and was so wrapped up in his own medical work that he was more than happy to be spared the details of anybody else's. 'I won't tell him much and I'll arrange for you to move tomorrow. We'd both better be in early.'

At least Wendy was gratified to see that he was as excited by her find as she was. She placed all the cultures and glassware in a wooden cupboard with special care, and they scrubbed their hands meticulously.

'It's gloves from now on until we know a lot more about this clone,' Adrian warned. 'And don't forget – not a word to anyone. We don't want to make fools of ourselves.'

They did not embrace, as they would have done a few weeks previously. To Adrian's annoyance, Wendy had ended – or at least suspended – the sexual relationship after he had told her, almost with humour, that his wife, Gillian, knew of their affair. Under pressure, he had confessed that it was he who had informed his wife and Wendy had surmised that this was not only unnecessarily unkind but was, perhaps subconsciously, an act of sadism. She had never met Gillian and Adrian could not understand why the information should have suddenly made her feel guilty.

'Nothing has changed,' he had argued when she had resisted his last groping advance in his room. 'My wife is very understanding about what she calls sins of the flesh.'

'She may say she is but I'm sure she can be hurt like anyone else,' had been the sharp response. During her student days, on the fringes of far-left politics, Wendy had developed a deep sense of injustice.

As she drove down the wide, horse-chestnut avenue leading out of the fenced off area and on to the six familiar miles back to Salisbury, through countryside she had come to love, she pondered on the scientific possibilities of her discovery. Suddenly she realized that there was a potentiality of which neither of them had thought.

'Now that really would be something!' she told herself. She would have to discuss it with Adrian first thing in the morning. And with Julian Flickinger as soon as possible.

Driving home eastwards towards the village of Broughton, near Stockbridge, in his second-hand maroon Jaguar, Adrian, too, was visited by sudden inspiration.

'Jesus Christ!' was all he said aloud.

Chapter Three

The Allens lived in an old stone house, rented in the tucked-away village of Broughton, near the River Test, that Mecca of trout anglers, of which Adrian was one. It was always a delight when the bonnet of his car nosed into the short, gravelled drive. All that really mattered in his private life was there.

A dark, eye-turning woman who set great store by studied elegance, Gillian was completely confident of her ability to hold her husband. Whatever casual affairs might come his way, she knew they were trivial and that he would never leave her and their two children. From the time of their early courtship, when she had detected his problems, she had guessed that he would be occasionally unfaithful and he had quickly become dependent on her and her understanding. His sexual appetite was such that, in their former years, he would book a room for a couple of hours at a London airport hotel when she was meeting him on his return from a foreign trip, because he could not contain himself until he reached home. She had found it very flattering, and still did on the now rare occasions, but in spite of what he called his 'demon rider', he was really a sexual inadequate, forever in search of fleeting new experiences and with a persistent need to fantasize. There was an unresolvable conflict between desire and performance, due, perhaps, she thought, to some hormonal imbalance outside his control, and it was only with her that he felt able to admit it without losing his masculine self-esteem. Privately, he rationalized his promiscuous pursuit of women as being motivated by the same drive as his pursuit of science – his curiosity about the unknown, which had to be satisfied.

Gillian appreciated that she was married to something of a genius in his field and had no option but to put up with the consequences, for she needed an exciting man whose mind she could admire; a dull, faithful Fido would have bored her. So she was prepared to share him rather than lose him, as long as she had the lioness's share and he returned to the den, where she had always ensured that there would be no alternative attraction. The au pair girls they had hired when the children were young and the daily helps had all been selected for their plainness.

Because of her luxuriant, raven hair, Adrian called his wife 'my lucky black cat' and he was indeed fortunate to have such a partner. Friends who knew his proclivities could not understand why he wasted his time on anyone else.

The lecherous strains of Ruggiero Raimondi singing *La ci darem la mano* on a compact disc assailed Adrian's ears as he opened the heavy oak front door. It was, perhaps, just an unfortunate coincidence that Gillian's favourite opera should be *Don Giovanni* but a psychologist might have interpreted it as masochism. The music was loud but Adrian was too preoccupied with his inspiration for it to register. Usually, he was pleasurably aware of the small-palace environment which Gillian's care and taste had created but he did not even notice his favourite Siamese cat, which sidled, sinuously, to greet him.

He was uncommunicative during dinner, which was not uncommon when he had some academic problem on his mind, and Gillian did not press him. He remained preoccupied as they sat by the open French windows over coffee, savouring the warm breeze blowing from the water meadows of the Wallop Stream and scented by new-mown lawn grass. Gillian, content to repair a Victorian child's sampler she had picked up in an antique shop, could almost hear the cogs whirring in Adrian's head as he stared out over the garden, stroking the neutered Siamese cat on his lap. 'Bizzing', she called it.

'Sorry to be so preoccupied,' Adrian said eventually. 'I've acquired rather a problem.'

'That's all right, darling. You'll solve it.'

She was curious but knew he would unburden himself before the night was out: he always did.

Adrian was in the habit of discussing the day's events with his wife in bed, using her as a sounding board for his ideas. She was not scientifically qualified, her main intellectual interests being in music and omnivorous reading, but she had been reared in a household where her father's visitors conversed chiefly about science and she had picked up enough knowledge and jargon there, and from her husband and his friends, to understand basic issues and make common-sense suggestions. This kept Adrian on the ground when tempted to launch what she called 'his hot-air balloons'. While

25

scrupulously avoiding wild hypotheses in print, he found it creatively useful to throw them around in bed.

'I do hope you haven't brought any of that stuff in here on your shoes,' Gillian remarked, in a half-sleepy voice, when he told her what had happened. 'I'd hate it to attack our Georgian mirrors . . .'

'This is no joke, Gillian. It's not just a question of glass. The clone was developed from a bacterium which can attack elemental iron. Glass is a silicate, so the bull question is can the clone attack elemental silicon?'

'Are you thinking of the silicon chip?' she asked, suddenly becoming alert.

'You're damn right I am,' he said. 'And these days, to pervert a phrase, it's chips with everything.'

'I'm told they are even in my steam iron.'

'Never mind your steam iron! It's the computer I'm thinking about. Modern civilization has made itself totally dependent on computers. Nothing works without them.'

'You're worried what might happen to all the computers if this clone escaped and there was an epidemic?'

'That's not the only worry. The clone could be used deliberately as a weapon if it fell into the wrong hands. The defence implications are mind-boggling. Every aspect of defence relies on computers or on equipment that depends on silicon chips. It is clearly an aerobic bacterium,' he continued, thinking aloud. 'But it might be able to exist without oxygen as well, as iron bacteria do, deep down in bogs. In a sophisticated computer most of the chips are embedded in some kind of insulating resin. So could the bacteria reach the chips? I suspect they could. I don't know much about computers but I doubt that any seal between metal and resin could be proof against bacteria, particularly against such an invasive one as this.'

'You certainly have got yourself a problem, haven't you, darling?' Gillian commented. 'And all thanks to that young girl whom you didn't think had much talent.'

'It was just a fluke,' Adrian said, dismissively. 'Could have happened to anyone. That's the way science wags. Do the boys still have that computer game I bought them?'

'Yes, I saw it the other day. I don't know if it still works.'

'Well, if it does, they've lost it. I'll offer it as a sacrifice to Clone Fe 113.'

'Is that the name of the glass-chewer?'

Adrian did not reply; his mind was on another issue.

'If it does attack silicon I'll have to report it to the Ministry, you know. At the highest level. And in person. It will be top secret so don't mention it to a soul.'

Gossip in the village and in lovely Stockbridge, where Gillian shopped and hunted antiques with such enjoyment, was part of her daily life but Adrian knew that she could be relied on to be secure.

'Does that mean that Dr Payne won't be able to publish her discovery?' she asked.

'I'm afraid so.'

'Poor Dr Payne! Her very first breakthrough! How will she take it?'

'Badly. She's allergic to secrecy and she'll be absolutely horrified to learn that she has probably stumbled on a new weapon. What a turn-up for a pacifist! But that's life.'

Gillian snuggled up to him, as she generally did before going to sleep. At such times Adrian genuinely wished he could be free of the demonic desire that drove him to ephemeral satisfactions which he knew were disgraceful for a man for whom the discipline of intellect was paramount. As he expressed it himself, the difference between the qualities of lust and love was the difference between chipboard and solid oak, between breeze block and granite.

Chapter Four

When Wendy entered Adrian's office on the following morning he was hanging up his jacket, exposing one of the fancy waistcoats which were his personal logo, before donning his white working coat. She was bubbling with excitement.

'I've had a marvellous idea,' she announced, almost triumphantly. 'Clone Fe 113 obviously produces an enzyme which dissolves glass: glass is a silicate. The spicules in the lungs which cause silicosis in miners are silicates. Silicosis is incurable because silicates are insoluble and can never be removed. But, if this enzyme can be extracted and proves to be harmless when injected into the human body, it might dissolve the spicules and cure, or at least ameliorate, the disease! What do you think of that?'

'Ingenious,' Adrian replied, with some impatience. 'You must follow it up. But it will have to wait.'

'Why? I was reading up on silicosis last night. There are still new cases and a huge backlog of old coal- and gold-miners suffering terribly from the disease and getting no treatment. Asbestos is also a silicate and there's no cure for asbestosis either.'

'I'm afraid there is a prospect of far greater significance which has to take priority, Wendy. Your clone might also attack silicon chips. We must find out if it does – and quickly.'

'Oh Lord! I hadn't thought of that.'

From his trouser pocket, Adrian produced a small plastic box containing a few silicon chips and handed it to her. 'As soon as we have you installed in your new lab I want you to try to infect these chips. The technicians have supplied them: they don't know why. I need an answer as soon as possible. I'm sure you appreciate the implications. Your clone is much more than a laboratory curiosity now.'

'It certainly is – on the enzyme prospect alone. It's Julian's field. I should get him working on it without delay.'

'Positively not! You mustn't tell anyone anything at this stage.'

'But I should at least report it to the Public Health Laboratory Service. They are the people who pay me.'

'I appreciate that, but please don't say anything to anybody just yet.'

'What about my letter to *Nature*?'

'Forget it for the present. Anyway, we don't want to go off at half-cock.'

'We? Are you thinking of joining in with me?' Wendy could feel her hopes of full recognition slipping away. She had seen too many instances where professors and heads of departments had grabbed credit by insisting on having their names on the published research reports, always appearing as the senior author.

'I have no intention of stealing your thunder,' Adrian assured her. 'But I have to be in with you on this silicon business. Its potentialities are enormous.'

'I'll be grateful for your guidance,' Wendy acknowledged, with a wan smile. 'But it would have to happen to a woman, wouldn't it? Not being able to publish, I mean.'

'It has nothing at all to do with sex,' Adrian countered. He was not being unreasonable, as she was well aware. 'Now, to business,' he said. 'Your laboratory is already being prepared. Nobody knows why. I simply said that you had reached a further stage in your work. The conditions for a Category 4 are laid down in this document.' He handed her a small brochure. 'Computers operate at warm temperatures because of the heat they generate,' he continued. 'So try infecting your chips at about thirty degrees centigrade. We shall also need to know, eventually, whether your clone can exist without oxygen. But I suggest a more direct approach to the problem first, if your chips are attacked.'

He reached into a hold-all, produced a computer game and plugged in the lead. 'This used to belong to the boys. Come and see how it works.'

Adrian spent a few minutes shooting down space invaders on the game's small, built-in screen by operating a little joy-stick. 'I got quite good at this,' he said. 'I could usually beat the boys. See how you do.'

Wendy did not do so well.

'There's some skill in it,' Adrian said with enthusiasm, warming to the challenge. 'It's like a shooting gallery.'

29

'I'll bet he never let his boys beat him once,' Wendy thought, seeing that he was not immune to the weakness of always needing to win.

'Right,' Adrian said, disconnecting the game, 'if you get a positive result with the chips I'll bring this in and we'll inoculate it somehow. If it goes out of action we'll know we're not deluding ourselves and we won't be raising any undue alarm. Then, perhaps, we can try something rather more elegant.'

'I suppose we should pray that it all proves negative,' Wendy suggested.

Adrian raised his eyebrows. 'But it will be a lot more exciting if it doesn't!'

As he and Wendy moved off to the C4 laboratory she mused on the fact that this was the first time that she had stood really close to Adrian in private and he had resisted groping her thighs. Either he had lost interest in her or his mind was totally occupied by the silicon issue, which, she told herself, meant that it must be very important indeed.

Because of the increased sterility precautions, with the dressing and undressing, and her impatience to test the silicon chips, Wendy had decided to take a packed lunch into the laboratory. By mid-afternoon she was on the telephone to Adrian.

'The chips are beginning to etch,' she announced.

'I'll be right in.'

Entering through the air-lock, Adrian looked like a surgeon ready to operate in cap, gown, gloves and short white rubber boots in place of his Gucci-type shoes. He examined the infected chips under the microscope. 'They're quite deeply indented. I don't see how they could possibly work. Let's see if they do.'

He took the computer game out of his hold-all and connected it to a convenient socket, checked again that it was working and switched it off.

'Put a little of the culture on a scalpel and introduce it into that hole,' he said. 'Do the same with that hole there and the one on the other side.'

He reached into the hold-all and produced a small rubber-vaned electric fan. 'This is intended to simulate the cooling fans of a real computer.' He held it near each of the treated holes for a few minutes.

30

'It's crude but it might do the trick. Just keep the game running, try it from time to time and let me know what happens – if anything. I'll be in my room. I've told my wife I'll be home late.'

Nothing happened for about three hours but then, when Wendy tried to play the game again, it behaved peculiarly. After another thirty minutes, nothing showed on the screen at all, though current was still passing through the circuit. She alerted Adrian.

'Let's have it apart,' he said, briskly getting busy with a screw-driver. 'What we can't unscrew we'll break open. It's only thin plastic.'

He prised out an array of silicon chips.

'Right, you examine this lot and I'll look at the rest.'

They did not have to look for long. Several of the chips were etched and pitted to destruction.

'You agree there's no doubt about it, Wendy?'

'Absolutely. What doubt can there be?'

Though the consequences were possibly disastrous she felt nothing but exhilaration.

'One can guess how quickly it would spread in a big computer with the extra warmth and the internal cooling fans,' Adrian said, his voice betraying some excitement. 'I imagine there's some redundancy built into a big computer but I wouldn't think it could afford to lose too many chips. Anyway, those considerations are beyond our competence and our facilities.' He looked at the digital clock on the wall. 'Well, that's all we can do for tonight. I'll help you clear away.'

He selected several pitted chips, sterilized them with dry heat, slipped them into a small plastic box and pocketed them. Wendy busied herself collecting the pieces of the computer, put them into a heavy-duty plastic bag and sealed it.

'I reckon that must be the cheapest experiment ever carried out at Porton,' Adrian said. 'It's like the old days of the early microbe hunters who had to do everything on a shoe-string budget. Not very elegant but it worked. I suggest you start setting up some anaerobic conditions tomorrow. By the way, I won't be here.'

Wendy waited for him to explain.

'I'm going up to the Ministry of Defence. I fixed a tentative appointment with the Chief Scientist, Sir William Brook, and now I'll have to keep it. I must tell him what's happened. I can foresee all sorts of problems.'

31

'Such as?'

'Surely you've realized the defence implications, Wendy? That this clone could possibly be used as a weapon, to knock out computers?'

Her drained expression showed that she had not. 'Are you telling me that I've invented a weapon?'

'I'm afraid the odds are that you have.'

'But that's terrible,' she said, slowly, as her predicament struck home. 'I can't have anything to do with weapons. I detest them.'

'I'm afraid you've no choice, my dear. It's not your fault but you let this genie out of its bottle and you're stuck with it. Anyway, it isn't going to kill anyone. It only attacks inanimate equipments.'

Wendy was not to be comforted so easily. 'A weapon is a weapon is a weapon,' she pronounced, 'and all weapons are evil.'

The observation sounded naive to Adrian but it was convenient to agree. 'We must both hope it will never be used but, as Acting Director, I can't avoid reporting it to the Ministry.'

'How well do you know this Chief Scientist chap?' Wendy asked.

'We've met a few times but I don't know him well. The Director attends all the committees.'

Wendy could sense that he was anticipating the encounter with some eagerness and she was right. Unlike many scientists who are poor or reluctant communicators, preferring to work in isolation, Adrian fully appreciated the importance of people on the ladder to success and preferment. The meeting would enable him to make his mark with Brook. He might be the bearer of bad news but he would be bringing it without delay and there could be little doubt, because of its nature, that the bearer would be well remembered. He could also assure the Chief Scientist that secrecy had been thoroughly maintained. Brook would have major influence in deciding who was to be the next Director of the Chemical Defence Establishment.

Wendy wondered how much credit she would be given at the meeting or whether she would be even mentioned at such a level. She was worrying unnecessarily. Adrian had no intention of saddling himself with the responsibility for such a potentially disastrous development, only with the virtue of having dealt with it expeditiously.

'You'll appreciate that secrecy is now more important than ever,

Wendy, until we hear what the Ministry wants us to do,' Adrian remarked, as they walked through the Establishment, which was always quickly deserted after 5 p.m.

From being at the peak of exhilaration Wendy was cast down and her trainer-shod feet felt heavy as she dragged them across the clinically clean, polished floors. 'Secrecy is the negation of discovery,' she declared, mouthing another of her student-days slogans. 'Anyway, as I've never signed the Official Secrets Act, it can't apply to me.'

'Well, you might have to sign it now,' Adrian warned her. 'I know it's been a shock to you but promise me you won't say anything to anybody until we've talked again. And we'd better lock up your working notes. Let me have them. I should put them in the safe but you'll need them in the morning. I'll lock them in my desk drawer for tonight. My secretary has a spare key.'

Wendy obliged saying, despondently, 'I'm not so sure I want to publish anything now – my name would be mud with all my old friends.'

'Oh, a scientist is not responsible for what use is made of his or her discoveries, Wendy.'

'Well, I shall always feel responsible if any aggressive use is made of mine. What about Julian Flickinger? Can't I bring him into the picture on the medical side? He's secure enough. And so is Fort Detrick.'

Adrian shook his head decisively. 'Nobody, repeat nobody, can be told anything until we know the Ministry's views.'

Wendy agreed with deep reluctance. 'Like I said, it would happen to a discovery made by a woman.'

'Oh, you'll get your proper recognition one day,' Adrian said, putting his arm round her shoulders affectionately. 'This is too big to be kept secret for long and meanwhile you've plenty of work to do. But I agree it's a hell of a bore. I suppose we'll have the bloody spooks down here.'

'Spooks?'

'Yes, spooks – MI5 and that lot.'

Wendy drove back to Salisbury deeply depressed. What had she done? Whatever it was it could not be undone. Momentarily, she toyed with the idea of going into Porton early next morning and destroying all the cultures but quickly convinced herself that extinguishing knowledge was a bigger social crime than keeping it secret. Her mood brightened while she was preparing her fast food supper in her little kitchen, which sported several old CND posters, her old badge pinned to one of them. Maybe the clone would not work as a weapon. In any event, she would stick with it until the implications became clearer. Then she would make her stand. It was terrible that the defence aspects of her discovery should be given priority over the medical possibilities. She would certainly fight that, in every way she could. She had always taken pride in being known, among her North country friends, as a bonny fighter.

After a discussion with Gillian that evening, Adrian wrote a short report for the Chief Scientist and put it into his briefcase along with the pitted samples and a magnifying glass. Then, with two hours of light left, he went down to the river in the hope that there would be an evening rise. Izaak Walton had called angling 'the contemplative man's recreation' but its virtue in Adrian's eyes was that, while stalking a timorous trout in the Test, which, as the saying had it, was as clear as gin and twice as expensive, it was impossible to think about anything else.

Early the following morning, during the drive to London along the congested M3 motorway, he deliberated on a further problem of communication which he faced as Acting Director. The protocol of a long-standing agreement with the United States required complete interchange of information between Porton and Fort Detrick concerning any bacterial aspects of defence research. Adrian was in no doubt that Clone Fe 113 fell within the protocol and that the American scientists were entitled, not only to all the available information, but to a sample of the clone should they require it, as he felt sure they would.

Under normal circumstances, Fort Detrick would have been quickly informed, probably even by telephone. Wendy was quite right. Flickinger should be told and Adrian himself had a senior American colleague who could be guaranteed to be upset, even angry, if he found out that he had been denied such information. Fort Detrick had so much money to spend on research that what Porton could do was small by comparison. What pleasure it would give

34

Adrian to tell them something new, especially something as exciting as the silicon-eater.

It was a dilemma he could raise with Sir William Brook but, knowing the ways of Whitehall, he felt that the response was sure to be negative, leaving him eventually responsible for the failure of communication in the eyes of the Americans. The absent Director was a stickler for protocol, especially concerning Anglo-American co-operation, but he was far too ill to be consulted.

It seemed that he could not avoid offending either the Americans or the Ministry, but by the time Adrian turned into Horse Guards Avenue towards the North Entrance of the huge white edifice, so indicative of the size of the sums spent on defence, he believed he could see a possible solution.

The Chief Scientist was impressed as he read Adrian's report and examined the chips. He appreciated all the obvious implications without undue excitement and the two warmed to each other.

'What you say about that girl's hand lens being attacked interests me greatly,' Sir William said. 'You see, it means that the bacterium can work in dry conditions so it might be possible to dispense it as a dry biological.'

'I don't understand.'

'A dry biological agent is one which can be carried in the dry state and dispensed as a powder — you know, by aircraft or missiles to cause a local epidemic on enemy territory.'

'The trouble with epidemics, Sir William, is that you can never guarantee that they will stay local. And since this clone is able to live on glass, it could spread very quickly and be very difficult to eradicate.'

Brook did not reply as he moved towards a cupboard and produced a tray of bottles and glasses. While biological and chemical warfare was officially outlawed by Britain and America, though not yet by the Soviet Union, it was his duty to consider the defence potential of any new development and he found it fascinating. That was why he had accepted the post of Chief Scientist, which involved him in every major new development in defence hardware.

'Gin and tonic suit you?' he asked.

'Fine, just a small one. It's a bit early for me and I'm driving.'

'I'm very grateful that you approached me directly, Dr Allen,' Brook said, passing him his drink. 'So often I'm told what's happened at the scientific out-stations by other civil servants here – the Permanent Secretary and such like. It's most irritating.'

What Sir William meant was that, this time, he would have the satisfaction of doing the telling at the highest levels in Whitehall.

Chapter Five

The ultra-secret meetings of the Joint Intelligence Committee, held in the Cabinet Office, were always likely to produce a staggering pronouncement from one of the security and intelligence chiefs attending. But the revelation made that hot August morning electrified those present to a degree which none of them had experienced before, accustomed as they were to alarming knowledge withheld from the public 'in the national interest'.

Their feelings and fears were accurately expressed by the Chairman, Sir Richard Carlton, when he declared, with some bitterness, 'Without exaggeration, gentlemen, this silicon business is potentially the most devastating and most sensitive secret since the atomic bomb and somebody can be guaranteed to make use of it. The more one thinks of the possibilities, the more horrendous they become – on all counts, political and economic as well as military.'

Austere, precise, somewhat humourless and always smoothly professional, Sir Richard, Deputy Under-Secretary at the Foreign Office and currently heading the nation's most secret assembly, was not given to exaggeration. A career diplomat with impeccable qualifications, he deplored the late twentieth-century situation in which international politics were conditioned less by statesmanship and ideals than by military hardware and scientific discoveries.

'Like the wretched atomic bomb, I profoundly wish this clone thing had never been developed,' he continued in his rather peremptory manner. 'Let us hope, indeed let us pray, that the secret of its existence will be better kept.'

Sir Alexander Pryce, the Director-General of the Security Service, commonly known as MI5, a rather obese, button-nosed, sad-sack figure, tending to look hung-over whether he was or not, and noted for being monosyllabic at all meetings, nodded his agreement. The much sharper looking Chief of the Secret Intelligence Service, MI6, did not betray his thoughts even to that extent, while the Director of Government Communication Headquarters, GCHQ, and the Deputy Chief of the Defence Staff, an air marshal expert in defence intelligence, simply looked at each other with blank expressions. Before the Chairman's briefing, none of these key officials of the secret domain had known anything about the extraordinary development which had caused the intelligence crisis.

There were others from Whitehall who would normally have been present but were on summer holiday. There were also some, like the representatives of the United States, Canada and Australia, who had been deliberately excluded from the meeting, which was extraordinary. It was strictly for 'UK Ears Only'.

The only one anxious to give tongue was Oliver Taylor, the other senior Foreign Office 'mandarin' who, by regulation, was always a member, intelligence being so essentially a matter of foreign affairs that the Committee responsible for briefing ministers usually had a numerical Foreign Office bias.

'The diplomatic and political implications are the most immediate,' he declared emphatically. 'If the Soviets find out about this discovery they will never believe that it was made by accident. They will say that it was all deliberately contrived, with evil intent, and that we have been cheating on solemn international understandings. I know that it had nothing whatever to do with defence research but it was made at a defence establishment and you know what the Soviets are like.'

Sir William Brook, who had been co-opted for the meeting, was in agreement and his utterances always commanded respect. His collars invariably looked as though they had never seen an iron and his suits were crumpled, their trouser-seats polished by desk work, but there was nothing untidy or worn about his mind.

'The Russian scientists might believe the truth of the matter but the politicians certainly won't,' he asserted. 'They'll make a meal of it.'

The Chairman's glumness indicated his concurrence.

'And it won't only be us who'll be in trouble,' Taylor continued, believing that he had the meeting with him. 'It's the Americans who will really get the stick from Moscow. The Soviets simply won't believe that the Americans were not involved in developing this clone, especially given our intimate relations in that field. The whole détente situation between the US and the Soviet Union, on which we've all worked so hard, is at risk. It could put us back to the Cold War just when everything is looking so rosy.'

'Have the Americans been told yet?' Brook asked, the usual half-smile playing round his full lips. 'We haven't done anything on our net.'

It was known to all present that Brook had high standing in the Pentagon, which he visited frequently, and would be anxious not to upset his contacts there.

'The answer is no,' Carlton responded crisply. 'And for the time being it must stay that way.'

'I would like it on the record that I profoundly disagree,' Taylor interjected.

He had previously discussed with Carlton the stand which the Foreign Office should take and they had not been in agreement. 'Washington will be furious if they find out that we have delayed telling them about this appalling development for even a single day,' he continued. 'And they will be justified. It's the Americans who have the most to lose, and especially the President – a fairly new President, may I remind you, who is soon to face a summit meeting in Moscow, where this dynamite could explode right in his face. I would like it recorded in the minutes that it is my opinion that Washington should be given the fullest information immediately.'

Carlton showed his irritation with a steely look as he made a note. 'Of course Washington will have to be told, but not just yet,' he said, emphatically. 'That's the surest way to make the silicon secret leak and we can't tolerate a leak until we have considered all the possible consequences, especially with Parliament in recess and ministers and half the staffs on holiday.'

Carlton had served in the Washington Embassy and was familiar with the difficulty of concealing sensitive issues from the American media.

'Some wretched senator would dine out on it,' he went on. 'I wouldn't give it three days to be all over the *Washington Post* and *New York Times*. And then what? Apart from the security aspects, it would cause a furore in the whole world of commerce.'

Nobody had cause to disagree with that prognosis so Carlton pressed home his argument. 'There's a further reason for delay. If, and when, we tell the Americans, it will put them in a dreadful dilemma. With their summit coming up they might feel under obligation to inform the Russians, which would hand them the secret on a plate. It's simply too early to tell anyone. We need more time for thought, especially about the defence issues. We need to foresee all the possible contingencies, for ourselves and for our allies, and we don't want to raise alarm until we have to. I'm sure that a pause for deliberation would be in the best interest of everybody concerned.'

Brook had a reservation. 'What makes you so confident that it won't leak here? Quite a few in the Ministry of Defence know about it already and it has unlimited potential for the left-wing press, Labour backbenchers, the pacifists and the demo brigade.'

'Are you thinking of another Ponting?' the MI6 chief asked, mischievously, referring to a former civil servant who had caused a commotion some years previously by leaking embarrassing information to Parliament.

As Ponting had been quite senior in the Defence Ministry, Brook preferred not to reply. There were some present, Sandy Pryce in particular, who were not too sure of Brook's own ability to keep his mouth shut. A sociable, much-liked bon viveur of lower-middle-class origin, having won his way to Cambridge, he had a reputation for indiscretion and unnecessary association with defence correspondents who, he believed, deserved to be well informed in the interest of maintaining public support for the heavy defence expenditure.

'I suppose there's no way of stifling the whole thing permanently?' the GCHQ Director suggested, rhetorically.

A physicist by training, Brook gave a pathetic smile. 'You can't disinvent knowledge. Not even the Renaissance popes could do that.'

Everyone looked at Carlton, whose ardently professed Catholicism extended to assisting *The Tablet* newspaper, but he did not take the remark personally. 'The Renaissance popes did at least manage to delay things,' he commented drily. 'And I take it we are broadly in agreement that is what we must do. Ministers have no need to know at this juncture and that includes the Prime Minister, who's on holiday anyway. We must take ministerial advice eventually but not just yet. I will take responsibility for not informing the Foreign Secretary. We are only thinking of a few weeks at the most. By that time we will have had further meetings after more reflection. It's a British discovery and we are entitled to set the pace.'

Taylor sighed and, with the exception of him and Sandy Pryce, those present nodded assent. There was a shuffling of papers being stuffed and locked into black briefcases, watches were looked at and lunch dates anticipated. Only one man reached for a hat, Pryce, who unhooked a battered black homburg from the hatstand. It was joked in Whitehall that it had been second-hand when he had bought it three years previously, when he had been the surprise choice to head MI5. The last homburg in Whitehall, it had become his badge of office and he was never seen outside without it. Pryce was a bachelor, so he had no good woman to look after him and his hat or nag him into buying a new one.

The two Foreign Office men walked back in the sunshine past Downing Street, where Carlton gave unusual vent to his feelings. 'Bloody scientists! Why can't they leave things alone? Why must they always be tinkering with what they don't understand? We're expected to foresee political problems but how the hell could anyone have foreseen this one?'

He had always resented the intrusion of scientists into Whitehall life. Now they were about to ruin his holiday, a week's salmon fishing on the River Spey, in what had become perhaps the most productive month of the year. He was tired and stale and yearned for the delight of fishing his favourite pools.

As they glanced up Downing Street at Number 10, Carlton re-marked, 'There's no point in disrupting her holiday. We all forget she's an old age pensioner and she still takes so little time off.' He sighed and added, 'She'll have to deal with it all soon enough.'

'Where is the PM?'

'Only Cornwall, poor dear. Going abroad when she doesn't have to causes a security problem and she flits around the world enough in line of duty.'

'Aren't you taking a chance by not telling her?'

Carlton pursed his lips. 'That's what we are paid to do,' he said, though aware, as was the whole nation, that 'She of the We' as the Second Lady was known, through her gratuitous use of the royal plural, was unforgiving.

'How do you think she'll react when she is told?'

'It depends on the position by then. Right now I'm confident she would agree with me – don't tell anyone before we have to.'

'No doubt the Opposition will try to make it into another banana skin for her if it does leak,' Taylor observed as they passed the Cenotaph.

41

'Yes, and it could be a mega banana skin, suddenly right in her path. Whoosh and she'd be on her backside, with her legs in the air and all the media watching!'

Carlton pronounced 'media' with scorn. His colleague shared his view that journalists and broadcasters were, largely, a squalid nuisance to the whole machinery of government.

'It's the timing of this discovery that makes it so potentially catastrophic, especially for the Americans,' Taylor said. 'It's the kind of accidental event that looks like one of God's little jokes.'

'That's one way of putting it, I suppose,' Carlton said, ruefully, as they reached the Foreign Office. 'If the Good Lord is trying to mock our puny efforts to preserve peace and goodwill He could not have timed it more precisely.'

Chapter Six

After the session of the Joint Intelligence Committee, Sir Alexander Pryce was driven back to his headquarters in Curzon Street, a *demi-monde* of gambling, gays, tarts, pimps and MI5. The traffic round Trafalgar Square was solid metal but he was in no great hurry. He needed to ponder on a personal communication problem. The time difference with Washington was five hours, so 8 p.m. would be a good time to ring the man with whom he needed to communicate – a certain Ross Pilgrim, who would then be back in his office.

Pryce had undertaken not to 'tell the Americans' but Pilgrim, the Deputy Director for Operations at the Central Intelligence Agency's headquarters at Langley, near Washington, was not 'the Americans'. He was one very special American who, in Pryce's view, could be told anything in absolute safety.

The two had become friendly when Pryce had been the MI5 representative in Washington some fifteen years previously, and Pilgrim had been in charge of the CIA's counter-intelligence. Both never ceased to express their total commitment to the Anglo-American alliance as the keystone of Western security and freedom. The raw intelligence reports they saw, daily, confirmed that the Soviet bloc was continuing its offensive against the true democracies by means of 'active measures' – the use of sophisticated techniques of deception to undermine governments and their leaders and grossly mislead those who elected them. Both were vocal in their distrust of the Russians and in their belief that up-to-the-minute intelligence, and the counter-operations which could be based on it, were essential if freedom was to be preserved. They had remained in close professional communication on that score but there was more to the relationship than that. Ever since his return from Washington, Pryce had functioned, virtually, as a CIA 'mole' inside MI5.

He was deeply indebted to Pilgrim for a personal service which the CIA man had rendered during his Washington tour, and telling him everything had not only been a subsequent requirement – the payment of a debt of honour – but had become a habit. It was a strictly private endeavour and essentially surreptitious, being against the MI5 rules concerning certain information classified as 'For UK Eyes or Ears Only'. Pryce would have fired any of his officers caught doing the same but he had never regarded his own behaviour as being treacherous, by any stretch of the imagination. How could keeping one's closest ally informed be treacherous, especially when Pilgrim was so secure?

This self-deception was further justified to Pryce's satisfaction by the information which Pilgrim occasionally fed him in return – when it suited the CIA's purpose. 'Our relationship has always been in the best interests of the Service,' Pryce told himself, whenever assailed by doubt.

He had never expected to become 'DG', as the Director-General was invariably addressed, and had been aware, when he had accepted the post, that he was not fitted for it. Essentially a plodder, his greatest asset as a counter-intelligence officer had been the phenomenal memory which had secured him a first class degree in history at London's King's College, but he suffered from many limitations in other qualities necessary for leadership, not the least of which was his withdrawn and buttoned-up nature. While achieving some secret successes, MI5 had suffered so many public humiliations that the Director-Generalship had ceased to be a prestigious post and nobody of eminence had wanted it when it had fallen vacant. Pryce had consulted Pilgrim when eventually offered it, *faute de mieux* to end the Government's embarrassment at receiving so many refusals, and he had urged him to take it, promising that he would give him every assistance to hold it. That he had certainly done. The few successes Pryce could claim derived essentially from tips from Pilgrim, gleaned from defectors to the CIA, from secret CIA sources or from decrypted messages. There had been many occasions on which Pilgrim had been able to brief Pryce about intelligence known to MI6 but withheld from MI5, allegedly to protect MI6's sources but more often in furtherance of the rivalry and distrust between the two British agencies.

Pilgrim had also been able to suggest ingenious actions, as he had done immediately following news of the death of the British traitor, Kim Philby, in 1988. Pilgrim had urged that, without delay, Philby should be awarded a posthumous CMG – Companion of the Order

44

of St Michael and St George, an honour commonly bestowed on loyal intelligence officers. This should be followed by an authoritative obituary notice in *The Times* stating that, in the author's opinion, Philby was the bravest man he had ever encountered. Pryce had agreed that the consternation this would cause within the KGB, which had buried the traitor with such public ceremony, would be prodigious. And, with the royal imprimatur which the honour would require, it could generate ridicule of the KGB in the international media.

With little hope of success, Pryce had put the idea forward as his own to the Chief of MI6, the service Philby had betrayed, but it went no further. The MI6 management was sure that those responsible for honours would reject it, as would the Queen's advisers, fearing that it would bring the system into disrepute. 'Gutless!' was how Pilgrim had described the response when told of it by Pryce.

It was the common view in Whitehall generally that Pryce's appointment had been a mistake but to Pilgrim it remained a Godsend, carrying the assurance that little British intelligence of consequence would be withheld from him. And intelligence was his venture capital.

The two had originally taken the precaution of communicating through a 'cut-out', an American friend of Pilgrim's based in London in the oil business. That had become unnecessary when Pryce became DG because he then acquired his own totally private and secure telephone on which he could call Pilgrim, who had correspondingly secure, 'scrambled' facilities.

It was no hardship for Pryce to stay late in his spacious office looking out over Curzon Street to make his occasional calls to Pilgrim; he stayed late most evenings anyway, being unattached and in no hurry to get to his flat, nearby in South Audley Street, or to the Travellers Club in Pall Mall. A previous incumbent had developed the habit in order to have uninterrupted time for philandering with his secretary but the staff never levelled that jibe at Pryce. The only birds for which he had passion were the feathered variety, his one serious hobby being bird photography, a fitting pursuit for a loner, demanding solitary hours in cramped hides and dark-rooms. His office reputation, therefore, was that of a total neuter devoted to his aged Scottish mother, whose fiery Welsh husband had died when their only son had been small. Pryce looked forward to his evening telephone talks with Pilgrim, in whom he was free to confide, and had become rather dependent on them.

The professional position of Ross Pilgrim was very different. Within the Western intelligence community he was a living legend and he was highly respected by his adversaries, especially the KGB. Trained at Princeton as a mathematician, his forte had been counter-intelligence and in his present position he was still responsible for overseeing that extensive activity as well as for covert actions.

A novelist's concept of an intelligence spook, he was tall, lean, inscrutable and intensely secretive, with an air of knowing all and telling nothing. He signed himself Ross M. Pilgrim but nobody knew what the M stood for and anyone who asked was told, half-jokingly, that he had no 'need to know'. It was a common remark that nobody ever really knew what was going on behind his thin-rimmed spectacles or in any part under that thick, prematurely silver thatch. He had a reputation for personal courage deriving from his three years of service in the CIA's Moscow Mission – 'sharp end' experience as a field officer in the most dangerous environment, running agents from the Mission located in the American Embassy under the usual diplomatic cover. He had never been caught in spite of operations regarded by his colleagues as unnecessarily audacious. 'I always walked towards my luck – and it held,' he explained, modestly, to his juniors, though they were aware that exceptional ingenuity was a likelier explanation. 'Pilgrim's Progress', as his steady promotions were termed in the Agency, had always seemed deserved.

Apart from the bow tie, which was his personal logo, he dressed soberly in well-tailored dark suits, as befitted his idea of a professional. He loved and lived for the ancient game of deception – what he called 'black diplomacy, the other side of the diplomatic mirror which nobody sees and shouldn't see' – and had developed it into an art form. His job satisfaction came from the contributions he could make in moulding history. Through secret operations he could accomplish twists and turns denied to diplomats and politicians, hamstrung by the fetters of protocol and the perils of publicity.

He had much to his private credit but was still in quest of the truly big operation which would really count in the human chronicle and on which he would be able to look back in serene, if silent, contentment. The circumstances for this supreme effort had not yet presented themselves. And with just two years to go before his

46

planned retirement they might never arise. But the search for them kept him going as enthusiastically as ever.

His particular speciality was the setting-up and manipulation of the 'willie' – a person who could be induced to play an important role in an intelligence operation without being aware of what he was really doing. Within the CIA, Pilgrim was acknowledged as the greatest willier of all time and it was said, among the many stories retailed about him, that this peculiar ability reached back to his schoolboy days when he had made a name for himself as an unusually artful prankster, displaying great ingenuity in staging embarrassing jokes against his teachers. He had been peculiar in that he had revelled in deceptions so secret that only he knew about them, while other boys would have found them pointless if unable to share the fun and take credit for them. It had been an early expression of his freedom from vanity and his eventual hatred of it, on the grounds that the vain were likely to be incapable of keeping secrets. In his experience, the leaker of secrets was usually motivated by a desire to let the recipients know that he belonged to an in-the-know élite. Even professional spies, whose lives might be forfeit from a leak, usually found a human need to confide in at least one other person, but Pilgrim had never felt the need to confide in anyone.

His face, excessively lined for his fifty-seven years, wrinkled further in fascination at what Pryce had to tell him that evening on the telephone. He was not at all surprised that the Foreign Office had insisted on holding the silicon information secret until the implications became clearer. That was how he would have behaved himself. As usual, he said little and both had become expert at speaking in riddles, but, on looking at the notes he had made, he asked himself, as he always did on such occasions, 'How can we take advantage of the situation?'

The potential for clandestine action was already inflaming his imagination but no operation would be possible without possession of Clone Fe 113. So a culture had to be secured with least delay. Pryce had indicated how this might be achieved without endangering his position or their relationship. Until Pilgrim heard more, he would not be informing anyone else in the CIA of this exciting development. This was intelligence from his own private network and he was not one to put his sources at risk by sharing it.

Pilgrim was married, contentedly in his view, but his wife, Betty, had always been excluded from his work, which he often continued at his home in Washington's fashionable P Street, a house made possible by inherited private means. A slim, harassed-looking lady with a slight, not-unattractive stammer – said by unkind friends to be occasioned by her perennial fear of revealing one of her husband's secrets – she was gregarious by nature. She enjoyed entertaining but, save for two or three trusted cronies, her husband classed the rest of their friends as 'homeopathic' – to be taken in small doses. Betty found comfort in her deep religious faith. She also sought earthly companionship and some measure of fulfilment through her church activities and Women's Clubs and was out attending one of her functions that evening when Ross returned home. Their two grown-up sons, on whom they both doted, were also away from home, the younger at the Harvard Law School, the elder abroad in the 'white' diplomatic service. To their father's deep disappointment, neither had wished to involve themselves in the game of 'black' diplomacy, though he had assured them that the 'white' form was often every bit as secret and underhand, with career diplomats as opportunistic and cynical, discarding friends and making common cause with enemies when it suited.

The only welcome, which was always excitedly warm, was from his dog, a yellow labrador called Dallas, not because Pilgrim had any affection for that city – he was a New Englander. When given it as a puppy, he had wanted to call it 'Dulles', after a former CIA chief who, like himself, had been a master of deception, but that could have given a clue to his profession to those who should not know it. So he had settled for the nearest safe name.

Pilgrim poured himself a stiff measure from his last remaining bottle of 25-year-old Macallan, a rare single malt whisky, lit yet another cigarette and stretched out in his armchair to indulge in what a close friend, who was given to quoting poetry, called 'the bliss of solitude'. There was a bundle of documents by his side but, first, he relaxed and thought over the day, twisting his wide-band wedding ring, as he was wont to do when pleased or puzzling out a problem. As Dallas intruded his welcome snout under his master's arm, Pilgrim remarked aloud, 'We had a good day today, Dallas. A very good day.'

He often talked to his dog. He thought better aloud and had a ready answer when anyone ribbed him about it. 'A guy called Francis was made a saint for talking to birds. So what's wrong with talking to a bird–dog?'

It looked like being an even better day. Waiting for him on his desk was a thin envelope, delivered late that afternoon by a CIA colleague, from his best current source, a Russian to whom he had given the code name Brown Derby – chosen from an approved list made up from the names of various hats. Brown Derby was known as Vinogradsky at United Nations headquarters in New York where he was listed as a diplomat in the Soviet mission, but his real name was Peter Ivashutin. Nor was he a diplomat. Clandestinely, he was the senior representative in the United States of the Chief Directorate of Intelligence of the General Staff – the GRU – and was the officer responsible for the acquisition of advanced technology computers and other equipment denied to the Soviets on defence grounds. Though posing as a civilian of modest grade, a scientific and technical attaché, he held the military rank of a senior colonel, in line to be major general, and was a close relative of the GRU's most famous former chief, after whom he was named. He needed the rank to lead the large team of 'techno-bandits', as the CIA and FBI called them – Soviet bloc agents dispatched to the United States in various guises to defeat the embargo on the export of strategic goods to the Soviet Union. The better known KGB was also involved in such operations but it was the GRU that was in charge of them.

Like some of his predecessors, Brown Derby displayed remarkable ingenuity in spiriting large items of high-tech equipment out of the United States, under the noses of the Customs and the FBI, but Pilgrim had secured a hold on him. In return for occasional 'chicken-feed' to enhance Brown Derby's reputation with his chiefs in Moscow – in the form of some genuinely secret CIA information which could be sacrificed or an easy run in acquiring some equipment deemed not to be too important – Pilgrim received an intermittent stream of information which he rated invaluable to his counter-intelligence activities.

The Russian also served a greater general purpose. As Pilgrim put it, 'You can't fight an enemy with whom you have no contact.' So, over the years, Pilgrim had built up a highly secret relationship with the GRU through a succession of conduits, of which Brown Derby was the latest and most senior. As with Pryce, his private conduit

49

with MI5, Brown Derby was deeply in Pilgrim's debt. Shortly after his arrival in the US, he had been caught in the act of trying to bribe an official of a computer company, with full photographic evidence, and was about to be prosecuted, which meant eventual deportation and disgrace, but Pilgrim had successfully intervened and stifled any publicity or complaint to the Soviet Embassy.

'Yes,' Pilgrim assured himself, as he drew deeply on his cigarette and assessed the day's achievements, 'one needs a hold on such people; gratitude is never enough.'

Brown Derby's latest information, in the thin envelope, had reached Pilgrim through his most trusted aide, who had travelled to New York to empty a dead-drop, a hiding place in a disused drainpipe by the East River front, convenient to the United Nations building, the glass-faced thirty-nine-storey block known to the Soviet intelligence men as 'their tallest observation tower'. Like several of his UN colleagues with military training, Brown Derby, at forty, was a keep-fit fanatic. 'Don't let the body go!' he admonished his staff. His habit of jogging during the lunch interval, or even at night, provided opportunity to pass such dead-drops and to slide in or remove a written message while adjusting a lace of his trainer shoes. As always, the message was in code based on a book cipher, sets of figures which could be deciphered only by someone with knowledge of the chosen book and a certain page in it.

As Pilgrim settled down to the boring business of deciphering Brown Derby's latest message, he was grateful that the Russian was such a pro: the report was mercifully short. He received its information with some delight but an attached message gave him cause for concern: 'Aquarium exerting utmost pressure fulfil quota without delay. Otherwise expect recall, which may be permanent, for consultations – repeat consultations. Can you assist? Repeat, utmost pressure.'

The Aquarium was the colloquial name for the Moscow headquarters of the GRU, a heavily glassed nine-storey building on the edge of Khodinka airfield, an old, rarely used airstrip generally unseen because it was surrounded by buildings with restricted public access. While everyone in Moscow was aware of the KGB headquarters in Dzerzhinsky Square, few even knew of the existence of the GRU. When the chiefs at the Aquarium cracked the whip they meant business and Brown Derby's deliberate use of the word 'consultations'

50

had been particularly worrying. 'Consultations' was the standard reason given for recall when an officer was under some suspicion.

It could be just a come-on but perhaps it was time for some more chicken-feed of such a special nature that it would allay any dangerous qualms about Brown Derby at the Aquarium. Pilgrim could not afford to lose such a priceless asset, especially in view of an operation which was beginning to brew in his mind. And the FBI had been enjoying rather a long run of success against the techno-bandits.

It was an additional problem at a time when he was already overloaded. But then he was always overloaded. And he was used to problems: in intelligence work the solution of one always created others. He would resolve it in the morning; possibly even that night in his bath, or in bed, for he slept alone. His sons claimed that he did so for fear of talking in his sleep and revealing some secret. While respecting his intellect and reputation they regarded him, affectionately, as something of a screwball.

He sat back with a second stiff Scotch at his elbow to read the proof of a document called the *Weekly Bulletin of The Nephews*. This was one of several publications issued by 'The Nephews' – short for The Nephews of Uncle Sam, an overt organization of Americans, led by retired military chiefs and some serving senators, who were suspicious of the relationship between Washington and Moscow, which seemed altogether too cosy for their peace of mind. Composed almost entirely of Republicans, it had given good support to the election of Clinton Rockwell as President in the previous November, but had since turned against his management of East–West issues and especially his closeness with the Soviet leader, General Secretary Vladimir Primarkov, who was almost as new to the job as Rockwell was.

In the ensuing power struggle after the ousting of the previous Soviet leader, who had lasted little more than a year, the hardliners had fought to regain control. They were the original radicals of the Gorbachev era who had mellowed into the new conservatives, opposed to further change for the sake of change and concerned about the extent to which Lenin's infallibility was now being questioned. But *glasnost* and *perestroika* had been sold so heavily to the Soviet people that the tide of popular demand could not easily be stemmed, much less reversed. The agile and highly intelligent thruster, Vladimir Sergeyevitch Primarkov, had emerged the victor, determined to pursue the 'bloodless revolution' with even greater speed. In his zeal for accommodation with the new Soviet leadership, President Rockwell seemed set to outdo his predecessors.

The Nephews regarded all arms control agreements with the Russians as a dangerous delusion, being sure that Primarkov's public image must be very different from his private Politburo face. They did not believe that the Soviet leadership had given up the imperial design it had inherited from Peter the Great and had pursued so effectively for so long. They could see no really significant reduction in military strength or in general arms production. Some nuclear and old conventional weapons had been scrapped but massive Soviet superiority still remained; high-tech tanks, submarines and aircraft were still pouring off the production lines, universal conscription still kept enormous armies in being and in place. Primarkov's seductive changes were aimed at presenting a less frightening face to the outside world to secure Western economic aid but the threat remained as potential as ever.

The Nephews' badge was Uncle Sam's hat in colourful enamels and, as regards sharing any American technology with the Soviets, their motto was 'Keep it under Uncle Sam's hat!' Their criterion was to help the Russians only if Uncle Sam was assisted in the process, and they saw little coming in return. On the contrary, Soviet subversion continued in the form of espionage, theft of technology, disinformation – what Pilgrim colourfully called 'bullshitsky' – and active measures generally. Whatever Primarkov might claim, there were others out there working as hard as ever to undermine America and show its Government to be untrustworthy.

The Nephews organization was well-endowed with money, being supported by certain billionaires, and formed a powerful political lobby of which Rockwell had to take note, in spite of his insistence that they were out of tune 'with the realities of our time'.

The main headline in the *Bulletin*, 'Uncle Sam Being Taken for a Ride', induced a nod of assent from Pilgrim. The writer could see no point in helping Primarkov with soft loans, cheap grain and advanced technology when the only hope for the free world was for the Soviet people to depose the whole Politburo and the communist system and disband its empire which, to those enslaved in it, was still evil. Putting Western goods into the Soviet shops, improving the disgraceful housing situation with American money or reducing the miseries of communist life in any other way would only perpetuate the system.

Pilgrim paid special attention to an article by 'Watchdog' calling for more money to be spent on counter-intelligence. 'Watchdog' was very suspicious of the joint Soviet–American verification arrangements to ensure that missile-reduction deals were being observed. 'What could the democracies do if the Russians were caught cheating?' the writer asked. 'The State Department would always find a reason for doing nothing because any action would confirm that it had made an error in the first place.'

The issue's centre-spread article was an up-to-date account of what the Russians were really doing about 'Star Wars' – what President Reagan had called 'the defence which kills incoming missiles not people'. It was illustrated with drawings based on intelligence photographs, showing that, in spite of their continuing denials, the Soviets were heavily engaged in the high-tech struggle for the new high ground of battle, with more than 10,000 scientists and engineers based at several research centres, the main one being Sary Shagan in Soviet Central Asia.

'Excellent stuff,' thought Pilgrim, as well he might since he had supplied the intelligence photographs and much of the data. As he scribbled his approval in the margin he experienced the sharp surge of exhilaration and involuntary in-take of breath symptomatic of sudden inspiration, which had come sooner than he had expected. He was no longer in doubt about the best way to make use of the Clone Fe 113 when he could get his hands on it.

'We really have had a good day, haven't we?' he said to Dallas.

He made a few more notes on the proof of *Bulletin* in his minuscule, spidery writing before returning it to the editor, who was a retired admiral. In his position Pilgrim could not be associated openly with The Nephews though, like various serving chiefs of staff, he was suspected of being sympathetic. He had a further reason for close liaison: the organization had its own, richly financed intelligence service and Pilgrim had access to it. His world was the Great Domain of Doubt and every scrap of information facilitated his task of converting possibilities into probabilities and probabilities into near enough certainties.

Chapter Seven

Sitting alone in his austerely furnished flat, which looked more like a room in a club with its black leather armchairs and sofa, Sandy Pryce was concerned to resolve his immediate problem – one he had created for himself. Like all his major leaks to Pilgrim, his tip about the silicon discovery had to be deniable if there was a backlash, as there would undoubtedly be if Pilgrim made use of it. So, the following morning, he called in the MI5 officer best equipped to arrange the necessary circumstances. This was his senior female officer, Lesley Barrington-Fuller, the Director of C Branch, responsible for Protective Security. Secrets were her currency and protecting them was her function.

Looking businesslike, as always, in a sharp suit, white blouse and court shoes with her auburn hair fashionably cut on the shortish side, she could have passed for one of the new brood of successful women in the City.

'Good morning, Lesley,' Pryce said affably as she entered his office. 'I must indoctrinate you into a rather remarkable development down at Porton. Have you ever been there?'

'Never, DG,' Lesley answered, settling herself in the lowish chair set in front of Pryce's impressive partners' desk, which was bereft of papers.

'Well, I want you to visit it – the Chemical Defence Establishment. It's on Salisbury Plain. We suddenly need to mark their card about security. Normally I wouldn't ask anyone as senior as you to do such a routine job but it's delicate and needs a woman's touch. There is also a special requirement.'

Lesley, who had achieved the highest rank of any woman, to date, in a service which had always been dominated by men, smiled her approval of the DG's choice. Her smile was attractive, being rather toothy in the way which, for some reason probably associated with certain television personalities, had become fashionable.

In her early forties, and with good Oxford degrees in both modern languages and law, she had risen through sheer ability as a field officer in counter-espionage work and felt too desk-bound in her present position, though it was pleasurably prestigious to be a director and part of the senior management.

'It will be a nice change to get out,' she observed, as the sunshine slanted through the windows and the dust motes danced in it.

'Yes, it's very pleasant down there. I once went there to see some bustards – huge birds they are trying to reintroduce on to Salisbury Plain . . .'

'Exactly what do you want me to do, DG?' Lesley prompted.

Pryce briefed her on the Joint Intelligence Committee Meeting. 'The Foreign Office is determined that the Americans should not be told because then this silicon business will leak,' he added. 'So we have to go through the motions of making the need for secrecy clear to the man in charge. He's not the Director. He's away ill. It's a scientist chap called Dr Allen. He's not used to dealing with secrets.'

'That seems pretty straightforward,' Lesley commented. 'But what's the special requirement?'

'Ah, you will appreciate that there are intelligence angles to this discovery and we should really inform the CIA about them without delay. That would be in the best interests of the Security Service. If the CIA finds out that we have been hanging on to a secret of such obvious importance to them there will be hell to pop.'

Lesley nodded. She too had served three years as a liaison officer in Washington, a usual appointment for those being groomed for stardom, and knew how touchy the Americans were on that score – with fair reason in view of certain events in the not too distant past.

'You know how strongly I feel about our relations with Washington,' Pryce continued, stroking the few hairs across his scalp. 'And I particularly don't want to raise any doubts about them in the mind of the new Director of Central Intelligence there. It's all very well for the Foreign Office but we're a small and highly vulnerable organization and we need all the friends we can get.'

Lesley agreed. To avoid offending the relatively new head of the CIA, appointed by the President on his election, was of the utmost importance. She had no knowledge of Pryce's personal obligation to Pilgrim, whom she knew and admired, but she was well aware of the extent to which her chief depended on the CIA for information. She was one of the very few colleagues with whom he socialized and exchanged confidences, remaining aloof from the others, which did not help his image in the office at large.

'You know, Lesley, we're still somewhat on parole with the CIA after the Peter Wright affair. They don't really trust us yet and I don't blame them after that catastrophe. The Foreign Office may have its problems but we have to protect our turf.'

'Of course, DG, but how do we do that?'

'Well, Bill Brook is absolutely right. This silicon business can't be kept secret for long, so it wouldn't do too much damage if someone from Porton told the Americans about it on the science net. The CIA would quickly hear about it through their own resources and then we would get a formal request for a briefing, which we couldn't refuse, whatever the Foreign Office said.'

'That's hardly compatible with telling the Porton people that they need to be secure, is it?' Lesley queried.

'No. Somehow you have to resolve that conflict. And do it quickly. We can explain a slight delay as simply due to the time taken for our inquiries.'

'Have you any suggestions?'

'Absolutely none, dear girl. I leave it entirely to you. There's more than one way of cooking an egg and the less I know about how you cook this one the better. All I know, officially, is that I was so impressed with the need for secrecy at Porton that I sent down the Director of Protective Security herself.' Pryce gave Lesley one of his rare smiles. 'We shall learn soon enough if you have had any success. I wouldn't trust anyone else with this, you know. It's entirely between us.'

The bald way Pryce had let her know his requirement surprised Lesley. Normally he was an ace exponent of what Whitehall knew as 'Not-quite speak' – the art of getting a message into somebody else's skull without quite saying it. But he had made it absolutely clear that he wanted the silicon secret leaked in a way that would enable him to deny that he or any of his staff had been responsible. It was not a task she fancied but she was anxious to assist and controlled leaks were common enough in her world. She would do anything to keep Pryce in his post until his Deputy was too old to succeed him, which meant another couple of years. Then she would be in the running for the job herself with a fair chance, if the appointment was to be made on merit and the Government could breach the psychological barrier of appointing a woman. That should not be impossible with a woman in Number 10 Downing Street. The first woman chief of any major security-intelligence service in the world! That was some target!

Though few in Whitehall would have believed it, Lesley knew that, though Pryce had four more years to run, he might take early retirement. Through her influence, her husband Dr Paul Barrington-Fuller, a prominent psychiatrist, had been appointed as a consultant to MI5 a couple of years previously, and Pryce was one of his occasional patients.

A man with a charming couch-side manner and distinguished both in his appearance and qualifications – he was on the senior staff at the Maudsley Hospital – Paul had originally met his wife through his study of the psychological aspects of treachery. He was particularly interested in the possibility of identifying the early signs – what he called the 'prodromal symptoms' – which might give an early indication of a person's susceptibility to becoming a traitor, like excessive drinking, greed, smouldering resentment, the chip on the shoulder. Before publishing a paper on the subject he had been wise enough to submit it to MI5, and Lesley, then more junior, had been assigned to deal with it. Having met him, Lesley had been relieved to find that he was immune to such Freudian fantasies as the claim that traitors were raping their motherland, and she arranged a meeting with Pryce. The DG had eventually been so impressed with Paul's special interest, competence and professional gravitas that he had offered him the consultancy post.

Having been positively vetted, Paul served as a kind of medical ombudsman. His services were available, on a totally confidential basis, to members of the staff with personal problems and they were so widely used that he was the repository of many secrets. After becoming friendly with him, Pryce had consulted him about a drink problem which was usually held in check but occasionally defeated his determination. As a result of several sessions, held in private consulting rooms in Wimpole Street, it had become clear to Paul that Pryce, whom he liked, was an intensely unhappy person, fully aware that he should never have taken on the onerous post of Director-General. And, while there was no pressure on him to depart, almost all his colleagues were of that opinion – and Pryce knew it. For his part, Pryce appreciated that Paul would probably have few secrets from his wife, who, though ten years younger, clearly dominated him, but he trusted her because she understood his predicament.

Paul did, indeed, have few secrets from Lesley because her knowledge assisted him in making judgements about his patients, who tended to be oddities, either because they were made that way and the Security Service attracted such people, or they had been warped by the strange nature of their work. His current research project, on which he hoped to publish a medical monograph, was a study of suspiciousness, the tendency to be suspicious of others which, in its extreme form, was a component of schizophrenia and what used to be called paranoia. He had coined the word 'sceptomania' for the tendency to be unduly suspicious, and his MI5 patients, afflicted with the condition in various degrees, were a rich seam of material. Their work required them to be suspicious but its corrosive effects on character had been greatly exacerbated since the discovery of the various 'moles' in their midst. Since Anthony Blunt and his like, nobody was above suspicion and sceptomania in a degree which could only be called pathological – what the MI5 officers themselves called Wright's Disease – had become more prevalent.

Paul was keeping a watchful eye on his wife to keep her well-balanced – with a chip on each shoulder, as she put it, laughingly. He took it more seriously. His MI5 knowledge proclaimed a central premise – all power corrupts and secret power corrupts particularly. The secret world offered power over others to people who would otherwise never achieve it and some were not fitted to wield it or cope with its effects on themselves. And the Official Secrets Act ensured that any excesses were unlikely to be exposed. He therefore ensured that in their social life Lesley met people from outside the intelligence community, mainly through their serious interest in bridge, at which they were a formidable pair, and she seemed to be wearing the professional hazards better than most. The only observable symptom was an excess of ambition, which had kept them childless with no genetic stake in the future. Lesley's insistence that they had both married too late for a family was either self-delusion or, more likely in Paul's opinion, a conscious pretext.

After making arrangements to visit Porton, Lesley spent some time quietly examining the file on Dr Adrian Allen held in the Registry's massive computer. The positive vetting which had taken place when he had joined the permanent staff at Porton, because of his necessary access to some top secret information, showed nothing of interest. But there were several quite detailed addenda, mainly concerning his behaviour when on foreign trips. He had never been under surveillance but it was surprising what had been supplied either by busybodies or by scientists whose habit it was to report matters of possible interest to the security and intelligence authorities.

She found some brief notes under 'Payne, Wendy – Student agitator, superficially left-wing militant, but not deeply political, a slogan chanter, a natural anti of any convenient cause. CND, Civil Liberties, Friends of the Earth, League Against Cruel Sports. Continued her agit-prop activities, though diminishingly, while taking a PhD in bacteriology.'

There was nothing recent.

It was a common enough syndrome in Lesley's experience and usually faded with maturity and immersion in the serious business of earning a living.

In MI5's computerized library of, literally, millions of photographs available for identification purposes and use by the 'watchers', the surveillance operators, she found pictures of Allen and Wendy taken at conferences, some by photographic agencies, others by amateurs. Glued to the back of the photographs were identifying notes. Three pictures included an American called Julian Flickinger, an eager-looking, trimly bearded man in his mid-thirties described as a scientist from Fort Detrick. Two were of Flickinger and Wendy alone and indicated a degree of close friendship. The third showed them both in earnest conversation with Allen.

To her surprise, Lesley, who was nothing if not thorough, found a record on Flickinger in the Registry. It had been started when he had been cleared for his service as liaison officer at Porton and contained nothing to his discredit.

There were several older photographs of Wendy, taken mainly by photographers of northern newspapers covering political demonstrations by students and anti-bloodsport activities. In one she could be seen struggling vigorously against removal by the police, though there was no record of any charge against her.

So this was the girl whose research was causing all the commotion, Lesley mused. Porton could have a problem on its hands.

By telephone, Lesley made an arrangement to see Sir William Brook at his club, the Athenaeum, off Pall Mall, immediately after lunch. They frequently met in connection with Defence Ministry security. She admired him, needed his advice and he was always pleased to see her. One thing they had in common was a dislike of the Foreign Office. Invariably anxious to preserve any secrets they had originated, those in the Foreign Office tended to regard any other department's as commodities which could be traded for diplomatic advantage.

The silicon secret was unlikely to be an exception.

Chapter Eight

At the Ministry of Defence that same afternoon, the atmosphere bordered on the hectic, at least for a Whitehall department on a hot day in the holiday period. Brook had sent his deputy down to Porton that morning to question Dr Wendy Payne and to make an examination of the evidence in her laboratory. The deputy had taken with him the Ministry's chief computer expert, who made arrangements with Adrian Allen for a more complex and expendable computer to be supplied for a larger-scale experiment. Neither of the visitors had any doubts about the gravity of Wendy's discovery, as they told Brook by telephone before returning to Whitehall in the early afternoon.

At short notice, Brook had called a meeting in his room on the sixth floor, the location of the so-called 'corridors of power' which, following heavy defence cuts occasioned by the East–West relaxation, were becoming corridors of impotence. The Chief of the Defence Staff and the First Sea Lord had been briefed hurriedly after being helicoptered down that morning from different grouse moors, but they had heard enough to realize that, in the wrong hands, the development threatened all their war plans. Without electronic communications, war simply could not be waged and, while even more remarkable alternatives to silicon were under development, that element would dominate the defence situation for twenty years at least. The First Sea Lord, who was noted for his lower-deck expletives, was particularly concerned with the vulnerability of the few warships left to him since they relied so heavily on computerized automation to launch their missiles and torpedoes and to fire their guns.

'It's the possibilities for sabotage that worry me most,' he said. 'It's tailor-made for high-tech terrorism. This bloody stuff could so easily be introduced into a ship's control system and it would be as good as sunk – a sitting duck unable to defend itself!'

The Chief of the Air Staff, whose bomber programme had been

slashed, pointed out, with some intensity, that not only were silicon chips in the essential computers on every aircraft, but the communication and radar systems which controlled them were highly vulnerable. 'If you are looking for high-tech terrorist targets, there they are!'

While the Army Chief felt rather less threatened, he agreed that communication and control systems were the prime targets for sabotage. He had in mind various underground headquarters, on which enormous sums had been spent to protect them from bombing and terrorist assault. 'Is there any possibility that this awful bug could become epidemic?' he asked.

Brook replied, 'It might. Porton can't be sure without further experiments. If it did become epidemic, with a computer, a word processor and at least a calculator in almost every home, and with glass everywhere, how could we eradicate it? Apart from our problems, the civilian mayhem could be catastrophic. Micro-chips control everything now – the telephone service, power stations, airliners, you name it. If this secret gets out, and it will, the response of the whole high-tech industry is going to be pretty brisk.'

'What about the intelligence computers?' the Chief of the Defence Staff asked. 'I hope they'll all be duplicated. You'd only need one of MI5's infamous "moles" to contaminate the main computers there to put them out of action and destroy everything in them.'

'Eyeless in Curzon Street!' Brook quipped. 'We may have to give some consideration to having duplicates on the old car index system until non-silicon chips become available. All the contingency plans are on computers these days.'

'Or go back to valves,' commented the First Sea Lord. 'Christ! What a bloody undertaking! But what's the realistic risk? What's the intelligence appreciation about the Russians if they got hold of this stuff? Would the buggers use it as a weapon?'

'It's anybody's guess,' Brook replied. 'They are about to sign an agreement outlawing bacterial warfare but would they be able to resist this thing in the event of war?'

'Not as a sabotage weapon, they wouldn't,' the Chief of the Defence Staff said assuredly. 'What do you think, Jimmy?' he asked, addressing the Army Chief who, as a former Director of Army Intelligence, was the expert on the Soviet *Spetsnaz*, the SAS-type forces which would be responsible for extensive sabotage in advance of a surprise attack in Europe.

'Oh, it's an ideal weapon for *Spetsnaz*. Would they even regard a method of destroying defence computers as bacterial warfare, which has always been thought of as essentially for use against people?'

'They'd do whatever suits them,' Brook said, emphatically. 'The temptation could be too great. We have to be prepared for that.'

'Meanwhile there is nothing we can do but rely on secrecy,' the Chief of the Defence Staff concluded. 'Thank God the secret was discovered in a secure Government establishment and not by some academic. You know how red some of these university scientists are. They would be only too happy to make a public issue of it, using that as the self-righteous excuse to blow it to their Russian friends.'

His military colleagues agreed that they could only put their faith in security, at least for the time being. Not only should all the information be held tightly secret but the clone itself would have to be specially protected.

The possibility of destroying all cultures of the clone was raised but quickly abandoned when it was realized that the Russians might stumble on it through their own genetic engineering research. The clone might then be needed as a deterrent. And it would certainly be necessary to keep it going for research on possible antidotes.

'What is the security situation at Porton?' the Air Chief inquired.

'Frankly, a mess,' said Brook. 'The chap in charge is helpful but he has little feel for security. And the girl who made the discovery has never even signed the Official Secrets Act.'

'Surely she'll have to do that now, and be positively vetted!' the Army Chief exclaimed.

'Sandy Pryce is putting that in hand,' Brook responded.

'There's one other problem that worries me,' said the Chief of the Defence Staff. 'What do we tell the Americans? In all honesty, we should inform them immediately. If anything, they are more threatened than we are.'

'The situation with Washington could hardly be more piquant,' Brook replied. 'There is a solemn agreement between the United States and the Soviet Union that neither of them will undertake any further research on bacteriological weapons pending a treaty to outlaw all such devices, which is due to be signed at the summit early in the New Year. The Americans haven't broken the agreement but if we give them all this information, it will be only too easy for the Russians to claim that they have done so. Therefore, the Foreign

Office is against telling them anything, until we know a lot more about the implications.'

There was a general murmur of disapproval.

'I agree with you,' Brook said. 'I think the whole thing is bound to leak and then we'll get the worst of both worlds. This Payne girl has been working in collaboration with a man from Fort Detrick and any mention of the Fort will send the Russians up the wall. They've been claiming for years that Fort Detrick deliberately invented the AIDS virus and let it loose in Africa! They'll say this new bug is for germ warfare and they will be widely believed.'

Each of the Chiefs had an opposite number in the Pentagon, the huge American defence headquarters in Washington, whom he could not afford to alienate and was, more often than not, a personal friend. The Chief of the Defence Staff looked glum. 'It won't help our relations at all. Why should the Americans go on supplying us with all their surveillance satellite intelligence if we hold back on something like this? They're as secure as we are.'

'I don't know that I would agree with that,' Brook said, 'but I wouldn't give the secret another month here anyway. Too many people know about it. However, I suppose we will have to follow the Foreign Office line, at least until the next meeting of the Joint Intelligence Committee.'

It was agreed, with reluctance, that perhaps the Americans did not need to know at that early stage.

The First Sea Lord gave a surreptitious glance at his watch and cursed silently. But for the silicon intrusion, he would have been in his butt in the Shipka Pass on Wemmergill Moor with high grouse bulleting over him. He was relieved that there was no action for him to take. He could not be helicoptered back to North Durham: that could raise nasty questions in Parliament about misuse of transport. But a quick dash up the Great North Road might get him there in time for dinner and to shoot the next day.

As the meeting adjourned, he was not the only one wondering why Brook was so certain that the secret would leak. They were all aware of his reputation for indiscretion. His remark, 'You can safely tell me anything, provided it has no entertainment value,' was part of the folklore of Whitehall.

Chapter Nine

Adrian Allen was not looking forward to the visit of the senior security officer, which had been arranged in telephone talks with the Ministry of Defence, but he brightened when Lesley Barrington-Fuller turned out to be a challengingly attractive, red-haired woman.

'I expected some dull old stick of a man,' he said after he had seated her in his office and eyed her slender, crossed legs in their gun-metal tights.

'They all do,' she replied. 'But I'm not the only female Security Service officer by any means.'

'Well, you are the first female spook I've met. I must apologize for the absence of the Director. He usually deals with these administrative matters but he's away sick.'

'I know and I understand that the prognosis is not good. So perhaps you had better get used to the admin,' Lesley said, deliberately indicating that she was aware of his interest in the post.

'How can I assist you, Miss Barrington-Fuller,' Adrian asked.

'Mrs Barrington-Fuller. I'm married. I'm also faithful to my husband.'

'What an extraordinary thing to say!'

'I suppose it is but it's relevant to my visit, Dr Allen. Not all spouses are faithful,' Lesley said briskly. MI5 officers were forbidden to resort to blackmail but encouraging hints were fair enough.

She looked at Adrian fixedly, trying to assess his response. Throughout her career she had been adept at establishing a moral ascendancy over those whom she interviewed or from whom she needed a favour, and she was never embarrassed by a direct approach if it would save time.

Shifting uneasily under the stare of his visitor's greenish eyes, Adrian appreciated that his promiscuous behaviour was not conducive to positive vetting and he had managed to get away with it so far.

'I need to talk to you about this silicon business, Dr Allen,' Lesley said in a friendly tone. 'I trust that you appreciate the security aspects.'

'In what particular way?'

'The possibility that some adversary might find out about the discovery and then misuse it against us.'

'I take it you mean the KGB?'

'Among others. Actually, the GRU is likely to be the most interested.'

Seeing his puzzlement, she explained. 'The GRU is the military arm of Russian intelligence and very formidable. You remember that Soviet delegation of scientists which visited you here recently? Well, at least two of those were quite senior GRU officers.'

'But that was long before the silicon discovery.'

'I know but it showed that the GRU has a special interest in this place and that interest will be greatly intensified if they get wind of it. Your clone, as I believe you call it, could make a very dangerous sabotage weapon and it's the GRU that's responsible for sabotage. So they might approach your staff. How many people here know about it?'

'As far as I am aware, only one, Dr Payne, who produced the clone.'

'That's Dr Wendy Payne?' Lesley asked rhetorically. 'It would be helpful, at this stage, if you could ask her, I might say require her, not to talk to anyone else about it – at least until you hear from me further. How well do you know her?'

She looked at him quizzically with half a smile, as though she might already know the answer. The look was not lost on Adrian.

'Pretty well. Our academic interests overlap. We've been scientific associates for several years.'

'I gather that you attend a few foreign conferences together and socialize outside the office.'

'You *have* been doing your homework,' Adrian said, a trifle testily.

'It's my job, Dr Allen. What I had mainly in mind was the kind of people with whom she might have become friendly at such conferences. You know, scientists from behind the Iron Curtain,' she said, gesturing with her arm, as was her habit.

'Oh, we all meet those. As you recalled, we even had some Russians visiting here, though we only showed them what we wanted them to see. And, of course, we communicate with others who are working in the same fields. You'd better ask Dr Payne about her contacts. I can call her in.'

'No,' Lesley replied, hastily. 'That job's not for me. I understand that the lady is going to be PV'd and that will be done by the Ministry of Defence.'

'She won't like that,' Adrian declared, emphatically. 'You see she's not employed by the Ministry of Defence. She really belongs to the Department of Health. I don't think she'll agree to be PV'd. You might even have some difficulty getting her to sign the Official Secrets Act.'

'She won't be able to continue her work unless she does. She would have to leave this place and she wouldn't be allowed to take any cultures with her.'

'That's correct but it might not stop her. She might decide to go anyway, in view of the secrecy. I know she's very opposed to it – the universality of scientific knowledge and all that. She's very hot on civil liberties. I believe she was quite an activist in her student days.'

'Nevertheless, I think you might persuade her otherwise,' Lesley persisted.

'Oh, she's a very determined young lady. And she's very sparky. She could cause trouble if she's pushed. She is most anxious to pursue her discovery in the way she wants to and she's within her rights to do that.'

'As a woman operating in a man's world I see her point, Dr Allen, but I'm sure you will manage if you try,' she countered, giving him her half-smile again.

'What makes you so sure?'

'Just a woman's intuition. It's a great asset.'

Lesley prided herself on being a good judge of character and being married to a psychiatrist had improved her insight. She had already sensed Adrian's insecurity, which explained the little she had gleaned from his file. He was another example of the multitude of men with whom, in her experience, sex cut clean across intellect and who were the natural prey of foreign intelligence agencies. Perhaps it was just as well that he had never been involved in much really secret work, she thought. He would have been a pushover for compromising KGB photographs behind the Iron Curtain. He looked like being a pushover for her.

In fact, Adrian was becoming rather irritated by Lesley's patronizing attitude. 'I don't think you fully appreciate that there are medical aspects of this discovery which are very important to Dr Payne. She needs to tell an enzyme expert about them so that he can press on with the research. I've stopped her doing that for the moment but she's quite concerned about it.'

'And who is this expert?' Lesley asked, sensing her opportunity to complete her task.

'It's a certain Dr Julian Flickinger, but in spite of his Middle European name he's an American – third generation I believe.'

'Doesn't he work at Fort Detrick?'

'Yes. How did you know that?'

'Oh, I keep myself informed, Dr Allen. Fort Detrick is very secure, isn't it?'

'It is but, like us, they are permitted to publish most of their researches.'

'But not all,' Lesley rejoined. 'And you would agree that secrecy in this matter is as much in the American interest as in ours?'

'Even more so, I gather.'

'You suggest that Dr Flickinger is a good American, so there shouldn't be much danger if Dr Payne told him just enough to enable him to get on with the medical research in secret.'

Adrian, too, saw his opportunity. 'I have to agree. In fact I'm really committed to inform our counterparts at Fort Detrick under the protocol arrangement. They get very testy if we keep anything from them, as we would with them. But the problem is that Dr Flickinger can't do the work without cultures of the clone and we are forbidden to let any of it out of Porton until further order. Surely you can see why.'

'Indeed! But couldn't Dr Flickinger be invited here to do the work? I gather there is a regular interchange of personnel between Porton and Fort Detrick.'

'Yes, certainly – if he would come,' Adrian replied with enthusiasm. 'He's worked here before and he likes England. Do you want me to ask Dr Payne to approach him?'

'I can't authorize you to do anything, Dr Allen,' Lesley said, with a cautionary wag of her finger. 'It is the considered view of my superiors that nobody should be told anything at this stage but that's a counsel of perfection and you and I have to be pragmatic. We need some initiative to solve the immediate problem of calming down Dr Payne and inducing her to sign the Official Secrets Act.'

'What the Americans call a trade-off?'

'Exactly. All I am suggesting is that a sensible compromise would be for someone to invite Dr Flickinger to come and do the enzyme work here and, in return, Dr Payne would sign the Official Secrets Act and agree to be PV'd. The Security Service would not want to be held responsible for holding up purely medical research.'

'You realize that Dr Flickinger would have to be given some idea of the reason for the offer before he could accept?' Adrian pointed out.

'Of course, but concerning the medical aspects alone. And couldn't that be restricted to him and anybody he might have to consult in Fort Detrick, along with the advice that the information has to be kept "in house" there, as much in American interests as in ours?'

'I suppose so. It's worth a try.'

'Good,' Lesley said, smoothing down her skirt, which had ridden above her knees. 'Life's all about compromise and gentle persuasion, isn't it? At least ours is. We have no real powers in the Security Service, you know, contrary to the fiction writers and some ignorant MPs.'

The turn of events had delighted Adrian because it meant that he would not be in personal problems for failing to inform Fort Detrick and he would not have to do that himself. The possibility of solving his communication difficulty with Fort Detrick by inviting Flickinger to Porton had occurred to him while he was driving up to see Sir William Brook at the Defence Ministry. The Director-General of MI5 was not the only one with turf to protect.

'I would be grateful if you would let me know how Dr Payne reacts,' Lesley said, picking up the capacious, black crocodile handbag which had been presented to her on a security visit to Kenya. 'She would, of course, have to move quickly.'

'When will she be required to sign the Official Secrets Act?'

'Within the next forty-eight hours, I imagine – that is if she agrees to. If you get wind of any adversary interest, I mean interest from people representing countries whom we don't entirely trust, perhaps you will let me know that too. Dr Payne, in particular, could be a target. Any approach would be quite sophisticated, at least in the first instance. I am sure she will confide in you.'

She gave Adrian another of her knowing looks. He did not rise to the fly.

From the handbag she removed the MI5 equivalent of a Filo-fax. 'You can get me on this number on your secure line,' she said, passing him a card with nothing on it but a telephone number. 'Just ask for Mrs Lesley or leave a message for me to ring you.'

'Mrs Lesley! Is that your code-name?'

'Not really but it's best not to use my full name on the telephone and it is rather a mouthful.'

Adrian watched Lesley climb into her chauffeur-driven car from his office window, her hair glinting in the sunshine. He smiled as he was reminded of a rather mature student at Cambridge who had told him, as an item of accumulated wisdom, 'There's always something doing with a red-haired woman.' He thought she had been showing rather more leg than she had needed, as Lesley herself had been well aware.

It had been an extraordinary discussion. He was in no doubt that she had been trying to induce him to leak the information to Fort Detrick. She had used the word 'pragmatic' with all the abandon of a politician seeking to excuse some reprehensible expediency. What was her game? Clearly, she knew all about his affair with Wendy and of his interest in becoming Director. No doubt MI5 would have some influence when possible candidates for the post came to be considered. He felt vulnerable, with a pressing need to acquire some merit by obliging her if he could. It should not be too difficult; and their immediate interests were the same.

He reached among his reference books for *Who's Who*. There was no entry on Lesley but there was a lengthy one on Paul Barrington-Fuller: *Professor of Psychiatry, University of London, Maudsley Hospital . . . Married Lesley, only daughter of Admiral Louis le Huray, of Jersey . . .*

The Admiral's entry showed that he had been Director of Defence Intelligence in the Ministry of Defence some years previously. So that was how she had got into MI5!

Adrian wasted no further time in summoning Wendy to his office.

'I told you we'd get spooks down here. I've just had a visit from Olga Polovska, the beautiful spy-catcher from MI Funf. They want you to sign the Official Secrets Act.'

'I won't do it,' Wendy said hotly. 'It would be tantamount to an agreement to work on weapons. And I'm absolutely convinced that

70

it is ethically and morally wrong to hold up the enzyme work, with all those old miners and asbestos workers coughing their lungs up and with no hope of any relief. I couldn't sleep last night for thinking about them.'

'I sympathize, Wendy. Believe me I do. But I have to point out to you that if you decline to sign you will have to hand over all the research to somebody else, including your working papers. You will have to leave this place and you won't be able to take any of the cultures with you.'

'I'm prepared to do that. I only went into a branch of medicine because I care about people.'

Adrian held up his hands in a calming-down gesture. 'I assure you we all do that. This establishment works to protect people – from war gases and war germs. I urge you not to be too hasty, my dear, because I'm sure you would regret it if you quit.'

'Maybe. But will I regret it more if I stay?'

'You mustn't be selfish, Wendy. It's in everybody's best interests, including your miners, that you stay. It also happens to be a most fortunate opportunity for you and you would be very foolish to throw it away. The security authorities are not being unreasonable. They believe that your discovery could pose quite a threat if the wrong people heard about it. But I think there is a compromise situation which would enable you to get ahead with your enzyme work and still remain secure.'

'What's that?' Wendy asked earnestly.

'I have a hunch that the authorities would not be too upset if your hirsute friend, Flick-Finger, came to work with you here. That way you could get over the problem of being unable to send him a culture. Do you think he would come?'

'He might,' said Wendy, brightening. 'Could you invite him?'

'No. You would have to do it. I can't authorize you to do it or encourage you in any way but, until you sign the Official Secrets Act, I have no power to stop you. Naturally, if Flickinger accepted and then applied to come I would agree.'

Wendy got the message. 'I would have to give him a clear idea of what it's all about. In fact, since we started publishing papers together, we have an agreement that we keep nothing from each other, especially anything as important as this.'

'Well, you must act according to your scientific conscience, as we

71

all have to. I cannot advise you otherwise. But, I repeat, it will have to be *your* initiative. And you'll have to act fast. I understand the spooks are coming down to see you within a couple of days.'

'That means I'll have to talk to Julian by telephone.'

Adrian nodded. 'As I must repeat, I can't authorize you to tell him but I can't stop you either. But you've probably only got forty-eight hours to do it before I *can* stop you and *must* stop you – that is if you want to stay here. You can use my secure line if you decide to go ahead.'

'How much can I tell him?'

'Only about the glass and the silicosis idea. You mustn't tell him anything about the chips.'

'But he's very bright. He'll probably cotton on to it.'

'That's no skin off our nose, so long as you can say you didn't tell him.'

'Just one thing, Adrian,' Wendy said mischievously before she left, without committing herself. 'What sort of a cat was your lady spook?'

He thought for a moment. 'A peke-faced ginger tabby with very sharp claws. Not to be trifled with!'

When Wendy had left he sat back with considerable relief and satisfaction. She had trimmed her principles, as he had guessed she would, when faced with the alternative of being dispossessed of her 'baby', a monster though it might be. He was pleased for her sake and relieved for his own. He would have been the scapegoat in Whitehall if she had quit in dudgeon and made her situation public. And he suspected that she could be vengeful. He had little difficulty in convincing himself that he had acted in Wendy's interest and was not being a shit. But he would not be discussing the matter with Gillian. He knew that she would spot the self-interest.

There was little doubt in his mind that when Flickinger informed his chief, the latter would feel duty bound to tell the Director at Fort Detrick. Then, without much delay, there would be a formal request for samples of the culture, even if Flickinger agreed to work at Porton. The news was bound to break soon, anyway. The Whitehall people were living in fantasy generated by their pathological preoccupation with secrecy.

Wendy was conscious that she had trimmed and it chewed at her, especially when she was alone, but she assured herself that there had been no option. She was genuinely ashamed of the implications of her discovery but nobody was going to take it from her if she could help it. Her desire for Adrian had been another factor. She still felt tingles in her flesh when he was near and expected to resume the affair one day – after a decent interval.

Chapter Ten

Being unattached, with no domestic ties, Julian Flickinger could not have been more delighted or more excited. The silicon project was an entirely new field, an irresistible challenge, and his own research on AIDS was at a stage which could be interrupted. He would be more than happy for another spell away from Frederick, the rather dull little town which serviced Fort Detrick. His chief proved to be extremely keen to get his team involved, though preferably at Detrick itself. If that were not possible then, certainly, Flickinger could move to Porton at short notice.

Meanwhile, tests on the larger redundant computer, sent down to Porton by the Defence Ministry, had quickly shown that, in spite of the more sophisticated insulation, the clone had little difficulty in infiltrating the various modules at points where wires, in contact with the printed circuits and other components, emerged. But those at Fort Detrick were given none of that information or, indeed, anything at all about the defence aspects.

As soon as 'Miss Lesley' received Adrian's telephone message that Flickinger had been invited to Porton, she told Sandy Pryce that her mission had been accomplished. She was denied the pleasure of telling him how it had been done because he insisted on not knowing, but she was privately pleased with her ingenuity. As usual, Pryce lost no time in dutifully informing Ross Pilgrim that matters were on the move. While avoiding explicit details, he was able to assure his friend that everything would be deniable, all round.

'Beautifully done!' Pilgrim responded. 'I owe you a case of the bourbon. Take it gently, Sandy,' he added, knowing Pryce's problem.

'I'll keep it for visitors,' Sandy replied good-naturedly.

Pilgrim did not comment. He knew that Sandy had few visitors.

In fact, Pryce was controlling his drink problem rather well. He allowed himself just one whisky per evening in the office, unlocking the little drinks cupboard, pouring one glass, relocking and then

74

dropping the key through the slot of a petty-cash money box, to which his secretary retained the key overnight. This unseen ritual had given him a reputation for being abstemious which, senior colleagues believed, was why he never offered them a drink. It also explained his tough attitude to hard drinkers among the staff.

Meticulous, as always, Ross Pilgrim made a note to send off a case of the special brand of bourbon whiskey for which Sandy had acquired a taste during his service in Washington. Pryce invariably responded with a case of 25-year-old Macallan Scotch, supplied by a Speyside distillery in the lee of the Grampian Mountains and hard to come by in the United States. 'Almost as rare as a cuckoo's nest,' was how Pryce had described the Scotch, until appraised by Pilgrim that some American cuckoos build their own nests.

When the CIA received the information about Wendy's discovery from officials at Fort Detrick, Pilgrim affected to be as irritated as any of his colleagues that it had not come, more quickly, direct from Whitehall.

'Goddamn Brits, hanging on to information as important as this,' he fumed at a meeting called to consider it and presided over by Stanley Arnold, the Director of Central Intelligence, who was still in his first year of office. Having had more than a week to consider the various implications, Pilgrim was able to give the impression of an exceptionally sharp grasp of an entirely new problem, as he had so often done in the past.

The Fort Detrick scientists immediately appreciated the defence potentialities if the clone proved able to attack silicon, and Pilgrim proposed using all his resources to finding out whether the British had already made any discoveries in that direction. Within twenty-four hours he reported that, according to 'a source with excellent access' but which he was not prepared to identify, the British had established not only that the clone attacked silicon but that it could quickly disable a computer into which it was introduced. Inevitably, this exacerbated the American response to being kept in the dark and Pilgrim joined in the general denunciation with gusto.

Alone in the airy, impressive office allotted to the CIA chief on the seventh floor of the main Langley building, and overlooking the woods surrounding it, Stanley Arnold had to be impressed by the apparent speed of Pilgrim's action but he did not like him, resenting his superior air, his excessive suspiciousness and exalted reputation.

Pilgrim's early training as a mathematician had not helped. 'Mathematicians are peculiar people,' Arnold had observed. 'Their minds are different. They don't think like we do.'

A lawyer by profession, Arnold was a puritanically religious man, whose dining table was graced with two silver cockerels – to remind his family and their guests of their sins. He dipped into the Bible each day, literally fearing God and the consequences of any failure to keep his Commandments.

On his appointment he had called a meeting of senior officers to enunciate his policy: 'I regard my prime function as to serve the President as his chief adviser on intelligence affairs. Unlike some of my predecessors, I intend to be one hundred per cent honest with the President and I expect you all to be one hundred per cent honest with me. You must all be accountable to me at all times, as I will be accountable to the President.

'Under my leadership the Agency will work strictly within the legal rules and no excesses or cowboy actions will be tolerated. That way the Agency should suffer no more of the public embarrassments which have done so much damage to its public image in the past.

'There will be no more interference by the Agency in the internal politics of other countries. That is not our function. Our job is to collect and evaluate information. How those in the State Department and elsewhere use it is their affair. It is not ours. I hope that is understood.'

As soon as the meeting had broken up Pilgrim had been openly scathing, with the word 'cowboy' fuelling his anger. 'How the hell can we be one hundred per cent honest with anybody in the deception game?' he asked his close colleagues. 'It's a contradiction in terms. Because of "need to know" we have to be economical with the truth even with each other. This Agency is no place for anyone obsessed with honesty. As for working to the rules, what rules do the opposition observe? In this game there are no rules.'

Arnold's restriction of the CIA role to collecting and evaluating information had particularly infuriated Pilgrim. 'Are we here just to collect intelligence which bureaucrats will file and forget? This idiot doesn't know what he's talking about. We've got to get rid of him – soonest.'

Believing that his function was to serve the security of the state – the entire state, the whole American people, not just one man –

Pilgrim always warned his staff that 'Presidents come and go but the same enemy remains'. When indoctrinating any new officer, he made use of the statue of Nathan Hale, which graced the front of the CIA headquarters. This patriot, hanged as a spy by the British during the War of Independence, had proclaimed as he mounted the gallows, 'I only regret that I have but one life to lose for my country.' Hale had it right, in Pilgrim's view. It was 'country' that mattered – the whole territory and all the people in it. Prime loyalty to the President was too narrow. 'Like Nathan Hale, any individual in this Agency is expendable in the national interest,' he warned his recruits. 'And that includes you. And me.'

Pilgrim had been prepared to dislike Arnold as soon as he had heard that he was a lawyer. He attributed his own physical, mental and financial well-being to staying away from doctors and lawyers. In particular, he disapproved of lawyers dabbling in the intelligence business because they were impressed only by legal evidence, hard enough and ethical enough to be brought into a court of law. They were besotted with proof when it was the balance of probabilities that governed most intelligence actions. And that balance depended on wire-taps, bugs, intercepted messages, circumstantial evidence, hunches born of long experience and informers who could never be produced as witnesses. Lawyers were also intent on prosecutions when the needs of counter-intelligence often demanded that a spy or traitor should be manipulated rather than sent to prison. No doubt the narrow-minded Arnold would be aghast at any association with the 'enemy', the KGB or the GRU, but some contact was essential if the enemy was to be known.

Pilgrim considered the appointment of an intelligence ignoramus such as Stanley Arnold an outrage, being firmly of the belief that the man in charge of the CIA should be a career officer, like himself, with wide experience of the 'game'. But then President Rockwell, who had appointed Arnold, had been a wimp himself during his own brief service as Director of Central Intelligence some ten years previously. Pilgrim had never forgiven him for vetoing one glorious opportunity to blackguard the KGB and the Soviet system in the eyes of the whole free world.

A senior Soviet defector 'with excellent access' had volunteered credible evidence of KGB involvement in the assassination of President John Kennedy. A contingency plan to kill the reigning US

77

President always existed and, early in November 1963, in a fit of anger, Khruschev had ordered its translation into action. In the previous year Khruschev had obtained a firm promise from Kennedy that Cuba would not be invaded if the Russians withdrew their nuclear missiles from there but the KGB had then obtained proof that the CIA was employing the Mafia to murder the Cuban leader, Fidel Castro, to cause a revolution 'with boom and bang on the island'.

Pilgrim had urgently recommended that the defector should be made available to the media but Rockwell, always a political animal, had taken outside advice. The White House, State Department, FBI, and the CIA top management, all with private reasons for suppressing the information, had insisted that it would be dangerously inflammatory. Pilgrim had no doubt that Arnold would bid goodbye to any similar opportunities with equal cowardice and relief.

Arnold's religiosity had been a further black mark. Pilgrim called himself a born-again atheist and had always felt that the Christian ethic and the requirements of counter-intelligence must be fundamentally at odds. 'In this game you can't be inhibited by any religious creed. For instance, you simply can't offer the other cheek to the KGB. They'll just think you are mad and smite it. Offering the other cheek to anybody is totally discredited by history. It's called appeasement these days and we know where that leads. "Off with their heads" has more going for it.'

In his view, the austere, teetotal Arnold was 'about as genuine as some of those TV hot gospel evangelists who get caught out'. He had him wrong, however: Arnold was essentially an Old Testament eye-for-an-eye man. He also meant business and had moved, swiftly, into executive action.

His method of reducing the risk of more Irangates or Watergates was to cut down on covert actions, the secret operations which were Pilgrim's lifeblood. In an effort to reduce the budget deficit, President Rockwell had ordered cuts throughout the Washington bureaucracy, with defence bearing much of the burden, and the CIA could not be excepted without a political explosion in Congress. To Pilgrim, this was perfidy for a former CIA chief, as Rockwell was. But Arnold's behaviour in choosing to concentrate the cuts on the sharp end of counter-intelligence, rebuilt over so many years following the mayhem inflicted by President Carter, was the act of a traitor. It was for that reason that Pilgrim was wont to refer to his chief, privately, as 'Benedict Arnold', after a traitorous revolutionary general of that name who was vilified in the annals of American history. Many of Pilgrim's senior colleagues agreed that, under Arnold, the Agency was rapidly sliding back into a negative organization more concerned with keeping out of trouble than with doing anything positive.

It was Arnold's zeal for pleasing the President which mainly motivated his policy, but a determination to reduce Pilgrim's singular independence and scope for autonomous action was no small part of it. Pilgrim even had his own cipher for sending and receiving secret messages which nobody, not even the CIA chief, was permitted to read.

In spite of Arnold's 'cowboy' warning, Pilgrim had continued to operate as before, regarding his position as being unassailably set in the concrete of long-established practice. He was confident that he would see Arnold off, or at least see him out, and that was the betting of most of his colleagues who were aware of the smouldering feud. But the new Director was a formidable opponent and had his own informers within the Agency – for there were many who disliked Pilgrim or resented his reputation. He was equally sure that Pilgrim was the kind of godless man who, if given enough rope, would eventually put it round his own neck. The danger was that in the process he might involve the Agency in another Irangate. He would already have removed him had he not been so entrenched and so prestigious. But if the opportunity arose . . . Meanwhile he would trust in the Lord to deliver his enemy into his hands.

With new-broom enthusiasm, Arnold lost no time in informing the State Department and the White House of the CIA's official deliberations on the Porton developments. He awaited their reaction before proceeding further.

Pilgrim waited for nobody. From the moment that Pryce had alerted him to the computer implications of the silicon secret, his mind had been brooding on 'contingency plans' for taking advantage of the opportunity. Ever since Harry Truman's 'The buck stops here', desk mottoes had been popular in and around Washington. That on Pilgrim's desk was a quotation from Henry Kissinger: 'Security without values is like a ship without a rudder but values without security are like a rudder without a ship.' Sometimes democratic values had to be traded off in the interest of security. The trade-off which had occurred to him while reading the *Weekly Bulletin of The Nephews* had such irresistible appeal that it was dominating his waking time.

What he had in mind was a 'dangle' operation which would make such willies of the Soviet techno-bandits that they would paralyse their own nation's defences. He would dangle, temptingly in front of them, some specially choice item of equipment which they needed for a high-priority military programme, hopefully at a Star Wars research centre like Sary Shagan. Then he would induce them to steal it after ensuring that it would become thoroughly infected with the silicon-eater once it was installed in the Soviet Union. With luck – always a major factor in any intelligence operation – it would cause such chaos that the whole establishment would have to be shut down.

Of all operations a successful dangle gave Pilgrim the greatest satisfaction. As a boy he had spent many happy hours, alone, angling for sucker-fish with various baits in muddy streams. The main excitement had been in wondering whether the fish would take the bait and sensing the first movement of the line. A good dangle offered the same delightful anticipation and the same thrill as the bait was swallowed by the human suckers.

If the techno-bandits could be fooled into taking his contaminated bait he could even bug the equipment and listen to the Russians' appalled reaction as they realized their predicament, especially if the pestilence should spread. What a sweet pay-off that would seem for thousands of operations by the KGB, which recently had planted so many bugs in the new American Embassy in Moscow that the building had to be demolished and rebuilt, using American labour!

Lenin had prophesied that capitalists would sell the rope with which to hang themselves. Perhaps the Leninists could be induced to *steal* a noose. As Pilgrim foresaw the project, nothing would be provable and the Russians could hardly complain publicly when they had acquired the equipment by criminal means.

Pilgrim had brought off many successful dangles but, with his extreme perfectionism, he regarded none of them as impeccable. He still hankered after the consummate operation, what he called, among his CIA intimates, the 'grand-daddy of all dangles'. This could be it. The parameters looked exceptionally promising. Blown open by the gale of change in the Soviet Union, the door of history was swinging on its hinges. How doubly satisfying if he could push it the way he

80

wanted through a perfect dangle! In any event, it was an opportunity that was too good to miss. And the urgent chicken-feed operation he was about to set in motion to strengthen Brown Derby's position might serve as a dry run for it.

His planning was entirely theoretical because the project was impossible without a culture of the clone. But that might well be forthcoming – and soon. In the intelligence game windfalls were always possible, especially if one could shake the tree.

Chapter Eleven

There was consternation in Whitehall. The Public Health Laboratory Service had received a formal request from the Scientific Attaché at the US Embassy for information about Wendy Payne's discovery and for a sample of the clone. Knowing nothing about it, the Laboratory Service had consulted Wendy who referred them to Adrian Allen. After brief reflection about his own response when questioned, Adrian had telephoned Sir William Brook at the Defence Ministry.

'The Scientific Attaché!' Brook had commented scathingly. 'I'll bet he's really acting for Charlie Yates!'

Charlie Yates was the popular head of the CIA Mission in London, based in the Embassy in Grosvenor Square. He had been in the post for several years, was widely known as an Anglophile, with a laudable love of the horse-racing scene, and had a reputation for being very astute.

Brook lost no time in alerting Sir Richard Carlton at the Foreign Office, resisting the pleasure of reminding him of his warning that the information would leak. In turn, Carlton immediately called in Oliver Taylor, his colleague on the Joint Intelligence Committee who, while expressing concern, was secretly delighted.

'What do we do?' Taylor asked.

'There's only one thing we can do now,' Carlton replied, resignedly. 'Observe the protocol, tell them everything; give them cultures and devise some excuse for the delay. That's in our best interests now.'

'They haven't mentioned the silicon chip business?'

'No, but we must tell them all we know. The balloon's up. There's no point in compounding our difficulties. Ministers, including the Prime Minister, must now be informed and we want everything ship-shape with the Americans before we do that.'

'I agree, absolutely. We can't risk any retaliation from Washington

82

on the interchange of information. They're holding enough back on need-to-know as it is.'

Carlton heaved a heavy sigh. 'It will certainly leak to the Russians now. Somebody will trade it off or that wretched Nephews outfit will hear of it and then anything could happen. They could use it against us. You know how isolationist some of them are. And the media will back them up.'

'I wonder how the Americans heard about it so quickly. Could it have been Bill Brook? To keep his friends in the Pentagon sweet?'

'I doubt it,' Carlton said. 'He's a funny chap and he drinks too much but his heart's in the right place. I suppose it was that damn woman down at Porton. We'll have to find out. But that's a job for the Ministry of Defence. She's their responsibility.'

Having wasted so much time in the past on the leak procedure, the Ministry's ritual action for tracking down the source of a security breach, Brook was against wasting any more. The old system of using charts to see which leaks coincided with which suspect had been 'high-teched' with computer graphics but it still hardly ever produced the culprit. 'Water over the dam' was Brook's usual reaction to a leak. Nevertheless, it was important to get Dr Payne constrained by the Official Secrets Act. There was still the Russians to think about.

Wendy had given a lot of thought to how she would react to the men from the Ministry. She was forthright by nature and also because that was what she had been brought up to believe North country people should be, so blank refusal to discuss the matter on the general grounds of her objection to secrecy in science had been her first choice. But that would have put Adrian in a difficult position and left him with no option but to ask her to leave.

Of the two security officers who turned up at Porton, the one who did the talking while the other made notes was pleasant enough in explaining why she would have to sign the Official Secrets Act or quit the establishment and leave her cultures behind.

'If I decline, what is to stop me from going to some university laboratory and simply repeating the experiment from scratch?' Wendy asked. 'I know exactly what I did and I would probably be able to do it again.'

Nonplussed, her visitors had no response.

'I could also emigrate to America and get a job at Fort Detrick,' she continued. 'I know I would be very welcome.'

The spokesman seized his chance. 'Talking about Fort Detrick, did you speak to anyone there?'

'I speak and write to them all the time. My collaborator, Dr Flickinger, works there. You can't do scientific research in a vacuum, you know. I wanted his view and to ask him if there was anything relevant in the literature.'

'Did you actually tell him about your discovery?'

'I told him about the effects of the bacterium on glass and invited him to come here and work on it with me. He's worked here before. He's completely cleared for security.'

'Nothing about, er, silicon chips?'

'Nothing whatever about silicon chips.'

The security officers, who knew little about science, seemed relieved.

'Well, you must make a decision, Dr Payne. Are you prepared to sign the Official Secrets Act?'

'What does it entail?'

The officer shrugged. 'It simply means that it would then be an offence if you said anything or published anything about your work without official permission.'

'I'm no Peter Wright,' she said, rather petulantly.

'It's not your memoirs the authorities are worried about, Dr Payne. The security problem is rather more immediate.'

'Are they really worried that I might spill the beans to the Russians?'

'Of course not. But you might say or write something which could reach their ears through some other route. You've already told this Dr Flickinger. Where did you first meet him?'

'At an international microbiology conference in Warsaw.'

Wendy thought that she detected a shudder as the silent partner made a note.

'I went there as a British delegate and the Government paid my fare,' Wendy added, mischievously.

'Have you any other contacts behind the, er, Iron Curtain?'

'Of course. That is the object of such conferences – they are international.'

From the look on the scribe's face Wendy assumed that the word international troubled him even more.

'Could you identify any of your contacts in Warsaw?'

'There's Professor Baranski,' she said, naming the most distinguished Pole in the field of microbiology.

'What's his Christian name?'

'I don't suppose he has one. I think he's a Jew.'

'Well, what's his first name,' the security man asked, irritably.

'Leon. I also met him in Beijing,' Wendy added for good measure.

'Beijing! That's Peking, isn't it? What were you doing there?'

'I was attending another international conference. The Chinese are rather good at microbiology. By the way, the Government paid my fare there too!'

'Do you remain in touch with any of these Chinese gentlemen?'

'Of course. And some of them are ladies.'

'You mean you write to them?'

'Yes. And send them separates.'

'What are separates?' the interviewer asked, suspiciously.

'When a scientist publishes a paper in a learned journal the editor provides some copies of the pages containing the paper stapled together. That way you can send off your paper as a "separate" to colleagues without sending the whole journal, which would be far too expensive.'

My God! What a way to transmit secret messages, the interviewer conjectured. 'Could you give me the names of some of these Chinese to whom you send these, er, separates?'

Wendy reeled off a few names which she eventually had to spell.

The two men looked at each other as though agreed that the interview could be brought to a close. 'If you need further time to think—' the spokesman began.

'No,' Wendy responded crisply. 'I'll sign your document now if you have it, but with extreme reluctance and distaste.'

The silent officer produced a printed form for Wendy to peruse. She went through the motions of studying it, having previously been shown a copy by Adrian, filled in the few personal details and signed it, the signature being witnessed by the spokesman, who seemed very relieved.

'You will of course need to be positively vetted, some time soon,' he explained. 'Just a few questions and a background check. In your case it will be purely a formality. You see, normally PV-ing is done *before* people engage on top secret work. But you are already on it.

We've never encountered a case quite like yours before. It was your discovery that made it automatically top secret!'

Wendy made no comment.

'Meanwhile your papers on this research should be marked "Top Secret" and locked away every night in a proper container.'

'I don't have one.'

'We'll see that one is provided. Meanwhile, perhaps you could use Dr Allen's – and his Top Secret stamps.'

Back at Ministry headquarters in Whitehall, the security officers submitted a quick report recommending MI5 to make a check on Flickinger and Professor Baranski. The first had already turned out to be the epitome of a good American. The second was a dear old soul of an academic at Warsaw University with no political history whatever.

Adrian was greatly relieved by Wendy's agreement. She had told him that she did not wish to leave and, much as she disapproved of secrecy, it did not suit her to be made publicly responsible for inventing a weapon. Still, he knew that she remained disturbed about it and might have become emotional when it came to signing.

It was already clear to him that Flickinger would not be transferring to Porton. Once Fort Detrick received the culture of Clone Fe 113, as he had been informed they would, he would undoubtedly be required as a key figure in a major team there working on every aspect of the possibilities. Adrian had previous experience of American 'crash programmes'. It was a term he would have to avoid using in front of Wendy. He had manoeuvred her over the immediate hurdle but shuddered to think how her outsize conscience might react if she learned that a multi-million dollar effort was being concentrated on the weapons potential of her innocent discovery. He could foresee a wide choice of impulsive actions – all highly explosive.

Chapter Twelve

Of all the assets which Brown Derby had patiently accumulated, the most valuable and the least expendable was the man he called The Dealer. He had to be used sparingly but Brown Derby had been sharply reminded by the Aquarium that his team of techno-bandits was falling short of its required quota of achievements. So The Dealer would have to take his chance. He had been paid long enough for fairly routine work. The Aquarium would be furious if The Dealer was exposed, when so much had been invested in him for a long-term purpose, but Brown Derby was the decision-maker in this instance and was confident that, in any showdown, he could convince his colleagues that he had acted in the best interests of the GRU.

The Dealer was a deeply established illegal agent who had been introduced from Canada, which was known to British Intelligence as the 'Clapham Junction' of espionage because of the ease of entry from it to the prime Soviet target, the United States. He had reached the US twelve years previously with a meticulously constructed and memorized 'legend' – a false account of his past – supported by what looked like impeccable papers prepared by professional Soviet forgers. They included a birth certificate really belonging to a child who had died in infancy. The Dealer was of Czech origin but the birth certificate showed his parents as being Canadian.

As cover, he had opened a discount store in the Californian town of Sacramento, with capital provided by Moscow. Being thus able to afford to undercut anybody, he had prospered so that he now ran three large stores in different cities, including one in San Francisco. Starting with videos, computer games, tape recorders and similar small items, he had progressed to equipment of virtually any size and, still being able to undercut rivals with his GRU subsidy, he was patronized by institutions like the University of California at Berkeley and commercial firms.

It was no coincidence that he had been originally instructed to set up business near Silicon Valley, the districts of Santa Clara and Palo

Alta, just south of San Francisco, where every major electronic firm had factories and laboratories, all beautifully landscaped to harmonize with the pleasant, sunny environment.

The Dealer was therefore an excellent source of high-tech electronic equipment for the techno-bandits for, while export might be prohibited, there was nothing to interfere with domestic sales. It was up to the techno-bandit chief, Brown Derby, and his men to scheme ways of smuggling the purchased products out of the country.

Brown Derby, a short but chunky, eager man, bright-eyed, as sharp as his pointed nose and looking as trim and aggressive as a cock robin, had received specific instructions directly from the Military Industrial Commission in Moscow to provide, without delay, an advanced computer for controlling special machine tools used for extremely fine work. As usual, no details of the Soviets' purpose were given but Brown Derby was technical enough to guess that it was needed for machining screws for the Soviet Navy's new, and more silent, nuclear submarines.

The Dealer's instructions from Brown Derby were always received through an intermediary and he had no knowledge of his controller's identity or of his connection with the United Nations. He had no difficulty in purchasing the computer from the manufacturer. He already had one in store for delivery to the University of California, where the engineering department wanted it for machining special nuclear research equipment. The manufacturer was only too keen to sell its products to any established bona fide customer. It was up to The Dealer to ensure that they did not fall into the wrong hands.

The Federal Bureau of Investigation was used to receiving tips from Ross Pilgrim. Though he held his sources tightly secret, he clearly had some good ones in the techno-bandit field and the FBI had achieved considerable credit on past occasions through acting on his advice. While the CIA had some authority to undertake counter-intelligence operations in the United States, the surveillance and arrest of techno-bandits was the FBI's responsibility. This time Pilgrim's information had been unusually specific.

Two FBI special agents were conveniently parked in sight of the warehouse serving The Dealer's discount store in Sacramento when a black delivery truck, with two men aboard, emerged at the expected time as night began to fall. Assisted by two colleagues in another car, the agents tracked it along the expected route towards the corresponding warehouse near San Francisco's international airport. In precisely timed movements, the Sacramento FBI then handed over the surveillance to the San Francisco FBI mission, which was fielding a bigger team – four cars, and two motorcycles. The delivery truck was parked for the night in the San Francisco warehouse and, having tucked away their own vehicles unobtrusively, the new team settled down to wait, taking turns to get some sleep.

Nothing happened until shortly after 8 a.m. the following morning when the locked gates opened, the truck appeared and headed north along the Californian Highway 101 and over the toll bridge to Berkeley. There it stopped and delivered a large crate to the Engineering Department of the University of California. There seemed to be nothing possibly illegal about that.

The handover completed, the truck headed south, as Pilgrim had predicted it would, crossing over the toll bridge at Mount Eden. With the FBI cars in carefully controlled pursuit, it then turned back on to Highway 101 towards San Francisco but this time sped north over the Golden Gate bridge.

From then on, the FBI men knew no more than that the expected illegal delivery would be made off the coastal road, somewhere near Gualala, a former hippie haven.

The target truck turned off the 101 by Marin City and on to the Pacific coastal road through Stinson Beach, Olema, Tomales, Valley Ford, and Bodega Bay, continuing along the coast road towards Gualala. It was obviously taking unusual care not to infringe the speed limits. With meticulous precision, the FBI vehicles kept ringing the changes so that none would be in view for long.

Around mid-day the truck turned down a sandy track. At the bottom of it the FBI men could see a leisure cruiser, of a type common enough round San Francisco, tied up at a mooring. The scenario was exactly what they had been told to expect and they checked their hand guns in readiness for action.

After emerging, quietly, from their cars, the arresting agents watched the proceedings through binoculars as a large crate was unloaded from the truck and was soon in process of being handed over to two men on the launch. Then they moved down cautiously, hand guns drawn, one of them carrying a bull-horn.

'This is the FBI!' roared the agent with the bull-horn. 'You are surrounded by armed agents. I want to see every hand on top of your heads. Do you hear me? Don't do anything stupid. This is the FBI!'

The leading agent, his gold badge displayed in his left hand, his pistol in his right, ran forward crying, 'I am a special agent of the FBI. Here are my credentials. We have warrants and you are under arrest.'

The men, who were totally surprised and looked astonished, made no effort to escape and, had the two from the launch attempted to do so, they would have seen a fast US Coastguard cutter bearing in from the ocean. The FBI men had been in car radio contact with it from the moment that the truck had hit the Golden Gate.

After the suspects had been frisked and handcuffed, without resistance, one of the agents appeared with a camera to photograph the crate which bore stencilling indicating that it contained marine navigation equipment.

Having overcome their shock, the captives began to protest their innocence in most vehement terms and insisted that the crate be opened without delay. This was done without ceremony, the lid being prised open and ripped off with a heavy-duty tool. When the contents had been photographed, their wrappings were removed exposing electronic items which meant little to the FBI men.

The captives from the launch then invited the agents aboard to see the existing navigation equipment, which they had disconnected because it was unserviceable. No technical knowledge was needed to see that the new equipment being supplied was an identical replacement. And the papers and instruction documents showed it to be of no great technological interest to anyone and exportable anywhere.

In considerable anger, the frustrated senior FBI agent telephoned headquarters from his car, which had been brought alongside, and, after a longish delay, during which Pilgrim was consulted by the FBI, he received instructions to terminate the operation and release the captives.

A quick reference to the central police computer in San Francisco showed that the owners of the launch were who and what they said they were – honest American citizens going cruising to test their new navigation equipment.

The senior FBI agent's apologies, when the men were released, were, inevitably, met by threats that their victims would be consulting their lawyers.

Meanwhile a second computer, identical to that left at Berkeley and in a crate also marked to indicate that it contained marine navigation equipment, had been delivered during the night, direct from The Dealer's store in Los Angeles. It had been carried in a large, private estate wagon towards the coast at Port San Luis, far south of San Francisco. There, out of sight and off the road, it had been transferred to another estate wagon driven by one of Brown Derby's agents so that, in the event of a disaster, The Dealer would not be directly involved. The agent had then delivered the crate, without incident, to a launch moored off Lucia, higher up the coast. The launch had passed it before daylight to an East German freighter outside the twelve-mile limit.

As the FBI officers suspected would be the case, the crate delivered in Berkeley contained sensitive equipment which would have been banned for export to the Soviet bloc but was perfectly proper for purchase by the University of California. The authorities there confirmed that they were in the habit of buying equipment from The Dealer, who was perfectly straight and above board in their experience. 'A bum steer,' was the chief FBI agent's scathing comment to his colleagues.

The Dealer had encountered no problem in purchasing two of the computers from the manufacturer – one for the San Francisco store, the other for the store in Los Angeles. He was an American citizen running an established business and could buy what he liked.

A full report of the operation, submitted by Brown Derby to the Aquarium, stressed the very genuine interest of the FBI and how it had been countered, with the area FBI specialists and even the Coastguard cutter being engaged in a fools' errand. Later, he was able to inform Pilgrim that the tone of the congratulatory note from Moscow had allayed his fears that there was any suspicion about his loyalty. For the time being, at least, the danger of the curt summons home 'for consultations' had faded. So had any fear that he might be fed alive into the Aquarium's incinerator, normally used for burning surplus secret documents. Whether it was true or not that GRU officers convicted under Article 64 of the Soviet Criminal Code – 'Betrayal of the homeland' – were really burned alive, feet first, they were all encouraged to believe it.

While Pilgrim received Brown Derby's news with pleasure, the note from FBI headquarters was not so friendly. He was prepared to apologize and admit that his information had been flawed, ending his reply with a condolent 'We can't win 'em all'. But that was just what the FBI Director expected his staff to do.

Fooling the FBI in the Soviet interest was not Pilgrim's usual form but it had been something of an emergency and his intimate staff agreed with him that it was to the long-term advantage of the United States to keep Brown Derby 'in place' and productive. Nevertheless, Pilgrim appreciated that he would not be able to make a willie out of the FBI like that again – at least not for some time. The operation had been too straightforward to have much appeal for him. He always avoided over-complication but any enterprise needed a greater measure of ingenious sophistication to give him satisfaction.

For his part, Brown Derby did not tell Pilgrim everything – only what he needed to know to stay the CIA man's hand and keep the money coming in. As a senior GRU officer, Brown Derby was well paid by Soviet standards but, like all the UN staff, he was required to kick back to Moscow a substantial part of his United Nations salary, which continually angered him. He needed as much as he could save against the day when he might have to defect. Pilgrim had made grand promises concerning such an exigency but, being an intelligence officer himself, he did not put much faith in the word of another. Whatever was said in such secrecy could so easily be denied.

The trouble with regular extra money, as Pilgrim fully understood and exploited, was that one slowly became dependent on it. And on the person supplying it, especially when he possessed handwritten receipts.

Chapter Thirteen

The Pentagon was so vast that, according to a standing joke there, a heavily pregnant girl found wandering in its several miles of corridors insisted that she had not been in that condition when she had entered the building. Nevertheless, the silicon secret emitted shock waves through all the crucially interested departments, which was most of them.

Pentagon officials were not concerned with the diplomatic implications of the silicon discovery. That was a matter for the State Department. What concerned the senior forces chiefs were the defence implications and a crash programme to examine them had been mapped out even before the culture of Clone Fe 113 had arrived. There was need for haste against the time when the State Department might rule that research on the clone contravened the moratorium on germ-warfare research which had been agreed with the Soviets.

The crash programme was called Project Drumbeat, a name which happened to be the next on an approved list, but Pilgrim thought it eminently appropriate when told of it. He had first heard of the subject on his private bush telegraph.

After being briefly interviewed by Pilgrim's chief aide, Julian Flickinger was detailed to fly to Britain to collect the culture and maintain the line that his interest was essentially scientific and medical, concerning silicosis. His chief knew that he would not be fooling anybody but it would 'preserve the appearances'. He was flown by the US Air Force to Brize Norton, as though passing through on a routine visit to examine the possibility of another tour of duty at Porton.

Waiting for him at the airfield was Charlie Yates, the head of the CIA Mission in London, his purpose being to mark Flickinger's card in more detail concerning his coming conversations with Wendy Payne, Dr Allen and anyone else he might meet.

Charlie, a mid-Westerner from Saint Louis, was the kind of extrovert who, off duty or for golf, would sport black trousers adorned with pink dolphins and a garish jacket as a contrast to the well-cut suit and American brogues he usually wore. Of medium height and useful looking, with dark, curly hair greying at the temples and a ready smile, he was much liked and respected by his colleagues as an able operator.

Before he set off for Porton by chauffered transport, provided by the airfield, Flickinger had been briefed by Charlie to capitalize on his friendship with Wendy to find out all he could.

'You know how much the Brits have told us. Probe around and find out if they have held anything back. I don't think they have but they might still be working on strict need to know.'

'Would we?' Flickinger asked.

'We would and we are. So nothing whatever about any crash programme. What I would like to know is whether they have any evidence of leaks. Who has Dr Payne told, apart from you . . .'

Charlie waited at the airfield to debrief Flickinger on his return, working in the quiet of the officers' mess on some documents he had brought. A conscientious officer, he left nothing to chance.

As Julian stepped from his car outside the main entrance to the Chemical Defence Establishment, the field guns on the Larkhill practise ranges could be distinctly heard and he recalled that, as a keen environmentalist and Friend of the Earth, it was the one thing about the area which Wendy disliked.

His reunion with her was joyous. He gave her such a mighty hug that he whirled her off her feet.

'Gee, it's great to see you again. Isn't she a clever girl, Adrian? Not just creating the clone but seeing the possibility of extracting an enzyme for the treatment of silicosis!'

Adrian agreed, admiringly.

'I'm sure looking forward to getting my teeth into this one,' Julian said. 'How's it all going?'

'I'm rather held up at the moment,' Wendy replied. 'I'm relying on you to get moving on the silicosis aspects.'

'But surely you're doing something?'

'I'm culturing the clone under anaerobic conditions but I want to get enough data for a paper.'

'Will you be able to publish?'

'I hope so, eventually.'

They both looked at Adrian who did not commit himself.

'It's a damn shame about all this secrecy,' Julian said. 'Have you discerned any interest from the other side of the Iron Curtain?'

'Not a thing,' Adrian replied. 'Why should they have heard about it?'

'I just wondered. When can I see the monster?'

'Right now.'

Suitably robed, he was taken into Wendy's C4 laboratory and shown the effects of the bacterium on glassware, the original flasks, slides and magnifying glass, now being treasured as future museum pieces.

'Amazing! I would never have believed it.'

'It certainly is versatile,' Adrian observed.

Seizing his cue, Julian asked, as casually as he could, 'Any evidence that it could attack a silicon chip?'

Adrian and Wendy glanced at each other. They both knew that the Pentagon had been told everything so there was no point in prevaricating with Julian. In confidence they told him everything they knew, showing him the numerous silicon chips which had been used in various experiments, including those with computers.

'It seems to be able to attack any silicon chips at temperatures up to about seventy degrees centigrade. Some big computers might be too hot for it but it could invade them when they are turned off,' Adrian explained.

'What a turn-up, Wendy, that you, of all people, should have invented a potential weapon,' Julian exclaimed, well aware of her pacifist commitment.

'I'm not proud of that,' she said quietly. 'In fact, I'm ashamed of it.'

She opened a cupboard revealing an array of plastic flasks and dishes. 'These are your wet cultures. They are all ready for you. I take it you brought a container.'

'Sure did,' Julian replied. 'I have it in the automobile.'

'Any chance that you'll be coming to work here?' Adrian asked.

'Not for a few months, at least,' Julian replied, with genuine sadness. 'The Chief wants me to press on at Fort Detrick. He's very excited about the medical possibilities and asked me to congratulate Wendy on her breakthrough into a new field. But whatever I'm required to do at the Fort, it will be in the closest collaboration with Wendy.'

Wendy was clearly delighted by the prospect but Adrian did not respond. He knew that the military authorities would be in charge of the crash programme and they, not Flickinger, would decide what could and could not be imparted to the British.

'Your friend looks more piratical than ever with that new shape to his beard,' he said to Wendy after Flickinger had gone. 'I hope that he doesn't pirate your discovery.'

'Julian would never do that,' Wendy insisted.

She invariably rose to the support of her friends but Adrian had an irrational suspicion of young men with beards. He thought they must have something to hide, though Julian had not been very clever at concealing the instructions he had been given to probe the situation at Porton.

Flickinger had left with several cultures in sealed flasks packed in his low-temperature container and, after his debriefing by Yates, was flown back the same day to Andrews Air Force Base, near Washington. On the long flight he wondered if he would be permitted to angle his enzyme research towards the silicosis problem, which interested him as much as it did Wendy. With some sorrow, he anticipated that it would be in the discard until all the defence implications, and possible applications, had been thoroughly probed. He was at one with Wendy in thoroughly disliking secrecy in scientific research, especially when it impacted on medical possibilities.

A refrigerated van was waiting at Andrews Air Force Base to speed the container to Fort Detrick, where several groups of scientists of various disciplines were waiting to examine it without delay. Within days, one of the teams had confirmed the clone's ability to inactivate silicon chips. Another, using a really big, expendable computer, proved its offensive capabilities after dismantling it, under extremely secure conditions, to see exactly what had happened. It was worse than they had expected. Under the influence of the warmth generated by the computer and the continuous flow of air needed to cool it, the bacteria had managed to infiltrate at almost every possible entry point.

The immediate consequent question was could the infestation spread from one equipment to another? If it could, how far could it 'jump' and under what conditions? Experiments to resolve these questions were too hazardous to be carried out at Fort Detrick, if only because of the menace to all the glassware, and the remote bacteriological proving ground in the distant desert in the state of Utah was designated for them.

When Pilgrim learned the result of the first experiments from an informant inside Fort Detrick some two weeks later, he was captivated by the possibilities. Like any highly infectious bacterium, the clone could 'jump' from one equipment to another in a building, being spread by the current of the air conditioners, but seemed incapable of spreading from one closed building to another unless introduced by contaminated material or by human agents, accidentally or deliberately.

That, of course, was purely an interim judgement but, on the basis of it, the Pentagon steamroller was set in motion. Under the all-embracing name of Drumbeat, several secret committees with their own code-names were set up to explore every offensive and defensive aspect in case the Russians should ever acquire the clone. What if the Russians develop it and we don't? was the question dominating all the proceedings. Recent intelligence had confirmed that, in spite of the moratorium, the Soviets were continuing with an offensive biological warfare programme, the major facility being near Sverdlovsk. So none of the defence authorities felt any qualms. On the contrary, they assured themselves that they would be derelict in their duty if they failed to explore every eventuality.

Mass production appeared to present no difficulty. The clone seemed eminently suitable for production by continuous culture machines. So, on the urgent recommendations of the committees, the research programme was rapidly expanded to examine how the bacteria might be deliberately disseminated. Could they be released surreptitiously from civil airliners over major cities? What was the potential for dry powder cultures disseminated from spray tanks, delivery by drone aircraft or by warheads releasing biological bomblets? How realistic was the danger that the clone could be spread manually by enemy agents or terrorists?

Experts who had become redundant when offensive biological research had ceased were recalled from retirement to help speed the programme, the topmost priority being given to studies of the clone's possible use for sabotage and high-tech terrorism. For instance, could a passenger disembarking from a long-distance airliner secretly disseminate enough dry powder to incapacitate it during its next

97

flight? Other scientists were co-opted from the universities, increasing further the growing number of people who had to be let into the secret to varying degrees. They were subjected to the highest security and warned of the severest penalties for leakages. It was decided that, in the best interests of the United States, the amount of Drumbeat information supplied to the British should be restricted to what they needed to know, which at that stage was considered to be very little. Time was needed, first, for deep deliberation on all the implications.

From reports provided by MI5 and Charlie Yates' debriefing of Flickinger, the CIA specified Wendy Payne as the weakest point in the whole security screen. She was rated a soft, tempting target, with her student record of agitation, commitment to internationalism in science and with foreign friends who were under communist control.

Further concern was expressed that the secret might leak from some 'pinko' British civil servant who might supply a document to the Labour Party, which would make maximum political use of it to create a banana skin. If the British Government was accused of pursuing 'germ warfare', the charge would be levelled at the Americans with greater international ferocity.

It was, however, felt necessary to involve the British in one aspect. It was agreed that all major defence computers would eventually have to be germ-proof as well as dust-proof, not only because an adversary might use silicon-eaters but because a natural mutant of some bacterium able to attack silicon might suddenly arise. So with more research to that end being needed, an ultra-secret joint UK–USA committee for computer protection was set up to secure British expertise.

The CIA was deeply concerned in Drumbeat from the start; senior intelligence agents were instructed to discover what, if anything, the Soviets might be doing in the general field of computer protection and to report on any indications of an upsurge of interest in the bacteriological defence field. The National Security Agency, the global eavesdropping organization, was alerted to keep close watch on the volume of KGB clandestine radio traffic and to analyse it for any indication that the Russians might have got wind of the developments. The Fort Detrick experts had decided that, even if the KGB or GRU received a detailed leakage, the Soviet scientists would have great difficulty in creating the clone and the chances of repeating the same experiment by accident were negligible. There would therefore be an immense Soviet effort to secure a sample of the strain by surreptitious means and the FBI in the US and intelligence agents abroad were urged to look out for signs of attempts not only by Soviet agents but by surrogates, such as the Poles, Hungarians, Czechs and Cubans.

So Drumbeat proved to be aptly named for another reason – it reverberated throughout the American defence and intelligence communities in thousands of coded signals throbbing through the ether via repeater stations and satellites, from Langley to the CIA Mission in Moscow, from Maryland to the remotest out-stations of the National Security Agency, from the Pentagon to a score of specialist establishments.

Again, Britain, and Porton in particular, was seen as the area where the Soviet bloc agents would concentrate their effort. This danger inflated the importance of Charlie Yates, who made it his business to conjure up reasons for conferring with the numerous friends he had made in the intelligence and diplomatic world in London.

The subject of Yates' first report back to CIA headquarters, from his office on the second floor of the US Embassy, was his discovery that there had been an extraordinary meeting of the Joint Intelligence Committee from which he had been deliberately excluded. Charlie was not pleased but, as an old campaigner, neither was he surprised and agreed with Pilgrim that it was water over the dam and not worth a formal complaint – at least at that stage. After all, the main objectives had been obtained and hurt feelings would be held in reserve against the day when the Brits might have some justifiable bleat.

Charlie's likeliest source of detailed information on the security and intelligence aspects of what had become known as the 'silicon threat' was Lesley Barrington-Fuller whom he saw fairly frequently for an 'exchange of views'. The personal conversational network, which every Resident worth his salt develops, produced much that would never have been forthcoming on paper on the give-some-to-get-some convention. He rarely had the opportunity to meet the Director-General, who kept his distance, except when very senior CIA officers visited London, but this was no great loss to Charlie who did not like Sandy Pryce.

It was not Charlie's experience that women were less secure than men: on the contrary, they were usually immune to the 'peacock factor' – that streak of vanity which induced men to air their secret knowledge, especially when they had a few drinks inside them. And he knew that Lesley was dedicated to the Anglo-American alliance on security and intelligence affairs. So he had no reason to withhold from her the secret that he had been fully briefed on the events at Porton and had been involved in Flickinger's visit. Lesley, however, was able to resist acquiring merit, at least at that stage, by refraining from telling him that she had been responsible, as she genuinely thought, for ensuring that the Americans had been informed of the silicon discovery. A more opportune moment might arise. In such matters timing was everything.

Over lunch together at the Travellers Club, which still barred women members but permitted them as guests, the conversation was the usual fencing match at the beginning to see how much the other knew. 'Have you any evidence of any Soviet interest?' Charlie asked.

'Nothing. GCHQ is watching the traffic. Are there any signs at your end?'

'No, but we're keeping our fingers crossed. I've no doubt that the opposition will be busy eventually. Have you set up any special precautions in the Porton area?'

'Yes, we're keeping a close watch. There is a *Spetsnaz* subversion unit trained for action in war and manned by some local creatures who call themselves British but are committed to operate as *Spetsnaz* auxiliaries and knock out the communications services at UK Land Forces at Wilton, just up the road from Porton. We think that if anybody had been instructed to snoop around it would be them and there are no signs of that.'

'Have you managed to infiltrate the unit?' Charlie asked.

'No comment,' Lesley answered, with a toothy smile that said enough. 'We've also increased our surveillance of the satellite agencies, especially of the Hungarians, who seem to be used most by the Soviets for keeping tabs on our scientific defence establishments. There's no special activity there either.'

Charlie then guided the conversation to his main interest – the weakness of Wendy Payne as a source of leakage. He revealed that Flickinger had been questioned in the United States and had indicated that, through her open nature and beliefs, Wendy could easily be induced to talk, though not with any evil intent.

'Such people are always the most dangerous,' Lesley observed.

'They mean well but can do terrible damage. The trouble with some scientists is that they feel more loyalty for their profession than for their country, if it comes to a choice.'

She allowed Charlie to tell her all that he wanted to without interruption. Then, as judged by his facial reaction, she staggered him by remarking, 'In our view there may be a greater danger than Dr Payne – an American danger. She has an American lover who has relatives behind the Iron Curtain. He's of Polish origin,' she added, darkly.

'The United States is full of Poles,' Charlie commented. 'What's his name?'

'Jerzy Malinowski.'

'What does he do?'

'He works in your Embassy.'

'Then I know him. We call him Joe. He's a nice guy. You needn't worry about him.'

Charlie had not told any lies. But he knew Joe Malinowski rather better than he had indicated.

Chapter Fourteen

President Clinton Rockwell, known to his wife and friends as Clint but to the media as 'Rocky', was also rather better informed than he pretended when he was officially told of the silicon discovery and its implications at a meeting of the National Security Council in the Situation Room in the White House.

'If only the goddamned scientists would leave things alone,' he groaned.

'You sound like that Pope complaining about Galileo, Mr President,' the Secretary of State remarked.

'I suppose I do,' Rockwell responded, his bronzed features creasing with good humour. 'But it comes at such a difficult time for my personal relations with General Secretary Primarkov. But then it's always a bad time when these things happen,' he added, resignedly.

When Rockwell had first been informed of the silicon threat by a close, personal source, shortly after Pilgrim had first heard of it, his immediate reaction had been to tell himself that he did not need to deal with the problem that day and to let others do the thinking until he was faced with it officially. He was a 'hands on' leader who enjoyed the business of government but, with so much in his in-tray, he could never afford the luxury of concentrating on any one problem for long or of dealing with anything which could safely be delayed. He had learned to delegate earlier in life, in his varied business career and during his stint at the CIA in particular, and was confident that the problem was in good hands. Up-to-the-minute intelligence was essential to anyone in such a highly responsible political position but it was often advantageous to plead ignorance and to be able to say in public 'I didn't know'.

This self-indulgence, however, was short-lived. When the Secretary of State was officially informed of the events by the British Foreign Office, he immediately appreciated the full horror of the implications. The moratorium under which the Soviet Union and the United States refrained from all research on biological and chemical warfare had been signed by the previous President only a year before and the signing of a full treaty, outlawing both types of weapons for ever, was to be the highlight of the forthcoming summit. Britain and the other NATO countries were to be signatories in later accords. Rockwell and the whole Republican administration were setting the greatest store by this treaty, to which nobody, not even The Nephews, could possibly object. Now it was seriously threatened by the chance British discovery, and the position of the President could only be described as invidious. There could be little doubt how the Russians would react if Drumbeat came to their notice.

With the summit in the detailed planning stage – there had been one brief encounter with Primarkov in Washington to get acquainted – the meeting of the National Security Council had been called to consider all the implications of the silicon threat. As so many people in so many departments were now involved, it was more than likely that the secret would leak, possibly before the summit. So which would be the lesser of two obvious evils – to risk letting the Russians find out and put an enormous propaganda initiative into their hands or to tell them?

The Council had little difficulty in agreeing that if the Soviets found out the facts from their own resources Moscow would claim, and might well believe, that Clone Fe 113 was the result of illicit research with silicon chips as the deliberate target. In the peculiar circumstances, most other countries, and especially their media, would believe the Russians and not the Americans. Most perilously, that could give Primarkov's opponents on the Politburo a powerful weapon to disrupt the blossoming relationship between him and Rockwell by pointing to the perfidy of the Americans. Primarkov had been assuring his political opponents and the Soviet people that the Americans could be trusted and had to be trusted, mutual trust being essential to the whole thrust of his policies.

If the Soviets were given the silicon information, the onus for developing the clone could at least be put on the British, where it truly belonged. The concomitant danger lay in the certainty that, if they were deliberately told, the Soviets would request cultures of the clone. In the view of an interim Pentagon report, that could put a powerful weapon in their hands, especially for sabotage and terrorist purposes.

It was a difficult dilemma requiring careful thought from all angles and the President quickly settled for the inevitable bureaucratic suggestion: the issue would be referred to a hand-picked study group, which would examine the options in detail and make recommendations as to the most advantageous course of action for the United States. Such a study would normally stretch into weeks but, because of the forthcoming summit, the President needed a quicker than usual response. Meanwhile total secrecy would continue, hopefully, to be maintained.

After the meeting had broken up and Rockwell was stretching his long legs, the Secretary of State for Foreign Affairs requested a few minutes entirely alone with him.

'It's difficult for me, Mr President, but I must raise a delicate matter concerning the First Lady . . .'

Rockwell half suppressed a sigh, knowing what was coming. 'I guess it's about her Polish interest?'

'Yes, Mr President. It could create an additional difficulty at the summit and we already have enough.'

'You want me to tell her to pipe down?' Rockwell asked, good-humouredly.

'Something like that – but only until after the summit.'

'OK. I'll see what I can do but you know Baby!'

The First Lady was a forceful figure known to all as 'Baby' Rockwell, the nickname deriving from her maiden name, Martha Babinski. It had become incongruous in middle age, especially in view of her physique which was tall and amply upholstered. She was a second-generation American Pole and, inevitably, had been called 'Baby' at school in Chicago. Intensely political, she had long been active in America's large Polish community, spoke the language and had been responsible for attracting a sizeable proportion of the Polish-American vote during the Presidential campaign, having been far more vocal than most potential First Ladies. She was also an ardent Catholic and that, coupled with her championing of a downtrodden country where Roman Catholicism was a potent political factor, had helped with the Irish-American vote.

With her deep sense of grievance about Poland's postwar treatment by the Russians, she had virtually promised her supporters that her husband would try to alleviate Poland's lot, if elected. After he had won, with a large majority, she had encouraged her husband's friendly approach to Primarkov, hoping that he could put pressure on him to loosen control of Poland, a move to which the Soviet military chiefs were strongly opposed. She now expected him to deliver and never stopped trying to work on the Secretary of State in that respect whenever they met.

She had been a strong supporter of The Nephews because of their firm anti-Soviet stand and had worn their Uncle Sam badge with pride until required by First Lady protocol to commit it to a drawer. This, too, dismayed the Secretary of State whenever The Nephews made propaganda out of it, as they still did, regularly.

Rockwell confided in her deeply, needing a non-official, non-technical, common-sensical view on many issues where he might feel he was being overborne or bamboozled by the bureaucracy. For that reason, apart from his need for her marital support – throughout their thirty-five years of marriage she had been fiercely protective of her husband's welfare – he was determined that she should accompany him on the trip to Moscow but there was a problem.

At the meeting with the Primarkovs in Washington, Baby had tried to gain the support of the Soviet leader's wife, Tamara, in securing greater freedom for Poland, both domestically and in its dealings with the West, and that First Lady, who gave an impression of equal political aptitude and superior intellect, had reacted with some spirit.

'Poland is an essential buffer state for the security of the peace-loving Soviet people, who have been subjected to terrible suffering by invading armies, something Americans cannot really begin to understand,' Tamara had replied, tersely, in English. 'I am afraid that, for the foreseeable future, the Poles will have to go on doing what they are told.' The exchange had soured relations between the two wives.

They were ill-matched, their discernibly Slavic features being all that they shared. Baby's height, exaggerated by her bouffant blonde-dyed hair, made her the proverbial galleon in full sail as she bore down on the small-boned, slim and elegant Tamara. 'Some baby,' Tamara had remarked in Russian behind her back but audibly to others, so that it was duly reported in the press. Baby's alleged reaction to the fulsome media praise of Tamara had also appeared in print: 'Just because she's not a bag tied up in the middle, like some

105

other Russian First Ladies, they call her beautiful. She'd never turn a head on Fifth Avenue!'

The President's problem was Baby's continuing pressure to induce him to raise the Polish issue with Primarkov as a human rights scandal and he was disinclined to risk souring the summit by doing it.

'We have to move gently, Baby,' he said on returning to the family quarters, upstairs, after the National Security Council meeting. 'There are more urgent problems for the United States than Poland. Maybe at the next summit but one . . .'

'That's always Poland's fate. Always on the back burner!'

'But, honey, I just can't rock the boat when the little man's position is so precarious.'

They always referred to Primarkov as the 'little man' because the contrast between his height and Rockwell's was as great as that between Tamara's and Baby's.

'Is his position really precarious or is that what he tells you when you talk to him on the telephone?' asked Baby, who was not prepared to trust any Russian.

'Oh, it's precarious all right. Half the Politburo is rocking the boat and if we're going to make any progress on arms control I need to keep the little man in it and fully in command. So I don't want you rocking it as well.'

Rockwell had new reason for relegating Poland to even lower priority. As an additional item on the agenda that day, the National Security Council had considered the rapidly worsening Mexican economy. Intelligence reports suggested that if it suddenly collapsed, as seemed highly possible, there could be such a mighty surge of illegal immigrant Mexicans across the 1,800-mile US border that it could not be stemmed. As a precaution, miles of deep ditches were to be excavated under the cover that they were for keeping out vehicles used by drug smugglers, though they would, in fact, also serve that purpose. The Council had decided that it might be necessary to withdraw troops from Europe to man the border and contingency arrangements for doing so, with practise exercises, were to be put in train. So further deals with the Soviets to ensure peace in Europe were more urgent than ever.

The President explained the Mexican threat to his wife, with whom he shared most of his secrets, but she responded only by peering at his temples. 'There are some more grey ones beginning to show,

106

dear. She's coming tomorrow. I'll make sure she stays until she's had time to deal with you.'

'She' was the First Lady's hairdresser, who attended the White House several times a week. Rockwell would never have bothered to have his dark hair dyed but for the pressure from Baby, who was sure that even the older voters preferred a young image.

Eventually Baby promised to behave diplomatically but what she would do when she got to Moscow was anybody's guess. With such a tempestuous temperament on such an inflammatory subject, anything was possible. And there were plenty of people to cheer her on.

Chapter Fifteen

The person appointed to chair the study group on the silicon threat options was a former US Army Lieutenant General, Daniel Blanchard, a big, bulky, florid and jovial soldier who, since his youth, had answered to the name Butch. Blanchard had been Director of Army Intelligence and, shortly after his retirement, had been snapped up by the President to serve as his Chief of Staff in the White House. It had been a surprise appointment, for his name had not been in the list of front-runners touted by the media, but he was proving a success.

He was everybody's friend, without guile or political ambition, and his general likeability compensated for political inexperience when forging the good relations with Congress which were so essential with a Democrat majority there. His integrity was unquestionable and, as a member of the National Security Council, his intelligence expertise was a bonus, helping to ensure that the CIA and the rest of the intelligence community did not pull too much wool over the President's eyes or deny him information. Through his many forces friendships, Blanchard had excellent sources and welcome access in the Pentagon and this was an additional asset when the public spending cuts were bound to cause so much painful blood-letting there. And he had long experience in controlling the flow of paper which, if unchecked in the White House channels to the President, could be suffocating.

In his youth, Butch had played American football for Notre Dame and the Army as quarterback, being something of a national hero at the time. To him, intelligence was another game in which you gained ground and lost it in an energetic ding-dong struggle, the ball being the current operation against the current adversary. Only occasionally did you score and, as often as not, that was due to a mistake by the opposing side. Few holds were barred. The game was very rough and, however much you tried to protect yourself, you could get hurt. The more you scored, the greater the determination of the adversary to defeat you. And he, or you, could move the goal posts. Return matches were not only inevitable but perpetual. It was very much a team effort and the strategy, devised in a huddle, had to be kept secret from the adversary until it had to be shown and even then it should be disguised in some manner. There was far less scope for individual enterprise than readers of spy fiction generally believed. Unless you played unselfishly, as a team, you were bound to lose.

A complex character, Butch's other intellectual interest was poetry, which he described as potted wisdom, and he was renowned for his ability to produce the apt quote at the right time.

Blanchard and Rockwell had become friends when the future President had been Director of Central Intelligence and Butch had been the senior Army Intelligence representative in the Pentagon, positions which frequently brought them together. But it was Baby who claimed the responsibility for his appointment as Chief of Staff, a plum post for which several influential Washington wives had canvassed on behalf of their husbands. She had become fond of Butch, an outgoing huggy-bear prepared to devote a lot of time to friendship. Way back, Blanchard was of French origin and, as a fervent Catholic, worshipped at the same church as Baby, who attended alone since the President was of the Protestant faith. But Baby's deep affection had been for his wife, Patsy, a pert little woman of great energy and charm. In the freer days before Rockwell's accession to the Presidency, the two women, who could not have looked more dissimilar, had liked nothing better than to spend a few days together in New York, staying at the all-female Colony Club, shopping, seeing a few shows and enjoying much laughter.

Tragically, but swiftly, Patsy had died of acute leukaemia and with Butch pining so much, Baby had pressed her husband to give him the post into which he could throw his prodigious energies. With two other politically ambitious Republicans pressing for the powerful position, it had suited Rockwell to seize on her suggestion and give them other appointments. He needed a Chief of Staff who would not only be entirely dependable and unflappable but would be commonsensical and even-handed in deciding who got access to the President and his limited time.

There was a rogue factor in this personal equation: Butch was also on intimate terms with Ross Pilgrim, though the President saw nothing wrong in that. On the contrary, there were advantages in it for him. As Chief of Staff, it was Butch's duty to liaise with the CIA and especially with Stanley Arnold, the Director of Central Intelligence. Arnold did not like the close nature of Blanchard's friendship with Pilgrim but there was nothing he could do about it since it was, as Butch put it, 'grappled with hoops of steel'. There was some comfort for Arnold in the hope that Blanchard might restrain Pilgrim's rumoured excesses.

Pilgrim had been delighted for Butch, and for himself, when the Chief of Staff appointment had been announced, but the choice had astonished him. In his view, Butch, though a fine soldier and an outstanding authority on the GRU, did not appear to have much political sense. Pilgrim was confident that he would enjoy continuing access to Butch's 'facilities'. In return, Butch could expect to learn certain CIA matters which the President might be deemed, within the Agency, as having 'no need to know'.

Butch had already benefited by being informed of the British silicon discovery as soon as Pilgrim had been told about it by Sandy Pryce. It had been safe to inform Butch because his personal commitment to security was a byword. 'The security buck stops with you!' he used to tell his staff, stabbing a pudgy finger at them. Throughout his career, he had insisted that every officer under his command, and that included himself, should be personally responsible for destroying his surplus or outdated secret documents. This meant a personal trip to the shredder and the incinerator and the sight of a general burning papers became a cause for ribald comment at the Army Intelligence headquarters at Fort Meade in Maryland. The General's response had always been robust and to the point: 'If everyone had done as I do then that goddamn Walker family would never have been able to sell the Navy's secrets to the Soviets by the bagful.'

Though Pilgrim had advised Butch to be 'very selective' about whom he informed concerning the silicon chip discovery, he knew that he would immediately tell the President, not only out of loyalty but to show that he was on the ball. But it would put Butch in his debt and casting his bread upon the waters was a well-tested Pilgrim principle.

They had become intimate professional colleagues when Butch had been Chief of Army Intelligence, with an annual budget almost as big as the CIA's; their interests had often coincided or been complementary. Blanchard's headquarters had not been far from Washington or from the CIA headquarters at Langley. His main adversary and target had been the GRU and, with Pilgrim as the acknowledged authority on the KGB, the two had been a formidable combination.

With his far-flung military facilities, Butch had often been able to assist CIA operations – indeed to make them possible. His military attachés behind the Iron Curtain had travel facilities denied to civilian CIA men working under cover and they had co-operated in various ingenious counter-intelligence operations, sharing their failures as well as their triumphs. Among the latter had been the planting of eavesdropping sensors, known as 'sneakies', in many areas of the world. These were devices which came in all sizes and could be disguised in many ways, as items of desk equipment, laboratory tools, domestic objects, even as stones and logs, and would pick up information and relay it to satellites over long periods. The radio signals emitted by a sneaky were difficult for the adversary country to detect among the many ordinary Soviet radio transmissions. As some of even the smallest sneakies were atomically powered, by radio isotopes, they lasted for years – unless detected.

What had really cemented the friendship, however, and thrown them together for whole days at a time, was their common interest in hunting, especially for duck and quail. These were times for triviality and escape from the seriousness of their work. They would set forth before daylight in their red shooting caps with their over-and-under shotguns, Pilgrim's bird dog Dallas, and decoys and duck-callers. Pilgrim cast a long shadow, literally as well as metaphorically, and Butch had difficulty keeping up with him as they strode along foreshores or through marshes.

With his unusual power of concentration, Pilgrim was a brilliant game shot, laughingly attributing his exceptional success with the elusive quail as they exploded away in front of the pointing dogs to a personal stratagem: 'To kill a quail I pretend it has a hammer and sickle on its ass.' When a couple of drakes came over, while they were in a duck-hide together, Pilgrim was wont to whisper, 'You take Primarkov on the left and I'll get Chevalsky on the right,' referring to the current head of the KGB. The hype usually worked, with both birds tumbling down shot in the head, to a muffled cheer from both men.

111

Pilgrim had good reason to detest Oleg Chevalsky, whom he had encountered when both had been young and operating in Vienna, at the East-West crossroads which had become the trysting ground for adversaries of the intelligence game. There they could meet and contest on neutral ground. The Russian had been responsible for the only serious blot on Pilgrim's career.

With common need to know the enemy, they had indulged in badinage at the Embassy drinks parties and Pilgrim had taken a dangle and assumed that Chevalsky was prepared to defect. He had run him for a few months, giving him chicken-feed, and then the Russian had announced that he was under suspicion and needed to 'jump'. With a senior colleague, Pilgrim had gone to a discreetly situated flat in the eastern extremity of Salzburg to pick up Chevalsky and smuggle him to West Germany but, when they had entered it and switched on the light, all that had greeted them had been maniacal laughter from a tape recorder hidden in a ventilator which could not be reached without a ladder. They had left in a hurry and the laughter had continued to ring in Pilgrim's ears down the years. It had been an eerie experience and he had never been able to see the funny side of it. His colleague, who had later been killed in Vietnam, had managed to suppress it within the Agency.

They had assumed that Chevalsky had been arrested but intelligence soon showed that he had been promoted and he eventually out-ranked Pilgrim by emerging as the KGB chief. The defector who had described the KGB involvement in the assassination of President Kennedy had offered one explanation: as a field officer in those days, Chevalsky had been associated with that stunning success.

In spite of the deliberate air of boyish flippancy between Pilgrim and Butch on their hunting days, more than one delicate operation against the adversary had been conceived and honed during the long wait in a duck hide. Early in their acquaintance, while shooting on a foreshore, Butch had been particularly impressed by a dissertation by Pilgrim comparing the inevitability of the ebb and flow of the tide with the inevitability of the ebb and flow of power. They had pledged their joint determination to stop it flowing from the United States to the Soviet Union.

Before his political appointment, Butch had shared Pilgrim's fear of the former President's trust in the new-style Soviet leadership and both had been clandestine supporters of The Nephews in this regard.

But as the ingenuity of the strategy had been revealed to him he had changed his mind. He had come to realize that, as in the intelligence game, foreign policy is not always what it seems.

As he now understood the East-West relationship, the welcome Soviet preoccupation with internal change derived directly from the Star Wars programme, introduced by President Reagan as a deliberate political ploy. He and his advisers had been well aware that the system for shooting down incoming Soviet missiles would probably not work effectively enough against a heavy attack. But the Soviet leadership would not dare to bank on that and would be forced to realize that it would have to compete even more intensively in that field. So enormous were the sums being actively invested in Star Wars by the US Government, and so superior was the American technology, that the Soviet leadership quickly appreciated that effective competition was beyond its economic and scientific resources. If the American Star Wars concepts worked, as they just might, the Soviet Union would lose the military pre-eminence in nuclear missiles which was its sole claim to superpower status. If forced to rely on its economic strength it belonged to the Third World.

So, when threats and propaganda failed to stop the American programme, the Soviets had been forced to the negotiating table in a bid to find safe ways to reduce defence spending and so release money and resources to build up the economy. It could not be done without major social and political changes, which would concentrate the energies of the leadership on internal problems for many years. The relatively new Soviet leader, Vladimir Primarkov, seemed dedicated to promoting the less aggressive policy which he had inherited and Rockwell was keen to assist him in the interest of peace and human rights.

Pilgrim's reaction to this exposition of foreign policy by Butch had been typically brusque. 'I don't buy it. The Soviets have been busy with Star Wars research far longer than we have.'

'But they don't seem to have got very far with it.'

'How can we be sure of that? Remember how they fooled us over the long-range missiles with all that bullshitsky about technical bottlenecks that never really existed. Then, suddenly, what do you know? Nuclear missile supremacy!'

'Yeah, they certainly caught us out there,' Butch admitted, recalling his own part in the way the Pentagon had swallowed the ingenious Soviet deception.

'And if Clint Rockwell has his way, they'll catch us out again. You, of all people, Butch, should know that in the communist world nothing is ever what it seems. This guy, Primarkov, is a lineal political descendant of Peter the Great, as Lenin was, and empire-building is still the long-term goal. What's happening superficially is just long-term window-dressing, another tactical response to desperate domestic circumstances. *Glasnost* and all that crap are part of the most elaborate deception operation ever foisted on the West. What was it you once quoted to me? "To the honourable a word is a bond but to the communist a bond is nothing but words."'

'But the Soviets have got to change some time,' Butch argued. 'This could be it. The President believes that what Primarkov is sponsoring is not so much another Soviet revolution as the Soviet Renaissance – the questioning of authority which has been stifled by the Communist Party, just as it was by the Catholic Church way back in time. It could lead to all kinds of changes. Let's give Primarkov a chance.'

Pilgrim shook his head, decisively. 'Real change would mean the collapse of communism and the end of the Politburo dictatorship. Do you really think that Primarkov, a product of the communist system, is working for that? Do you really think the Red Army and the KGB would permit it?'

'I see the State Department intelligence reports and there is nothing in them to suggest that Primarkov does not mean what he says. We should help him along. He's even more of a genuine reformer than Gorbachev was.'

'Alas, poor Gorbachev! I knew him well, Butch,' Pilgrim mocked. 'The State Department didn't foresee his departure, did it? But we did. The trouble with State Department intelligence is that it's put together by credulous diplomats and others who deliver what they think the State Department wants to read. Our intelligence is very different.'

'But you can't deny that there really are major changes going on in the Soviet Union. Democracy is on the march there!'

'A slow march, maybe, but the changes are all short-term and cosmetic to suit the immediate Soviet purpose into which Primarkov has been forced by circumstances. He's after a Marshall Plan and he could get it. It's as plain as daylight what they're after – our technology and massive cheap loans to underwrite their economic reforms so that they can carry on with their military spending.' Pilgrim continued when Butch had no response: 'Then, when they have completed all this *perestroika* crap, which has been forced on them by the failure of communism, watch out! We need to know their true intentions, and that's my task. Your trouble, Butch, is that you've been got at by those gullible goons in the State Department. With them, hope will always triumph over intelligence – in both senses of that word.'

Blanchard, a more rounded figure than Pilgrim in more ways than one, had the highest regard for his friend's flair and steadfast devotion to his country and still went along with much of his philosophy, but he was prepared to grant the other side some degree of sincerity, especially when Primarkov had gone so far. An avid reader of prose as well as poetry, one of his favourite admonitions to his staff, when he had been in charge of Army Intelligence, had been Talleyrand's '*Pas trop de zèle*'. He often felt that Pilgrim could benefit from the wily diplomat's wisdom.

If literature was a mirror of reality, the obsession responsible for most human excesses was passion, with control jettisoned and judgement in the discard. Pilgrim was passionately obsessed by his precious 'game' and such a zealot could drive himself to excesses which he could always justify, if he recognized them at all, especially when they could be kept secret.

Chapter Sixteen

As Adrian Allen had fully appreciated, Wendy Payne was no more capable of celibacy than he was. He had surmised, when their affair had ceased, that she would find another lover, or a philanderer would find her, but he had no idea who his successor might be and Wendy had not enlightened him. With the CIA attaching such importance to the secrecy of Project Drumbeat, Sandy Pryce had seen to it that Wendy was placed under MI5 surveillance and it had not taken the watchers long to discover that her lover was an American, a fact which caused Pilgrim to wonder what advantage might be seized out of that situation when Pryce appraised him of it.

There was no difficulty whatever in discovering all about Joe Malinowski because it was on record in the American Embassy, where he worked in the US Information Service. His real first name was Jerzy and his parents were second-generation Polish immigrants. Charlie Yates knew him rather better than he had admitted to Lesley because both the CIA and the FBI used him as a conduit with the British media for information and, occasionally, disinformation. In Charlie's book Joe was everybody's nice guy, a good American, conscientious in his work and with nothing whatever recorded to his discredit. He was also extremely obliging when convinced that a course of action was in his country's interests.

Joe had met Wendy during the Warsaw microbiology conference, which she had described to MI5. At that time, being a Polish speaker, he had been serving on the staff of the US Embassy in the Polish capital and had attended some sessions of the conference as a matter of courtesy and to be on hand for assistance to the American delegates.

The encounter had developed, on his initiative, some time after their return to Britain and it was fortuitous that he pursued his interest just when she was lonely after her traumatic break with Adrian.

Being unattached, somewhat overweight, lethargic by nature, a jeans and trainers man off duty, Joe offered a comfortable change to the smart and hyperactive Adrian, with his marital ties and other demands on his time. Joe was in his early forties but Adrian had given Wendy an intellectual taste for older men.

Wendy had yet to encounter love outside her family. She had been infatuated with Adrian, had enjoyed flings with Julian Flickinger and a few others. It was not that she was wanton: she simply disliked being alone for long and the physical enjoyment of sex was a human right. So at weekends Joe regularly stayed with her in her flat in Salisbury. There was still a framed photograph there of Julian and some of her student friends but Adrian's had been consigned to the underwear drawer in the bedroom. Small but cosy, the bedroom also served as the show-place for Wendy's sizeable collection of ethnic dolls acquired on her foreign trips. The Polish doll, which Joe had presented to her after they had visited the Warsaw Catholic Cathedral, totally rebuilt from the rubble of the war, had been given pride of place, usurping a Mountie doll which Adrian had brought back for her from Canada.

On the occasions when Wendy visited London she used Joe's furnished apartment in Wimbledon, which was larger and more elegant. She was relieved to have a lover for whom sex was a straightforward, natural business, to be taken, without domination, as the mutual mood arose.

The way Poland kept intruding into the picture worried Lesley Barrington-Fuller, who remained in active charge of the 'Payne case' on Pryce's instruction. There was a great deal of respect in Curzon Street for the UB, the Polish intelligence service. To Lesley's mind, Joe was just the person who would be targeted by the KGB if they got wind of the silicon discovery, perhaps using the UB as a surrogate. Someone close to Wendy who might find out what they wanted to know through pillow-talk would be irresistible, once the KGB had a lead. Indeed, he might already have been recruited while he was working in Warsaw, and could be cultivating Wendy under UB instruction. There would be no harm in putting him under surveillance. It would not be easy to obtain a signed warrant from the Home Secretary for the surveillance of an American official but it could be done to some extent without that, as part of the surveillance of Wendy for which a warrant had already been secured.

As was his practice while serving in any foreign country, Joe seized every opportunity to see all he could, provided it could be done in leisurely fashion, and it was not the first time that he and Wendy had wandered about Salisbury's graceful, grey stone cathedral. He could not get over the extraordinary fact that the enormous edifice – all 120,000 tons of it with its soaring spire – stood on foundations resting on gravel only four feet below ground level. Whoever the thirteenth-century architects were, they had achieved a miracle of engineering as well as of art.

Wendy agreed but, for sheer beauty and atmosphere, it could not compare with Durham Cathedral, which was so much more impressively sited on a bluff overlooking the River Wear, close by her old university.

'I must visit Durham one day,' Joe had responded.

'We could stay with my parents in Darlington, which isn't far away. They only have a little house. They are very ordinary folk.'

'Same as mine, back in Indianapolis.'

'We could go up the Dales. You'd love them, Joe – the heather, the villages and the dry stone walls.'

They were eavesdropping on a woman guide who was explaining to her party that the brightly coloured figures of Sir Richard and Dame Catherine Mompesson, lying uncomfortably in their stiff, seventeenth-century ruffs, were facing west instead of east because the whole elaborate monument had been moved. In the half-gloom behind them Joe noticed a man whom he thought he had seen before when he and Wendy had been together at an avant-garde theatre in London. It could have been coincidence but Joe spotted him again later, a nondescript middle-aged figure, wandering about the Close. He did not detect the woman watcher who, like her colleague, had been on the look-out for a possible brush contact with a Soviet-bloc agent, an event well suited to the dark corners of a cathedral.

Joe did not mention his suspicion to Wendy as she enthused, a few minutes later, about the houses in the Close, to her the most desirable in England, with their warm, pink brick and crisp, white stone, shining in the early autumn sunshine, in an incomparable setting.

He had almost dismissed the incident as of no consequence until the following day when the same man turned up for a drink in the Hatchet, a tucked-away, thatched pub in the village of Lower Chute, near Andover, which they used for occasional evening meals.

'Can you think of any reason why that man standing by the bar should be following us?' Joe asked quietly as they scanned their menus.

Wendy could certainly think of a reason but had not enlightened Joe in any way about the silicon business, save to say that she was working on a development in genetic engineering which could be of great medical importance.

Appalled by his whispered explanation, Wendy asked, 'Are you sure that was the same man in the cathedral?'

'Absolutely. I deliberately dropped my guidebook when we were standing by that tomb and I got a good look at him as I picked it up. It was the same man I saw in London the week before.'

'I'm just not putting up with it,' Wendy announced, as she moved towards the bar.

'Excuse me, but are you following us?'

The man made no reply, finished his ale and left hurriedly.

'Bastards!' Wendy exclaimed as she rejoined Joe at their window seat.

'Who?' Joe asked, artlessly.

'MI5, the security people.'

'Why would they be following you?'

'Oh, they're insisting on positive vetting me now that I work in a secret establishment.'

'That seems fair enough.'

'Like hell it is, following me here and snooping on us. What do they think we are?'

'I guess he was only doing his job – but not doing it very well.'

'Balls to his job! These blood spooks have no shame.'

Joe shrugged. 'I guess they couldn't do their job if they had.'

'Well, I'm not having it,' Wendy said decisively. 'Not when it comes to intruding into my private life.'

It was brave talk but, at that moment, engineers representing MI5 were planting 'bugs' in both her flat and Joe's. The purpose of the watcher, who had not been too clever, had been to ensure that Wendy and Joe remained remote from the scene while the intruders completed their task. He had reported that all was well as soon as he had reached his car. The engineers could safely complete their work because the watcher had overheard the couple preparing to order a meal.

On the following Monday morning, Wendy marched into Adrian

119

Allen's room in some dudgeon to complain about being followed.

'Unless it is stopped I intend to consult my union,' she declared. 'I have my civil rights.'

'Please, don't do that,' Adrian pleaded. 'I'll have a word with the security people. If you tell the union it will be in all the media and then the whole business will blow.'

It was not easy, at that moment, for Adrian to explain that an MI5 officer was on the way down to Porton and would almost certainly wish to see her but there was no alternative.

'Good,' Wendy said, with relish. 'I'll give him a piece of my mind, especially if it's that idiot who has been following me.'

'It's not a him, it's a she. And she's far from being an idiot. It's the ginger tabby with the sharp claws.'

Though Wendy had promised Adrian that she would not blow her top, she was in no way subdued when eventually confronted by Lesley, who had chosen to see her because she felt that a woman-to-woman talk might be the most productive. To a North country 'bonny fighter', such a challenge was always welcome.

A sun-worshipper, still brown from the good summer, Wendy was surprised by the paleness of Lesley's skin until she spotted the freckles which had earned her that nickname at school and were exacerbated by sunlight. From the tone of her voice she sized her up as a rather superior southerner who had enjoyed pecuniary and social privileges. She was prepared, in advance, to dislike any of her sex who could make a profession out of the snooping business.

Lesley noticed all the signs of the ardent feminist in the intellectually truculent look about Wendy, apart from her unsexy clothing. From the accent, which Wendy had never consciously tried to modulate, and what she had read in her file about her antecedents, she could harbour some social resentment. Was it heavy enough to be a chip? It could be a difficult encounter.

'We are interested in your friend, Mr Malinowski,' Lesley said. 'Did you know that he is of Polish origin?'

'So is America's First Lady,' Wendy responded. 'Have you objected to that?'

Lesley remained calm. 'The point is that he still has relatives behind the Iron Curtain and could be, well, leaned on. Have you told him anything about your work?'

'You mean about the silicon chip business?'

'Yes.'

'No, we never discuss my work and he doesn't discuss his. We have other things to talk about. He's totally non-scientific.'

'I understand your annoyance at my intrusion into your private life, Dr Payne, and I assure you that it gives me no pleasure. All I ask you is to be on your guard and to let us know if Mr Malinowski, or anyone else, tries to pump you.'

'He won't.'

'Probably not, but he might,' Lesley persevered. 'I would, of course, be grateful if you could refrain from letting Mr Malinowski know that I have questioned you about him.'

Declining to commit herself on that score, Wendy retorted, 'And I would be grateful if you would refrain from putting your hatchet man on my trail.'

'Hatchet man? I don't understand.'

'That man you sent down to spy on me in the Hatchet pub.'

Lesley denied all knowledge of the Hatchet or the man, being honestly confused, though she would have denied it anyway. Once she had set the surveillance in motion the details had been left to others. But Wendy did not believe her.

'I signed your wretched form, very much against my principles, and I'm repaid by being spied on,' she persisted. 'You should know that I don't have to stay here any longer.'

'Why not?'

'Now that Fort Detrick has my clone I could go and do my work there, couldn't I?'

'I'm sure that you would find yourself governed by secrecy there as much as you are here,' Lesley told her, picking up her handbag.

The realization that the watchers had bungled the surveillance, without reporting it, had put her at too great a disadvantage. She had intended to ask Wendy if she would undergo a polygraph, 'lie-detector' test, which had been introduced in specially sensitive areas a few months previously after a savage battle with the trade unions, but that was no longer opportune.

If pushed too hard, Wendy really might resolve her problems by emigrating, Lesley suspected. And Malinowski's intrusion into the picture might make such a move more likely if the relationship became serious. Then she might even do what had become known

121

in MI5 as 'a Peter Wright', putting herself outside the jurisdiction of the Official Secrets Act.

It had been a long way to go for such a brief encounter but as Lesley rose to take leave of her somewhat triumphant quarry, she consoled herself that she had gone through some of the necessary motions.

Wendy felt disappointed. The claws of the peke-faced ginger pussycat had not been so sharp. But then she had never extended them.

The bugging of Joe's flat produced an early result which dismayed Lesley when she read the transcript of the tape. Joe was on intimate terms with the newspaper journalist most feared by MI5, Barrie Gordon, known to his colleagues as 'Wolf', because of his lone wolf tactics. He eschewed the company of competing journalists, knowing that he would learn nothing from them and the first they usually knew of his activities was a late night call from their newspapers alerting them to yet another Gordon 'scoop' and curtly requiring action. With his heavy jaw, receding hair and aggressive-looking features, 'Bulldog' might have been more descriptive, especially as he was disinclined to let go once he had his teeth into a 'story'. He would have preferred that nickname but, as an item of self-advertisement, had bought himself a wolfhound, which he called Scoop and took to the office and, on occasion, to the local pubs. Those with the temerity to look at the inscription on its wide, spiky collar read 'I am Barrie Gordon's dog. Whose dog are you?'

After apprenticeship as a crime reporter, he had specialised in disclosure. The British media were obsessed with secrets, including the so-called 'secrets' of the private lives of show-biz stars and royals, but Gordon concentrated on the genuine articles, the defence and intelligence information expressly banned under the Government's draconian Official Secrets Act of 1989. Such secrets were the occasional sustenance of other journalists but were Gordon's daily bread and his source of fame and professional satisfaction.

While most reporters had to wait for events before they could distil their golden words, there was always a mass of secrets awaiting Gordon's attention. They were like nuggets to be mined and refined and during those stages nobody took greater care to guard them. Gordon was aware that MI5 was not the only Government department to penetrate the media offices, bribing reporters, sub-editors, printers and even cartoonists into the service of giving advance warning of incipient exposures, so that pre-emptive action might be taken against them. He was one of the few to know of the appalling case, hushed up by the newspaper concerned, in which the office lawyer, who saw all copy in advance, had been reporting directly to ·MI5 and, where feasible, had been spiking sensitive copy to order on 'legal' grounds.

Gordon remained tight-lipped until his nuggets were completely ready to be sold, first to his editor then to his readers, and then barred no device or stratagem in exposing them. There was virtually no secret which was immune to being leaked through self-interest, vanity or drink-induced stupidity and while the new Official Secrets Act made publication more hazardous there were ways round it.

His favourite gambit was kite-flying – the publication of a story far enough from the truth to be immune from action under the Act but near enough to cause a public commotion, from which the truth could eventually be made to emerge. Another was to plant a disclosure in an obscure American or Australian newspaper and then to send a cutting of it to an obliging Opposition MP who would ask, in Parliament, how the Government had been so remiss as to allow such a secret to leak. The resulting exchanges would be privileged so that all newspapers could publish them, and Gordon always held enough back to make his story the most revealing.

He exploited the special advantage that his stories would rarely be denied, however inaccurate, for the standard official reaction to disclosures involving secrets was to remain silent. So it was rumoured that the Whitehall press officers who were pestered with telephone calls about his sensations asked themselves, each morning, 'What fact-fudging mission is Gordon up to today that will keep us awake tonight?'

The frank dishonesty of his methods worried him not at all and he justified them by insisting that he had been driven to them by governments intent on suppressing press freedom and that he would rather not be forced to work in such devious ways. But it was transparently obvious that, without secrecy, he would have been out of his particular business, which he enjoyed, particularly when putting the skids under his rivals.

He was not only a door-stopper, with no feelings whatever for the recently bereaved or disgraced, but was prepared to rake through dustbins for documents or climb through windows, if necessary, and to believe the worst about anybody – which always made for sensational copy. While devoting much time to acquaintances who might be productive, he set little store by friendship, cheerfully admitting that his best friend was his word processor. He could, however, be guaranteed never to reveal a source.

It was inevitable that Joe Malinowski would meet Gordon regularly in his press duties but the bug transcript suggested that the relationship was close. Lesley was not aware that Joe cultivated Gordon on Charlie Yates' instructions, because he was such a sucker for CIA disinformation. Like a vacuum cleaner sucks up dust and anything else in its path, Gordon welcomed news of any kind from all quarters.

He had not endeared himself to Joe when he had 'bought' and projected under big black headlines the KGB lie that AIDS was caused by a virus deliberately concocted by American genetic engineers to reduce the population of black Africa. And he seemed to delight in accusing the CIA of every kind of skulduggery, however fanciful, in spite of Joe's useful snippets, which, as Gordon suspected, originated from that same Agency. His usual excuse was to claim that he was presenting both sides of the 'debate' so that his readers could come to their own conclusion. His libertarian posturing was always supported by his editor, who 'stood by' his reporter. Gordon was no fool and had not believed the AIDS information but it had made a good exclusive, repeated on television and bringing high praise from his editor and proprietor, who also disbelieved it. On Charlie Yates' instructions, Joe continued to use Gordon because of his newspaper's large circulation and the fact that other journalists tended to follow up his stories.

What would Gordon make of the silicon chip story if he got wind of it? Lesley wondered, with a mental shudder. She had good reason to suspect that he might do so because the bug tape recorded a dinner given by Joe, at his flat, for Gordon and his wife, with Wendy present. Lesley simply did not believe that Wendy had told her lover nothing about the silicon chips.

When Gordon had gleaned that Wendy was a medical scientist at Porton, involved in AIDS research, he had tried to pump her about her work and her reticence had told him that there was probably some kind of story to be dug out if he persisted. Lesley judged, from the tape, that Wendy had not been good at dissimulating in front of someone as perceptive as Gordon. Being unprepared to lie, she had not denied that her research might be of press interest.

Disarmingly charming when he wished to be, Gordon had then steered the thrust of the conversation into the general area of official secrecy, with Joe pointing out that American journalists would never accept such constraints. Wendy had responded, heatedly, by urging him to counter that curse whenever, and however, he could in his newspaper, especially when it involved weapons. Though she had given nothing specific away, Gordon's suspicion that Wendy must have some particular reason for such vehemence had obviously been aroused, and it was not like him to leave the matter there. He would be having a quick opportunity for further probing because Gordon and his wife had invited Wendy and Joe to a return dinner at their smart home in Docklands.

Gordon's own telephone had been bugged at intervals in the past. Perhaps it was time to do it again, Lesley thought. Wendy Payne might as well inform the KGB directly as tell Gordon.

Lesley decided that she would have to mark Charlie Yates' card about this further unwelcome development – once she had devised a way of explaining how she had come by the information. The official surveillance of Wendy could be used to cover a multitude of MI5 sins.

Chapter Seventeen

A short, 'Most Urgent' CIA report was sitting on the President's desk when he arrived for work in the ground-floor Oval Office at 8 a.m., after his morning swim in the White House pool and his usual cereal breakfast. Submitted by Director of Central Intelligence Arnold, and based on 'a usually reliable source with excellent access', it revealed nothing less than a serious attempt to assassinate General Secretary Vladimir Primarkov.

Some weeks previously, it stated, the General Secretary, accompanied by his wife, had been visiting Volgograd, the name by which Stalingrad was known since the Kremlin's demotion of Stalin's image. In his usual defiance of KGB advice, Primarkov and his wife had done a walk-about to meet some ordinary people face to face. A sniper's bullet, fired from a distant window, had struck Tamara Primarkova on the right arm causing a nasty flesh wound and bone damage requiring surgery. Primarkov had been unharmed.

Immediate efforts to find the would-be assassin had failed but, some days later, the KGB had arrested a local man of limited intelligence who had not been heard of again. The CIA's informant believed that the man was being used to cover the KGB's inefficiency in preventing the attack and in failing to find the true assailant.

CIA inquiries in Moscow had not confirmed the event but the report recalled that, immediately after the Volgograd visit, the couple had disappeared from public view for several weeks. When Moscow correspondents had sought the reason they were told, variously, that the Primarkovs were on holiday on the Black Sea; that the General Secretary was preparing an important speech; that his wife was convalescing from appendicitis. Nothing suggesting that there had been an attack had appeared in the Soviet media but that meant little. Other Soviet leaders, Brezhnev and Andropov in particular, and, more recently, Gorbachev, had experienced assassination attempts which had been stifled by the censorship machinery to which the media still had to submit in spite of *glasnost*.

The President liked a few minutes to himself before the arrival of his Chief of Staff, with time to think in shirt-sleeved comfort before having to don his jacket for some more formal visitor. He was inclined to believe the report because it fitted so many facts and assassination was a daily risk for political leaders, including himself. Any attempt, however unsuccessful, must leave its mark and that could have been the cause of the distinct air of depression which the Soviet leader had projected during their recent confidential exchanges.

On his visit to Washington he had manifested such a jaunty, restless personality that the press had likened him to the film star James Cagney, to whom he had some resemblance, being short, dapper, springy of step, with a ready smile and a quick, eager voice yet with the mien of a man who could take care of himself and was not to be trifled with.

Checking with his diary, Rockwell confirmed that he had spoken with Primarkov on the telephone on two occasions since the alleged assassination attempt, once from the White House, once from Camp David. The hot-line connections had been improved and extended by their predecessors and secret White House–Kremlin conversations had become an essential component of the expanding 'frank political dialogue to find common ground', of which both participants made such capital. Primarkov was the first Soviet leader to speak reasonable English and Butch Blanchard, who was usually on hand, had qualified as a Russian speaker on an Army Intelligence course, taken when he was much junior. So their interchanges were meaningful and lively. What transpired, however, was never disclosed and, however significant the consequences in shaping events, they remained part of the hidden history of the world from which the public would forever be excluded.

Before receiving the report of the Volgograd incident, Rockwell had attributed the Soviet leader's downbeat mood to the events outlined in the routine intelligence briefs, which were always on his desk, each morning. These had recorded a succession of clamorous demonstrations in the Soviet Union about shortages of food, clothing and other consumer goods, even soap, for, while prices had risen much faster than wages, the long queues had not been lessened much by *perestroika*, the economic reconstruction which was going to take a long time to work through a system so heavily encrusted by

127

outworn practices. Indeed, the briefs described the Soviet economy as 'now in desperate shape'.

The whole Soviet state and crucial countries of the empire seemed to be simmering with discontent. There had been a wave of strikes and racial riots. Religious leaders, having been permitted an unusual degree of freedom, were pushing their luck in the churches and there was a menacing upsurge of religious feeling among the huge Muslim populations. Generations of communists had been brought up to despise religion as the 'opium of the people'. Now their political leaders were being photographed with the Patriarch of the Russian Orthodox Church and other religious dignitaries, seeking their assistance and promising freedom of worship and freedom of conscience. In Poland and Czechoslovakia the Catholic churches were filled with young as well as old, as the alternative faith in communism appeared to be losing its appeal. It was all very confusing to ordinary Soviet citizens and dangerous to the élite of the *nomenklatura*, the list of some 300,000 Party functionaries who still ran the state in their own interests. If their masses came to disbelieve in communism and, through their upbringing, could not believe in God, they had nothing to believe in. And where would that lead?

The increased freedom allowed to the media was proving to be like sex; having tasted it, people wanted more of it, and the press was bombarding the leadership with a barrage of demands. A frankly rebellious attitude was expressing itself in the widely-read magazines and *samizdat* publications which escaped censorship and were rapidly growing in readership.

The intelligentsia, who had been allowed to become respectable again, were busy demonstrating why, in a hardline, Marxist–Leninist dictatorship, Stalin had been wise in suppressing them. Student unrest, which had been unheard of in the Soviet Union, was widespread and gathering momentum in the university cities. Protestors holding placards were on the streets chanting, 'We are not slaves of the Communist Party', implying that, in the past, they knew that they had been.

Mikhail Gorbachev had been defeated by the ungrateful impatience and excessive aspirations of the people – or rather by his political opponents who had exploited his predicament. His successor, quickly dubbed 'Boris the Brief', had attempted a degree of suppressive clampdown but, being unprepared or unable to be harsh enough, had also been deposed. Primarkov was making a second attempt to keep the bloodless revolution moving at an acceptable rate, hectoring his colleagues with the argument that it was safer to face a succession of social explosions which they could control than a cataclysm which could destroy the whole system and themselves along with it.

In fact, some blood had been shed during the KGB and police reaction to the unrest on the streets and in the factories, but not enough for the hardliners who felt that the second phase of *'glasnost'*. the so-called 'new path to the future', should be radically curtailed by really tough action against demonstrators, including those in the satellite states.

Primarkov's critics genuinely believed that the leadership was allowing itself to be pushed headlong to disaster by American pressure regarding human rights. They saw grave danger in encouraging citizens to go where they wanted, to read what they liked and think for themselves. As Primarkov's deputy and chief ideologist, Nikolai Borovik, put it to the Politburo, 'Two hundred and eighty-five million people thinking for themselves – that's unplannable, undisciplined chaos. We, the Party, must do the thinking for them, as Lenin did.'

The strongest and the most dangerous resentment lay in the KGB where, after years of prejudice, the United States was still regarded as a deadly enemy dedicated to destroying communism. Yet there was talk of trimming the KGB and even of its submission to the law, a major tinkering with the engine of Soviet power which would diminish its capability – the Sword blunted, the Shield shattered.

The outspoken Chevalsky, who shared Borovik's conviction that the strength of the communist state lay in the discipline of its peoples, was appalled by the growing lack of subservience and the blatant objection to being pushed around, beaten and arrested. Indeed the blue uniform which had once commanded such respect – and fear – was becoming an object of scorn and, occasionally, of assault. The bureaucrats of the *nomenklatura* were increasingly being told by ordinary folk to go to hell without redress or retribution, which in the past had been swift and effective.

Inevitably, it was the young who were forcing the pace of dissent. 'Curb the hotheads like the Chinese leaders did!' was Chevalsky's prescription but they spoke for a generation which Primarkov needed to win over if he was to have a secure work force committed to the long uphill slog of *perestroika*.

The formidable Borovik and the other guardians of the Party ideology feared that the foundations of Marxism–Leninism, invented, refined and inculcated over so many years, were being dangerously undermined. They were used to having their previous leaders – Stalin, Khruschev, Brezhnev – brought into disrepute, but when it came to Lenin it was nothing less than desecration.

If Marxism–Leninism was eroded, then communism had no reliable foundation. So, understandably, the conservatives were asking themselves what had been the point of all the struggle, sacrifice and suffering of the past if the Soviet Union was to end up as a semi-capitalist democracy?

They were supported by Red Army generals who hated losing their missiles, chemical weapons and tanks in the succession of American–Soviet deals and were having to rethink their whole strategy. The military chiefs were the most aware that the Soviet Union was a superpower only because of its military strength. It would be a couple of generations, at least, before Primarkov's policies could turn it into an economic superpower, *if* – and it was a big if – they succeeded, and anything could happen in the meantime if Soviet military strength was sacrificed in the financial interests of the economy. There was China to worry about, with more than a billion people on the Soviet doorstep, who would one day need to expand. Only one thing would stop the hordes if the Soviet Union began to disintegrate and it wouldn't be human rights.

All this had Clint Rockwell deeply concerned about Primarkov's position inside the Soviet Union even before the CIA report on the attempted assassination appeared. He had gone to extreme lengths to cultivate a special relationship with the brave little man in the drive to improve East–West relations. Now the signs that Primarkov might also be removed from office were becoming really ominous. According to the most recent CIA count of the Politburo line-up, the Premier, the two Party Secretaries and several of the First Secretaries representing the main regions, as well as Chevalsky, were ranged against him, while the Foreign Secretary seemed to be wavering.

While the little man was undoubtedly beleaguered, he was still in a position of great intrinsic power as Commander-in-Chief of the Armed Forces and Chairman of the Defence Council, as well as chief executive of the Communist Party, and the President had not been prepared for quite such a pessimistic prognosis when he had been telephoned again from the Kremlin, while staying at Camp David.

'I thought I should give you notice that we may have to delay our next round of talks,' Primarkov had said, rather wearily.

'Why?' Rockwell asked, trying to disguise his concern.

'Some of my supporters are wavering. They want to slow down the pace of progress – to snail's pace.'

'Oh, there are always people like that, General Secretary. I have exactly the same problem. We have to carry them with us.'

'It's rather more difficult here, Mr President,' Primarkov countered. He paused before adding, 'I am feeling very isolated.'

The President looked anxiously at Butch who had been with him at Camp David and had been listening in. Primarkov must be meaning that his adversaries were closing in on him, with even the 'moderates' joining them. Because of the very liberalization he was promoting, he could not liquidate his enemies, as Stalin and Khruschev had. But they might liquidate him – with a 'heart attack'.

'If I should have to depart, the discussions we have planned would be cancelled,' Primarkov continued. 'It would be a tragedy because everything we have accomplished would be lost and my country desperately needs progress.' He paused again, then added, with discernible emotion, 'It will come, you know, given time! It will come!'

'I know it will and that's why you mustn't even think of quitting,' Rockwell assured him, determined to steel the Russian's resolve. 'Right is on your side. Stick to your principles and your policies. Keep your nerve, and move against your opponents when opportunity offers, as I have no doubt it will. The good Lord may deliver them into your hands.'

'As you know, I have no faith in the good Lord,' Primarkov replied.

'Then trust in the Goddess Fortune. She might present you with a windfall.'

'What's a windfall?'

'An unforeseeable event or a set of circumstances which will be to your advantage. It's like a ripe plum falling into your lap off a tree.'

Primarkov knew all about ripe plums. He had been brought up in the belief that the capitalist societies would fall to communism like ripe plums and in more than seventy years it had not happened.

'I hope you are right,' he said.

The President sensed that Primarkov had nothing more to say. Apart from confirming the precariousness of his position, he seemed to have telephoned for reassuring support, which he could get from nobody of political consequence in his own country.

'I will be proved right, General Secretary,' Rockwell averred. 'Keep smiling and let us press ahead with our plans for our meeting. We will hold it! Nothing and nobody is going to stop us. The world is behind us.'

'You sound very confident, Mr President. Have you been consulting that astrologer?'

Rockwell laughed as he said goodbye. He had more than the advantage of faith – in God, in fortune or in the stars. He had the benefit of his experience and expertise as a former Director of Central Intelligence. In the secret world, windfalls occurred all the time.

'At least the little man hasn't lost his sense of humour,' he remarked to Butch.

'No, but he seemed very pessimistic. Things must be pretty desperate for him to sound off like that about the struggle inside the Politburo.'

'Yeah. Like he should jump the gun and depart with dignity rather than wait for the gun to go off.'

Butch looked puzzled. 'It's not like him, or any other Russian, to be as frank as that. I wonder what's really behind it.'

'He's a human being. It could be a desperate cry for help.'

Butch remained unconvinced.

'Well, whatever it is, we'll have to snap him out of it, Butch. And soonest! If Primarkov goes, our foreign policy and the defence cuts are for junking.'

Rockwell was re-reading the report of the assassination attempt as Butch entered the Oval office, on time to the second, with his bluff 'Good morning, Mr President'. Since his wife had died, Butch was usually the first member of the White House team to reach his office in the West Wing, his morning staff meeting always being called for 7.15 a.m. He sat himself down in the chair on the right of the President.

'Take a look at that,' Rockwell said, pushing the CIA paper across his desk. 'It's a shocker,' he added, clasping his hands behind his head and stretching out his legs, while watching his aide's face.

'What do you make of it?' he asked, as Blanchard handed back the document.

For once, Butch did not have the advantage of prior briefing by Pilgrim who had supplied the report to Arnold.

'I don't know what to think, Mr President. It certainly explains that mysterious disappearance that worried us so much. I wonder if the KGB organized it and bungled it. That would fit the facts. We know that Chevalsky would like to be rid of the little man.'

'I was wondering that myself,' the President responded.

There was sound intelligence evidence of an irreconcilable rift between the affable General Secretary and Oleg Chevalsky, the KGB chief who was a hangover from the stonefaced school. They were similar only in that each had become possessed by overweening ambition and had used his talent to achieve it. In their respective positions of enormous power, a conflict of ideals, objectives and personalities was inevitable.

As the son of a peasant, Chevalsky had been the perfect subject for inculcation into Marxism–Leninism and, throughout his life, had never questioned the Party line or wavered from it. When communism appeared to fail, it was always attributable to the capitalist and imperialist powers and he remained convinced that Western 'subversive circles' were still working, harder than ever, to discredit and destroy the communist ideology.

In contrast, Primarkov, the only son of a professor of applied physics at Leningrad University, was a born critic with a burning need to know, to question and to probe. His early life had been in the mould of any good, young communist with service in the Komsomol youth league and trusting belief in what he was told. But his father had been required to travel abroad in the interests of securing Western technology and had returned stunned by his first-hand experience of conditions in the United States, Britain, France, West Germany, Scandinavia and Japan.

With political history as his chosen special subject, the young Primarkov had been shattered to learn that his tutors and their textbooks had fed him a mass of lies about life in the true democracies. If the Dickensian picture of the West was so false, what was the real truth about his own country? he wondered. But he was prudent enough to wonder in silence.

His discreet inquiries convinced him that his tutors believed what they taught him and were innocent victims of a colossal deception foisted on the entire nation. The main government newspaper, which was called *Truth* and in which he had put his faith, had mangled the truth ever since its inception. And the *Great Soviet Encyclopaedia*, the official record of the nation's history which he had read with such proud absorption, was essentially a massive fabrication.

Like a deeply religious man stricken by doubt, Primarkov had become severely depressed and had taken to long solitary walks trying to come to terms with his devastating enlightenment. There could be no escaping the conclusion: Marxism–Leninism simply did not work, to such an extent that its failings had constantly to be covered up by fraud. And it had demanded a cult of secrecy and suspicion which had kept the Russian people in isolation for more than seventy years and warped its mentality. Where had it all started? Primarkov had found himself forced to accept the heretical answer. It was not with Stalin but with Lenin.

While others, including his father, simply tried to make the best of an implacable system, he determined to do something about it. Defection could be no more than a gesture. With so much military might in the hands of the Soviet leaders, no change could be enforced from outside. It had to come from within. So he vowed to stay and change it. He would practise deception to defeat deception. From then on he led a secret, introverted life dedicated to achieving political power and flung himself into Party affairs.

His necessity to guard the secret of his dangerous heresy, and to trust nobody on the road to his ambitious intention, profoundly affected his character. He had been outgoing, jocular, given to badinage and hurdling life with an easy, loping stride.

As he rose in office through merit and application, taking the utmost care to offend nobody, he came to believe himself destined to bring his country to a degree of freedom which it had never possessed in its history, being unique among the great powers in that respect. Eventually he had reached the Politburo, ostensibly as a moderate conservative in favour of such reforms as the economy demanded but at a rate consistent with the continuation of the glorious Marxist–Leninist ideals.

When Gorbachev, having achieved power by similar methods, revealed himself as motivated by comparable purpose, Primarkov gave him support but never so much as to be forced out with him if he was ousted, as he was when the impatience of the people overflowed and swept him away in a tidal wave of protest and demands. Still a Leninist at heart, Gorbachev had sought to compromise but that had never been possible in any revolution, bloodless or otherwise. The final push had been made by a Politburo clique headed by Borovik and Chevalsky but, in the mêlée for the leadership, the KGB Chairman's recipe of rugged repression had been rejected as impracticable in spite of its success in China.

The Politburo had then chosen a man who had proved even more indecisive, trying to play both ends at once, and, after disposing of him, had settled for Primarkov, who could be counted on to pursue reforms which could no longer be denied but at a pace less destructive of the status quo. But once Primarkov believed himself to be securely installed, and his true nature could safely reassert itself, they found themselves with an iron-willed, charismatic leader, with a ready, disarming smile, determined to swim with the popular tide and reform at an even faster rate, whatever it might do to the system. As Chevalsky put it to his dismayed colleagues, all they had got from the change was 'Gorbachev with hair'.

They had got much more. They had got Gorbachev with fire. Gorbachev had never been able to rally the masses with one unequivocal slogan, as revolutionaries must do to succeed. Primarkov's chantable, rhyming slogan *'Derzanie cheloveka – zalog uspekha'*, meaning 'Achievement through individual initiative', had instant appeal to a people weary of working to order for ideological goals which did not benefit them. He had not quite dared to make it 'Individual prosperity through individual initiative', but that was what the people believed he meant and what he intended.

While the KGB Chairman had been appalled, he had not been too disappointed: he expected Primarkov to go the same way as his predecessors – and quickly. The terminal error for Gorbachev had been the increasing vehemence of his tilts at Lenin within the confines of the Politburo, which the ideologues could not tolerate. Primarkov was challenging the light of the communist world in public.

Chevalsky was not the only one to wonder, privately, whether the new leader was, at heart, an agent of the West. Before becoming

135

head of the KGB, where he had twenty years' service in lesser capacities, he had kept continuous tabs on all the KGB records about the new General Secretary and everything seemed to conform with his suspicions. Now Primarkov was even having private telephone conversations with the American President, talks which the KGB was forbidden to monitor. In the older and more certain days, he would undoubtedly have been branded as a 'counter-revolutionary'. Even in quite recent times, people had been declared insane for less – for far less. At best, the leader of the Soviet Union, with his wild talk of a parliamentary and presidential democracy, was being manipulated by the American President.

There was little doubt in Washington as to the reason for the continuing anti-American disinformation campaign, which Primarkov had promised to stop. The KGB, and Chevalsky in particular, were using the AIDS myth and any other slur to convince the world that the United States was villainous. General acceptance of this in the Soviet Union would seriously undermine Primarkov, who was basing his foreign and domestic policy on the grounds of trust in America for, without improved relations with the United States, the injections of Western money and technology which were essential to upgrade the Soviet economy in a hurry and allow initiative to flourish would not be forthcoming.

His early-morning routine conference with his Chief of Staff completed, the President returned to the subject which most intrigued him.

'Whatever really happened in Volgograd, it makes the summit that much more urgent,' he observed. 'We have to get the biological and chemical warfare treaty signed and some commitment on more arms reduction deals before someone takes another poke at the little man and makes a job of it. If it was the KGB who tried, someone will.'

'Surely, with all his power, he won't just sit on his fanny and let Chevalsky take him,' Butch said. 'He ought to be able to find some way of firing him.'

The President shook his head doubtfully. 'Chevalsky has too many supporters in the Politburo – and among the military. Just one other thought, Butch,' Rockwell added, as his aide rose to leave. 'Assuming that this report is true, can we be absolutely certain that the CIA was not involved? I wouldn't put it past your friend, Ross Pilgrim.'

Butch was genuinely shocked, as he settled his heavy frame back

136

in his chair. 'I'm absolutely sure that Ross would never be that irresponsible. And it's not his style. Assassinating a head of state! No way!'

'I agree with that but the head of state was not assassinated, was he? It was his wife who was hit, and not very accurately. Maybe she was the target and it was not intended to kill her.'

'The chance that Ross would be party to firing a gun at a woman is even more unthinkable,' Butch replied, assertively.

'Not even to ditch Chevalsky? You must know how much he hates him.'

'You mean by setting him up to get the blame?'

'Sure,' the President replied, his hands again clasped behind his head. 'The whole scenario is vintage Pilgrim. And you know he's something of a law unto himself, as I discovered during my brief sojourn as his chief. Make a few discreet inquiries.'

'I will, Mr President, but I can tell you right now that there's no finer or more loyal patriot than Ross Pilgrim. He's much maligned. "My man's as true as steel."'

Rockwell smiled as he stood up and put on his jacket. Butch was so loyal himself he could not stand any impugning of the loyalty of his friends.

'Got any ideas about how we might help the little man, Butch?' he said, staring out at the garden through the window between the draped flags – the Stars and Stripes and his own Standard.

'Not at the moment, Mr President.'

'Well, give it thought. Operation Skinsaver is what we need.'

The remark sounded like a signing-off quip and Butch was inclined to pay it no attention, but the report of the assassination attempt induced second thoughts. He had no ideas for action but knew someone well qualified to produce a scenario, and he agreed with the President about windfalls.

Chapter Eighteen

That same evening, by a telephoned invitation, Pilgrim took his personal diary round to Butch Blanchard's large apartment in Wyoming Avenue. Ostensibly his purpose was to arrange their duck-hunting schedule – something that had to be planned well ahead, as far as they could, given their commitments. They always had an agreed social excuse for their unofficial meetings and, as usual, each had something rather more important on his mind.

Since being widowed, Butch could not do much formal entertaining, as his wife, Patsy, had done with such verve and skill. They had been delightfully happy but had produced no children, so his loss was total. While friends were kind and no doubt some, like Baby Rockwell, would be wife-hunting on his behalf once a decent interval had elapsed, he was often alone in the evening. There was a limit to the time he could spend reading poetry so he welcomed a visit from an old friend like Ross.

The very comfortable apartment was much as it had been, with many framed photographs of Butch and his wife and some of Butch and Ross on their hunting trips, with broad grins under their funny hats. It had been cleaned by the daily help but, with a practised eye for detail, Pilgrim noticed the differences. It was lacking in the caring touches that had brought man out of the cave: there were no flowers, the cushions were not plumped up, the odd curtain hook was loose, Butch's slippers were where he had kicked them off, some of the many books were out of place on the shelves, and the newspapers of several days were on the guest armchair. The place looked like Butch still was inside – mournfully sad.

'What do you make of the attempted assassination report?' Butch asked, to start the shop talk rolling.

'Very interesting. But it could be bullshitsky. That's why I didn't tip you off about it. When I passed it to Arnold I urged him to hold it away from the President's desk for a few days until we made some checks. But you know what he's like. He couldn't wait to impress the Chief.'

'Do you think it's true, Ross?'

Pilgrim scratched his head. 'Yeah. Could be. It came from a very good source.'

'A trusted agent?'

'Very much so.'

'Then who would you think organized the attempt?' Butch asked.

'Wish I knew. Could have been a lone nutter. Could have been someone who objected to Primarkov's policies. Might have been someone who didn't like his wife! She was the one who got hit. I gather that she's not very popular.'

'Do you think it could have been the KGB?'

'That's always possible when there's a power struggle,' Pilgrim said, adjusting his glasses. 'But I would have expected Comrade Chevalsky to employ a better marksman. As it is, I imagine that it must have done the KGB a lot of harm – that's if it's true.'

'Could it have been the Brits?' Butch asked, sensing a way of avoiding the direct question.

Pilgrim shook his head decisively. 'MI6 is out of the assassination business, like we are. If either of us had organized it we would have gone for something more elegant, more sophisticated. Violence is the antithesis of sophistication. The satisfaction is in setting up the circumstances so that somebody else is induced to do what you want and makes a job of it. There are plenty of different ways of cooking that egg,' he said, purloining a phrase much used by Sandy Pryce. 'I'm sure I could think of a dozen – though I never have,' he added, hastily.

Sure that he was telling the truth, Butch took two stapled sheets of paper from a drawer and passed them to his friend, who was lighting a cigarette.

'I thought you'd like a glimpse of this – under the usual arrangements. It's a copy of the interim report of the study group which the President set up, under my chairmanship, to advise on the silicon threat, vis-à-vis the Soviets.'

Pilgrim's eyes lit up, as they never failed to do when presented with information that was specially secret. While Butch refilled their glasses he settled back in his armchair and read:

The Group puts forward three options for possible action:

Option 1

To do nothing with respect to informing the Soviets about any aspect of the silicon chip situation.

Should they learn about it through their own intelligence resources, and then complain that the United States has been engaging in bacterial warfare research in contravention of the moratorium agreement, they should be told that the discovery was entirely British and that any complaints should be lodged in that direction.

No samples of Clone Fe 113 should be supplied to them, its use as a possible weapon being thereby denied.

The major disadvantage to this course of action lies in the probability that the Soviets may learn about the silicon situation and exploit it to its maximum propaganda value. The United States could be made to look perfidious and, if the propaganda action was in the hands of the KGB or some other department with a special political interest, it could undermine General Secretary Primarkov's position in favour of his opponents in the Politburo.

Both domestically, in the Soviet Union, and internationally, the propaganda could point out the danger of dealing with the United States, which would stand accused of cheating on a solemn understanding. The chances that the Soviet Union would then be prepared to sign the proposed treaty outlawing chemical and biological weapons might be slim.

Option 2

The Soviets could be informed of the developments but be denied cultures of Clone Fe 113.

The Soviets could then publicly accuse the United States of producing a new offensive biological weapon and of keeping it for unilateral use. The whole propaganda potential would be intensified and General Secretary Primarkov's political survival would be endangered as with Option 1.

Option 3

The Soviets could be informed and also be given cultures of the clone.

That way the spirit of the proposed treaty would be honoured and the United States would be 'clean' in all respects. General Secretary Primarkov would be able to present this action to his opponents in the Politburo as evidence of the sincerity of the United States and of its President in particular.

Only simple wet cultures need be supplied, all information about progress towards producing a dry powder form of the clone being withheld, along with all other advanced information of defence significance.

The study group is unanimous in recommending Option 3. We must face the reality that a secret of this nature cannot be kept for long, particularly in view of the commercial implications. We are informed that Soviet microbiologists have a high reputation in the field of genetic engineering and when they learn that a bacterium which attacks silicon can be produced they may well find out how to make it. The general techniques are public knowledge.

If it is conceded that the Soviets will eventually acquire the clone or something like it, there is little to be lost by giving it to them but a great deal to be lost by failing to do so.

If Option 3 is accepted it would be advantageous to implement it quickly. There would seem to be no advantage in holding on to it for much further time, with preparations for the next summit meeting so advanced. The worst that could happen would be for the Soviets to learn of the information just prior to the meeting.

We express concern, however, about the facts becoming generally known to other countries sooner than they need be. We are thinking, particularly, about the risk of cultures falling into the hands of certain countries which promote subversion and terrorism. Perhaps, in return for supplying the information and cultures, the Soviets would enter into an agreement to keep the secret to themselves.

Exhaling a cloud of smoke, Pilgrim was in no doubt that the President and Secretary of State, being politicians, would seize on the study group's support for Option 3. They would do anything to avoid offending Primarkov or undermining his position.

'This is a wimp's solution, Butch. Give them the clone! It's just putting a weapon into their hands. You know these bastards can't be trusted. I'm amazed that you've gone along with it.'

Blanchard shrugged. 'I was impressed by the arguments, Ross. With the summit so near, one has to take notice of the State Department. They are the experts in diplomatic matters and we have to go along with foreign policy.'

'Foggy minds from Foggy Bottom,' Pilgrim said scathingly, referring to the location of the State Department buildings in Washington. 'What guarantee could we possibly get that the Russians won't twist the situation to their advantage somehow? The KGB will do what it likes propaganda-wise. Primarkov gave a solemn undertaking that the lies about our creating the AIDS virus would cease but the KGB are still at it. Think what they'll do with this one.'

'Nobody ever expects the KGB to play ball, Ross.'

'Or the GRU! And they won't play ball when they realize that we've presented them with a subversive weapon which their *Spetsnaz* forces would not hesitate to use. This advice that the secret can't be kept is a counsel of despair. Of course the bloody secret can be kept if we plug all the leak holes.'

Butch remained silent but unrepentant.

'What was Arnold's view?' Pilgrim asked.

'He was in favour.'

'He would be, wouldn't he? You know what I think about him. I'm not sure he's on our side. They say that the CIA has never been penetrated by the Soviets. But do they need to penetrate us with a destroyer like Arnold in charge?'

'That's harsh, Ross. You've really no grounds for it.'

'No grounds?' Pilgrim grunted. 'At least you'll admit he has no stomach for the fight. Him and his Christian principles! "Blessed are the meek: for they shall inherit the earth." They sure will – all six feet of it!'

Butch was concerned about the feud. Like everyone else on the intelligence circuit he had heard of Arnold's recent remark that 'Pilgrim should do a Hirohito and publicly declare that he is not a god'. Ross had failed to see the humour of it and it was his judgement which was showing the worse signs of wear.

Pilgrim handed back the document and stubbed out his cigarette in the ashtray with unnecessary force. 'Well, that's it. The secret's as good as gone: after all the effort we've made to preserve it. Talk about a tale told by an idiot! We'll all be made to look very stupid. There will be hell let loose in the Pentagon. When will the President be making his decision?'

'He hasn't seen this interim report yet and, if he wants to, he can put off a decision until he's read the full report, which won't be ready for a week or two.'

'Why bother with a full report when the decision is already as good as made?' Pilgrim asked.

Butch shrugged his ample shoulders. 'They need it for the record.'

He poured Pilgrim another whisky, wishing to change the subject. 'Have you ever considered the possibility that, if Primarkov was toppled, the President might want him rescued out of the Soviet Union?' he asked.

'You have to be kidding, Butch.'

'Not really. The President has got rather fond of him. He told me we might need "Operation Skinsaver".'

Pilgrim was smiling to himself like a schoolboy. 'It would be one hell of a coup,' he said. 'I guess it could be done if they just pushed him into retirement and didn't lock him up or write him off. But I can't see Benedict permitting it.'

'You shouldn't call him that, Ross. In fact, he'd go along with anything the President wanted.'

'Yeah, he's an asshole creeper, I grant you that.'

Butch shook his head, despairingly. 'Anyway, give it some thought, Ross, just as a contingency plan, of course. But you never know. It might just be needed. And in a hurry.'

Pilgrim did not commit himself. But it was one hell of a challenging concept.

On the short drive home Pilgrim indulged in some possible scenarios for a rescue of the General Secretary but soon descended to earth and became his philosophical self. It should be possible to snatch some advantage, somehow, from what he had described as the impending disaster of giving the silicon secrets to the Russians. As Butch would have said, 'Sweet are the uses of adversity.' He would give it more thought in his 'think-tank' – his bath, where some of his most ingenious ideas had come to him.

It did not let him down.

Chapter Nineteen

While Pilgrim could run his large, far-flung department, involving several thousand officers, agents and other employees, only by delegating almost all the active work, there were some specially sensitive operations which he held to himself. For those he had selected a few favoured officers, dubbed within the Agency the 'Disciples', their super-secret operations being known, equally sardonically, as 'Pilgrimages'. All CIA activities were supposed to be subject to scrutiny by the two 'oversight' committees of the Congress and the Senate but they never seemed to get wind of the Pilgrimages. They were unofficial with nothing whatever about them recorded on paper, everything being, as Pilgrim put it, 'in the head and the heart'.

The Disciples were led by Al Quest, a well-built, clean-cut, bronzed Southerner, who looked at though he would be at home on a surfboard, as indeed he was. It was Al who was called in to hear about his chief's latest brainchild, the following morning.

One of Pilgrim's many axioms was 'Favouritism is the secret of success' and some eighteen years previously, when Al had been fresh out of Tulane University, Pilgrim had selected him as a bright and ingenious recruit who would take orders without demur and would make the Agency his whole career. He had cleverly caught the young man's imagination with his exciting assertion that involvement in covert operations would give him a hand in determining the hidden history of international events, knowledge of which was denied to ordinary mortals.

To the envy of other officers, he had trained Al in his own likeness, devoting much time to conditioning him in avoiding the Seven Deadly Sins of intelligence theology. In Pilgrim's Good Book these were Intellectual Cowardice – in planning operations; Physical Cowardice – when running agents in the field; Moral Scruple – doubt for conscientious reasons; Objection to Lying – the right to lie being a crucial weapon; Putting Private Life Before Duty; Breaching 'Need to Know'; Having Regrets – whoever might have suffered in a secret operation.

The underlying requirement for all his Disciples was the total absence of any sense of shame. 'Consider yourself as soldiers,' Pilgrim told them. 'They must feel no shame when they are ordered to kill in battle. You must have no shame when you incapacitate the enemy in unarmed combat.'

Aware of his own deficiencies, Pilgrim had ensured that Al spent time in the Technical Services Division, which produced the ingenious equipment for high-tech intelligence. He had also been posted abroad to hyperactive intelligence centres like Vienna, for a few months at a time, to gain field experience in running agents. This involved occasional contacts with his KGB and GRU opponents, especially when fishing for possible defectors.

It had not been by chance that these foreign postings had usually occurred soon after the appearance of a serious girl in Al's life. Still unattached, Al was available to Pilgrim all day and night.

Genetic engineering might be high tech but there was more than one way of producing a clone and professionally Al, at thirty-nine, was as near a behavioural clone of Ross Pilgrim as could reasonably be expected, a daring, can-do guy who could improvise an operation at short notice, using the 'tools' which happened to be to hand. He, too, was a clam and almost as mysterious as his master. He was also a sharp dresser but his hallmark was not a bowtie but protruding cuffs with heavy gold links.

It was a commonplace that, by and large, secret service officers had little liking or respect for each other so it was a tribute to Al's character that he remained generally well-liked, being 'Al' to all at Langley, where he occupied an office next to his chief's.

'We need a field test of this silicon chip business to see how these bacteria act in a real-life situation,' Pilgrim announced to Al. 'And where better to carry it out than in the Soviet Union? Those stupid bastards in the State Department have decided to give the clone thing and all the information about it to the Russkies. So I see no reason why we shouldn't present it to them first, through a dangle. This is what I have in mind.'

Dragging deeply on a cigarette, Pilgrim explained his plan. It was delightfully simple, as the best deception operations always were, like all the best conjuring tricks. He worked on what he called the

KISS command which, as originally formulated, meant 'Keep It Simple, Stupid' but which he had changed to 'Keep It Skilfully Simple'.

The Soviet 'techno-bandits' were still as busy as ever, with high-tech items purloined from Silicon Valley a speciality. 'We'll help them again,' Pilgrim said, referring to his recent Brown Derby success. 'I want you to give me a note of the main equipments that are occupying their attention and we'll select the one that suits us best. We'll need a name for this dangle. What's the next on the approved list, Al?'

'Turbid, sir,' Al answered, after consulting a file. In view of what was to occur it could hardly have been more fitting.

'Right. Operation Turbid will be a contingency plan for the time being but, as I see it, there is nothing to be lost in putting it into effect soonest. What the hell are we here for if we don't take our chances when they offer?'

Pilgrim grinned in anticipation as he twisted his wedding ring. 'With resources for counter-intelligence cut to the bone, we have to take up all our opportunities and this one will cost the Agency next to nothing.'

While used to Pilgrim's surges of enthusiasm when a good deception programme was in prospect, Al could sense that this one was something special, as indeed it was. If Operation Turbid could be accomplished, it would do the Soviets a great deal of harm and at the same time undermine the chief of the GRU, one General Yuri Yakushkin, possibly to the point of his dismissal in disgrace.

'Pity it couldn't be Chevalsky,' Pilgrim observed to Al. 'But Yakushkin will do for now. His humiliation would cause one hell of a shake-up. With this one we could really leave our mark on the pages of history.'

'Could this be your grand-daddy dangle, sir?'

'It has all the makings of it. But then I've thought that before and been disappointed.'

Butch's gossip about the President's recent talk with Primarkov made the injury which Operation Turbid might inflict look even more severe.

'We might even destabilize the Soviet leader and push him off his perch,' Pilgrim told Al, with almost boyish glee. 'That would put paid to his cosy relationship with the President. And it would be much easier dealing again with the hardliners – you know where you really are with them. Primarkov could turn out to be anything.'

He watched his assistant's face for his reaction. Nothing was observable behind the piercing blue-eyed stare though, inside, Al had grave doubts about the wisdom of doing anything to displace a Soviet leader who, on the surface at least, appeared to be doing so much to dispel the risk of war and the need to spend such huge sums on defence.

'We wouldn't be interfering in the internal politics of another nation, would we, sir?' Al ventured, laconically.

The remark brought a broad grin to his master's face but, privately, Al thought the whole concept far too serious for humour.

No other members of Pilgrim's staff were privy to such adventurous thoughts. Nobody was ever told more than he needed to know. It was another of Pilgrim's axioms that the only real secret was something known to just one person. A secret known to two was already half-gone, even if the confidant was as totally dependable as Al.

Chapter Twenty

As always, when the chief raised the banner for another Pilgrimage, Al and the other Disciples moved quickly. They had two good starting points. The first was an up-to-date photocopy of the Kremlin's Red Book, officially entitled 'Co-ordinated Requests for Technological Information', a twenty-seven-chapter catalogue of equipment which the Soviet bloc techno-bandits were instructed to acquire. It had been supplied by Brown Derby from the loose-leaf volume in his office at the UN building in New York. The second was Brown Derby himself, who could always supply Moscow's most recent and highest priority requirements. Additional leads were also suggested by the FBI records of surveillance of the known techno-bandits, which frequently indicated what they were after.

The team came up with a short list in which one item stood out for a special reason and looked a likely answer even before the detailed search was launched.

The Russians had devoted a great deal of diplomatic and propaganda effort in trying to buy a very advanced American Star Wars simulator, which its manufacturers in Silicon Valley called the Mockingbird. This permitted research scientists to simulate, in the laboratory, many of the acquisition, tracking and kill techniques which an effective defensive system against ballistic missiles would have to possess. Its several screens provided chilling three-dimensional displays of nuclear missiles rising from distant enemy territory, arching over the Arctic and being destroyed – or not – by space-based interceptors in transit to their targets.

The name of the apparatus was apt on two counts. Like the much-loved grey and white mockingbird, common in many states, it had a versatile ability to imitate and, when fully assembled, it happened to resemble an enormous long-tailed bird put together by some Cubist sculptor.

The Soviet Government had officially requested permission to buy it under the share-out concept originally put forward by former

President Reagan, perhaps tongue-in-cheek, on the grounds that it was not in the interest of safe East–West relations for either side to get too far ahead of the other in Star Wars research. As Reagan had expressed it, 'Too big a lead could be dangerous to the West because understandable anxiety that the US was getting too far in front might induce some irrational reaction by the Kremlin through fear. The hardliners might authorize a pre-emptive strike fearing that we might do just that ourselves, once we have an effective defence against their missiles.'

The manufacturers of the Mockingbird had been pressing for the sale to the Soviets, because it was worth $110 million, and Rockwell had been publicly in favour. 'Trade is the cement of peace,' he argued, 'and for the sake of the balance of payments we need to sell more to the Soviets. The equipment is only a simulator: it can't shoot anything down.'

While the Mockingbird was on the Pentagon's 'Critical Technology List' of equipment banned from export, except to close allies, the President, in his role of Commander-in-Chief of the Armed Forces, had the power to overrule it and had seemed set to do so. Uncharitably, it had been suggested by political opponents that he favoured the sale because California was his home state. In reality, he genuinely regarded the sale as an earnest of his goodwill to convince the Russians that the United States was sincere in not trying to secure a dangerous superiority and was only developing a means of defending its people from ballistic missiles, to which Soviet citizens were also entitled.

In all this the President had been strenuously opposed by the US military chiefs, who argued that the highly sophisticated Mockingbird was 'state of the art' and could be used in other military research by the Russians. They were supported, privately, by those like Pilgrim who were in favour of US superiority in every field as the most effective deterrent to Soviet foreign ambitions, which they believed had not really changed.

The Nephews organization had seized on the theme publicly, in their *Bulletin* and in speeches, accusing the President of wanting to 'give away our ace-in-the-hole' and of 'taking chances for so-called peace' with the Soviets giving nothing, apart from the money, in exchange. They recalled the 'Great Grain Robberies' of the Brezhnev era when millions of tons of cut-price American grain had been sold

149

to the Russians to spare the Politburo the mass resentment of empty bellies, with no beneficial political results whatever to the West. The conflict had thereby become a major public issue, with opinion polls showing a big majority of the American people firmly opposed to the President's intention of selling Mockingbird to the Soviets.

'Keep it under Uncle Sam's hat!' had proved to have wide public appeal, with a new surge of membership for The Nephews. With their muscle so strengthened, the organization went so far as to threaten to prevent the export of the Mockingbird physically by organizing lie-downs in the path of the delivery vehicle. Members picketed the Silicon Valley factory and the White House with placards proclaiming 'Our Mockingbird was paid for with American tax-payers' money', 'Rocky loves Primo', 'Rocky in the Peace Casino'.

The President had stood his ground but when his opponents in Congress and the Senate had seized on the issue, and his anxious advisers had warned him of the alienation of his right-wing support, the sale had been halted, though he had continued to argue that his stand was in the best interests of the United States. He remained determined to supply the equipment, eventually, and told Primarkov so during one of their telephone conversations. The Soviet media had made known the Kremlin's disappointment but criticism of the President had been subdued on Primarkov's orders.

When the public argument had still been raging, and to thwart The Nephews' threat to hijack the Mockingbird, it had been quietly transferred from the factory to Vandenberg Air Base, a short distance down the Pacific coast, where it was secure and from which it could be transported by air. It was sitting there in limbo, disassembled in its crates, when the frustrated manufacturer received an inquiry from a Swiss contractor offering to purchase the simulator for a West German company which was already involved in American Star Wars contracts. There could hardly be any Government objection to supplying it to a close ally when the President had judged it safe to supply to the Russians. So the manufacturer was pacified; he would have no difficulty producing another Mockingbird for the Soviets if the President subsequently got his way. One had already been sup-plied to a British company to assist its contribution to Star Wars research.

The sale to West Germany was given only modest publicity in American newspapers and The Nephews were not concerned about the danger of technical leaks to the Soviet spies infesting West Germany. It was the hardware they had been worried about, not the know-how. Their intelligence network had told them that the equipment was based on silicon chips of a quality which the Soviets could not match.

The Mockingbird's incarceration in Vandenberg Air Base meant that Turbid could not be modelled on the recent successful operation which had been set up in San Francisco to assist Brown Derby. Still, the simulator was too ideal for Pilgrim's purpose to be abandoned – provided he could get access to it. It would be certain to end up at a Star Wars centre, maybe even Sary Shagan, and the instruction manual showed that it was full of silicon chips which could be infected by the clone. If expertly dangled, the techno-bandits should find it irresistible.

With Al's technical assistance, Pilgrim was nothing if not inventive. 'Now that the GRU has heard that this equipment is going to West Germany, it's a certainty that they will be planning to intercept it and I can't wait to help them,' he told his Disciples, who were well practised in his axiom that the essence of willieing an adversary lay in being able to read his mind and foresee what he would do.

'We have to devise some means of inserting a sneaky into the equipment so that it looks like part of it,' Pilgrim continued. 'I don't want to be denied the pleasure of overhearing our Russian friends when they find out what they have really got – a Mockingbird with some special salt on its tail!'

Between them they worked out a detailed plan for Turbid, which, like all the Pilgrimages, had to be a plausibly deniable operation, should it backfire.

'The beauty of this operation is that all the evidence will be safely behind the Iron Curtain,' Pilgrim enthused. 'And there it will remain.'

If 'beauty' meant an assembly of qualities giving intense pleasure to the senses and profound satisfaction to the intellect, then, for Pilgrim, there *was* beauty in a deception operation, successfully accomplished, especially when it had been a dangle, with the opponents well and truly willied.

The scandal which had attached to people like himself over the Irangate affair occasionally entered Pilgrim's mind but was quickly dismissed. There was a difference between gung-ho irresponsibility and adroit executive action, in neglect of which, he believed, he would have been derelict in his duty. With a wimp like Arnold in command he had to work on his own initiative or quit and he had no intention of quitting. He knew, in his heart, that he would be incapable of fulfilling his promise to his wife to retire early, at sixty.

Chapter Twenty-one

On the KISS principle, Pilgrim liked the absolute minimum of people involved in any one operation, with none of them outside his firm command. In an operation as controversial as Turbid, the danger from a leakage was compounded by the reaction which could be expected if one of the oversight committees got wind of it. But the removal of the target, the Mockingbird simulator, to such a secure airfield as Vandenberg Air Force Base demanded some relaxation of this precaution. It was apparent that he would have to seek the collaboration of his friend, Butch, but under deceptive circumstances. He was confident of getting it: Butch had maintained his fascination with counter-intelligence ploys and had admitted suffering some withdrawal symptoms since his retirement from active participation.

The autumn day on which he invited Butch to his house for an evening drink was hot and humid, the all too common consequence of the fact that Washington had been built on a swamp. In the late afternoon Al, dressed in casual summer clothes, called, at Pilgrim's request, carrying a suitcase. He opened it on the floor of the study to reveal a fairly large replacement module from a Mockingbird simulator. Like most complex electronic equipment, the Mockingbird was built of several hundred separate, inter-locking modules so that, in the event of a breakdown of a component part, the whole affected area could easily and quickly be pulled out and replaced. Through his CIA resources at the manufacturers in Silicon Valley, Al had experienced no difficulty in securing the module, which he had selected after studying the structure of the Mockingbird from the detailed instruction book.

He had chosen an easily portable, rectangular module, some 2 feet by 18 inches by 6 inches, with spare space inside and apertures to permit the easy entry and exit of cooling air. There had been little difficulty in inserting an eavesdropping sneaky in the form of one of the CIA's latest micro-sensors, provided by his friends in the Technical Services Division. The 'Little Wonders', as they were known in the Agency, had the capability to communicate any overheard conversation in 'real time' – directly to a satellite, which relayed it immediately to one of the National Security Agency centres located in various parts of the world. The eavesdroppers could listen to conversations thousands of miles away virtually as they happened.

The latest Little Wonder had a further attribute which was highly advantageous to the operation. Its more advanced microchips were not based on silicon but on gallium arsenide, which was immune to attack by the clone. Not even the rapacious Fe 113 could survive on arsenic.

Al took the lid off the module by removing only four screws, and pointed to where the micro-sensor had been fitted. It had been camouflaged to look like a normal part of the internal equipment, which was a maze of printed circuits, silicon chips, and other electronic marvels.

'Gee, they really have miniaturized it,' Pilgrim remarked, admiringly. 'I've never seen a long-range sneaky that small. Are you sure it will work?'

'Certainly will, sir. They don't call it the Little Wonder for nothing. State-of-the-art, you know.' Al pointed to another similar sneaky, ingeniously intruded among the electronic parts. 'So we also have a back-up in case that one fails, sir.'

Always a belt and braces man, Pilgrim expressed his appreciation. 'This Mockingbird is going to be more like a parrot, Al. It's going to talk!'

Al then produced a small, stainless steel vacuum flask, unscrewed its lid and withdrew a black, rectangular, heavy-duty plastic capsule fitted with a stout screw cap.

'This contains the culture of the clone – the silicon-eater,' he explained. 'It's in powder form, a dry biological. State of the art again, sir!'

His chief was suitably impressed. 'And it won't attack the sneaky?'

'Definitely not. It's all been tested. The capsule's very robust so that it will stand knocking about,' Al continued, 'but Technical Services have designed it so that the local heat will melt it when the Mockingbird starts working.'

'And the air-conditioning system does the rest,' Pilgrim observed with satisfaction.

'Right. When the simulator is switched on, the heat generated by the electrical parts will melt the plastic and the cooling fans will blow the bacteria out of the module all over the place. The powder is very light and I told them to put plenty in.'

'Is it full?' Pilgrim asked.

'As full as it can be. It's a bit like one of those Russian dolls. There's another phial inside containing the powder sealed in a vacuum. That way the bacteria can last indefinitely until the vacuum is destroyed when the whole thing melts.'

'Very ingenious.'

Al pointed to the module. 'It clips in here,' he explained, fitting it in. 'The capsule has been designed to look like a component.' He removed the capsule and handed it to Pilgrim. 'Don't unscrew the plastic stopper, sir. If the phial broke you might lose your windows or, worse still, your whisky glass.'

'Ah, the risks we take for America!' Pilgrim responded. He weighed the object in his palm, admiringly. 'It's like a silent atom bomb, Al. Properly distributed, there's enough in here to put a modern city out of action – no light, no heat, no telephones, no banks, no business!'

'Yes. And the way things are going it could soon be produced by the sackful.' He recovered the capsule. 'Until you need to insert it in the module it's safest in the steel flask, especially in this weather,' he said, slipping it in and replacing the lid.

'Where did you get the culture, Al?'

Al smiled. 'Through good friends at Fort Detrick, as you suggested. They've got a little pilot plant going there.'

'Any questions asked?'

'No questions asked, sir, and no answers expected.'

'Long tongs, Al?'

'Long tongs, sir.'

A long tongs operation, in Pilgrim's parlance, was one in which so many cut-outs were used that the ultimate recipient was untraceable. Long tongs were an integral part of any good dangle.

'How are you going to get the sneaky into the Mockingbird?' Al asked.

'I think another good friend will oblige.'

'Will he know what he is doing?'

'Up to a point, Al. Up to a point. But that's not for you to worry about.'

Al did worry about it. He was confident that he knew the identity of the 'good friend', for whom the operation could be decidedly perilous. The friend was one of Nature's gentlemen and in the intelligence world they were so rare as to be an endangered species.

'This is an awesome moment, Al,' Pilgrim said holding up the capsule. 'The first use of a new weapon in anger and you and I are the only witnesses.'

Al did not seem at all happy and Pilgrim looked at him quizzically. 'I don't think you really approve of Turbid, do you?' he asked.

'Mine is not to reason why, sir,' was his sole and crisp reply.

'You know the British SAS has a great motto, "Who dares wins". That needs to be our motto, Al.'

Again Al did not reply. He did not disagree but felt that the circumstances which were due to unfold when Pilgrim received his next visitor hardly reflected the CIA slogan carved in capital letters on the marble wall of the main lobby at Langley: 'And ye shall know the truth, And the truth shall make you free.'

What was happening to the old man? Al wondered, and not for the first time. He seemed to be taking the most reckless risks. He was becoming more and more autocratic, cynical and arrogant, as expressed by his open feud with his chief, Stanley Arnold, and his talk about pushing Primarkov off his perch. And ludicrously suspicious. Al was used to Pilgrim's habit of looking around to check if he was being followed but when they had lunched at the Mayflower Hotel, on a recent visit to downtown Washington, he had even taken the pepper-mill apart, looking for a bug.

Like most of the CIA staffers, Al was ever conscious of the Irangate affair. The repercussions of that covert hassle with a petty power had been horrific; the Turbid ploy was with a superpower. He felt that if the operation should go sour and heads had to roll, as they surely would, Pilgrim's would somehow remain on his shoulders. Men may come and men may go but some seem to be permanent fixtures whatever happened.

'I'm afraid I won't be able to take Dallas out,' Al said, apologetically. 'I have a date.'

'That's OK. I'll take him. I could do with some air.'

After Al had left, and been seen to drive away, Pilgrim removed the cover of the module and took out the plastic capsule from the vacuum flask. He toyed with it for a while then inserted it in its allotted place, replacing the cover and screwing it up.

156

A little later, Butch arrived, having driven himself there. He was allowed a few moments to make a fuss of Dallas. He had given the dog to Pilgrim as a puppy and it had grown into a personable companion with what his master called 'a great dogality'. Butch would have loved such a dog of his own but an apartment with no garden access was no place to have one. So he shared Dallas in the shooting field and it had become another bond between the two men. It was carefully excluded, however, when its master ushered his guest into his study and poured a couple of drinks.

'By the way, this room was swept again this morning,' he said, referring not to domestic chores but to the weekly electronic examination by CIA technicians which ensured, as far as was possible, that the room was not being bugged by any adversary. Pilgrim had a reputation for having his office at Langley searched every morning for sneakies though this was, in fact, an exaggeration. He felt that twice a week was probably enough.

Pilgrim was faced with telling Butch more about Operation Turbid than he liked but he had no alternative.

'You remember that Star Wars simulator that was the centre of The Nephews' row and is now going to West Germany?'

'Yeah, Mockingbird.'

'Right. Well, I want to make it sing.'

'What do you mean?'

'I want to put a real-time sneaky in it.'

'What the hell for, Ross, what's the idea?'

'I have a hunch that the Russians are going to hijack it and, if they do, it would be useful to have a sneaky in it. You recall that we agreed we all need to know more about what the Russians are really doing on the Star Wars front? Well, a sneaky in this Mockingbird should let us know which research centre they take it to and give us some idea what they are doing there.'

'Where do you think that might be?'

'My money is on Sary Shagan.'

Butch was startled. Sary Shagan, the main research and development site for Star Wars weapons, located north of Lake Balkhash in Soviet Central Asia, was a familiar intelligence target.

'That would be quite a coup, Ross. We were never able to penetrate Sary Shagan. We used to reckon it was the most secret place they'd got.'

157

'I thought it might excite you.'

'It sure does. I boned up on Sary Shagan a couple of years ago. It looked like they had two prototype ground-based laser-beam systems for shooting down satellites and they were building particle beam weapons — synthetic lightning bolts, we called them. There was also one of those huge radars. Of course, that was all from satellite reconnaissance. We could never get anything from inside.'

'Well, now we have a chance, not to see inside but to hear inside,' Pilgrim said, enthusiastically. 'You know, like we did at Tyuratam.'

Butch grinned as he recalled the details of that difficult and dangerous operation in which several sneakies hidden in telephones had been introduced into the heart of the huge Tyuratam missile-space complex near Kazalinsk, just east of the Aral Sea. But his features quickly registered doubt. 'Is this one a good idea, Ross, with the summit coming up?'

Pilgrim had prepared himself for the question. 'It wouldn't be if the Russkies had bought the Mockingbird with the President's blessing but, if they hijack it, they deserve all they get.'

'I guess so. But why not just stop the hijack?'

'I can't guarantee to be able to do that, once the Mockingbird's out of the country. Anyway the President wants the Russkies to have it, doesn't he? And, as we both know, Presidents always eventually get their way if they think the political advantages outweigh the intelligence losses. So why should we waste CIA resources in stopping the hijack? It's only a simulator. As the President says, it doesn't shoot anything down.'

'I see your point, Ross, but why tell me about it? It's not like you, with anything so technical, when I don't need to know.'

'Because I can't accomplish it without your help, Butch. The Mockingbird is being held at Vandenberg Air Force Base. My guys can't get at it there to put the sneaky in. Yours can.'

'What do you mean, mine can? I don't have any guys any more.'

'No, but your old guys would do anything for you. And keep quiet about it.'

Butch relished the compliment and his curiosity and old enthusiasm had been aroused but Pilgrim sensed that he needed more encouragement.

'You'd be doing Army Intelligence a great service, Butch. It's something they'd try themselves if they had the opportunity. Something you'd try, if you were still there.'

That was undeniable. 'Just what do you want me to do?'

Pilgrim opened the suitcase and took out the module. 'The sneaky's inside this. All you have to do is to get some technician to fit the whole module as a replacement to the one that's there now. The module's numbered. It can't be confused with any other.'

Butch inspected the module, turning it over in his hands. 'Won't the Russians open it up and examine it?'

'I don't think so if they hijack the Mockingbird, of which this is only a tiny part. They probably would if they were getting it direct from us: they'd look any gift horse very carefully in the mouth. But in any event, I don't think they'd spot anything. My guys have been very ingenious. This sneaky is the latest in micro-sensors: state of the art. It has been engineered to look like a normal part of the equipment.'

'But if they do spot it won't you be making them a valuable present?' Butch asked.

'Not really. There's quite a few of these Little Wonders in place behind the Iron Curtain already and there are better ones coming up. These things have to be expendable. It's an acceptable risk.'

Butch was well aware that sneakies were expendable – in his intelligence career, he and his officers had expended hundreds – but his face still looked as though he was by no means convinced that he should be involved.

It was time for Pilgrim to make his bull sales pitch. 'I'll cut you in, personally, on anything we learn about the Soviet Star Wars progress. Then you could mark Rockwell's card before he goes to the summit. Wouldn't it be in his interest to know if the Russians were really telling the truth about their Star Wars work or if they're lying?'

There was deep division among Rockwell's advisers as to the effort being made by the Soviets in the Star Wars field. One group was convinced that intelligence gleaned by satellites showed conclusively that they were making a huge effort, cheating on agreements in the process, while lulling the West into believing they were opposed to the whole concept. The other insisted that the intelligence was being misinterpreted and believed the Soviet claim that various suspect installations, such as giant radars, were not for Star Wars but for satellite communications and other peaceful space purposes.

159

It would certainly do Butch no harm if he could resolve that doubt for the President before the summit. Sary Shagan was exactly where the issue might be settled. If the evidence indicated that the Russians had been telling the truth, then the President's line would be re-inforced and The Nephews and the rest of the doubters could be dismissed. On the other hand, if it showed that the Soviet leadership had been lying, then the President still ought to know. Facts were facts, whichever way they pointed.

Suddenly Butch needed no more coercion. He wanted to be part of the action.

'Even if I could arrange it, Ross, which I'm not sure I can, how would I explain why this module needs replacement?'

'No problem! It's a last-minute high-tech modification supplied by the manufacturer and only the best is good enough for our West German allies.'

Butch smiled. 'You've got it all figured out, as usual. I'll see what I can do but I can't promise. There's no way, in my position, that I can be personally involved.'

'Of course not. You don't have to be if you have a long enough chain of command. That's the virtue of dealing with soldiers. Civilians ask questions: soldiers just do what they are told.'

Pilgrim paused and asked, 'What's that quote of yours about evil men, Butch?'

'All that is necessary for the triumph of evil is that good men do nothing.'

'As of now, I couldn't agree with it more.' He knew his Butch and felt he was home and dry. 'I thought this dangle would appeal to you,' he said, replacing the module in the suitcase. 'It's in the interests of your old Service and it's time these goddamn techno-bandits were taught a lesson. Naturally, if there should be any come-back of any kind you know nothing whatever about it. For that matter, neither do I,' he added with a smile. 'It has to be a plausibly deniable operation for us both. But there can't be any come-back. How can the Russkies possibly complain about a sneaky when they hijacked the whole apparatus?'

'You seem to be remarkably confident that they will hijack it, Ross. Have you heard something?'

'No, I just reckon that, after all these years, I know my Russkies.'

'Well, I'll think about it and see what I can do. Where did you say the Mockingbird was?'

'Vandenberg Air Force Base.'

'I know the commandant there. He could fix it but I won't be able to deal with him direct. I'm with you all the way in spirit in doing the techno-bandits a bit of no good but I mustn't get too close to it. I don't want to get involved in a Silicongate!'

'Absolutely not,' Pilgrim agreed. 'And I can promise you that you won't. If the sneaky comes up with the goods I'll camouflage what I give you in the usual way so that you can simply tell the President that the information originated from a human source – a source with excellent access.'

The more relaxed expression on Butch's face suggested that the ploy had worked. 'By the way, does Arnold know about this operation?' he asked.

Pilgrim smiled. 'Need you ask? It needs to be kept secret, really secret, and Arnold is so vain that, if it succeeds, he would be bound to talk about it to someone, probably the President. Lawyers are like actors, aren't they? They wouldn't have become lawyers unless they were vain. Anyway we mustn't overload the DCI with detail he doesn't need to know.'

Butch was not misled. He knew, well enough, that Arnold was not being told because he would forbid the operation. 'How urgent is the action?' he asked.

'It needs doing soonest. I gather that the Mockingbird could be shipped to West Germany any day now.'

He poured two more Macallan Scotches. 'It's just like old times, Butch,' he said handing him a glass. 'Just like old times!'

Butch rolled the mellow gold whisky round his tongue, savouring its flavour, malty, slightly smokey and with a hint of peat. 'That's very good. Where do you get it?'

'I get it from a special contact, a Brit. I did him a service once.'

As Butch stowed the suitcase carefully in the trunk of his automobile he did not notice Pilgrim watching from his study window, dragging deeply on a cigarette and with the kind of satisfied look he displayed when he achieved a right and left at high ducks. Pilgrim remained confident that, as an old intelligence compaigner and being so eager to make his mark in his new career, Butch would find the challenge irresistible.

Nor did Butch notice an automobile, with Al at the wheel, parked out of view of Pilgrim's windows. As Butch drove home Al followed him at a discreet distance.

The following day Butch made certain dispositions and within forty-eight hours was able to telephone Pilgrim to announce 'Mission accomplished'.

The module had been flown down to Vandenberg from Washington on a regular flight by the US Air Force, on the orders of a brigadier general, with whom Butch had done Forces intelligence business in the past. The officer who had received it at the base treated the task as a routine Pentagon matter, which was none of his business, and passed it to a top sergeant who selected a skilled electronics artificer, familiar with other simulators in use for general training. He had experienced no difficulty in finding the correct crate among the twenty-five containing the Mockingbird parts, since the contents were all marked in conformity with the manual and parts schedule.

The old comrades' Armed Forces network had operated smoothly and without hitch. It had been a nod and a wink arrangement with need to know fully applied and Butch 'cut out' several times. A good 'long tongs' operation.

Pilgrim was jubilant. Good old Butch! Friendship was one of the real joys of living – especially when friends were in the right places.

162

Chapter Twenty-two

Like most firms in the export business, the American manufacturer of the Mockingbird simulator had commercial agents who held the franchise for the sale of its products in various parts of the world. They worked on a commission basis and, once having signed contracts with them, the manufacturer was required to deal through them with respect to all sales in their designated areas. The man responsible for West Germany, Austria and Switzerland called himself Rolf Schneider, a German-speaking Swiss who had wide experience of electronics deals but was fairly new to the American company. He was not, however, entirely new to the CIA. Reference to the computerized checklist held in Pilgrim's department showed that his name was there as a suspected diverter – a person involved in the diversion to prohibited countries of equipment intended for legitimized customers. What evidence there was showed him as being suspected of diverting products to South Africa, Israel and Iran but Pilgrim was in little doubt that, given the right financial inducement, he would divert anything anywhere.

There was not enough evidence for the CIA to warn American manufacturers against him. That might not only result in a legal action, which they could not sustain in a court of law, but might prejudice their sources. To Pilgrim, however, the paucity of information simply meant that Schneider was unusually clever in his use of bogus companies, subcontracts, forged papers and other devices used by those who assisted, and exploited, the techno-bandits.

Schneider had ordered the Mockingbird through his Zurich-based company for onward delivery to a West German electronics firm, located near Frankfurt. The firm was engaged on Star Wars contracts under the arrangements brought in by President Reagan for involving the European allies in the project. At the same time, being also the agent for Austria, Schneider had bought from the same American company a substantial amount of routine, exportable communications equipment for sale to a different, unnamed customer. Because these goods were saleable anywhere in the world, the eventual customer did not have to be specified. The sale was simply marked down to Schneider.

'It's sticking out a mile,' Pilgrim commented, when he heard of the double order from one of his scouts. 'He's going to do a switch.'

Because of the importance and value of the Mockingbird deal – $110 million meant a massive commission for him – Schneider made it his business to fly to New York where the simulator was to be delivered to the dockside. The twenty-five crates housing the separate parts had been collected from Vandenberg Air Base and returned to the factory in Silicon Valley for checking and loading into a container for transport by road to New York, where a West German freighter was waiting. For convenience, Schneider had arranged for the communications equipment to be delivered from the factory in a separate container at the same time. As he had anticipated, the manufacturer used the same delivery firm to transport the two containers across country to New York so, naturally, they were of similar size and design. Both containers, locked and sealed, were destined to be offloaded at Hamburg.

'More interesting coincidences,' Pilgrim observed, when appraised of the arrangements.

With their customary efficiency, the manufacturer and the transport firm delivered in good time and, with his, Schneider was at the bustling New York dockside to meet them. It did not surprise Pilgrim to learn that he had made preliminary arrangements to accompany the containers to Hamburg on the freighter.

Unknown to Schneider, the loading of the containers in California had been surreptitiously and skilfully recorded on video and still camera by Pilgrim's men. The CIA had been barred from undertaking any domestic intelligence by President Jimmy Carter but, by an edict of President Reagan, it had been permitted to resume a certain amount of intelligence work inside the US under limited circumstances. Having no wish to involve the FBI in Operation Turbid, particularly after the Dealer episode, Pilgrim reckoned that photographing a couple of containers destined for foreign parts fell within that dispensation.

The clandestine procedures continued on the New York waterfront, as cranes hoisted the containers aboard the freighter, which was not a specialized container ship. All the photographs were faxed to Pilgrim, personally, at Langley, and through his communications network he was able to oversee the operation hour by hour. The surveillance officers were given no indication of the purpose of their activities and, obeying the 'need to know' rule, did not seek enlightenment. To them it was a routine job, probably connected with some techno-bandit counter-ploy.

The CIA was also surreptitiously represented when the two containers were unloaded at Hamburg, though again the officer had no knowledge of why he was required to report in such detail on their safe arrival and subsequent departure. Through binoculars, he was able to confirm the identification numbers boldly painted on each container, showing that those offloaded in Hamburg were those that had been delivered in New York.

He also watched Schneider as he made himself amiably busy at the Hamburg quayside. Being heavily built and rather obese for a man in his early forties, the Swiss was easily recognizable·from photographs. As was his sensible practice, he had consulted the Customs authorities in advance to ease the passage of his imports. He provided papers for one container which stated that, enclosed within it, was a Mockingbird simulator, packed in twenty-five crates, which was not to be re-exported but delivered to Frankfurt. He offered to open the container for inspection by the port authorities but when they saw the origin of the equipment and the prestigious West German firm for which it was intended, they waived that formality. The Hamburg Customs authorities had good liaison with the CIA and the FBI and, had there been anything suspicious about Schneider's goods, they would have expected to have been alerted in advance of their arrival.

Once that container had passed Customs, Schneider personally oversaw its movement to a locked area of the port, from which it was to be picked up for delivery to Frankfurt in three days' time.

The port authorities were much more interested in the second container which, according to the American papers Schneider supplied, contained routine, fully exportable communications equipment, but they were forbidden to open it by international law. During the voyage from New York, by radio telephone and fax machine, the contents had been sold to the Soviet Embassy in Vienna. Schneider produced the faxed documents to prove the sale and a representative of the Soviet Consulate in Hamburg was on hand to oversee the dispatch of the sealed container, for which a vehicle was waiting. He

165

was accompanied by another 'diplomat', who was a junior GRU officer located at the Soviet Embassy in Bonn and delegated to travel with the vehicle as a courier.

Before this second container left the ship, the Soviet Consulate official, accompanied by a Customs officer, had gone aboard to secure it with red seals and label it 'Diplomatic Mail of the USSR. Despatcher – Soviet Consulate General, Hamburg'. The impressive looking papers which he supplied to the Customs officer were signed by the Minister of Foreign Affairs, and stated: 'In the name of the Union of Soviet Socialist Republics the Minister of Foreign Affairs of the USSR requests the governments of friendly states and their military and civil services to allow the diplomatic mail of the USSR to pass freely without it being subjected to any interference or Customs examination, in accordance with the Vienna Convention of 1815.'

The port authorities were quite unaware that, during the voyage, the Customs papers relating to the two containers had been switched, after attention by a skilled GRU forger who had travelled aboard the ship as an assistant to Schneider and who, with the captain's well-paid connivance, had never left it in New York.

The container allegedly housing the communications equipment was transported along the autobahns via Hannover, Wurzburg, Regensburg and Linz to Vienna, with the GRU officer 'riding shotgun'.

'Good old Vienna, I would have bet on it,' Pilgrim had commented.

The border crossing presented no problems. The Austrian Customs men were curious to know what was inside the container but had no hope of finding out because of the need to observe the diplomatic niceties. It was the usual practice of a skilled diverter to confuse the issue by involving a third country. When Soviet intelligence was involved it was mandatory to keep Moscow right out of the scenario.

On arrival at the Soviet Embassy in Vienna's Reisnerstrasse, the container was whisked inside the compound and the crates housing the components of the simulator were taken out behind locked doors. The empty container was then returned by its lorry to Hamburg.

Meanwhile, a larger, empty container had arrived by truck from the Soviet Union for the routine collection of the Embassy's diplomatic 'mail' which included parcels or crates of any size. That same night, in the darkness, it was loaded with the crates, fitted with a new set of seals and papers. With new GRU couriers in command,

166

it set off south-east for the border with Hungary. Its papers showed its destination as the Foreign Ministry in Moscow. The Austrian police were used to such large consignments of Soviet 'mail' and, while they had developed a reputation for looking the other way to avoid conflict with the Russians, everything had apparently been above board.

Once on Warsaw Pact soil, the truck headed for the nearest military airfield, where an Antonov heavy logistic transport plane was waiting.

CIA agents, who were in plentiful supply in Vienna and had been appraised of the description of the container, watched the developments and reported back to Pilgrim as a matter of dull routine. Their messages were purely confirmatory, however. The Little Wonder sneaky had been working perfectly, both aboard ship and on its other journeys, and Pilgrim had been in receipt of occasional snatches of fascinating conversation. The ever-alert antennae of the National Security Agency had picked up the transmissions and passed them directly via the NSA–CIA link to Langley where, after being taped, Pilgrim had ensured that the translation and analysis had been conducted by his Disciples.

So much raw intelligence flowed into the NSA from the thousands of other sneakies and clandestine devices planted in so many countries that nobody else had been interested, or in any way disconcerted, when Pilgrim had insisted on having the reports dealt with at Langley.

Though disjointed, the snatches contained evidence enough of Schneider's switch, should it ever be needed, particularly during the offloading and reloading of the crates in Vienna. There were even sporadic items of the conversation of the drivers and guards during breaks in the truck journeys, but, once aboard the Antonov transport, the sneaky relayed nothing but the drone of the turboprops.

Pilgrim had high hopes for it once the Mockingbird reached its destination and was assembled. Meanwhile he could relax and await developments. He had some professional admiration for Schneider, who had accomplished an elegant 'end-user diversion' on the KISS principle but marked him down for professional destruction one day, when it suited.

Some four days later the West German firm discovered that the container delivered to it was packed with run-of-the-mill communications equipment. In some anger, a senior representative telephoned Schneider at his office in Zurich, to which he had returned.

'We have a load of junk here – communications equipment we haven't ordered and don't want. But we don't have a simulator. What goes on?'

Schneider had fully rehearsed his response. 'Good God! Are you sure?'

'Of course I'm sure. We've opened all the crates. They don't match the papers.'

'I just don't understand it. I checked out all the papers at New York and Hamburg and so did the Customs. I travelled over with the container and saw it off at Hamburg. The manufacturers must have mixed up two orders, or it could have been the stupid transport company.'

'Maybe so. But where's our Mockingbird? It's flown.'

'I'll ring the manufacturers right away.'

'Waste of time. I've done that. They checked and said that it had definitely been delivered to the New York docks.'

'Then I'll fly to New York tomorrow and make a personal, on the spot investigation. Leave it to me. It's my responsibility.'

'You're damn right it is.'

'OK then. I'll be in touch as soon as I've traced it.'

In spite of all his preparation, Schneider was sweating as he put down the telephone. What he needed was a breathing space. A couple of days previously he had been instructed to visit a flat in Zurich equipped with two suitcases. There, a junior 'diplomat' from the Soviet Embassy in Bern, whom he had never met before, had handed over $121 million in bundles of dollar bills – the manufacturer's price and his commission. He had immediately paid the manufacturer by banker's draft, so there should be no great pressure from that end. Now he would just have to play it by the day. He could gain some respite by delaying his departure to the United States because of pressure of urgent business. He had made contingency arrangements to go to ground in Rio, if necessary, but the 'diplomat' had warned him that his services might be needed again in the near future. It was agreed that he should visit the United States to 'go through some motions' and then to remain in New York until further orders.

Chapter Twenty-three

The four-engined Antonov had flown due east for more than 3,000 miles across Rumania, the Crimea, Georgia, Kazak, the Aral Sea and the Hungersteppe to a point north of Lake Balkhash, where several square miles of desert were surrounded by a perimeter fence. Its imminent arrival had been radioed to the control tower of the airfield and a ground crew was waiting. As the wheels were lowered, the chief pilot remarked to his co-pilot, 'They say there's over four thousand of our best scientists and engineers working in this dump. What a posting! Poor bastards!'

There were worse postings. Though the surroundings were bare and windswept, the climate was dry, with clear air, which was why the location had been chosen.

The chief pilot had not been there for more than a year and was surprised by the extent of the developments. There were more hangars, some of them with short lengths of rail track in front, indicating that they housed prototype weapons which could be rolled out for action.

He taxied the plane to a halt following the instructions of the batman. The rear doors were opened and, with minimum delay, the ground crew set about offloading the still sealed container housing the Mockingbird on to a self-propelled trailer.

'I don't know what we've brought here,' the chief pilot remarked to his Number 2. 'But they seem in one hell of a hurry to get hold of it.'

He was looking forward to a bath and some sleep. Just one night in that desolate spot and they would be off to Moscow to deliver the bag containing the genuine diplomatic mail, which had been carried from Vienna in the cab of the truck and handed over to him at the airfield in Hungary. A night in Moscow was a happier prospect.

Within a few hours Pilgrim's sneaky was able to tell him that his hunch had been correct. Mockingbird had landed at the Missile Test Centre at Sary Shagan.

169

Once the container had been transported to a large hangar the seals were broken, the crates removed, formally taken on the establishment's strength and opened with great care. Several scientists were on hand to oversee the process.

'It will be interesting to see how much better this is than ours,' one of them said. 'That is if it is any better.'

'It looks as though it will do quite a few things ours won't,' remarked a colleague, who was perusing the manual and the list of software.

'Well, I'll believe it when I see it doing them,' the first scientist responded.

Pilgrim smiled when he read these snatches of conversation. The NIH (Not Invented Here) Factor, which automatically denigrated anything developed at another establishment, seemed to operate with Soviet scientists as forcibly as it did with American.

'Touchdown!' Butch shouted when Pilgrim told him the news. 'A really great touchdown!'

'Yeah. After a brilliant interception by the other side! We'll just sit back now and see the score mount,' Pilgrim said, contentedly.

As the days passed and the odd reports from the sneaky arrived on his desk, Pilgrim became familiar with so many given names – Oleg Ivanovich, Boris Adreievich, Sergei Sergeievich – that the list began to look like the cast of *War and Peace*. He detailed one of his analysts to try to work out the surnames from known lists of Soviet scientists to see which might be working at Sary Shagan.

The sneaky overheard them assembling the equipment and commenting on the software. Within a week the Mockingbird should be completed and ready for starting up for trials. That was the moment for which Pilgrim was waiting with gleeful anticipation, which he would have to enjoy in the company of Al, and Al alone.

He showed the early sneaky reports to Butch, who, while rusty, could still comprehend part of the conversations in Russian, for both preferred to examine 'raw' intelligence. They felt confident that the information which the sneaky would provide, once the simulator was in routine use, would be immensely revealing.

'Have you any doubt now that your effort was worthwhile?' Pilgrim asked as they celebrated over a drink. 'I couldn't have brought it off without you.'

'None whatever, Ross. But how long before they rumble the sneaky?'

Pilgrim shrugged. 'We can only go on living in hope. No sneaky lasts for ever but, knock on wood, this one is state of the art.'

'I guess that this could be that grand-daddy dangle you've always been searching for.'

'Here's hoping,' Pilgrim replied, raising his whisky glass.

Pilgrim never doubted that he had been absolutely justified in going ahead with Operation Turbid.

'There is going to be one hell of a row in the Politburo,' he predicted to Al. 'All we have to do now is to wait and see whose head rolls. Somebody's will, without doubt, and we shall have been responsible. You see, Al, I was right. Who dares wins.'

With difficulty Al suppressed a sigh. He had been reading a learned paper published by a British psychiatrist called Barrington-Fuller which had been circulated round the Agency, as much for amusement as anything. It considered the effects of the secrets world on those working in it, suggesting that the peculiarities inherent in all human nature were more likely to express themselves there because of the tempting opportunities which secrecy offered. The conclusions had attracted ribald comments, written in the margins, about 'shrinkers' in general but in Al's opinion the Brit had it right. Secret power did corrupt. It corrupted principles, judgement and sense of responsibility. And nobody was showing its effects more despotically than his chief.

171

Chapter Twenty-four

A great deal more confusion was let loose than any sneaky, however wondrous, could possibly have revealed. Thirteen days after the Mockingbird left New York and five days after its arrival at Sary Shagan, the KGB Mission chief in Washington, customarily known as the Resident, received an anonymous letter. It had been sent, folded in four, inside a small envelope attached to a bunch of flowers delivered by taxi to the Resident's apartment, but addressed to his wife. Inside the envelope was the usual card, bearing the message 'From an Admirer', and another envelope addressed to her husband and marked Secret.

Written on headed CIA paper, the secret letter stated:

To the Resident,

Whatever your reservations about this letter, which has not been easy for me to write, I urge you to take action on it in the interests of world peace.

As we are aware, you have diverted a Mockingbird simulator intended for delivery in West Germany. If you have not yet started up the machine by the time you receive this letter my urgent advice is that you should not do so. The silicon chips in the simulator would then become infected with bacteria which we have deliberately introduced to render them useless. The bacteria might then spread to other equipment in the vicinity, which is the main purpose of the operation.

The simulator has also been fitted with surveillance devices.

I regard the operation as extremely irresponsible, particularly in view of the forthcoming summit, and because the possibility of an epidemic, though unlikely, cannot be ruled out.

The phenomenon of silicon infection was discovered accidentally by the British at the Chemical Defence Establishment at Porton, near Salisbury, England. If, as I expect, you need collateral evidence, Dr Wendy Payne, at that Establishment, may be prepared to provide it, though she knows nothing about the Mockingbird and what has been done to it. Dr Payne's interest has been entirely medical. There is some possibility that the bacterium can dissolve silicate spicules and might be effective in the treatment of silicosis.

I am not sympathetic to the Communist system. I write to you in what I believe to be the best interests of East–West relations and send this warning at considerable personal and professional risk.

The Resident's immediate reaction was to treat the letter as a crude CIA provocation. He knew nothing about the acquisition of any simulator but, if such a device had been obtained, then the letter could be a rather transparent gambit – a damage limitation exercise to stop the Soviet scientists using the equipment.

Whoever the writer was, he knew the Resident's name and his function, which few people did, as he was fairly new in post. The writer must also have known that he was in town. So he could well be in the CIA. The CIA had already suffered a few dissidents, such as Edward Lee Howard who had eventually defected to Moscow after supplying valuable secret information. The writer might be another.

The Resident's first move was to check the paper for forgery but there could be no doubt that it was genuine CIA notepaper. However, that meant nothing: the KGB rarely found difficulty in securing a supply of such headed paper for their own forgeries. The suggestion that silicon chips could be infected by bacteria sounded ludicrous and that stuff about silicosis sounded like typical CIA dressing. Nevertheless, the Resident decided that it would be wiser to risk making himself look foolish at Moscow headquarters than to hold up the information. Within the KGB Oleg Chevalsky was known as the 'Horseman', not only because of the obvious connotation but because he rode his staff so hard. The Resident passed the contents to Moscow by radio, following up with the actual letter in the next outgoing diplomatic bag.

In Moscow the KGB Centre quickly established that the GRU had indeed pulled off such a diversion. A joint KGB–GRU team was set up to go through every step of the acquisition. Because of the grave political implications if the warning turned out to be true, the KGB Chairman, Chevalsky, was immediately informed and took personal charge of the situation.

His first order was that, as a precaution, no further work should be done on the simulator, which had been almost completely assembled by the time the letter arrived. The senior Soviet scientist working on the Mockingbird was called to the station commandant's office and returned to the hangar in haste to motion all his colleagues to remain silent and to follow him outside.

'We have to drop everything and get out of this area immediately,' he said quietly.

'Why?' a colleague asked.

'I wasn't told but we can't even go back in to get our personal possessions. They will be collected for us.'

'Do they think the equipment's booby-trapped or something?'

'I have no idea,' the scientist replied, impatiently. 'All I know is that the whole area is being evacuated until further order.'

As the scientists marched away, a truck arrived carrying two security men with electronic sweeping equipment. They entered the hangar silently and swept all round the Mockingbird including those few parts not yet assembled. Watching the dials and listening with earphones, but communicating only by gestures, they detected the presence of the sneaky and located its position.

When this discovery was reported to Chevalsky he was more and more inclined to accept the letter as genuine.

'Why should the writer tell us about the bug if the rest is not true?' he asked himself. 'The bug is the last thing the CIA would want us to know about – unless, of course, the letter is just a hoax to stop us using the apparatus.'

There was a small chemical and biological warfare detachment at Sary Shagan for decontamination duties in the event of such an attack and the five men under an NCO were required to work in their full decontamination suits to stow the Mockingbird back into its large container. They towed it to an unused corner of the establishment remote from any activity, where it was cordoned off. The container was then completely sealed in a plastic covering sprayed on under pressure.

Chevalsky needed some collateral information, and quickly. There was one immediate source – the latest reports on the secret CIA radio traffic. If the letter was an official CIA hoax there should be an additional increase in the secret coded traffic between Langley and the US Embassy in Moscow because Pilgrim and his crew would be needing feedback from their human sources in the Soviet Union about what was happening there to the Mockingbird. But if the letter had been sent clandestinely by a disenchanted officer, as it claimed, there would be no such increase. Chevalsky's inquiry showed that there was, in fact, no observable increase. This was a pointer but it was not enough. If the letter was a hoax, he reasoned that his old enemy, Ross Pilgrim, would have been responsible for it and he would know what the KGB would be looking for. He might have forbidden any increase in the CIA traffic. The KGB chief despised Pilgrim but he also respected him as a professional and set a lot of store by reading his mind.

Chevalsky's next step was to find out all that the GRU knew about the Mockingbird business. He anticipated resistance for, apart from the long-established rivalry between the two organizations, he was no friend of the GRU chief, Army General Yuri Yakushkin. Though Chevalsky was the grandson of a revolutionary who had been famous in his day in his native province of Chelyabinsk, he remained conscious of his peasant origin and resented the apparent arrogance of Yakushkin, who was descended from a line of distinguished cavalry officers going far back into Czarist days.

The GRU senior management did indeed object to revealing their secret operations so, determined to exert his authority and rank, Chevalsky appealed personally to Primarkov as Commander-in-Chief of the Armed Forces. He was able to do this at a special meeting of the Defence Council, called because of the importance of the issue and the impasse between the heads of the KGB and GRU. This brought Primarkov into the picture, which Chevalsky would rather have avoided at that stage: until the doubt was settled the General Secretary had not needed to know.

As Chairman of the Defence Council, Primarkov, who always relished the opportunity to knock heads of warring factions together, ruled that the GRU must disclose all it knew in such a pressing circumstance.

The elegant, steely-eyed Yakushkin who, unusually for a modern Soviet officer, wore a small, trimmed moustache, did so with pride, claiming credit for a daring diversion, brilliantly executed by his men, to secure an item of equipment which could be of great value to the scientists at Sary Shagan. In Chevalsky's opinion the operation had been all too easy; it was almost certainly a deliberate dangle by

175

the CIA for which the GRU had fallen. Fortunately, as a result of the KGB's remarkable sources and his own quick action, any danger had been averted.

Under Primarkov's guidance, the Defence Council then fell to discussing possible options for action.

The whole suspect machine in its isolation area could be destroyed by fire, which would kill off any bacteria. That crude solution was quickly rejected when the Council learned that the Mockingbird had cost $121 million and was probably irreplaceable.

Alternatively, scientists could dismantle it and search each module for the bacterial cultures with which the machine had, allegedly, been 'booby-trapped'. The trouble with that answer was that the scientists would not know what they were looking for. If the bacteria had been inserted in the form of a dry powder they could be anywhere and everywhere in the three-dimensional maze of electronic components. The dismantling might have to be so thorough that the machine could be seriously damaged or effectively destroyed. Further, if the CIA 'dirty tricks' department had been on its usual form, the traps might be sprung and the bacteria disseminated in the dismantling process.

The doubt could be resolved, most simply and most safely, by completing the assembly of the Mockingbird within its container on the isolation site. It could then be started up and observers, wearing protective clothing, could see what happened. If all was well then the best result for the Soviet Union would have been achieved. It would be tragic if the simulator was destroyed or irreparably damaged when there had really been nothing wrong with it. That way the CIA would win.

Primarkov preferred the last solution mainly because, as he told the assembly, he could not believe that the Americans would have committed such an irresponsible act so close to the summit. With difficulty, Chevalsky stopped himself from pointing out that the GRU had been rather irresponsible in hijacking the Mockingbird at such a time.

The whole issue really depended on the credence to be given to the claim that silicon chips could be effectively destroyed by bacteria. Those Russian chemists and physicists who had already been approached had scoffed at the idea of such an inert substance as silicon being susceptible to attack but the bacteriologists had taken a more

176

cautious view, pointing out that, with genetic engineering, almost anything was possible.

In the usual way of committees, the Defence Council opted for delay, agreeing that no action of any kind should be taken until that basic question had been investigated further. There could be no harm in sounding out this Dr Payne, who had been mentioned in the anonymous letter to the KGB, so long as it could be done quickly and by a cut-out who had no direct connection with any Soviet service. Until then the Mockingbird simulator would remain safely and completely isolated.

As he left the meeting Chevalsky was deliberating on the inevitable question – what advantage the KGB could take of the extraordinary situation. The immediate tactical bonus, if the letter was correct, was to discredit the GRU and wipe off that air of superiority which Yakuskin and his officers always affected. But a strategic advantage of far greater significance was cooking in his mind, which was every bit as devious as Pilgrim's.

Chapter Twenty-five

Professor Leon Baranski, head of the Department of Microbiology at Warsaw University, known to all bacteriologists through the Baranski serum test, was a delightful old gentleman with a friendly face, topped with a mass of white hair standing out like an aurora borealis. Even as a student, in a country traditionally racked by international politics, he had been staunchly apolitical, claiming that his exacting subject left no time for such extraneous matters which, like bacteriology, were best left to experts in the field. His leadership of the Polish research into AIDS had brought him to the fringe of politics, because of the Government's involvement in that threat, but he had managed to remain aloof from politicians. He was, however, very much an internationalist in the field of science and nothing gave him greater pleasure than conferences at which he could meet colleagues from other countries and especially young ones whom he could encourage. He had been particularly kind to Wendy Payne when they had met at the international conference in Warsaw, her first visit to Poland, and they had remained in touch by letter, exchanging 'separates' as their researches came to publication.

Her youthful enthusiasm appealed to him and they had cemented their relationship during an AIDS conference in Beijing. Baranski had been to Beijing University before, knew the various professors there and introduced Wendy to them. There had been no Russians at the meeting. They were still averse to admitting that AIDS was much of a problem in the Soviet Union. Baranski had sat next to Wendy at a Chinese dinner where, as novices with chopsticks but determined to master them, they had shared great fun. They had also shared an unforgettable visit, provided as a conference sideline, to the Terracotta Army in Shanxi Province where, in subterranean vaults carved by 700,000 men working from 219 to 209 BC, stand the 7,000 sculpted warriors, horses and chariots guarding the tomb of China's first Emperor, Qin Shi Huang.

The professor had a good sense of humour and Wendy guessed

that he must have been very attractive to women when he was younger, if only because he could make them laugh. He had a habit of putting his hands on his knees and patting them when he was excited or amused and she found this a nice change from the old men who were inclined to put their hands on her knees.

Wendy was, therefore, most pleasantly surprised to receive a telephone call from the Embassy of the Polish Peoples Republic in London, inviting her to an evening reception for Professor Baranski in two days' time. In apologizing for the shortness of the notice, the Scientific Attaché at the Embassy explained that the Professor was night-stopping in London on an unexpected trip to the United States.

'I do hope that you can come because Professor Baranski specifically asked that you should be invited,' the Attaché explained. 'Obviously, he is very keen to meet you again. Try to get here promptly, 6.30 p.m., if you can because the Professor is likely to be very tired and will not want to stay too long.'

Wendy was delighted to accept. Not only could she look forward to meeting Baranski again but there would, no doubt, be opportunity to talk to other British scientists who would also have been invited. She had learned from Adrian that in the world of science, as in the world of business, whom one knew could be as important as what one knew.

It was a pleasant autumn evening when Wendy, suitably clad in a red suit, which suited her long blonde hair, blue eyes and trim figure, presented herself at 47 Portland Place, having made arrangements to spend the night with Joe. Being punctual by temperament, she was not too surprised to find that she was the first Briton to arrive, the rest of the small crowd already assembled being composed entirely of Soviet bloc diplomats and others posing as diplomats.

She was offered either wine or vodka from a tray and chose the wine. Introducing himself, the Scientific Attaché, who was in fact a career officer of the Polish Secret Service, the UB, explained why the reception had been a last-minute arrangement.

'Professor Baranski had originally intended to fly straight on to Los Angeles but, the journey being so long, his doctors insisted that he should have a night stop. He's not as young as he used to be,' the Attaché commented as Baranski entered the room.

'Ah, my dear young lady, how kind of you to come,' Baranski said in excellent English, kissing her hand. 'Let us sit over there and

179

have a talk before the others come. I can't stand too long these days.'

He motioned her towards a rather old-fashioned red settee. 'You are looking very pretty,' he said, noticing the special effort which she had made. 'What are you busy with now?' he asked as they sat down. 'I hear you've moved your laboratory.'

'Yes, how did you know that?' Wendy asked, flattered that the eminent gentleman should be so interested.

'I can't remember who told me but you know how news travels on the academic grapevine. Nothing stays secret for long.'

'We're all inveterate gossips, I suppose,' Wendy agreed.

'Why did you have to move?' the old man persisted.

'I needed a Category 4 lab and there wasn't one available in my building.'

'Ah, you're dealing with something rather more infectious?'

'Yes, it could be,' Wendy replied, without being more informative.

'Not to do with AIDS research?'

'No,' Wendy fenced. 'Something quite separate.'

'Virological?'

'No, bacteriological.'

Baranski felt the time had come for a more direct approach. 'It must be important for it to interfere with your AIDS programme. I heard it has something to do with silicosis. A possible treatment?'

'One fine day, maybe,' Wendy countered, appreciating that she was being pumped.

'I gather there's a possibility of an enzyme that might dissolve silica spicules. That would be a major breakthrough. It would make your name, you know.'

Wendy smiled but said nothing.

'What have you got that's certain so far? A bacterium that attacks silicates?'

'Something like that but it's very early days,' Wendy said, diffidently.

Baranski looked at her fixedly. 'Wouldn't it be exciting if it attacked elemental silicon?'

Wendy did not reply but her dismay was eloquent enough.

'When do you think you might be able to publish something?' the professor asked.

'Oh, not for a long time.'

'Why? Are the authorities forbidding you?'

'I'm not ready yet,' Wendy replied, dodging the question.

'Well, the sooner you can publish the better. You know we have a terrible problem with silicosis among our coalminers. Hundreds of tragic cases.' He shook his head sadly. 'And all hopeless at the moment.'

'I am working on it, Professor. As hard as I can.'

'But couldn't you publish a preliminary note? The more people who work on the problem the quicker it will be resolved.'

'I appreciate that but my senior colleague, Dr Allen, doesn't wish me to publish anything just yet.'

'Why not?' Baranski asked, almost sharply.

'He has his reasons,' Wendy replied, with a vague wave of her hand.

'I hope they are very good ones. You know the first loyalty of any scientist involved in medical research is to humanity. You also owe it to your profession to publish and make cultures of the strain available to other researchers with the minimum of delay.'

Baranski could see that Wendy was not relishing the sermon.

'You must excuse an old man if he gets carried away, my dear,' he said, patting her hand. 'Breakthroughs seem to be in short supply these days. I hope to hear good news from you soon. Indeed, so does the whole world!'

It appeared to Wendy that the professor had ended the conversation with some relief. She was perceptive: he had confirmed all that had been required of him during his briefing by the KGB in Warsaw and this had been recorded by the permanent microphone which, as he had been told, was fitted inside the back of the settee.

By that time, three or four more British scientists had drifted into the room to be presented. They were not late. They had not been invited to attend until 7.15.

Wendy stayed for the sandwiches and canapés, which were being passed round, and was chatted up by a couple of young Polish diplomats who apologized for the small number of people present, which they said was no doubt due to the shortness of the notice. She left shortly before 8 p.m. to join Joe at a favourite restaurant in Knightsbridge.

At 8.30 Baranski was whisked away to dine at the Polish residence in the company of two men with a special interest in his conversation. One was from the Polish intelligence service, the other from the

181

KGB. He was congratulated on his performance in carrying out instructions and required to keep his mouth shut but was given no other explanation.

While he did not relish the company, he was in no haste to get to bed for he did not really have such a strenuous journey to make in the morning.

Joe noticed that Wendy was unduly silent as she toyed with her spinach lasagne but eventually he induced her to unburden herself. Following the MI5 'Hachet-man' episode, she had already put him in the picture about her silicon work to some extent, and she was anxious to know if Joe thought that the Baranski meeting had been contrived and, if so, why and by whom. As Joe heard the details of Baranski's pointed questioning he was in no doubt that it had been contrived and that some aspect of Soviet Intelligence was behind it.

'They've got wind of your work, Wendy. What are you going to do?'

'I don't know. I suppose I should report it but it might get me into trouble and I went there in all innocence.'

'I know you did. I don't really know how to advise you. I guess you could tell Dr Allen and ask his advice.'

'I thought about that but he'd be bound to tell that MI5 woman and we'd have the spooks down again. I don't think I could stand another encounter with them without losing my temper. They can't do anything to me if I don't tell them.'

'I suppose not,' Joe said, but without conviction.

'Oh Joe, why am I mixed up in all this when I've done nothing wrong? There I was doing my own thing in the peace of my little lab and it's as though a bomb hit me. I'm quite disorientated.'

Later, as Joe cuddled her in bed, he did his best to console her.

'There's nothing you can do but stay quiet for a while and see how things develop. Just play it by ear. It will probably right itself. These things usually do.'

He was in a position to sympathize. He had started life as a journalist on a small newspaper and after moving into the Government information service, which had seemed so straightforward, had been dragged into the vortex of the secrets world himself.

But while Wendy remained confused about her duty, he had

already made up his mind where his lay. It was his duty to report the incident to Charlie Yates.

Charlie was all ears. Joe's information spelled only one thing – someone in Soviet bloc intelligence, in the GRU or KGB, had been informed about the whole silicon business and Baranski had been required to confirm it at first hand from Wendy Payne. The details were classic – the use of a surrogate agency, the UB, to distance the Soviets from the action. It was automatic that Charlie would have to put in a report to headquarters but he decided that, first, he would acquire local merit, personal satisfaction and, perhaps, some more information, by passing on what he had learned to Lesley Barrington-Fuller.

Lesley was in immediate agreement. 'Someone has leaked and it can't have been Dr Payne, otherwise the Poles would not have gone through all that rigmarole with the professor.'

'Could the Baranski episode have been a charade to cover Dr Payne as the source?' Charlie asked, thinking aloud. But he had already dismissed it as excessively elaborate.

'No, this was a confirmation exercise,' Lesley said, emphatically. 'I'd love to know who leaked but it could have been any one of a hundred people or more. What is of more immediate interest is what will the adversary do next?'

'I know what I'd do in his position,' Charlie said. 'Try to secure a sample of this goddamn clone. It's ten to one on that is what he will do.'

'So physical security will have to be tightened up all round,' Lesley observed.

'Right!'

Neither Lesley nor Charlie knew that the US Government was preparing to make a gift of the clone to the Soviets. Neither did the Soviets – as far as anyone knew.

Ross Pilgrim knew and within a few hours he also knew all about the Baranski episode – long before a copy of Charlie Yates' report reached his desk. Lesley had reported the matter in haste, and in person, to Sandy Pryce and, with his usual quick service, he was soon on the telephone.

Pilgrim instructed Al to study all the contingencies that came to mind. The first thing to do was to try to confirm that the Soviets really had got wind of the silicon business. There was no proof of it: just surmise. Baranski's questions might have been no more than scientific curiosity resulting from the gossip for which such people were notorious.

Al's first check was with the central CIA computer which stored and analysed all the details of passenger flights fed into it, continuously, by informants who supplied copies of the manifests from the world's major airports. It showed that Baranski had not travelled on to the United States but had returned directly to Warsaw.

He then consulted the National Security Agency concerning any sudden increase in the coded radio traffic between the headquarters of the GRU and KGB and their out-stations, following the meeting between Baranski and Dr Payne. He found it in both cases. So there could be little doubt that the Russians had got some wind of the British silicon development.

'That Payne woman is indeed a pain – in the ass,' Pilgrim remarked to Al on reading the reports of his inquiries. 'Why did she tell Baranski anything? Exactly how much did she tell him? What more might she tell him? Is she a fool or something else?'

He rubbed his chin as he checked Al's findings against Charlie Yates' report of his interrogation of Joe Malinowski. He did not buy Malinowski's explanation of Dr Payne's behaviour. Why should he? She was his mistress. In delicate and complex operations like Turbid, Pilgrim needed everything and everyone to be under his control and Wendy Payne wasn't. He couldn't have this silly girl fouling up Turbid when, as he had briefed Al with such smiling satisfaction, it seemed to be going so perfectly. The stakes were too high. With Turbid, timing was everything. And Turbid needed more time to run.

Chapter Twenty-six

On receipt of Baranski's tape-recorded evidence the GRU chief, Yakushkin, had to admit that the KGB's information could well be correct and that the Mockingbird should be left severely alone until further information became available. Operation Turbid had really been dead in the egg.

The anonymous writer's statement that Dr Wendy Payne might be helpful and the degree to which she had confirmed the silicon discovery caused the KGB to wonder if she might be part of an official CIA damage-limitation exercise, a hoax to prevent the use of the hijacked simulator. So Baranski was consulted again. He greatly doubted that she was or would be party to any kind of deception.

Chevalsky, who was taking the deepest personal interest because of a potential advantage of possibly historic significance which he had detected, urgently needed proof that the contents of the anonymous letter were genuine. He could not risk making his move until he was completely satisfied that they were.

The KGB Mission in the Soviet Embassy in London, which had been required to investigate Dr Payne, had reported on her association with Joe Malinowski. To Chevalsky's suspicious mind, the fact of Malinowski's presence in the US Embassy in Grosvenor Square was *prima facie* evidence of his involvement with the CIA – meaning that Wendy Payne could well be a tool under CIA control. So a close-check surveillance on Malinowski was ordered and his association with Charlie Yates came to light.

Because of the urgency, the KGB had no alternative but to show part of its hand to provoke a quick response which might be revealing. Baranski, who did his best to demur, was instructed to telephone Dr Adrian Allen, whom he knew, to fish for information as blatantly as would seem credible.

'I've just been told something about Wendy Payne which worries me,' he told Adrian. 'You know I'm fond of her. What is it all about?

Is she in some trouble with security? With the CIA? I gather that she is from the kind of questions I'm being asked here.'

'Who by?' Adrian asked.

'I'm not allowed to say but if I tell you that I could be in serious trouble for making this call you can guess who I mean.'

Adrian made a note. 'No. Wendy has nothing to do with the CIA or anything like that. She detests anything to do with secrecy or secret services.'

Doing his best to avoid betraying that he was reading from a list of questions which had been written for him, Baranski asked, 'Do you know anything about a man called Malinowski? I know that Wendy knows him. I remember seeing them together here, when he worked in Warsaw. I suppose he could be a CIA man. Do you think that Wendy could be under some kind of control by him?'

'Professor, I don't know anything about Mr Malinowski, but Wendy is the last person in the world to be under anybody's control. I can assure you of that.'

'Thank you, Dr Allen. You have reassured me.'

The KGB, which had monitored the conversation, was only marginally reassured. Its agents in London were instructed to devote greater resources to the Payne-Malinowski-Yates association and to report on any reactions with the utmost urgency.

Baranski had been heavily questioned about Wendy's Chinese connections but had been forbidden to mention that to Allen. The KGB was expressing great disquiet that the Chinese might learn the silicon secret. It was just the kind of weapon they would be adept at using in an emergency situation and there could be little doubt where their targets would be located. The London Mission's report to Chevalsky gave special prominence to Baranski's statement that Dr Payne had several friends among Chinese bacteriologists and was in regular touch with them.

When Adrian told Wendy of Baranski's concern, as the KGB had assumed that he would, she made a gesture of despair. 'What the hell have I got myself into? All I was doing was minding my own business and now I'm being accused of working for the CIA of all people.'

'I know. It's ridiculous.'

'Silly old fool, but I suppose he means well.'

Adrian was not so sure but did not say so.

'This is what comes of being mixed up with secrets,' Wendy said, despondently. 'I told you I would regret ever getting into this damnable business. It never pays to do anything against conscience.'

The KGB had also calculated that Wendy would lose little time in telling Malinowski about Baranski's strange call and he would immediately inform Yates about it. And Yates, no doubt, would inform MI5. The degree of agitation should, therefore, reveal itself in the increased volume of secret radio traffic, both American and British. Chevalsky set great store by the analysis of radio traffic, even when it could not be deciphered.

To the curious wonder of his close personal staff, Chevalsky, who was normally taciturn and unhurried, was vocal and impatient. This Mockingbird business could be a windfall which offered a key to all his problems and aspirations. And there it was sitting doing nothing in a remote corner at Sary Shagan.

Throughout his long service in the KGB he had modelled himself on a recent predecessor, Yuri Andropov, who had also been consumed with political ambition but had concealed it by his mastery of patient calculation. The KGB suited Chevalsky's temperament but Andropov might not be the only Chairman of it to reach higher and grasp the Soviet leadership. Of course, it went without saying that if events developed as Chevalsky hoped, his personal interests would be secondary to those of the Soviet state and the Communist Party.

So much was at stake that he had to be sure of his information and he did not have much faith in the London Mission to come up with the convincing collateral evidence he needed. In fact, he did not have much faith or trust in anybody. Time was too short to wait for further windfalls. They did not occur that often. There was some further action he could take himself, a provocation which would give him some incidental personal pleasure.

He called in the senior member of his close entourage. 'Find out the name of the GRU man who heads the military equipment acquisition programme in New York and see what we have on him in our records. Find out all that you can about him. You have one hour to do it.'

When the results of that inquiry were rushed to his desk, Chevalsky read them with some satisfaction. It was the man's habit of jogging alone round the streets of Manhattan, sometimes at night, which set his antennae quivering. Very strange behaviour for a full colonel! The KGB chief, who was unconcerned by his flabbiness, did not indulge in physical exercise. He was happiest sitting at his desk with all the buttons at his fingertips.

The light covering of snow crunched under Yakushkin's black jack-boots as the GRU chief, in the winter uniform of a four-star Army general, climbed into his car outside his headquarters on the edge of Khodinka airfield. Yakushkin was getting too old to enjoy snow but the cold, which could be guaranteed to increase steadily over the weeks and months ahead, would end the street demonstrations. A long succession of Russian leaders had reason to be grateful for the harsh conditions imposed by General Winter.

The distance to Chevalsky's office to which he had been invited – summoned would have been more accurate – was short and Yakush-kin had not smoked much of his cigarette before the car swung into Dzerzhinsky Square, dominated by the statue on a high, columnar plinth of the founder of what had become the KGB.

While nobody was more conscious of the need for secrecy and deception in the military sphere, Yakushkin had never been able to stomach the savage way the KGB had been used as a secret police force to spy upon, deceive and coerce the Soviet people. From Dzerzhinsky onwards, the KGB chiefs had been ruthless sadists and the 'Horseman' seemed to be no exception. The Horseman! The image of that rather wooden figure astride a charger was ludicrous. Whatever it was that Chevalsky wanted, the encounter was not likely to be pleasant. Yakushkin guessed that it must be about the Mockingbird business but, having been fully briefed about it, was confident he could cope with any queries.

A senior officer was waiting for Yakushkin; he whipped up a smart salute and escorted him to the KGB Chairman's office, which was on the third floor of the extended ornate, ochre-coloured building which had once housed the Lubyanka Prison. It was a forbidding room, plain, with stark lights and bullet-proof windows which could be covered by steel shutters at the press of a button. Chevalsky was seated at the grandiose desk. He rose and greeted his GRU counterpart who, having shed his round, cossack-style hat and double-breasted greatcoat in the outer office, sat on the appointed chair, which was lower than Chevalsky's.

'Do you mind if I smoke?' Yakushkin asked.

'Not at all.'

Chevalsky watched his visitor fix a cigarette into an old gold and amber holder, a habit which was as distastefully bourgeois to him as the atavistic moustache, and looked for any sign of tremor in his hands. There were none. Then he pushed across the controversial CIA letter, which Yakushkin had been told about but not allowed to see. He read it rapidly, too rapidly in the KGB man's view; he had studied its every word a score of times, looking for possible leads and inspiration.

'If that letter is genuine, the GRU has been responsible for importing a potentially disastrous Trojan horse,' Chevalsky alleged.

'If it is true, which I doubt,' Yakushkin replied, dismissively.

'I think that your man in charge of the acquisition programme in New York must have been involved in getting that Mockingbird here. He could not have been so incompetent as not to know about it. Who is your head man there?'

'Colonel Ivashutin.'

'Well, be so good as to get him back here. He has a lot of questions to answer.'

Yakushkin's insistence that Ivashutin had not been personally involved in the diversion had no impact on Chevalsky.

'Please get him back immediately! We need his opinion about whether this thing is a plant.'

'But he knows nothing about it, comrade. It was all done from this end. I've looked at all the papers. We employed a private diverter, a Swiss. We didn't tell Ivashutin because he had no need to know. He still has no need to know.'

'Did he know it was going to happen?'

'He had advised us, as a matter of routine, that the Mockingbird simulator was going to be exported to West Germany, but only because he had read it in the American newspapers and it was his duty to report it.'

'Get him back, and quickly,' Chevalsky persisted. 'Then we'll find out just what he knows and doesn't know and when he first knew it. I'd like to have him questioned at length.'

'I would remind you that he is a close relative of our most illustrious commander, General Peter Ivashutin.'

'Do you remember your traitor, Penkovsky?' Chevalsky asked with obvious relish. 'Wasn't he closely related to a general?'

The GRU chief did not respond. He recalled that, following the proof of Penkovsky's treachery, the head of the GRU had been dismissed in disgrace.

As Army generals, the two chiefs were of similar military status but though Chevalsky was only a *nomenklatura* general with no soldierly experience, as a full member of the Politburo and KGB Chairman he heavily outranked his visitor. On paper, Yakushkin had no political clout and that was what counted in the Soviet hierarchy. Grudgingly, he agreed to order his man back to Moscow.

'Tell him to bring his family with him,' Chevalsky added, as though it was an afterthought. 'He might be here for some time and I don't want to penalize them.'

Yakushkin was not taken in by the apparent solicitude. He was well aware of the KGB's habit of leaning on the wife of a man who might be reluctant to talk.

On the drive back to his office the GRU chief saw a way of preserving appearances. He was not going to appear to his staff to be obeying orders from the KGB. To hell with that! He was a soldier and he answered only to the Chief of the General Staff. Colonel Ivashutin would be recalled properly – for promotion. That would be the most eloquent way of letting that thug, Chevalsky, know what he thought of his suspicions about one of his best and most loyal men.

In fact it was exactly what Chevalsky had wanted him to do. The KGB had its own word for a willie – *peshka*, the Russian for a pawn in chess. Like most of the military generals, Yakushkin was not very bright in Chevalsky's opinion. Making a *peshka* out of him should not be difficult and would be immensely satisfying.

As for the Chief of the General Staff, Yakushkin would be in the discard if it came to a showdown with Chevalsky. A firm alliance between the KGB and the Army was essential to the interests of both.

Immediately Yakushkin had left his office, Chevalsky called in his chief aide. 'Instruct our New York men to make the surveillance on Ivashutin a bit obvious, but not too obvious,' he ordered.

Like the rest of his close staff, the aide could not quite understand why he was so insistent about Ivashutin's return and was attaching such importance to it. 'Why do you wish them to do that?' he asked.

'I want him to bolt.'

Seeing his aide's astonishment, Chevalsky explained, 'If there is nothing wrong with that Mockingbird equipment he'll come here like a shot for his share of the glory in acquiring it. If he daren't come, because he knows it's infected, he'll jump, won't he? Then we'll know. Really know.'

As the aide nodded his understanding, Chevalsky added, 'I don't usually encourage defectors but he's not one of ours, is he?'

It would be no skin off the KGB's nose if the GRU was disgraced, and Yakushkin along with it. Chevalsky permitted himself a thin smile at the prospect. Usually he was so humourless that Primarkov had said that he was incapable of pulling anybody's leg without breaking it.

Chapter Twenty-seven

As Ivashutin was officially a member of the United Nations Mission, the Aquarium was required to operate through the Soviet Ambassador to the UN, who was not one to risk offending either the GRU or the KGB.

'You are being recalled to Moscow,' the Ambassador told him.

'Any idea why, Ambassador?' Ivashutin asked, trying to look unconcerned.

'None whatever. Consultations? Promotion, perhaps? You have been here three years now. Your time's about up anyway.'

Ivashutin did his best to look happy. 'It will be good to get back. My wife is very homesick and it's time my children saw some more of their own country and their friends.'

The Ambassador, who liked and admired the GRU man, cordially agreed.

'How long have I got to pack up?'

'Just a couple of days. They seem to want you right away. I wouldn't keep them waiting, if I were you. I gather that your replacement will soon be on the way.'

'Who is he?' Ivashutin asked.

'I don't know yet. You know the Aquarium. They don't tell anybody much.'

'But it will take me at least a couple of weeks to hand over to him. I have projects in progress. There are secret sources and contacts I'll have to introduce him to, personally . . . three years of effort . . . we can't just throw that away. It can only be done on a personal basis. It's against the rules to leave written instruction about such secret matters.'

'OK, I've given you the message and you are the expert. I'll let Moscow know that you say you'll be home within two weeks. But don't make it any longer. And I'd book a flight now, if I were you.

Ivashutin immediately asked his clerk to book a flight for himself and his family a fortnight hence and cabled the Aquarium to that effect.

There was to be no complaint from Moscow about the delay. The GRU chiefs at the Aquarium assured the KGB that, in the essential interests of the service, Colonel Ivashutin did indeed need two weeks' notice and would report in person at the end of that time. Chevalsky affected to be angrily disappointed but was only more suspicious – and more excited.

On the following day and by the usual process, Pilgrim received Brown Derby's message that there was something urgent in the dead-drop in current use. This process, which had been effective for so long, was simplicity itself.

Over the years, the CIA had acquired most of the floors of a large building close to the UN complex through a chain of nominees. The ground floor was taken up by a small arcade of shops, one being a flower shop, the other a tour operator's bureau. Both catered for the UN staff as well as for the many residents in what had become a fashionable area. The Soviet bloc countries, in particular, used flowers extensively as a means of paying compliments and social debts – to men as well as to women. And there were always delegates, their families and visiting officials who wished to take advantage of tours of various parts of the United States. Both businesses flourished and both were CIA 'proprietaries', as was most of the rest of the building.

The upper floors, ostensibly let to lawyers and property companies, formed a CIA counter-intelligence centre, including the staff and apparatus involved in movements analysis. This was the recording and timing of the movements of members of UN missions, mainly of the Soviet bloc, which enabled the CIA to decide which were genuinely employed in UN desk jobs and which were using them as cover for outside activities. The office had a direct link with central computers at Langley and was in constant touch with cars and what looked like taxis parked in the streets and on parking lots so that suspects could be followed. Some of the windows could be used for binocular and photographic surveillance.

That was how Peter Ivashutin, alias Vinogradski, had been detected as the chief techno-bandit and had then been set up, with incriminating pictures, to secure his recruitment as 'Brown Derby'. His habit of emerging from the staff entrance on East 43rd Street for a lunchtime

193

or early evening jog, even in snow, and returning down 42nd Street offered an easy system of communication. He always wore a bright red headband and if he had deposited a message in a dead-drop he simply adjusted it as he passed the front of the flower shop. If there was a message in a dead-drop for him, a large, green Chinese vase in the shape of a fish with a gaping mouth filled with flowers was lodged in the front of the window display.

Pilgrim knew what to expect as soon as he saw the minuscule message from the dead-drop which Al had emptied, for it consisted of one set of numbers repeated three times. When deciphered it read 'Hat-check, Hat-check, Hat-check', which was a prearranged signal that the time had come for Brown Derby to check in. The number of times the word was repeated was an indication of the urgency and three was maximum.

Ivashutin had noticed that he and his family were being followed and that his apartment in the mid-Manhattan Soviet Mission building on East 67th Street was being watched.

The loss of such an asset was a body blow but that was the way of the counter-intelligence world. Nothing was more dynamic and no asset lasted very long. Casualties had to be taken philosophically and any possible advantage seized.

Smart action was needed to get Brown Derby and his family out to a safe place. The GRU had not given up the assassination of traitors on whom the death sentence had been passed, as it undoubtedly would be on Ivashutin once he had disappeared. The boast of Soviet Intelligence that its avenging arm was longer than the traitor's leg was well-founded.

'I fear it's bad news from Brown Derby,' Pilgrim announced to Al, after he had decoded the message.

'Meaning what, sir?'

'Meaning it looks like he'll have to jump. I want you to handle it, Al.'

As always, Pilgrim had a contingency plan in the pipeline and he decided to put it into immediate effect.

With Brown Derby almost certainly under heavy surveillance he would not be able to empty any more dead-drops but there was no need for that. As Ivashutin jogged through mid-town Manhattan in the early November air, steam was rising from the sewer manholes, reminding him of the anti-American joke, which always went down so well in Moscow – that it was the Red Indians smoking in their reservations. As always, he glanced at the flower shop window and there was the green Chinese vase, filled with gladioli, but placed in a corner pointing towards the tour operator's office across the arcade, where it had never been before.

As a result of standing instructions, Ivashutin knew exactly what to do. He walked into the office to book a weekend tour for himself and his family to the Florida Disney World, something which he had promised his children that he would do before they left America. Being interested in advanced technology, he himself had been keen to see that part of the huge exhibition called Tomorrow's World.

When he gave his name as Vinogradski he was dealt with by an efficient and attractive middle-aged woman, who took all particulars and was so caring that she insisted on delivering the tickets, vouchers and brochures personally to him at the UN headquarters.

There, in the visitor's lobby of the Assembly Building, she explained where to catch the bus which would take them to La Guardia Airport for the two and a half hour flight to Orlando International Airport, and described the hotel arrangements and other details. She made no mention of a special envelope which Al Quest, a personal friend, had given her to include in the bundle of documents. But she did tell her customer, laughingly with a wagging finger, not to open the packet of Mickey Mouse candies, which were very strictly for the children to eat in Disneyland.

Ivashutin had no certain knowledge how his wife, to whom he was devoted, would react to his plan to defect: she might not want to join him for she had always looked forward to returning home to Moscow and to the dacha in the birch woods. He had never taken her into his confidence about his work and had managed to keep his fears from her. One of his UN predecessors, Shevchenko, had been forced to ditch his wife when he had defected. But the CIA's neat solution should solve that difficulty – as long as it worked.

The two young children talked excitedly as they pored over the illustrated leaflets of Disney World's Magic Kingdom – 'a place where dreams really do come true', with Cinderella's Castle and the Haunted Mansion, a house of 'ghosts, ghouls and goblins'. As their father leafed through the brochure of Tomorrow's World, the complex of

195

buildings and exhibitions in an area called Epcott, it seemed aptly named. Tomorrow's World was going to be very different for him and his family.

Chapter Twenty-eight

Ivashutin's colleagues, with whom both he and his wife were popular, were envious rather than surprised when he informed them about the tour. On Pilgrim's instructions, he had occasionally told them that he was being badgered by his children to take them to Florida's Disney World. The youngsters had heard so much about the Magic Kingdom from other children and on television.

His KGB watchers, who knew nothing of Chevalsky's purpose, were perturbed when they heard of his plans but there was little they could do about it in view of his rank, his international position in the UN and the fact that they had been warned not to spook him too obviously. Their concern was slightly reduced when, again on Pilgrim's previous instruction, Ivashutin talked another Russian couple and their child into joining the same tour group. It all seemed very normal. Nevertheless the KGB made arrangements to tail them all.

The surveillance men had no particular reason for suspicion as they picked up the group when it landed at Orlando and followed the bus, which took the tourists to their hotel at the Walt Disney World Resort, some twenty miles away.

After the signing-in formalities, the tourists unpacked in their rooms, rested and took lunch. They were then bussed to the Magic Kingdom for the first leg of the tour. They followed the woman guide, who was carrying a raised and gaily-coloured parasol, through Liberty Square past Cinderella's Castle and watched the children's encounter with Mickey Mouse, Minnie, Donald Duck and their other favourites.

The KGB tailers kept a close eye on the Ivashutins but found it more convenient to wait outside while the tour boarded the mini-vehicles taking them through the African jungle, the Red Indian country and other adventures on the hundred acres of the Magic Kingdom, though they did accompany them on the Big Thunder Mountain Railroad, a simulation of Gold Rush days.

Ivashutin, whose professional eye had picked up the tailers at the airport, was relieved to see that they did not follow the family into the Haunted Mansion, which the younger children affected to enter with some noisy trepidation, but decided to lounge outside in the sunshine awaiting the family's emergence.

When the Mansion's forbidding oak doors swung open, a small group, including the family, was let in by a villainous looking butler and motioned, through a dark, cobwebbed hall, into a room where a disembodied voice challenged them to find an exit. Eventually an exit did appear and, at that moment, Ivashutin affected to remember the packet of Mickey Mouse candies. He popped one into the mouth of each of his children.

Within a few seconds the tour was piling into black, hooded carriages which would take them slowly through the Mansion's many rooms and corridors where, they were promised, nine hundred and ninety-nine ghosts would manifest themselves. The promise was fulfilled; transparent phantoms conjured up by laser beams, holographs and mirrors cavorted with abandon as though recently risen from their graves.

The Ivashutin children were watching out for the ghost of a top-hatted man playing an organ, which they had seen in the brochure. 'There he is,' one of them cried as they spotted him urging on the dancers in the haunted ballroom.

It was the last ghost in which they had any interest because, seconds later, when they were about halfway through the Mansion, both children began to be violently sick. Not by chance, there were helpers on hand to get them and their parents out of their carriages and through a service door down into one of the large underground tunnels housing the technical equipment which produced and operated the ghosts, while the rest of the tour wound on. It was the first time that Al had ever had the opportunity to speak to Brown Derby.

From there the two parents and their still retching children were ushered through further rooms and tunnels, used by the Disney World staff, to the open air some distance from the Mansion. A closed vehicle was waiting for them.

The tour guide, who had mothered the rest of her flock together outside the exit from the Mansion, waited for the casualties to emerge but was quickly assured that the Vinogradski family would be joining them back at the hotel when the children had recovered from the effects of 'something they must have eaten'. She was not dismayed: such events were common enough, especially with children. The KGB men, however, were near-frantic, especially when the family failed to return to the hotel hours later.

The KGB was not in evidence later that evening when a helicopter arrived to conduct Ivashutin and his family, accompanied by Al, to a safe location in Virginia – a large country house with extensive grounds, set in rolling country with a good view around and surrounded by a high wooden fence. The tour guide had been told that the Ivashutins had decided to opt out and return privately to New York, in case the children had contracted some infection.

Recovered from their brief sickness, the children were thrilled with the helicopter ride but Ivashutin's wife, who was normally supportive of everything he did, was terrified. She had been given no warning and it was not easy for her husband to convince her that his life was in danger if he returned to Moscow because he was being unfairly accused of being a traitor to cover for someone else's stupidity. He resolutely denied that he was any such thing.

'You know that I would never betray my country,' he assured her above the noise of the helicopter blades. 'General Yakushkin knows that an Ivashutin could never be a traitor. I am the victim of the KGB who are using me to discredit the GRU.'

While completely confused, she at least appreciated his fears, having been told in the past about the crematorium. She had always been given to understand that, in the GRU, to be simply under the shadow of suspicion of treachery could be fatal.

Sympathetically, Ivashutin promised his wife that, once the danger had passed and the frame-up had been exposed, it would be possible for them to return to Russia in full safety and in honour. 'It should only be a short time, my darling,' he said assertively, holding both her hands. 'Friends in high places are working on my behalf, including General Yakushkin.' Meanwhile, he explained, they would all have to be grateful to the CIA for saving them from the KGB, which had been following them, even in Disney World, to take him away by force. This was all confirmed to her by Al as best he could, mainly with gestures, since she understood little English, having spent almost all her free time with the wives of Soviet colleagues. His pleasant manner and appearance helped to calm her fears for he was very different from her concept of a CIA thug.

She remained confused but she trusted her husband and there was nothing she could do but defer to him, as she always had. She knew how dedicated he was to his career and that he would never have taken such a step without overwhelming necessity.

Once the family was safely installed, President Rockwell had to be told of the defection and agreed with his advisers that news of it should be withheld from the media until after the summit, not that the CIA had any wish to release it. Meanwhile, formal proceedings were put in hand, secretly, to accept Ivashutin's request for political asylum.

As both Ivashutin and Pilgrim had anticipated, the Soviet Mission reacted vigorously to the family's disappearance, being in no doubt as to what had happened. The Ambassador was instructed to seek no publicity but to make the strongest private protest to the State Department at the kidnapping of a prominent Soviet official and his family. When he did so, the State Department denied all knowledge of the event.

The Soviets went through the motions of demanding access to their man to assure themselves that he had not been coerced. This would have to be granted eventually but it could be delayed – until after the summit, if possible. The State Department promised to make full inquiries and, most unusually, the Soviet officials accepted the delay with the minimum of fuss. The Kremlin did not want to give the Americans the public kudos of a major defection prior to the summit.

In Moscow the most immediate effect of the defection was to convince Chevalsky that Ivashutin had been deeply involved in the plot to plant the infected simulator on Sary Shagan and that there could no longer be any doubt about the KGB's interpretation of events. The simulator would stay where it was and serve the purpose he had so ingeniously devised for it.

The KGB Mission in New York had done exactly what he had hoped but he saw to it that it received severe censure for allowing Ivashutin to escape. Never one to pay much attention to staff relations, Chevalsky was not in the habit of thanking his minions for doing the duty for which they were paid. As he put it in his earthy, peasant style, 'You don't thank anyone for putting the paper in the lavatory: you just raise hell if it's not there.'

As a matter of routine, Pilgrim had to have Brown Derby subjected to intense debriefing, including polygraph tests, to ensure that he was not a false defector – a GRU plant. There was always Fedora to remember, a Soviet intelligence officer who had also been code-named after a hat.

Fedora had fed the FBI with so-called intelligence for more than ten years, receiving valuable chicken-feed in return to keep him going, and then had suddenly returned to Russia. There was no doubt that Fedora had been a phoney planted on the FBI, who had 'bought' him in the biggest possible way. Ever since that debacle, Pilgrim had been in the habit of warning his aides, 'Remember Fedora! You can never be entirely sure about a Soviet defector.'

He had savoured a certain sweetness from the Fedora affair, though. It had cut the self-righteous FBI chief, J. Edgar Hoover, down to size. He had been so taken in by Fedora that he had submitted much of the defector's information direct to the White House as it came in. God knows what effects on policy it had exerted there, and years later it had turned out to be bullshitsky! What a *peshka* the KGB had made of Hoover! Since then, the unwitting transfer of false information to another Government department had become known, in Pilgrim's vocabulary, as 'doing a Hoover'. It was one thing to hoodwink another department deliberately in the interests of the Agency but doing a Hoover was one of the worst crimes in the book.

The FBI had enjoyed a later laugh when the wretched Yurchenko – the KGB man nurtured by the CIA and then trumpeted as a 'big fish', one of the most important defectors ever – re-defected to Moscow amid worldwide publicity, falsely claiming he had been kidnapped, drugged and beaten up by CIA men.

By definition, defectors were traitors with divided loyalties and you could never be sure where that dividing line was drawn. With Ivashutin, though, the preponderance of probabilities seemed to be overwhelming. Only Pilgrim knew how much the CIA had learned from him. He had fed it into the system over the years as information from 'sources with good access'. Still, someone had to play the devil's advocate with any defector of such seniority, and Pilgrim detailed his best interrogator to put Ivashutin through all the hoops – the doubts, the allegations, the insults, the threats. He was confident that the Russian would negotiate them faultlessly.

Chapter Twenty-nine

Chevalsky wasted no time in exchanging a few words with General Yakushkin.

'I see that New York man of yours has gone missing. With his family. Very interesting, General.'

Yakushkin seemed surprisingly composed. 'I'm afraid it happens, comrade. It's happened to plenty of your people. There must be something about the air in America. Remember your fellow, Yurchenko?'

'Ah, but he had second thoughts and came home, didn't he?'

'Well, you never know, maybe Ivashutin will.'

'That'll be the day,' Chevalsky scoffed, the corners of his mouth turning down even more than usual.

Having no cards to play, the GRU chief had no option but to bluff and to do so lamely. At least, that was how Chevalsky interpreted the exchange.

There was no disagreement between them, however, on the immediate action which should be taken in case the Mockingbird was infected, as the CIA letter had warned. Some advantage had to be seized from the situation and it could be considerable. Counter-deception was the correct response and Chevalsky directed his best resources in that field to inflicting it. As a result, Pilgrim's sneaky and his human intelligence sources in Moscow were subjected to the heaviest and most concentrated load of bullshitsky ever to descend on the CIA.

A scenario was drawn up by the most experienced operators from the KGB's disinformation department to induce the Americans to believe that the Soviet Star Wars programme had been set back by many months when, in fact, the interference had been marginal. The two most senior of the scientists who had been involved with the Mockingbird were flown to Moscow to assist.

Professional actors on the KGB payroll were withdrawn from whatever normal work they were engaged in and pressed into the service. Cast as scientists and other staff at Sary Shagan, they were scripted and rehearsed to give the impression that the Mockingbird had been started up with devastating effect on the whole research programme. Working round the clock, the performances had been recorded on a series of tapes in a hangar on Khodinka airfield, where most of the background noises could be simulated. These included a re-run of the decontamination exercises, which had actually been carried out at the Sary Shagan establishment. Those sounds which could not be exactly simulated were recorded at Sary Shagan and inserted into the tapes.

The result was compelling disinformation of the highest quality. From the time that the scientists had been called out of the Sary Shagan hangar in silence, the sneaky had relayed nothing but undiluted misinformation from tapes played to the Mockingbird in its splendid isolation in a remote area of the establishment. It ended only when it was time for the sneaky to fall silent in accordance with the programme.

When analysed, the intermittent sneaky reports received by Pilgrim pointed to a catastrophic breakdown of the assembled simulator within two days of testing. The deeply disappointed scientists had gone through all the fault-finding procedures prescribed in the manual without success. There seemed to be not one fault but dozens in every major part of the apparatus. The reports indicated that it had not taken the scientists long to discover that the trouble was in the silicon chips themselves and that the cause was something that was physically eating them.

From his service in Moscow, Pilgrim's Russian was good enough for him to translate some of the curses expressed by the Soviet staff though prodigious efforts by his colleagues to match Oleg Ivanovich, Boris Andreievich, Sergei Sergeievich and the rest with known scientists met with no success.

The general panic indicated that the whole Sary Shagan area had been shut down with everyone terrified that the silicon infection might spread. American reconnaissance satellites confirmed that work there seemed to be at a standstill. There was also some collateral feedback from a CIA human source in Moscow indicating that the KGB and GRU had been consulted about site security at Sary Shagan and that a delegation of senior officers from both organizations had been sent down in a hurry. It looked as though the entire Soviet Star

Wars programme, at its main centre, might be closed down for months.

When Butch asked for the latest news Pilgrim had to dissimulate. 'It's rather disappointing at the moment. Having assembled the Mockingbird they seem to be incapable of using it.'

'The usual teething troubles, I suppose,' Butch suggested.

'I guess so. They should resolve them eventually. Then we'll be back in business.'

Pilgrim was able to be rather more forthcoming with Al who, alone among his staff, had needed to know something about every aspect of Operation Turbid. 'They've certainly bought it,' he confided, his eyes sparkling. 'And in the biggest possible way. It's just beautiful, Al. Really beautiful! There's no other word for it. And the great joy is that they are absolutely powerless to do anything about it. How the hell can they complain when they brought it on themselves by hijacking the Mockingbird?'

Al seemed puzzled rather than pleased but then he never did say much.

'What have you told the Department of Defense, sir?' he asked.

'Nothing yet – too early. I gather from a human intelligence source that there's been one hell of a row about it between the KGB and the GRU. And that's always good for business.'

Working together, Chevalsky and Yakushkin also obliged with all the collateral evidence they reasoned Pilgrim would anticipate. They delayed any scheduled laser-beam or particle-beam experiments when American reconnaissance satellites were known to be in visual range of the establishment. Sary Shagan had its own satellite-tracking station for its work on anti-satellite weapons so there had been no difficulty in suspending visible work, by rolling back equipment into hangars, during the transit of the American robot spies. Similar precautions were taken with respect to US satellites specializing in picking up sound or radar emissions. So, by the judicious retiming of shifts, the work had progressed much as usual.

The Sary Shagan scientists, except for those flown to Moscow, were never put into the picture concerning their strange orders and dutifully obeyed them without asking why, though they wondered among themselves and could be in no doubt that they were connected in some way with the Mockingbird, which had been spirited away from them so mysteriously. There was no danger that the actors who had made the tapes would gossip, save, perhaps, among themselves. *Glasnost* or no *glasnost* you kept your mouth shut when you worked for the KGB – if you were wise.

Relevant verbal disinformation was put around Moscow where the CIA duly picked it up. The military commandant of Sary Shagan was seen twice in Dzerzhinsky Square by a CIA spotter, who operated there regularly. He was in uniform carrying a briefcase and had obviously been called there for urgent discussions with he KGB. The outward flight of the delegation of KGB and GRU officers to Sary Shagan was judiciously leaked, as was its return with the two senior scientists.

The volume of radio traffic going out to KGB and GRU agents in the UN and the Soviet Consulate in New York was deliberately increased, as it also was to the major signals station on the roof of the Riverdale complex, the seventeen-storey Soviet residential building in the Bronx. The same was happening with the signals post on the roof of the Soviet Consulate in San Francisco, close to Silicon Valley, whence the Mockingbird had originated. It was all in one-time pad code but, had it been translatable, it would have been seen to be nothing more than nonsense, what the intelligence world called 'cabbages and kings'.

The CIA movements analysis men were induced to note a substantial increase in the activity of KGB and GRU agents operating out of the UN building, with all manner of fringe operatives being obviously pressed into the service of saturating the CIA and FBI defences. The same occurred in Silicon Valley.

When Pilgrim consulted Sandy Pryce in general terms, but with no mention of Operation Turbid, he discovered that similar symptoms were being observed in Britain. The electronics array on the roof of the Soviet Embassy in London had been unusually active. For many years a tunnel driven under the Embassy had enabled MI5 to listen to the chatter of the cipher machines there but the Russians had long been aware of it and had ensured that the volume was suitably increased.

'Something's up,' Sandy observed sagely. 'Any idea what it is?'

'Not a clue,' Pilgrim lied.

The analysis of the feedback information to Moscow continued to give Chevalsky intense satisfaction. Pilgrim and his associates appeared to be delighted with the mythical damage they had inflicted which, surely, was final proof that the Mockingbird was infected, as the anonymous CIA informant had advised. All doubt evaporated. But he would not be having the Mockingbird destroyed. It had been intruded into the Soviet Union as a weapon and that was just what it was going to be. He could use it to strike now – and not just to wound.

Chapter Thirty

After her meeting with Professor Baranski, Wendy expected an encounter with MI5 and she soon found herself confronted in Adrian's office by Lesley.

'I understand that you had a conversation with Professor Leon Baranski, recently; have you any reason to think that he might have been trying to interrogate you about your silicon discovery?' Lesley asked.

'Yes. He seemed to have heard about it somehow – not through me I assure you. He was interested in the medical possibilities for silicosis.'

'Did it occur to you that he might have been pumping you on behalf of Soviet bloc intelligence?'

'Do you mean the KGB?'

'Something like that.'

'I don't know. He was just passing through London on his way to the United States and wanted to meet a few friends.'

'I think you should know that he was not going to the United States, Dr Payne. He returned to Warsaw on the following morning. He made a special visit to London just to see and talk to you. We are certain of that. He was sent by Soviet Intelligence to check something they had heard about your silicon discovery.'

'I find it hard to believe that he would do that.'

'One never knows what people will do when they are under pressure, Dr Payne. And the Soviets are very ruthless. Did the professor ask you to send him a sample of the clone?'

'No, and I wouldn't have done so if he had asked.'

'But would you have reported it if he had asked you?'

'Yes, I think I would have told Dr Allen.'

'But you didn't tell him about Professor Baranski's visit?'

'I had no reason to,' Wendy said wearily. 'It all seemed so innocent.'

She then recounted everything she could remember about the conversation with Baranski, and Lesley was left in no doubt about its purpose.

'Have you any idea how Soviet bloc Intelligence could have heard of your discovery?'

'No. Except that a lot of people in the Ministry of Defence know about it.'

'I know it wasn't you who leaked it to the Soviet bloc,' Lesley assured Wendy. 'But could it have been your friend Mr Malinowski? He is of Polish origin.'

Wendy bridled. 'Joe would never do anything to hurt America.'

Lesley shrugged. 'If there are any further approaches from Professor Baranski or anyone else, will you let me know? It is important. Dr Allen has my telephone number.'

Wendy agreed that she would, but without enthusiasm.

'There is just one other question, Dr Payne. Did the professor say anything about your mutual Chinese friends when you had your chat?'

Wendy thought back. 'I don't think so. He had no reason to.'

'And do you happen to have written to any of your Chinese friends recently?'

'I haven't told any of them anything about the silicon research, if that is what you mean.'

Her interrogator seemed satisfied.

When Sir William Brook, the Chief Scientist, heard that MI5 was still pursuing the leak, he thought that it was a pity that they did not have better things to do. He had just been informed that all the information about the clone, and wet cultures of it, were going to be being passed to the Soviets by the US State Department with the full agreement of the British Foreign Office. He telephoned to inform Lesley, who had not heard of the development. She was shocked by it and immediately passed the news to Sandy Pryce.

'They might have let us know,' Pryce remarked glumly to Lesley. 'I'm sorry you've been wasting your time. Anyway, it gets the issue off our plate. Don't spend any more effort on it.'

Pryce wondered if Pilgrim had known in advance about this extraordinary decision by the politicians and had avoided telling him.

In the interim, Charlie Yates had taken the precaution of having Joe's flat swept. They found the two MI5 bugs hidden in lightplugs, one by the bedside. Charlie, who felt sure that it had been an MI5 operation, had the satisfaction of telling Lesley about it by suggesting that they might have been planted by the KGB.

'It's all academic now, but what did you get out of Dr Payne when you saw her?' Charlie asked.

Lesley gave him the guts of her interview. 'She's no problem,' she pronounced, with a dismissive wave of the hand. 'Except in so far as she almost certainly leaks to your man, Malinowski. Wagging tongue pillow-talk, I suppose. Nothing sinister.'

Her analysis of the tapes recorded by the MI5 bugs had worried her for a while because Wendy seemed to have a grudge against society – one of the major causes of treacherous behaviour, according to her husband's studies. Typical of many remarks to Joe was: 'The sleep of the just is a romantic myth – the just shouldn't be able to sleep for worrying about injustice. It's the unjust who sleep soundly because they don't give a damn.' When Paul was asked his opinion he replied, 'People who go through life expecting social justice invariably end up with a chip on their shoulder.' But Lesley concluded that Wendy's trite comments were little more than attempts at clever repartee by a girl who, while ingenious in her work, was immature in other ways.

For reasons of which he was kept ignorant, Charlie Yates was instructed by Pilgrim to lean on Malinowski to discover all he could about Wendy Payne, particularly about her political beliefs and any left-wing friends. Though Joe was not in love with Wendy and there was no question of any permanent relationship, he put up token resistance but, under Yates' pressure he agreed, in the interests of his career, to find out if there had been anything more to the Baranski episode. Charlie had suggested a possible opening for him in the CIA and, while entertaining serious doubts about such a switch, Joe was keen to keep the option open.

He was well placed to delve, for Wendy needed someone with whom to share the guilt she was feeling about having discovered what might be a weapon. He had done all he could to reassure her that she was not in any way to blame but she was not easily consoled. Melodramatically, she was comparing her plight with that of the scientists who had discovered atomic fission. They, too, had only been following their calling and were not to 'blame' but they had changed the world in a way which she, and millions of others, believed to be ruinous.

In spite of his modest journalistic experience, Malinowski was not a professional interviewer and Wendy quickly sensed what was behind his too obviously repeated efforts to talk about the Baranski visit, which she wanted to put from her mind. At the fourth clumsy attempt she let him know what she thought about him.

'You're nothing better than a bloody CIA stooge!' she cried and stormed out of his flat late one filthy night to drive miserably back to Salisbury.

A few days later she was beginning to think that she had been unkindly harsh and was almost ready to ring Joe to apologize when Julian Flickinger telephoned her, late at night, in alarm.

'What the hell cooks, Wendy? I'm being asked all sorts of questions here about you. Who's this guy Malinowski? I'm being questioned about him too and I've never heard of him.'

'Who's questioning you?'

'I guess it's the CIA.'

'Why should they be interested?'

'Because of the crash programme.'

'I don't understand. What crash programme?'

'Haven't you heard? There's a major high-priority programme here to evaluate all the military possibilities of your clone.'

Wendy's stunned silence was eloquent. Adrian had been careful to conceal the extent of the military developments from her.

'I hadn't heard,' she said, eventually. 'It's like being told that your child is a murderer.'

'I'm sorry, Wendy. I was just worried that you might be in some danger. Are you getting any attention from your security people?'

'I thought I'd resolved that. But it doesn't matter. I'm so sick of the whole thing that nothing matters.'

When she had bid him goodbye she put her head in her hands and broke down in tears, something she rarely did.

Julian's call had convinced her that her parting taunt at Joe had been more justified than she had really believed at the time. After the way she had confided in him, when she had needed support and sympathy for her predicament, she could never trust him again or even see him again. She felt very alone and, with nobody to occupy her time in the evenings, the unpalatable truth of what she had set in train intruded ever more insistently into her consciousness.

Wendy's dejection was exacerbated by the attitude of the Defence

210

Ministry men following routine inquiries they had made in connection with her positive vetting. They had discovered some incidents in her left-wing student past which merited further questioning. They travelled down to Porton and waylaid her during her lunch hour while she was picking horse-chestnut 'conkers' in the avenue to fulfil a promise made to the small son of a neighbour. After protesting again about the invasion of her privacy, she dismissed the incidents as part of growing up. 'I wasn't an agitator: I was a protester. It was an outlet for my energies. I grew out of it.'

But her tormentors seemed unimpressed.

There was worse to come. Joe Malinowski's journalist friend, 'Wolf' Gordon, had met him for one of their regular, fully licensed lunches and learned that Wendy was being harassed by security. He could not induce Joe to tell him why but sensed that his reticence concealed some big news and, with no more to go on, decided to use the common media gambit – a 'mystery story'.

Knowing that Wendy was working on AIDS and that AIDS was always news, he induced his editors to print, under the banner headline 'AIDS Scientist Gagged', a front-page account of an alleged plot by MI5 and the CIA to conceal an important development in the field of AIDS research. He indicated that, since the Defence Ministry was involved, it might be in connection with research on the possible use of AIDS as a weapon. The fact that the alleged victim was an attractive young woman intensified the editorial interest.

The story was projected as a follow-up to his mythical scoop about the original development of the AIDS virus by American scientists and hopefully would diminish some of the scorn which had been poured on it.

Gordon had deliberately avoided telephoning Wendy because a straight denial from her would have weakened the story.

As usual with all scientists in such accounts, Wendy was projected as 'brilliant' and her gagged discovery as a 'major breakthrough'. According to Gordon, she wanted to disclose her findings about AIDS to the world but was being 'hounded' by MI5, probably in conjunction with the CIA.

He had made a guess that, as a dedicated scientist, Wendy had objected to signing the Official Secrets Act when recently transferred to the 'top-secret Government research station', the Chemical Defence Establishment at Porton. He claimed to know, as he did, that she was opposed to the 'prostitution' of science in the development of weapons.

The story was illustrated with a large photograph of Wendy with Adrian Allen, taken at some international conference and provided by a picture agency. In the caption Allen was described as her 'brilliant boss'.

Gordon had gleaned only a fragment of the true story but had fabricated a fantasy with it. The fantasy caused a political furore.

Whether or not Wendy could truly be said to have been 'hounded' by MI5, she was certainly hounded by the media. Knowing that there was always some fire at the base of Gordon's smoke, the rest of the newspapers and radio and TV reporters tried to follow up his report, hoping to 'harden' it, and Wendy was deluged with late-night telephone calls and with journalists and photographers hammering on her door.

She was so confused and distraught that after making one late-night call to Adrian, who advised her to continue in silence, she left the telephone off the hook and let the visitors hammer. This served only to assure Gordon's competitors that his story was probably correct. Most of the late editions of the rival newspapers contained versions of it, some even more embroidered.

Representatives of the foreign press in London were quickly on to the story, so Wendy found herself the subject of worldwide publicity and speculation. The Soviet disinformation service lost no time in claiming that, according to the British press, the British Government had an AIDS breakthrough which it was deliberately withholding because the United States was planning to use it to spread the 'killer disease' in the Third World and reduce the populations there.

For good measure, this development was 'surfaced' in Third World newspapers as proof of the previous Soviet claim that the AIDS virus had been deliberately created by the Americans as a germ-warfare weapon, using the techniques of genetic engineering.

The political opportunity presented by the reports was seized on by those MPs who formed what was known in Westminster as the 'Band of No-Hopers'. This was a motley group of backbenchers, mainly of the Labour Opposition, who, lacking in ability and with no hope of preferment, latched on to every sensational topic as a means of bringing themselves to public notice. The more outrageous the topic, the rougher the scrimmage to be first in alerting the media with the news that they were going to raise it in Parliament. Nobody took them seriously, least of all the journalists who publicized their activities, but they made copy on a dull day and their nuisance value was often appreciated by their party leaders, especially when they harried the Prime Minister.

Several No-Hopers quickly tabled private notice questions for the Prime Minister, using the usual gambit: 'To ask the Prime Minister when she expects to visit the Chemical Defence Establishment at Porton Down.'

The Prime Minister: 'I have no plans to do so.'

Then came the inevitable permissible supplementaries: 'Will the Prime Minister explain why an important development in AIDS research made by Dr Wendy Payne has been suppressed?'

'Will the Prime Minister explain to the House why AIDS research is being carried out, secretly, at a Ministry of Defence establishment?'

The Prime Minister: 'There is no secrecy whatever about any work concerning AIDS beyond the normal convention in which scientists do not publish their results until they have something definite to report.'

Howls of protest greeted this response, with the Prime Minister shouting wearily above the clamour – 'stridently', the press called it – to accuse the Opposition of supporting foreign disinformation services.

All this attention only exacerbated Wendy's distress as she was 'door-stepped' and followed around by photographers snatching pictures and reporters pursuing her for quotes until she felt besieged, as indeed she was.

It did not help when a Ministry of Defence security officer telephoned her at Porton to ask if she had been speaking to the press and to warn her about the danger of doing so. 'Go to hell!' she cried, in a voice which sounded near-hysterical. 'I'm sick and tired of these bloody accusations.'

She finally exploded when Adrian called her in to his office to give her some news relayed to him by Sir William Brook.

'You are not going to believe this, Wendy, but with the Government's agreement, the Americans are giving the Russians all the information about Clone Fe 113, including cultures!'

Wendy was flabbergasted and opened her arms in despair. 'What sort of idiots are we dealing with? Here we are being subjected to all this degrading pressure, being questioned and followed around to keep everything secret from the Russians and they give them it all on a plate. Am I free to talk now and tell the truth if the press come back again?'

'Positively not! That's what I've been asked to tell you. The Government has cleared the Russians to know but nobody else. The Russians have agreed to keep the whole issue secret, so we have to go on doing so.'

Wendy could not believe her ears. 'We're in a madhouse,' she declared. 'What the hell's the point?'

Adrian felt deeply sorry for her but could only shrug helplessly. 'I have no idea. They wouldn't tell me. Maybe they don't want people like the Libyans to know. Anyway, we're still forbidden by the Ministry to publish anything or say anything. It's bloody frustrating, I know, but there we are.'

'Bloody frustrating? It's bloody lunacy! As far as I am concerned the Official Secrets Act can go to hell and all the spooks along with it. If I get the chance to clear my name and reputation I'm going to take it. I should never have agreed to move here in the first place, then I wouldn't be in this position. It's your fault. You talked me into it.'

She flounced out of the office while Adrian stared helplessly at the polished top of his desk. He sensed that she was so deeply hurt and disturbed that she might do something really foolish.

He was right. Wendy had lost faith in everybody and it was in that mood of searing emotional tension that she had gone into her little office and fatally licked the envelopes.

Following Gordon's 'disclosures' about Wendy's mysterious death, Adrian's worst fears had been realized. Porton was invaded again by the media and subjected to mass demonstrations on a scale formerly restricted to the nuclear bases, which no longer offered even unreasonable pretext for protest. The Band of No-Hopers had several field days, with the CIA and MI5 at the centre of their censure.

While Adrian continued to wonder, there was one man who was immediately prepared to believe that Wendy had been murdered and was in little doubt that, if she had been, the KGB was responsible. That was Professor Leon Baranski, who was suffering agonies of remorse after reading newspaper accounts of Wendy's death in the

Polish press where it was blown up as proof of Britain's continuing interest in germ warfare.

Without seeking permission, he telephoned Adrian to express his grief.

'Whoever did it, what a dreadful waste of a young life,' he said.

'It is possible that she took her own life,' Adrian suggested.

'I can't believe that,' Baranski said, emphatically. 'She loved life and loved her work. And she knew she had so much to do.'

Aware that his telephone call was almost certain to be monitored, Baranski did not tell Adrian about a more recent interrogation to which he had been subjected by the UB, acting, he felt sure, in Moscow's interests. Though he was unaware of it, the questioning had quickly followed the receipt by Soviet scientists of wet cultures of Clone Fe 113 and all the information about it.

Because of his visits to leading bacteriologists at Beijing University, Baranski was asked about China's capability in the field of genetic engineering and particularly about the possibility that their scientists might produce a silicon-eating clone if they got wind of the fact that such a clone was possible. His response had been to point out that the Chinese were eminent in the field and highly ingenious.

'What if anyone told them how to do it?' he was asked.

'Then I am sure that, given time, they could.'

'Even without being given cultures of the clone?'

'Yes, given time.'

'Do you think that your friend, Dr Payne, might have told any Chinese bacteriologists about her discovery?'

'I have no idea.'

Had this been the KGB's motive for the murder? Baranski wondered as he ran his hand through his hair. Who had been most anxious to release the details – not just to China but to the whole world? Dr Payne. And which country would be threatened most if the Chinese leaders, who had demonstrated their military ruthlessness by a massacre of their own dissidents, ever chose to use the clone as a weapon? The answer was obvious and the scenario by no means incredible. Like all its predecessors the Soviet Empire contained the seeds of its own destruction and the symptoms of its disintegration were already manifest.

Baranski was quite sure, from the severe way he had been ordered to keep his mouth shut on all aspects of the silicon business, that the

KGB did not want anyone else to know anything about it, least of all the Chinese. It was far-fetched, perhaps, but it made more sense than any other reason he had heard for Wendy's death. So much sense that he was more than a little concerned about his own safety.

He was equally concerned about his own behaviour. If the KGB was guilty then so was he, to some degree. His involvement had been forced on him with threats which did not need to be spoken, but had he protested sufficiently? His oppressors had granted him the pretence of appealing to his patriotism and, ostensibly, he had obliged. But he could find little satisfaction in that sophistry. He had known, from the first, that the appeal was not in the interest of Poland but of the Soviets. And like most Poles, and most Jews, he detested the Soviets.

It would be too dangerous ever to seek relief by confiding in anyone. For the rest of what had been a highly principled and intellectually disciplined life he would have to live with his contamination alone.

Chapter Thirty-one

A chill November wind was blowing hard from the snow-covered Steppes as the thirteen men of the Politburo stood on the reviewing platform atop Lenin's marble mausoleum in Red Square for the annual celebration of the Revolution. The Russians called such a wind 'thin', meaning that it could edge its way through anything. All the civilians were thickly clothed in heavy overcoats, scarves, fur hats and boots but Primarkov and his colleagues were still glad of the chance to clap their hands to keep warm.

There was plenty of opportunity for that. The marching ranks below, moving towards St Basil's Cathedral, with its onion domes cheerfully garish in the bleak sunshine, were putting on the usual display of enthusiasm as the General Secretary smilingly took the salute. Those standing on his right and left, however, did not even attempt to look content. The Defence Minister, relegated to one end of the line, looked particularly grim and disheartened. There had never been a parade in which the military had been so poorly represented. There were plenty of marching troops but no missiles, no guns, no heavy tanks, nothing that could possibly savour of aggressive intent. The concept that the Soviet forces should be slashed just to make them less frightening to the West was anathema. It required a complete change of the offensive strategy which had made the country a superpower and had brought it international respect.

The diminishing role of military power was equally obvious to the diplomats and defence attachés among the guest observers. Clearly, one major purpose of the parade was to convince the West, and America in particular, that the Soviet Union could safely be given the economic help it so desperately needed. This procession was no celebration of the Revolution or homage to its prophet. It was blatant propaganda for a quickening pace to *Derzanie cheloveka – zalog uspekha*, 'Achievement through individual initiative', a slogan portrayed on a thousand banners brandished by the marchers.

Borovik, the ideology chief, was shocked even more by the paucity of banners displaying the head of Lenin. To him, to Chevalsky and to almost all the others, the November procession was a reverent and grateful tribute to the founding father, lying below them, embalmed, permanently in state. To Primarkov the mortal remains were more representative of the mummification of the whole Soviet system. He felt both the chill of temperature and of isolation. He had stood on that rostrum in the past with Gorbachev and with 'Boris the Brief'. He seriously wondered if he would be there for the next anniversary, or even for the May Day parade.

Bored by the procession, which was still grossly over-long in spite of his military cuts, he felt some security from his knowledge that the crack contingent always stationed secretly in the mausoleum in case of an assassination attempt were *Spetsnaz* troops belonging to the GRU and not to the KGB. As Lenin had done in his day, Primarkov had forged a friendship with the GRU chief to protect himself from the chief of the secret police.

Warming up in his office after the last ranks of the procession had mercifully marched away, Oleg Chevalsky, who had some physical resemblance to the former KGB chief, Beria, and was determined not to suffer the same fate, made a final check on his assets. He decided that Destiny, in the form of the Mockingbird, had stacked the cards for him in a way that should enable him and his supporters to get rid of Primarkov. He had a duty to act, on behalf of the KGB as well as the Communist Party. Pandering to so-called human rights was threatening the role for which the KGB had been created. His officers looked to him for leadership. Their parents had encouraged them to enter an élite force, which was what he had inherited. It had always been understood that the work of the KGB was so important to the continued existence of the Soviet state that it could command any funds it needed. Yet Primarkov was insisting that the KGB's spending had to be cut, along with the rest of defence, and had even described the hallowed organization, publicly, as an 'infinite sink' for money. If Primarkov was not checked, what was going to be left for him to pass on to his successor?

Sitting at his desk, Chevalsky listed those on whom he could rely for support: the several conservative hardliners led by Borovik, the General Secretary's deputy, possibly the Foreign Minister and, certainly, all the military chiefs, whose power was being eroded by progressive disarmament while China, the real long-term danger, was rapidly gathering both military and economic strength.

Like all good plans, Chevalsky's was simple: to use the Mocking-bird situation to discredit Primarkov by demonstrating, in the most dramatic manner, that his trust in the Americans, and in President Rockwell in particular, was totally misplaced. Primarkov could then be formally accused of weakening the USSR's position as a super-power through his naive reliance on Rockwell and his henchmen, who had tried to wage germ warfare on the Soviet people in a most insidious way. The American admission of the existence of the silicon-eater and the offer of cultures had banished any lingering doubts in his mind about the Mockingbird's condition.

Chevalsky chose the regular Thursday meeting of the full Politburo to launch his challenge because he wanted all the other members to witness it. Only Borovik, who believed himself first favourite to succeed the General Secretary, knew that it was coming. Both felt very confident as their black limousines were driven along the roads, which had been cleared of heavy snow, and through the Troitskaya Gate into the Kremlin. With Primarkov humiliated in Council, the facts could be then leaked worldwide through the propaganda machinery. He was so popular that the Soviet people had to be convinced of his criminal gullibility before he could be ousted, hopefully by resignation, otherwise by force.

The chandeliered room in which the Politburo met had wit-nessed many confrontations with historic, and sometimes bloody, consequences but most of the delegates were unaware of any ten-sion as the Chairman, Primarkov, looking spruce in a well-cut suit and radiating the aura of leadership which had been of such service in his rise to power, called the meeting to order. All went normally until they reached the 'Any other business' end of the agenda.

'I wish to raise a most important matter of urgent political concern, Comrade General Secretary,' Chevalsky announced, grimly.

'Then raise it, Comrade Oleg Borisovich.'

'You will recall that, at the last meeting of the Defence Council, it was agreed that I should take action to discover whether or not the Americans had developed a bacterium which can attack silicon and so put computers and other electronic equipments out of action.'

A stickler for protocol, Primarkov replied, 'I do recall it but you would seem to be out of order, comrade. That subject should be reserved until the next meeting of the Council.'

Not to be deterred, Chevalsky responded briskly. 'No, General Secretary, this is no longer just a defence issue but a matter of such exceptional political importance that it demands immediate attention by this political committee. The situation has been brought to a head by the official American confirmation that the bacterium *does* exist. In case certain members here are not yet aware, the Americans are in process of handing over all the information about this extraordinary development, together with cultures of the bacteria, as they should have done weeks ago.'

Observing the intense interest of Borovik and the others, Primarkov allowed the KGB chief to continue.

'From other evidence which has come my way, I am now absolutely certain that the American device, the so-called Mockingbird, which the GRU managed to deliver to our research station at Sary Shagan, is heavily infected with these very bacteria in such a way that it poses a danger to all the other electronic equipment in the area and perhaps in other areas if the infection spreads. It could, in fact, cause an epidemic which would be catastrophic, not only to our defence effort but to our economy.'

The non-technical members of the Politburo were clearly impressed as they sought more detail. In simple terms, Chevalsky listed his evidence, culminating in the belated American admission that the clone did exist.

'There can no longer be any doubt that Mockingbird has been used by the Americans in a deliberate attempt to wage germ warfare on the Soviet defences and the Soviet people. There is no escaping that stark fact.'

He paused to let the charge sink in.

'When you say the Americans perpetrated this alleged crime, I take it you mean the CIA,' Primarkov said.

'No doubt the CIA carried out the action but, in view of the political circumstances, I find it difficult to believe that President Rockwell was not party to it. And if he was . . .'

This was Borovik's cue to intrude. 'If he was, then he is not to be trusted on any matter.'

When this remark was greeted by general muttered agreement from the other Politburo members, Primarkov felt he should being

220

the meeting back to more pragmatic considerations. 'Is not our first priority to decide what should be done to remove the alleged danger at Sary Shagan? If what Comrade Chevalsky says is true, shouldn't the apparatus be totally destroyed without further delay?'

'Will you take the responsibility for sending 121 million dollars up in smoke, General Secretary?' Chevalsky asked, anxious to deter any action which would destroy his evidence. 'I have discovered that the GRU paid that out in cash from scarce foreign currency provided by the Military Industrial Commission. It might still be possible to save the equipment.'

'Well, what other action do you propose?' Primarkov asked.

It was the question for which Chevalsky had been waiting. 'What I would put to this meeting is that you, Comrade General Secretary, confer personally with the President of the United States, without delay, and ask him what is meant by this offensive behaviour at a time when we are supposed to be talking peace.'

Primarkov paused, and then asked quietly, 'But supposing you are wrong?'

'I know I'm not wrong,' Chevalsky replied, striking the table with his fist. 'There are matters which I may not tell anyone, when secret sources are involved, but the facts are beyond question and I must ask you all to accept my word for that. How can we contemplate doing business with a man representing a state which would perpetrate such a thing? What I am saying is that we now have the clearest evidence that the United States is not to be trusted. And I think our people should know that – and soon.'

Primarkov appreciated the gravity of Chevalsky's deliberate threat to his whole foreign policy. He looked round the table and saw that others seemed to be in agreement but it was Borovik who intervened to lend his weight to the request. 'Comrade General Secretary, I think that you should find out if the President is personally aware of this contemptible event. If he is not, then you should make him aware of it and let us all know how he responds before any further arrangements are made for a summit meeting.'

Primarkov seemed reluctant. 'But surely that would be a confession that the GRU obtained the equipment by surreptitious means and — '

'I appreciate that,' Chevalsky interrupted. 'But this is an instance where our need to know the truth is so urgent that we must afford a trade-off. It will be worth it for the political advantage of knowing whether or not the US President has been party to this outrage on the Soviet people.'

With a heavy sigh as he realized that he would have to oblige, Primarkov said, 'Whatever the CIA might have done, and I repeat *might*, I am sure that President Rockwell had no part in it whatever. He would not do such a foolish thing, particularly at such a sensitive time.'

Chevalsky pounced. 'May I remind the meeting of the infamous U2 incident which happened on the eve of a summit conference? The President of the day, Eisenhower, denied that spy planes were being sent over the Soviet Union and then had to admit that he had lied and that he had agreed to the flights when we produced the evidence in the form of a shot-down pilot.'

Everyone at the meeting knew of that sensational incident, which figured prominently in the Soviet history books, though some, including Primarkov, had been boys at the time.

'This situation is even more iniquitous,' Chevalsky went on. 'You, Comrade General Secretary, are about to sign a treaty outlawing bacterial weapons and the Americans choose that very time to assault us with what is possibly the most devastating bacterial weapon ever conceived.'

Clearly nonplussed, Primarkov flicked some non-existent dust from his sleeve and commented, 'I will be appalled if it transpires that President Rockwell knows about any adulteration of this simulator but I have to agree that it would alter the whole political climate if he does.'

Chevalsky relaxed as he saw that he had won his point. 'Even if he does not know, it will strengthen our position if you tell him that *you* know, General Secretary. You can then be suitably aggrieved and the CIA will be in tremendous trouble, with another Irangate-style inquiry. We could leak the situation to the American media . . .'

Holding up his hand, Primarkov urged, 'First things first, comrade. If it is the wish of the meeting I will do what you suggest.' He looked at his colleagues in turn and, though no vote had been asked for, each had a hand raised.

Chevalsky looked hard at Borovik. Their faces remained impassive but both were smiling within. Rockwell would have no option but to deny the charge and then he could be proved to be a liar simply by starting up the Mockingbird machine under safe conditions. It was not just Rockwell's credibility that was on the line but Primarkov's.

Later that day Primarkov made an excuse to telephone Rockwell about a procedural issue and then made a bald statement of Chevalsky's assertion and his threat to tell the Soviet public that the Americans had been cheating in a most dangerous and unforgivable way.

With some difficulty, Rockwell refrained from saying, 'If your fellows had not stolen the apparatus in the first place this problem would never have arisen.' Instead he expressed surprise and horror. 'You may be sure, General Secretary, that I will be making immediate inquiries at the highest levels – and the lowest levels. I'll call you back when I know the facts. Whatever they are, I will tell you the truth. You can depend on that. You have my word of honour for that.'

'I sincerely hope it is not true, Mr President. If it is, it will make my position here very difficult indeed.'

'I appreciate that. And anything that's bad for you is bad for me – policy-wise, I mean. We must get to the bottom of this extraordinary business.'

Rockwell and Butch Blanchard spent an hour going over all the possible implications, and the following morning – to allow a credible interval – the President returned Primarkov's call, reading from a carefully worded statement.

'Your KGB Chairman is utterly wrong about this alleged infection. He is either trying to undermine our relationship, and your position, or he has fallen for a stupid hoax, in which there is no truth whatever. I have had the situation checked out at every point. It is absolutely impossible that the Mockingbird could have been infected by us. And the British, who were the only other people who possessed the bacterium, had no possible access to the equipment. I urge you to instruct your scientists to start up the machine and then inspect it. You have my word of honour that there is nothing whatever wrong with it.'

'I can rely on that?' Primarkov asked.

'Positively and totally. As I said, I give you my word of honour.'

Then, more slowly and deliberately, he added, 'You have your windfall, Mr General Secretary. You have your ripe plum.'

As he had been aware for some weeks, Primarkov had needed to move decisively against his enemies. He possessed the political and military power to do so, power for which he was indebted to the infamous Stalin, but he had lacked a viable reason. Now he had it. He realized that he would be staking everything on Rockwell's word but felt confident that he could do so. He had not come so far in Soviet politics without being a sound judge of character. And with so much to lose himself, in political prestige and credibility, Rockwell would never have been so adamant had he not been certain.

Primarkov had no alternative anyway. Chevalsky had manoeuvred him into a position where action was unavoidable. If the KGB Chairman was right, he was finished, with most of the Politburo and the Army chiefs lined up against him and the rest who mattered dithering. If Chevalsky was wrong he could be discredited, absolutely and fatally.

Chapter Thirty-two

Wasting no time after his talk with Rockwell, Primarkov called a meeting of all the interested parties – the full Politburo and the military chiefs.

'Comrades, I have spoken with the President of the United States,' he announced. He paused and the rest of the meeting could sense, by the smile on his lips, what was coming.

'After making the fullest inquiries, he has assured me, on his personal word of honour, that when the Mockingbird simulator left American custody it was not infected or otherwise defective in any way. I have decided to accept his word without reservation and recommend that you do the same.' The delegates looked at Chevalsky to respond, which he did with vigour.

'The President's statement has to be a lie because we have already proved that the equipment is "bugged" and that could only have been done by the Americans – almost certainly the CIA.'

Only momentarily discomforted, Primarkov answered, 'That may be so but the matter at issue is whether the equipment is infected. I have the President's personal word that it is not.'

'No doubt,' Chevalsky replied, scathingly, 'but he must have consulted the CIA and the CIA would not necessarily have told him the truth.'

The General Secretary leaned forward in his chair. 'Would you have told me the truth in similar circumstances?' he asked.

'We do not behave like the CIA,' Chevalsky lied. 'What matters is that we have the hardest evidence that the Mockingbird is infected and only the Americans could have done it. The equipment was under Soviet control from the moment it was shipped from New York.'

Prompted by a list in front of him, he began to recite, again, the collateral evidence which the KGB had secured since first receiving the anonymous CIA letter.

As the general tension mounted, the General Secretary remained

225

unimpressed. 'Your industry is most admirable, Comrade Oleg Borisovich, but your collateral is not *proof*. We have to trust the President's word or he won't trust mine when I speak to him on behalf of all of you. I move that we put the issue to the test by starting up the Mockingbird. There should be little danger if it is done in isolation. If there is any, I accept full responsibility for it.'

Chevalsky's face betrayed no emotion but he was triumphant: his enemy had bought the ploy. The scientists would decide. A fair gamble was often necessary in intelligence work: Chevalsky was convinced that he was on a certainty. He sensed that he had his man on the spit and it only remained to roast him – and roast him in public.

He and Primarkov looked at each other in mutual awareness of their predicaments. Each had crossed his Rubicon. Each knew there could be no turning back. And there could be only one victor. Both tried to smile. Chevalsky had his collateral. On the face of it, all Primarkov had was Rockwell's word.

Primarkov was well read in Russian literature and it did not escape him that his situation was reminiscent of one of those stories in which a nobleman stakes his estate and fortune on the turn of one card.

Always a pragmatist, Primarkov was not prepared to leave arrangements for the test in Chevalsky's hands. Cultures of the silicon clone had already reached the Soviet Union and he knew the ways of the KGB. It was not beyond their wiles to ensure that the result was positive. So on the General Secretary's suggestion, it was agreed by the meeting that a neutral team of scientists, electronic engineers and bacteriologists, with both KGB and GRU representation, should be sent down to Sary Shagan immediately. It would report direct to the Politburo through the General Secretary.

A few days later, a portable generator with long leads was driven out and parked alongside the container housing the Mockingbird. Attached to it was a 'white noise' device which, when switched on, would effectively blanket any sounds picked up by the sneaky and make them meaningless.

With the scientists and engineers dressed in protective clothing supplied by the Army and required, for reasons they did not understand, to remain silent, the plastic covering was stripped from the container and the assembly of the Mockingbird completed. When the final modules had been connected to the top and sides, the reason for its name became apparent to them. It did have an abstract art appearance of an enormous long-tailed bird.

Two men entered the bird's great belly where the controls and visual displays were located, and the simulator was switched into action, with the others standing at a safe distance and still in their protective clothing. The equipment worked perfectly and continued to do so for seventy-two hours. It was then switched off for twenty-four hours and restarted. Again it worked. After a further forty-eight hours it was closed down. Parts of the equipment were then dismantled and ferried away to be minutely examined, under sterile conditions. When these proved to be perfect, more sample parts were examined. Everything was normal except for the sneakies which were spotted, removed and appropriated by the KGB. There was no sign whatever of any bacterial culture or any container which might have held one.

During the operation, the edgy Chevalsky could not resist telephoning his representatives at Sary Shagan for progress reports. Each dismayed him more than the last. He had enjoyed a brief moment of triumph when the Mockingbird had hiccuped and stopped but it had proved to be just an electronic malfunction which was quickly remedied. As the results proved to be negative, day after day, Chevalsky began demanding more time, suggesting that the incubation period might be longer than expected, but the team agreed that, after six days of such exhaustive investigation, a halt should be called and the report completed.

On receiving it, Primarkov telephoned Rockwell to announce, 'I have surmounted all obstacles and climbed to the top,' meaning that he would definitely be at the summit.

Restored to his jaunty, eager-voiced self, the 'little man' went into no details and expressed no thanks or gratitude. All he was prepared to concede was, 'The Mockingbird simulator was as you said it would be.'

'I told you that you could trust me,' Rockwell responded, delightedly.

'I only have one complaint, Mr President,' Primarkov said, jokingly. 'Your equipment was bugged.'

Rockwell laughed. 'I guess that's par for the course.'

227

Not being a golfer, Primarkov did not understand the remark. When his translator explained, he grunted and set it in his memory store of English idioms.

It was not in Chevalsky's nature to admit defeat with good grace. He realized that he had been hoaxed out of sight by the CIA and appreciated that in the process he had enormously enhanced Primarkov's position with his colleagues. Somehow he would have to try to ingratiate himself – and quickly. After all, he had only been doing his duty to the best of his ability and in the interests of the state. But while he was pondering on possible action, Primarkov, who knew that he would have received no quarter, made his strike. He quickly called a meeting of the Defence Council to which the KGB chief was not asked and issued copies of a brief summary of the scientific report. Then, from a prepared statement, he accused Chevalsky of extreme professional incompetence in having been so easily and comprehensively hoaxed by the CIA in what had been no more than a palpably obvious ploy to deprive Soviet scientists of the use of most valuable equipment which the GRU had obtained with commendable ingenuity. Further, he claimed, Chevalsky was guilty of unforgivable political misjudgement in having forced the General Secretary of the Communist Party into a dangerously embarrassing position with respect to the President of the United States. National face had been lost; Chevalsky, and those who had supported him, were entirely to blame.

The Politburo members present were not slow to appreciate that they had all been party to the loss of face and it was quickly agreed, unanimously on a show of hands, that the KGB Chairman should be dismissed.

Preferring conciliation to unnecessary conflict, Primarkov did not press for the dismissal of the defence chiefs who had sided with Chevalsky, as he could have done as their Commander-in-Chief. Their prestige and influence had been sufficiently undermined and in the Soviet Union, as elsewhere, dogs that are known tend to be safer than dogs that are not. As for Borovik, the co-conspirator, he was no threat without Chevalsky and the Army chiefs and could be removed within a few months, on the grounds of age or some other pretext.

Adept at converting political minuses into double pluses, Primarkov then asked himself what further advantage he might take of the situation and it did not take him long to make a decision, which he quickly cleared with those whom he cared to consult.

The first that Chevalsky heard of his fate was a statement on Moscow radio announcing his dismissal. It was brief but clear:

In pursuit of the reforms required for the modernization of the State, it has been decided that the Committee for State Security will be subjected to a change of policy. While remaining the Sword and the Shield of the State and the Soviet people, its responsibilities are to be reduced in conformity with the general reduction in defence spending, which the economy demands. This reduction will particularly apply to the responsibilities of the KGB within the Soviet Union.

The changes, which will be far-reaching, will be accomplished gradually.

As part of the restructuring, the present Chairman of the Committee for State Security, General Oleg Chevalsky, is to step down. He is replaced by General Yuri Yakushkin, who is widely experienced in the protection of the Soviet Union against external threat.

In view of the revised nature of the KGB, General Yakushkin will not be a member of the Politburo.

As was still customary in the Soviet Union, the media were unable to obtain any further elucidation. Nor were they permitted to speculate. The statement committed the leadership to a reduction in the activities of the KGB against the Soviet people and this was underlined by the removal of its Chairman from the Politburo. Clearly, the political power of the KGB was to be radically curtailed.

The Soviet people were the most experienced in the world at reading between lines and the news was immensely popular, save in the KGB itself. To be put under the command of a GRU man was the direst disgrace for the KGB, a studied insult which was not lost on perceptive Soviet citizens. Primarkov had not only used the opportunity to bring the KGB under firmer control and score a popularity point: it was a pay-off to Yakushkin for a very secret service rendered. Chevalsky had not been the only one to see that the defection of Colonel Ivashutin would seem to be proof of the authenticity of the CIA letter.

Among his Politburo colleagues Primarkov's position was hugely strengthened. His courage in laying his fate on the line was much admired and his prestige as an astute political operator greatly enhanced. Most importantly, the claim that the Americans, and the President in particular, could not safely be trusted had been disproved in a most dramatic manner.

Summoned to the General Secretary's presence to be formally dismissed, Chevalsky was dejected and chastened, with little to say for himself beyond the lame claim that he had made an honest error in line of duty with no personal animosity towards the leader. Primarkov too said the minimum. 'I needed to make these changes public as a matter of policy, comrade,' he explained. 'Otherwise you could have gone on health grounds.'

As he cleared out his beloved desk, Chevalsky was vain enough to believe that the CIA's prime purpose in the whole Mockingbird episode had been to get him out of the KGB leadership. All that collateral evidence could not have been coincidence. It had been contrived. But who had been responsible? Ross Pilgrim must have been involved but had Yakushkin been part of the act? It was probably no coincidence that Yakushkin had slid into his job.

Ruefully, he recalled how he had planned so ingeniously to make a *peshka* out of Yakushkin; now it seemed that Yakushkin had somehow been involved in making a *peshka* out of him. Clearly, he had underestimated Yakushkin, who had probably known the truth about the Mockingbird while he and the KGB had been spending so much time and effort trying to find out if that letter was genuine. It was possible, of course, that the GRU chief had been doing no more than the bidding of someone else. Could that someone have been Primarkov? He was the big winner. Had he been in collusion with Yakushkin? And, maybe, even with President Rockwell? Whatever the answers, Chevalsky was convinced that his departure and the reinforcement of Primarkov's position constituted a major defeat for communism, to which he had devoted his life and spirit. It was a black day for the Soviet empire and for the Union itself, for nobody knew better than he did the extent to which both were held together by the coercive power of the KGB and the Red Army. The whole Soviet system rested on three legs – the Party, the KGB and the Red

Army; Primarkov seemed intent on weakening at least two of them and, probably, all three.

From a position of enormous personal power and influence, he was going into obscurity from which there would be no return but he still had loyal friends in the KGB. They might, at least, assist him to take Pilgrim with him if he could move fast – before those friends were removed in the inevitable clean-out by Yakushkin.

The new KGB chief was too professional to swing an axe before being certain as to whom he wished to chop. He spent much of his first few days at Chevalsky's old desk being briefed on the immediate past activities of his predecessor concerning the Mockingbird operation. Among the less attractive endeavours which Chevalsky's former aides were anxious to offload on their lost leader was an exercise in which the gum of certain envelopes had been loaded with *botulinus* toxin and dispatched, via the diplomatic bag, to a deep undercover agent residing near San Francisco. This man had sent them, with their enclosures, to the British scientist who had discovered the silicon bacterium, with the required result.

The method of using a toxic substance which produced the symptoms of a fatal infection was not entirely new to Yakushkin. The GRU had applied it several times in the past to dispose of problem people, such as the British Labour leader, Gaitskell, who had been denounced by Khruschev as 'a traitor to the working class'.

As a soldier, deeply concerned about the long-term China threat, Yakushkin appreciated the motive in eliminating Dr Payne. And he had no objection to assassination in military necessity. On the contrary, he had been chief of the *Spetsnaz* forces who were rigorously trained to murder military and political enemy leaders in war and, occasionally, in what passed for peace. In recent years he had, for instance, been responsible for the operation in which President Zia ul Haq, the dictator of Pakistan, had met his death when a transport plane, carrying him and several other generals had crashed in the desert soon after take-off. Zia had been deeply involved in supporting the Mujahideen guerrillas who were taking such toll of Soviet troops in Afghanistan. It had been a perfect operation, superbly conceived in collaboration with high-level dissident Pakistanis and executed with a posion-gas bomb which had knocked out the entire flight crew.

With daughters of his own, though, he thought it a pity that Chevalsky's victim had been a young girl, but there was never room for sentiment in the intelligence world when genuine military issues were involved. Briefly, he wondered if Primarkov had been party to the murder. In the past, the GRU and KGB had been required to secure the approval of the Defence Council for the assassination of foreign nationals, as it had with the Zia project in Gorbachev's day. And he knew from his recent dealings with Primarkov that he certainly had the necessary streak of ruthlessness within that bland exterior.

Primarkov's feelings were a mixture of relief and triumph which he could share only with his wife Tamara. 'I felt very confident but now that it's over and I can see all that might have gone wrong, I feel like a gambler who has pulled off a long shot,' he said. 'Fortune does favour the brave – so long as they can keep their mouths shut.'

He had disposed of his most dangerous enemy and subdued the others. There were younger ones whom he would choose to replace the residual opponents, like Borovik, but some of them were likely to be thrusters, as secretive about their personal objectives as he had been. 'We are all right for the present,' he assured his wife. But, as some historian had said, history was just one damned thing after another. And the only certainty in life was uncertainty. He still needed to move quickly with positive construction if he was not to suffer the same fate as his two predecessors. Disposing of Chevalsky had removed the man with the knife but he could still be drowned in the tidal wave of impatience and frustration. It was unrealistic to expect people to wait a generation for changes, which were human rights of which they had been forcibly deprived, once they had been promised. And, as Yakushkin had agreed, the days of stifling protest by strong-arm repression were over. He had to get the masses with him, especially the young. And he could do that only by providing some material results in reasonable time.

There was only one way ahead and it involved the abandonment of cherished Soviet ideals: the belief that people should find enough satisfaction simply in working for 'socialism', and the continual spending of enormous sums on military power, subjugation and subversion to promote the Leninist concept of world communism dominated by the Soviet Communist Party. There had to be more freedom to produce and create for personal reward. And colossal cuts in military spending to free the resources to make it possible.

Lenin, Stalin and the rest had sown the wind and it had fallen to him to reap the whirlwind. If, in managing the crisis, Leninism and the power of the Party had to be undermined and the dogma of its infallibility discarded, then so be it. The times ahead would be hazardous but, with Yakushkin in place, he would at least have some protection from the KGB instead of its enmity, if he needed it.

The media pundits of the West had no idea of the real reason for Chevalsky's dismissal. They hailed it as a straightforward political victory for Primarkov and his policies, the culmination of a long ideological struggle inside the Politburo, which had ended in triumph for the General Secretary. There would be no documents for anyone to find: all the participants, Yakushkin, Ivashutin, Primarkov, Pilgrim, Al, Butch and Rockwell had ensured that what little had ever been committed to paper had been burned on reading or very soon afterwards.

Unable to take any credit, publicly, for his part in Primarkov's political survival, though privately there was much mutual congratulation with Butch Blanchard, President Rockwell discussed the coup with his wife, in whom he had previously confided.

'Well, Baby, Skinsaver worked,' he told her breezily. 'The little man is safe. We shall definitely be going to Moscow.'

Baby was delighted on all counts. 'What a pity the world can't be told how clever you have been, honey.'

Rockwell did not deny the compliment. 'That's one of the penalties of the job. Your mistakes nearly always speak for themselves; your triumphs often have to be dumb.'

'Do you think that the little man would have been deposed without your Skinsaver?'

'More than likely, I guess. They were certainly gunning for him.'

'Then at least you should be able to exact some reward now. Saving his skin should be worth something.'

Rockwell had no doubt what was in her mind as he shook his head. 'There will be no gratitude,' he predicted. 'That's not the way human nature works, least of all political nature. Nobody likes being beholden or having to admit that they are. There'll be no favours on Poland or on anything else. Do you know what your friend Butch said?'

'Tell me.'

'The gratitude of men hath oftener left me mourning.'

233

Baby was unimpressed. 'But Primarkov owes everything to you now. I still think you should try and lean on him when we get to Moscow.'

Her husband did not reply but was in no doubt that Baby would be leaning on the little man and, if he did not watch it, on his wife.

A few days later, Primarkov telephoned the President again, ostensibly for failing to apologize, during the previous call, for the way the simulator had been obtained. 'I assure you that under the new KGB leadership such a thing will not happen again,' he promised.

'I'm pleased to hear it,' the President responded, good-naturedly but without conviction, while Butch raised his eyes to the heavens, knowing that the GRU under Yakushkin had been responsible for the hijack.

'In fact, I feel so badly about it that we are sending your Mockingbird back,' Primarkov said. 'It's already on its way to you – not flying home, sailing. It's coming by sea. Let us have it on the proper terms or we do not want it at all.'

Rockwell was momentarily nonplussed and suggested that they might as well keep it but Primarkov was adamant. The President shrugged. He could not foresee any new problems and the West Germans would be able to have their simulator.

'I never expected to hear that, Butch,' Rockwell remarked when the telephone conversation was concluded. 'A Soviet General Secretary apologizing and doing the decent thing! What do you make of it?'

'I don't know. But I wouldn't take it at its face value. The little man is still a Russian.'

Chapter Thirty-three

Ross Pilgrim exulted at the elimination of Chevalsky. He assured Al that the KGB chief must have been fired because he had been held responsible for falling for the CIA 'dangle' and causing such technical mayhem at Sary Shagan.

'I aimed at Yakushkin and got Chevalsky. And he was a better bird. A much better bird,' he added, with immense satisfaction. 'It would have been great to have achieved a right and left and got rid of Primarkov too, but Chevalsky is reward enough, on top of all the damage to the Soviet Star Wars programme. The shake-up is sure to lead to other dismissals and demotions and put the KGB in chaos for months.'

Shaking Al's hand in mutual congratulation, he said, 'Turbid has been a superb operation. A classic dangle, one of the best ever.'

'The grand-daddy?' Al asked, expectantly.

'Could have been. Let's get a bit more feedback before we give it that accolade. In any event, you did your part wonderfully, just as I knew you would. Yakushkin is a much more straightforward character. He'll be easier to cope with than Chevalsky.'

His triumph was rudely tempered, however, when he heard from Butch that the Russians were insisting on returning the Mockingbird. He confessed that he had not foreseen that possibility. They had never admitted a hijack before, and it made for severe complications.

Schneider, the Swiss agent, was insisting to the Mockingbird manufacturer and to the West German customer that the equipment had never reached the Soviet Union and had never, in fact, left Vienna, but Pilgrim knew that could not be true. So why were they sending it back? He cudgelled his brains and twisted his wedding ring without much success.

'It's bloody awkward,' he said to Al. 'This Mockingbird is coming back infected up to its eyeballs and that spells trouble for us. Somehow we have to stop it being opened up where it could do any damage. Why the hell are they returning it?'

With no suggestion forthcoming, Pilgrim tried to answer the question. 'It can't just be a clumsy attempt at revenge. They know we infected it so they must realize that we are not likely to put it where it could do any damage to our installations. It makes no sense, Al. It makes no sense at all. There must be some kind of trade-off that we haven't tumbled to yet.'

He concentrated his thoughts for a few more minutes, rotating his wedding ring rapidly as though conjuring up some genie to assist him, as Al had seen him do so many times before. Then from the slight nod and the relaxation of his features Al knew that inspiration had not been sought in vain.

'There's one thing that's without doubt,' Pilgrim said eventually. 'Stanley Arnold is going to be very inquisitive when the infection is discovered. So this is how we play it. It was against my advice that the Russians were given the clone. I warned everybody that the bastards would use it as a weapon. So we shouldn't have any difficulty in convincing Arnold, Butch Blanchard and the rest who matter that the KGB has wasted no time in using the clone we gave them to infect the Mockingbird and return it here to cause damage. As I have always said, Chevalsky or no Chevalsky, Primarkov or no Primarkov, the KGB is incorrigible, along with the Soviets in general. It makes no difference who is in command of either the KGB or the country, the Russians will play it dirty. It's their nature.'

Remaining silent as usual but intensely alert, Al waited for the next instalment of Pilgrim's counter-ploy.

'If anyone is to be held responsible for any danger posed by the simulator on American soil it should be the President and his advisers, including Arnold – for giving the Russians the clone. Our remaining problem, Al, is to figure out a way of ensuring that when the Mockingbird container arrives here it is not opened in a place where it could damage anything else.'

Al was deeply embarrassed but was unable to inform the man he admired, and to whom he owed so much, that the Mockingbird had never been infected.

From the moment that Pilgrim had unveiled the details of Operation Turbid, Al had wanted to save his mentor from committing what he believed to be a highly dangerous and irresponsible excess – in short, to save him from himself. It was Pilgrim's repeated remark

236

about pushing Primarkov off his perch which had persuaded him that he had to intervene. The old man was behaving as arrogantly as people like Philby had done in deciding what was in the nation's interest.

He had been close to telling him so, particularly after handing him the clone capsule, but the resolution which had seemed so positive had deserted him in Pilgrim's compelling presence.

So after leaving the module and the clone culture at Pilgrim's flat, he had waited, out of sight in his car, until Butch had emerged with the suitcase and had followed him back to his apartment. It was, perhaps, a cowardly alternative but he was not prepared to see the Chief of Staff, whom he liked and respected, plunged into such political danger, along with the President.

'I just think this whole operation is crazy and far too risky, sir,' he had explained to Butch. 'Mr Pilgrim's talking about toppling Primarkov! I'm sorry to have to do this behind his back and I hate being disloyal to him but I know you are a good friend of his and will appreciate my motive. I can't understand what has happened to him lately.'

'He's gone over the top?'

'I certainly think his judgement is defective. And he's become more and more obsessive, especially about "need to know". I get less than the minimum of information required for action now. Maybe he's subconsciously ashamed of what he is doing. Some of my colleagues are becoming very concerned.'

With a considerable effort of will, Butch had avoided showing the intense anger he had felt at the incredible way Pilgrim had tried to implicate him so much more dangerously in the Mockingbird operation.

'Did you object when Mr Pilgrim asked you to get this clone thing?' he asked after Al had told him about the culture.

'How could I? Mr Pilgrim is the acknowledged master of the tradecraft. I was in no position to challenge him. Besides,' he continued wistfully, 'I never have.'

'Can we take this culture out?' Butch asked.

'No problem,' Al replied with enthusiasm as he proceeded to undo the module. He extracted the capsule and handed it to Butch. 'There, that's safe now. I can rely on you can't I, sir, not to mention this to Mr Pilgrim. He'd never forgive me. Worse than that, he'd be quite devastated that I, of all people, should have done this to him.'

'Of course. I can see that you are doing him a service. And your country, too.'

'I think you should destroy the capsule, sir. It should be incinerated. Do you want me to do it?'

'No, I'll do it tomorrow, in the White House incinerator,' Butch replied, wanting to hang on to the evidence of Pilgrim's duplicity towards him. 'Where should I keep it for safety tonight?'

'In your icebox. That's the best way of making sure it's inactive. Don't try to open it, whatever you do. You might break the phial inside and then you could create a major decontamination problem for the whole city. The culture's very light powder and it easily blows about.'

After Al had left, Butch gave vent to his furious disappointment. 'My best friend and he tries to make a willie out of me,' he exclaimed aloud to the walls, stomping up and down the room. 'The bastard would compromise his own grandmother if it suited his plans! To do such a thing at such a time, with the summit coming up! Toppling Primarkov, for God's sake!'

His hands trembling with anger, he put the capsule in a small cash box which he locked and placed at the back of his refrigerator. He would not be destroying it next day. He had made a decision about the action he should take and the culture would be evidence which he might require. As Pilgrim had always advised him, 'In the intelligence world no case is ever closed, so *never* destroy the evidence.'

He might also need it when the time came to confront Pilgrim with his duplicity. It would not be a pleasant encounter but, by God, he'd have it out with him.

Then Butch had gone out for a brisk walk to burn up the adrenaline of resentment and think through the more serious consequences for Ross Pilgrim of what he proposed to do.

With so much at stake, and so bitter about Pilgrim's behaviour, Butch had felt no compunction in informing Rockwell whom he saw that evening in his private quarters. His prime loyalty had always been to the democratically-elected President of his country. The President was his Commander-in-Chief and, with his long service as a soldier, the choice had presented little difficulty.

'God bless you, Butch. Thank heaven you stopped him,' Rockwell said after hearing what had almost happened. 'The man's gone mad.

He's out of control. The CIA's supposed to be *my* bag of tools, not his. We've got to get rid of him.'

'Sadly, I'm afraid I have to agree with you, Mr President. He's a great friend and he's been a fine public servant but he's become unbalanced. I suppose it's being in that kind of work too long.'

'And we must stop this operation,' the President said. 'I don't mind the Russians getting the Mockingbird, but not that way.'

'I've been thinking about that, Mr President. We don't want to get Mr Quest into trouble and it would still be a great idea to get the sneaky into Sary Shagan.'

Sitting back in his armchair, the President had been indulging in second thoughts of his own. 'Yeah, let's not be too hasty about Pilgrim. A few days aren't going to make any difference now. There just might be a way to put this situation to good use.'

His CIA experience had taken command and Skinsaver, conceived as a quip, had quickly become a requirement.

'Butch, you are an expert on these matters. Figure out if there is any way we might use this Mockingbird caper to discredit the little man's enemies in the Politburo. The KGB guy, Chevalsky, is the one I have most in mind. He's the danger man. But any others, like Borovik, would be a bonus.'

Latching on to the intriguing assignment with an enthusiasm that Pilgrim would have admired, Butch had called in Al next day, sworn him to secrecy and asked for his assistance. Al's years of training under the master deceiver did not fail him. Between them they worked out Skinsaver.

Through friends in the Pentagon and at Vandenberg Air Base, Butch had arranged the fitting of the module into the Mockingbird. For Skinsaver the sneaky was a must.

Though he could not be officially involved, the President had responded enthusiastically to the proposals, seeing the covert salvation of Primarkov as essential to the eventual public achievements which would assure him a place among the princes of peace in the history books. He was totally in agreement with the State Department that encouraging the collapse of the Soviet Empire was not in the world's best interest. The instability posed too many dangers which China, in particular, might exploit. As a safeguard should anything go wrong, he stipulated that Arnold must somehow be brought into the picture as the President could not be seen to have gone behind the back of his Director of Central Intelligence. Butch accomplished that by urging the necessity for damage limitation to thwart Pilgrim's purpose and, once assured that it had the President's private blessing, the Director had proved to be more resolute in pursuing a clandestine political operation than Pilgrim would have believed.

With Arnold's agreement, Al had concocted and sent the anonymous warning letter to the KGB resident in Washington. The rest had followed. Operation Turbid, converted to Skinsaver, had been far more momentous than Pilgrim had indicated so secretly to Al. A 'grand-daddy dangle' indeed! Chevalsky had been the prime willie but, in Butch's reckoning, Pilgrim had been a close second. Butch experienced no qualms about that. In fact, the situation gave him piquant satisfaction.

Chapter Thirty-four

Schneider, the Swiss agent who had diverted the Mockingbird, had gone through the motions of going to America and making tentative arrangements about container space on a German freighter to deliver the missing simulator once it had been located. He had telephoned his Zurich office to say he was travelling down to Silicon Valley and to Vandenberg Air Base to make on-the-spot inquiries. If the West German firm made any more calls, that was what they were to be told. He had then gone to ground in a quiet New York hotel, with the option of a quick flight to Rio in case of emergency. The only person who knew his precise whereabouts, apart from his office secretary, was a KGB deep-cover 'illegal' agent in New York who had been assigned to remain in touch.

The agent, a former Jewish refusenik who had been permitted to emigrate, ran a small kosher eating house off Second Avenue and carried out minor services for the KGB in return for promises, occasionally kept, that some of his many relatives would be allowed to join him. Schneider had been instructed to turn up for breakfast at the slack time of 10 a.m. carrying three books tied together with a strap and to order 'two eggs on a bagle'. The owner, fat, bearded and wearing a white apron, duly appeared from behind the counter, noted the books on Schneider's table and engaged him in brief conversation.

To his surprise and relief, Schneider was told that the Mockingbird was going to be returned to New York but the agent was unable to offer any explanation.

'If I could say that I found it in Vienna then it needn't come to New York,' Schneider suggested. 'I could deliver it direct to Frankfurt.'

'Absolutely not,' was the curt reply. 'The equipment is already on its way to New York on a Soviet ship. You are at liberty to explain to your West German customer that you have found the simulator and that, after examination by the manufacturer, it will be returned

241

to you. Just say that it has all been a lamentable mix-up but it's OK now.'

Schneider did just that, assuring the Frankfurt firm that he would be travelling all the way with it and would deliver it personally to the factory gates.

The peremptory summons to Arnold's office and the stark question, fired without warning, were intended to unbalance Pilgrim but, as usual, he had the necessary foreknowledge to disarm his opponent.

The Director was sitting at his desk in his usual interrogatory pose, with his hands palm to palm just under the pointed chin of his long thin face, so that he aptly fitted Al's jibe that he looked like a praying mantis.

'Mr Pilgrim, Mockingbird's returning home. Does that mean anything to you?'

'Mockingbird? What Mockingbird?'

Arnold derived considerable pleasure from watching what he believed was awkward dissimulation.

'It's an electronic apparatus which the Soviets diverted from Silicon Valley under our noses. What do you know about it?'

He had his adversary on the hook and was determined to make him dance. Though Turbid had been conceived and planned as a deniable operation, there was no way that Pilgrim could deny it now: the evidence was about to appear at a New York dock.

'How do you know they are going to send it back, sir?' Pilgrim asked. 'It's most unusual.'

'Sources I cannot reveal. Need to know! You of all people should understand.'

'Actually, sir, the Mockingbird was not diverted under our noses. We knew exactly what was going on and capitalized on it. The President was in favour of the Soviets having the equipment so I decided not to waste any Agency resources on preventing the diversion but to take advantage by bugging the machine. We have obtained some very useful data. I'm in the process of preparing a report for the Department of Defense.'

'I need to see that report. Let me have a brief summary today.'

'Yes, sir. Where is the Mockingbird to be delivered?'

'New York, by sea. Then to the manufacturer by road.'

'We mustn't allow that, sir.'

242

'Why not?'

'Well, the Russians have the clone now, don't they?'

'What clone?' Arnold asked, artlessly.

'The clone that infects silicon chips.'

'Ah, yes. The Soviets got that with the President's express agreement.'

'Then what's to have stopped them infecting the Mockingbird with it?' Pilgrim asked. 'They must have some ulterior motive for sending it back. If they get it to the manufacturer they might be hoping to start an epidemic in Silicon Valley. You can see what colossal damage that could do. There are hundreds of electronic firms there, tightly packed.'

Arnold sat upright in his chair and gazed at Pilgrim in amazement. 'I've never heard such a fantastic suggestion,' he scoffed. 'Only you could have thought of it. The Soviets would never do a thing like that with the summit coming up. Mr Primarkov wants cordial relations at the summit. He would never permit such a folly.'

'Maybe he would have no say in it. The KGB may be under new management but it is still a law unto itself.'

Arnold was tempted to retort, 'Like you, Mr Pilgrim,' but refrained.

Pilgrim continued, 'My professional advice is that the Mockingbird must not be touched or its container opened except in a safe area, remote from any other electronic equipment, and by people who are aware that it might be infected and can take all the necessary precautions.'

Arnold thought fast. When the Mockingbird was found to be perfectly normal, as he knew it would be, Pilgrim would be the subject of professional derision both within and outside the Agency. He was looking for proof that Pilgrim was paranoid and, sure as hell, this was it.

'Give me your advice in writing and I will think about it,' he said, bringing the encounter to an end.

'Sure as hell' was no idle simile in Arnold's book.

Before receiving the written advice, which Pilgrim delivered within the hour, Arnold had already decided to take it – with relish. He added a note to it expressing his agreement 'in view of Mr Pilgrim's unrivalled experience in such matters', and passed it to the Pentagon for action.

The Russian container proved to be large enough to accommodate the completely assembled Mockingbird. It had been recoated with a total plastic seal before leaving Sary Shagan. Remaining sealed at New York, it was picked up by a huge Army tank-transporter and taken, slowly, along the 2,500 miles to the Utah desert site belonging to Fort Detrick. The Army took its task seriously, knowing no more than that it had a potentially dangerous load, and supplied a convoy with warning flags. The police of the various districts, who had to be warned, seized their chance of action and, with motorcycle outriders and sirens screaming, the container passed over eight state boundaries.

As his representative Pilgrim had sent Al, who was instructed to keep in close telephone contact. Al was in no doubt that the whole pointless pantomime was going to make his chief look extremely foolish but he was in no position to pass comment on Pilgrim's assurance that 'once it is seen to be infected we'll both be in the clear'. When he had sent the anonymous letter to the KGB, on Butch's initiative and with Arnold's agreement, he had not foreseen his ultimate Soviet response, which was so out of character. Like his chief, he had been sure that the Soviets would never admit to a hijack, yet that was exactly what they had done. A sad end to the 'grand–daddy dangle' in which everything had really gone wrong for Pilgrim. As Pilgrim's side-kick, he would have to take the local flak when all the expensive precautions proved to have been unnecessary, but that was a minor penance.

On Pilgrim's advice, conveyed by Al, the container was taken to a remote area of the Utah establishment, among the sagebrush, far from any buildings. Scientists who had flown from Fort Detrick then donned protective clothing, tore off the plastic coating and opened the container, while a decontamination team stood by. The fully assembled apparatus looked normal but when they connected it to a power supply and tried to start it up it refused to function. They searched for malfunctions and found that it was full of them. No part seemed to be operable. Various modules were then detached and taken to the laboratory for examination. The silicon chips in all of them were eroded to destruction by bacterial contamination.

As telephone lines to the Pentagon and the White House hummed with the extraordinary news, Pilgrim was completely vindicated. There was unstinted praise all round for his brilliant perception and

Al had some difficulty in concealing his astonishment when he reported the triumph to him, personally.

'You sound surprised, Al,' Pilgrim said, on the scrambled telephone. 'Why? You read the sneaky reports.'

'Yeah, but I guess it's still remarkable when you see it,' Al replied lamely.

Julian Flickinger was flown in from Fort Detrick to take samples from the infected chips for culturing. He duly found that, genetically, the bacterium was beyond question the original Payne clone which the US Government had supplied to the Soviets. There could be no doubt, from the scale of the infection, that they had contaminated it deliberately.

'I thought that we were trusting these bastards now,' one of the Utah staff remarked to Al.

'Not yet,' Al replied, bitterly. 'Not this side of the year three thousand.'

Nobody was more astonished, or more irritated, then Director of Central Intelligence Stanley Arnold. The man he had been so ready to ridicule had been dead right. Though it stuck in his gullet, he had to go through the motions of congratulating him for preventing what might have been a major disaster in Silicon Valley.

'The Russians are always bigger bastards than you think,' Pilgrim replied, patronizingly. 'Maybe you'll believe me now. They take advantage of any situation. It was a thousand to one on that they would use that clone against us and I've no doubt that they'll use it again.'

He was jubilant and very relieved. It had been a close-run thing and only his quick thinking had saved him.

The Staff Chiefs in the Pentagon, who had been vigorously opposed to giving the clone to the Soviets, could hardly suppress a rueful laugh.

When the President was told he did not know what to think until Butch assured him that the Soviets must have done it deliberately. 'I was there when the culture was removed, Mr President, and I kept it. I still have it.'

Rockwell threw up his hands. 'I guess Churchill was right. These goddamn Russians are a riddle inside a mystery wrapped up in an enigma.'

Before conferring with Rockwell, Butch had taken the precaution of calling in Al for consultation. 'What the hell do you make of it?' he had asked. 'Is it possible that Mr Pilgrim could have slipped in another capsule?'

'Absolutely not. There was only one culture. I obtained it and gave it to him and, later, in your presence, I removed it. Nobody could possibly have slipped in another one once the module was in your hands. There's only one answer. Mr Pilgrim's explanation is right. He seems to have got himself off the hook, sir, for which I'm very thankful.'

'Well, I wouldn't be so sure about that, Al. The President is mad as hell about the whole business. But he's very grateful to you for all you did. I'm not permitted to tell you all the details, but you helped to change history. Never forget that.'

Al did no more than nod his appreciation. He, too, was aware that there was little real gratitude in public life and still less in the secret world.

At a special and highly restricted meeting in the Situation Room at the White House, Butch, Arnold and the Foreign Secretary discussed the significance of the Mockingbird's return.

'We got Primarkov off the hook, saved his skin, and with the very instrument we used to save him he tries to clobber us,' Rockwell complained. 'So what does it mean? I didn't expect any gratitude from the little man but neither did I expect a kick in the ass. Could it have been perpetrated behind his back?'

Both Arnold and Butch were in little doubt that Primarkov must have been privy to it and that it may well have been his idea. The KGB new broom, Yakushkin, would be leaning over backwards to avoid giving any offence to the man who had put him there.

They all listened to a replay of the tape of the hot-line conversation in which Primarkov had said that the Mockingbird would be sailing home. Perhaps, with hindsight, his tone did suggest that there was more to it than a straightforward return.

'I wonder if the name gave him the idea,' Rockwell suggested. 'He's certainly mocking us!'

The meeting ended with a consensus opinion that it was Primarkov's way of telling the President, in unmistakable terms, that he shouldn't expect any favours for services rendered at the forthcoming summit or at any other time.

'So it's back to Square One,' the President summarized. 'What he's saying is that, so far as the new arms control discussions are concerned, we start in Moscow with a clean slate. It's the political realities, and nothing else, that will govern our talks.'

'That's right,' Butch agreed. 'Put not your trust in princes . . . for there is no help in them.'

For once, as the quizzical look on the President's features indicated, the Chief of Staff's choice of a quote had not been opportune.

When Rockwell went upstairs to the White House living quarters, for lunch, Baby could see that he was disturbed and in some state of wonderment.

'What sort of a morning, honey?' she asked.

'Oh, this intelligence world gets beyond me sometimes. It always did. You know what I did for the little man?'

'Yes, it was very clever.'

Rockwell explained what had happened.

'What a son of a bitch!' Baby exploded. 'But for you he would have been in Siberia. How can you do business with such a two-timer?'

Rockwell shrugged in resignation. 'I have to do business with him. If I had been forced to do business with that hoodlum, Chevalsky, it would have been the end of our foreign policy. So I suppose I should be grateful in that respect.'

'I don't understand you, sometimes, Clint. You're far too forgiving.'

'In this job you have to face up to realities, Baby. Actually, I can see the little man's point. He didn't want to start at a disadvantage.'

'But couldn't you get one back at him?' Baby suggested. 'So you have a mark up before you begin the talks.'

'What have you got in mind?'

'That's for you and your experts to decide. All I can tell you is that a woman wouldn't let that little two-timer get away with such a dirty trick.'

Rockwell resisted finding an excuse to telephone Primarkov and then complain as an afterthought. Had he done so, Primarkov was ready for him. He was simply going to remark, 'It's par for the course, Mr President.'

In view of the circumstances and the intelligence reports, the President and his advisers were confident that the Soviets would not be giving the Mockingbird affair any publicity. That would result in the silicon secret becoming generally known and all the intelligence indicated that the Soviets were particularly anxious that the Chinese should not know.

The reports were accurate. Before his translation to the KGB, Yakushkin, with the support of the Red Army chiefs, had been pressing hard for the silicon discovery to be withheld from the Chinese on military grounds. He had produced a paper for Primarkov, who had studied it and agreed. Before his dismissal, Chevalsky had done likewise.

On seeing the first intelligence reports indicating this deep Soviet concern, Butch had alerted the President and senior friends in the Pentagon. To his satisfaction, he discovered that the issue was already under discussion by the military intelligence chiefs who felt that, since the Chinese posed no foreseeable threat to the United States but did to the Soviet Union, they should be told about the silicon discovery and given cultures if they asked for them. That would be the best way of counter-balancing the fact that the Soviets knew all about it, possessed the clone and were prepared to use it. The military chiefs had submitted a report to the National Security Council setting out their belief and recommendation, leaving it to the Council to determine the method by which the Chinese should be informed.

When Rockwell saw their report he was immediately reminded of Baby's forthright advice and secured the Council's agreement that the recommendation was sound on political as well as on military lines. He would not be going to the summit one down.

The Mockingbird, standing in the Utah desert, partly dismantled and 'dripping germs', as Al put it, presented a serious disposal problem. It was too hazardous to move it and too dangerous to leave it. So after various meetings and telephone calls to Washington, an Army flame-throwing tank was delivered to the site. From a range of fifty yards it spewed its liquid fire into the container until the contents were thoroughly incinerated.

From a safe distance Al watched the raging pyre through binoculars.

'What's in your mind, Al?' one of the Fort Detrick scientists asked. 'One hundred million bucks going up in smoke?'

'Yeah, just that.'

'It's worthy of some incidental music by Stravinsky.'

'I don't get it,' Al said, continuing to focus on the inferno.

248

'Highlights from the *The Fire Bird*!'

Al was too preoccupied for jokes. True to his training, he could not help wondering what advantage, if any, the Agency could snatch out of the situation.

Arnold was wondering the same thing; but not for long. As soon as the simulator had proved to be infected, the President had taken Arnold aside and whispered, 'This is *your* windfall.'

Chapter Thirty-five

While patiently awaiting an opportunity to pounce on his arch-opponent, Arnold had been set back in his tracks by the apparent accuracy of Pilgrim's foresight. Far from being paranoid, he had appeared to be outstandingly perceptive. The damage which might have been done had the Mockingbird been returned to Silicon Valley was on the lips of all who knew what had happened in Utah. This enhancement of Pilgrim's prestige was a further reason why Arnold felt he could wait no longer. Every minute that Pilgrim remained in office, he feared danger to the Agency and to his own position. Turbid was proof that the man was capable of anything. And he seemed to have the luck of the Devil, a power in which Arnold profoundly believed.

After a rehearsal in dealing with such a slippery opponent, Arnold called him to his office during the morning. He did not offer him a chair but left him standing, shifting his weight uneasily. Pilgrim had breached one of his own golden rules – never underestimate your enemy. He was about to pay the price.

'Mr Pilgrim, what can you tell me about Operation Turbid?' the Director asked, in his praying mantis attitude.

Very few people knew that code-name and one of them must have talked. Pilgrim paused for thought. 'Turbid was the Agency's counter-surveillance operation of the Soviet diversion of the Mockingbird simulator. It was a great success. We had the whole thing under control.'

'Yes. You told me that you inserted a listening device into that equipment. I believe you call such things "sneakies" in these parts.'

'That's right, sir. It worked extremely well. The Department of Defense is very pleased with my report. It taught them a great deal.'

'Did it indeed? Now tell me, Mr Pilgrim, did you insert anything else into that machine?'

'There was a back-up sneaky.'

'I'm not talking about sneakies, Mr Pilgrim,' Arnold said sharply, tapping the desk with his bony forefinger. 'Did you insert anything else? Something that was not, perhaps, er, electronic.'

'I can't really answer that question, sir, without treading on the dangerous ground of sources,' Pilgrim countered. 'As you know, my lips have to be sealed from anyone, even you, in that respect.'

'I thought that would be your defence.'

'I am not defending myself, sir, only my sources.'

'I hear what you say. I have your report here, the one you submitted to the Department of Defense,' Arnold said, lifting up a foolscap sheet. 'It's incomplete, isn't it?'

'All reports from the CIA to other departments are incomplete. There are always things we cannot tell anybody else.'

'And there are things that you cannot tell me. But other people do.' The time had come for dénouement. 'Isn't it a fact that you inserted a culture of the silicon-eating bacterium, called Clone Fe 113, with the intention of starting up some sort of epidemic inside the Soviet Union? Wasn't it you and not the Soviets who infected the Mockingbird?'

Pilgrim looked staggered. 'I'm sorry, sir, but an answer to that question could prejudice an on-going source.'

Arnold was very tempted to tell him all he knew and to shatter his blasted superiority by letting him appreciate that Operation Turbid, as he had conceived it, had been a total failure. But his own sources really were at risk and they could hardly be at a higher level.

'You may not be prepared to answer my question, Mr Pilgrim, but in view of what I know you did – repeat know – I have to tell you that you have been unforgivably irresponsible. You risked bringing the Agency as well as the country into catastrophic disrepute. It was a gross interference in a highly sensitive political situation at a most crucial time.'

Pilgrim's gaze remained blank behind his spectacles.

'I know everything about your so-called Operation Turbid, in fact a great deal more than you do. Operation Stupid would have been a better name. You have prejudiced the foreign policy of the United States and the position of its President, who is furious with you. You have also been dishonest with me. So, Mr Pilgrim, you have given me no option but to require your immediate departure from this Agency. You are not being suspended. You are being fired.'

Again, Pilgrim did not respond, save to stare more fixedly at his opponent.

'In the interest of the good name of the Agency I give you the option of going through the motions of resigning. You can send your letter round this afternoon but I want you off these premises right now, before you do any more damage. And you don't come back – ever. I suppose you realize what publicity about this affair would mean, for you as well as the Agency – a Congressional inquiry, and heaven knows where that could lead.'

'But there are sources and contacts to hand over,' Pilgrim protested. 'And I must be allowed to remove my personal effects from my office and from my personal safe.'

'No way,' Arnold said, emphatically. 'Just leave your keys right here and anything that is not Agency property will be sent round to your home. The same as if you had dropped dead, Mr Pilgrim. And so far as the Agency is concerned, you have. That is all.'

Pilgrim was devastated but followed the rule he had promulgated for any of his agents caught by the enemy: 'When a soldier is captured he gives only his name, rank and number. You do the same, except that you have forgotten your name and rank and you have no number.' He was concerned about certain documents in his personal safe but there was nothing he could do about them. He threw his office keys onto Arnold's desk, and turned on his heel to leave the office. In the anteroom he was subjected to the ultimate humiliation. There were two relatively junior officials waiting to escort him to his car and out of his beloved Langley.

Grim-faced, he stopped at the checkpoint, where the gatemen were bewildered as he handed in his identity badge and card with a curt, 'I won't be needing these again.'

That night Arnold went down on his knees and thanked God for delivering his enemy into his hands. For the sin of arrogance.

Butch had been told in advance what was coming. He knew that the Russians must have deliberately infected the simulator but that was not going to save his old friend. It had been a long-distance contest of heavyweights in which Pilgrim and Chevalsky had knocked each other out.

The news that Pilgrim had gone and would not be coming back quickly went round the organization and it was assumed that he must have been fired. His mutual animosity with Arnold was well known

252

and, with his total devotion to the Agency, he would never have retired prematurely.

Al was literally in tears, feeling lacerating responsibility for the professional assassination of the man who had treated him like a son. Pilgrim's personal secretary, who was weeping copiously herself, did her best to console him.

The following day Pilgrim sent round a very brief explanatory letter, handwritten in his minuscule style, for the staff noticeboard.

Dear Colleagues,

I have decided to leave the Agency for personal reasons. I do so with the deepest regret. I shall miss you all as I shall miss the Service and the work, which has occupied me so fully and satisfyingly for more than thirty years. I thank you for your unstinting support and know that you will maintain the Agency's fine reputation with the devotion and dedication to duty you have always shown.
Yours sincerely,
Ross M. Pilgrim

Arnold's comment was even briefer. 'Only four sentences and each one beginning with I. That should tell you something.'

Once the letter had been pinned to the noticeboard, out-of-office gossip and publicity were inevitable. The *Washington Times* and *Washington Post* were first with the story. Pilgrim declined to say anything to the journalists besieging his front door beyond a one-line statement, presented by a servant, that he had taken early retirement on personal grounds. The CIA would say no more. Arnold had ordered total silence. He would not even be giving any explanations to the oversight committees. The President had given instructions to the very few who had been involved that every aspect of Turbid-Skinsaver must remain secret for ever, a chapter of hidden history concerning which all records would be destroyed. At his press conferences, Rockwell refused all comment beyond remarking, 'It is an internal matter for the CIA.' The media were therefore restricted to speculation and comparisons with the known firing of James Jesus Angleton, the CIA counter-intelligence chief, many years previously, were inevitable.

The main effect of the publicity on Pilgrim was to increase his concern for his personal safety. In the interest of his cover, he had always eschewed any contact with the media and his staff had been enjoined to do the same. Now the attention of any potential assassins would be focused on his address, and those of Chevalsky's old friends who remained in the KGB would be keen to settle the score.

Pilgrim did not deny the bold media statements that he had been fired because there was bad blood between himself and Arnold, whom he believed to be wrecking the Agency. The White House was dismayed when one television commentator suggested that a major operation against the Soviet Union must have ended in catastrophe but that inspired line was not pursued.

Alone in his study with Dallas, Pilgrim was wondering exactly what Arnold had meant when he had said that he knew more about Turbid than he did. Why did he claim that the President was furious when he should have been delighted with his perspicacity? It might all be water over the dam and he had a fairly clear idea what must have happened but there were details he needed to know, for his peace of mind if for nothing else.

He reacted to the whole situation in the way he always had to any intractable professional problem. He prepared a deep 'chrono', putting down everything of consequence he could remember in chronological sequence. His personal diary was of small assistance. He needed help so he asked Al to visit him.

'In the circumstances, you'd better not let anyone know you are coming here,' he advised on the telephone.

'I don't give a damn,' Al replied.

Al was especially warmly welcomed by Dallas, who assumed he had come to take him for a car ride and a jog in the nearby park or in open country, as he often did. Pilgrim's welcome was even more affectionate. He embraced Al as he would one of his sons, a gesture to which Al was used but which, in the circumstances, made him feel what he was the 'Disciple' who had betrayed the master. He accepted a stiff Scotch and soda, thinking he might need it if his former chief had learned the truth. Though he had started the avalanche by informing Butch Blanchard about the culture concealed in the module, he had never expected that it would overwhelm the man he so much admired. His own judgement had been defective.

'I had an up and a downer with Arnold,' Pilgrim explained, when they were sitting comfortably. 'It was inevitable. I just couldn't take that creep any more.'

'Did you let him have it, sir?'

'Not really. I just treated him with contempt. I never fight below my weight, Al. And Arnold's a lightweight.'

'Who better to judge that than you, Sir?' Al responded. 'He's certainly too severe for my taste.' His mouth was unduly dry and he sipped his drink as he waited for further enlightenment.

'Your name wasn't mentioned, Al, so you've nothing to worry about. Your career should not be affected just because I have gone.'

Watching Al carefully, he asked, 'Did Arnold or anyone else question you about Turbid?'

'No, Sir,' Al answered, remembering Pilgrims insistence that the operation had to be deniable and realizing that the truth would devastate him. His reply was literally correct. He had volunteered the information.

'Why did the Soviets send the Mockingbird back, Al? I've looked at it all ends up. I was so sure that they would never admit hijacking it. They never have before.'

'Strictly speaking they haven't. I understand that they are telling the state department that it didn't leave Vienna.'

'Yeah, but they know that nobody's going to believe that crap.'

It was late in the day to realize it, but Pilgrim appreciated that 'never' should not be in the vocabulary of the deception game.

'I can only think that the motive must have been revenge on me for getting rid of Chevalsky. They reckoned that I would be held responsible for infecting the Mockingbird.'

'I guess that's so,' Al agreed.

Pilgrim rubbed his chin. 'On the other hand there must have been more to it than petty revenge. It doesn't really figure. It's academic now for me but this whole business will bother me until I get to the bottom of it.'

Al was in no position to explain that it must indeed have been the Russians who had infected the Mockingbird and that, but for Pilgrim's intervention, it could well have been sent back to the factory in Silicon Valley where the damage and panic it could have caused there was motive enough.

To provide thinking time he took another sip of his drink which was making him feel more relaxed. He had always prided himself on not needing the crutch of alcohol but, in recent weeks, he had been taking more of it. It was another abject way out but the time had come to end the probing if he could. 'I think you should know, sir, that I've decided to quit the Agency,' he announced.

'You mustn't do that, Al,' Pilgrim protested, assuming that he was acting out of personal loyalty. 'You must stay. You are my stake in the Agency's future. I've groomed you over the years. You're too young to succeed me now but next time round you should. Who else is there? Who else in the Agency could have handled Brown Derby like you did? We couldn't have accomplished any of the Pilgrimages without you. With Turbid we changed history, Al, like I always said we would.'

Al had never seen him so distressed but, while Pilgrim's dismay was genuine, he had an ulterior motive. If Al stayed in the Agency they would remain in touch and he could be a continuing conduit of information from the secret world, without which existence would have little meaning for him. There was no one else he could rely on. Without Al, and with Butch gone, he was going to be blind, out of business and with no hope whatever of fixing Arnold or exerting any other influence.

'I always told you that Benedict Arnold is out to wreck the Agency with all his cuts,' Pilgrim continued. 'He couldn't cut me so he got rid of me another way. The Agency is now disastrously short of seasoned campaigners. You can't possibly quit, Al. It's your duty to stay. You'll regret it if you don't.'

Al's silence asserted his determination. The brief encounter had confirmed his need to distance himself from Pilgrim before he found out the truth about Operation Turbid, which would be devastating for both of them. But his prime reason was more deep-seated. He was quitting because he could see what the game had done to the man he had hero-worshipped. Over the years he had watched an outstanding mind corroded and finally destroyed by deception and suspicion and could see himself going the same way.

'I'll think it over, sir,' he promised but had no intention of doing so. He was going and nobody, but nobody, was going to talk him out of it.

'Please do that, Al, not for my sake but for the Agency's and for the country's. Stay for a few more years – until you've groomed a successor, like I groomed you. Then you can quit, knowing you've done your duty. Maybe you shouldn't stay in the game as long as I did. Perhaps that was why I misjudged the Russians and was so sure they'd never admit hijacking the Mockingbird. Maybe I stayed in a bit too long.'

For Al, his chief's experience with Turbid had been the final eye-opener. The master deceiver who had devised it, organized it and ran it still appeared to have a totally false conception of what had really happened. He had been willied by his own side as well as by the enemy. It had been a case of he who had lived by deceit had perished by it. Al had begun to wonder whether any of their operations had been what they seemed. Looking back on his experience it could never be known, in the majority of instances, whether a secret operation had been successful or not. There was always doubt because you never really knew whether the other side was licking its wounds or laughing its head off.

He was utterly convinced that the time for him to go was now, while he was young enough to start a new career. He was not going to end up like Pilgrim, over-specialized in a game which could not be played anywhere else.

The parting, both from the master and his dog, was traumatic for Al who knew that he was unlikely to see either of them again, but it was tempered by his relief at avoiding the accusation he had feared.

After Al had left, Pilgrim thought that perhaps Al was right to quit before that bastard Arnold fired him. He would be after all the Disciples.

In fact, Arnold had tried hard to induce Al to remain. He had played an essential role in what, in the President's mind, was the most successful and significant operation ever undertaken by the Central Intelligence Agency. And he knew too much, particularly concerning certain matters which had been concealed from the oversight committees and, hopefully, always would be.

Chapter Thirty-six

As Al drove the eight miles back to Langley along the Washington Memorial Parkway and through the Virginia countryside, he took final stock of his position. He had enjoyed his years in the Agency working 'close to the horns', as Pilgrim used to put it. But it had taken savage toll. Because of his several, if brief, overseas postings and the continual inroads of Pilgrim's demands on his time, he had never married and was weary of playing the field and being deprived of parenthood. He was not short of women friends – he was the kind of man girls liked to be seen with, especially by other girls – but there was nobody close enough to confide in and he had become increasingly aware that such trust was a human necessity for anyone overburdened by too many secrets. He had become more and more withdrawn, was seeing less and less of the few men friends he cared about, stewing in the intricacies of Operation This and That. The social life that did remain was incestuous, usually spent with colleagues who were 'safe'. Even then there was the limitation of 'need to know' on what could be discussed. It was all so wearisome with colleagues whom one had to trust anyway, and sometimes it was ridiculous; like the rites of a farcical secret society. And those wretched random polygraph tests – an insult to anyone as dedicated and loyal as he was.

He was sick of dissimulating about his profession, fobbing off some stranger who was innocently interested in what he did for a living. Sure, it had become more sensible with the assassination abroad of CIA men whose cover had been maliciously exposed, but he wondered, in the current climate of opinion, how many of his colleagues kept quiet about the nature of their work because they were ashamed of it.

Al had been disquieted by the experience of one friend who had finally felt the need to tell his family that he worked for the CIA. His young daughter's reaction had been, 'But that's dirty'. As the man had expressed his feelings, 'I felt it was a pretty meagre reward for

twenty-five of the best years I could muster working for my country.'
It wasn't a career to be ashamed of. Yet his own shame was beginning
to weigh heavily. Al's mother had told him that he must never do
anything of which he would be ashamed in later life because it would
come to haunt him. She had been right.

Nothing scarified character more than the constant practice of
deception, with its lies and counter-lies. He could no longer accept
any statement or action at its face value. Automatically, he found
himself looking for ulterior meanings and ulterior motives, unable
to trust anybody and prepared to think the worst about everybody.

He had been too long away from the real world. If he stayed away
any longer he would not be able to adapt to it as, clearly, Pilgrim
was not going to be able. Now, Pilgrim would be full-time in the real
world, for which he was no longer fitted, after so long in the
demi-monde of shadows. In the real world people were, by and large,
what they seemed and meant what they said. For Pilgrim there would
be no more sneakies to intrude, no more secrets to decipher, no more
Joes to run, no more conspiracies to contrive. Nothing to stimulate
the adrenaline. After a life in which almost every minute had been
mortgaged, Pilgrim was going to have time on his hands and nothing.
to do with it. He would feel very deprived and, possibly, for the first
time in his life, afraid.

Secret service did attract odd people and Pilgrim was not the only
one. There were others in the Agency, though not quite so extreme
– yet. Why should he, Al Quest, be any different? Maybe he had
been odd to begin with but the work had certainly made him odder.
Under continuing contagion, he could end up as weird as his master,
unable to believe that two and two ever made four because it couldn't
possibly be that simple.

In what other profession would your boss keep telling you: 'We
only exist to do things which are ethically wrong. You must learn
to lie, convincingly. Conscience is a luxury we cannot afford. In our
business nothing is ever what it seems. Whatever you do in line of
duty, never regret it. Soul-searching is not for the likes of us.' Well,
there were things he did regret and if a sense of shame for bad
memories was evidence of conscience, then he had one. He would
go while he still possessed a fragment of soul to search.

He had been required to do some tawdry, degrading things in
fulfilling Pilgrim's oft-repeated request: 'Make this small sacrifice in

the interests of the Agency . . .' He was sickened by the memory of some of them and one in particular, when he had been required to take advantage of a fellow guest at a Thanksgiving dinner. OK, he had been obeying orders but that did not absolve him of responsibility when faced with being honest with himself. He had allowed himself to be used, most shamefully, in that hallowed atmosphere of goodwill and fellowship.

He had been concerned, too, about the death of that girl who had stumbled on the silicon secret. He couldn't really believe that Pilgrim or anyone else in the Agency had been responsible in the remotest way but the fact that he had been driven even to entertain the idea, however fleetingly, spoke for itself.

Pilgrim's original promise that he would find the career fulfilling had not itself been fulfilled. 'We changed history, Al,' Pilgrim had assured him but, as far as he was aware, all Pilgrim really knew was that one KGB chief had been changed for another. The game would go on as before and, for Al, the thrill had gone out of it. In fact, thrills usually meant that something had gone wrong in what was, mainly, tedious slog among the computered files. Suddenly, he couldn't face the hard labour of even one more 'deep chrono'.

Most of the so-called 'intelligence' was unintelligible. It was a matter of assessing the 'preponderance of probabilities' and looking for the hidden meaning which might not be there but could, self-deceivingly, be invented. Was the Great Game no more than an endless contest perpetuated by the adversaries for no other purpose than to keep it going? Like a game of American football with an infinite number of doubtful touchdowns – and no crowd. Or like an incessant feud between clans. The conflicting intelligence services spent half their time wreaking revenge on each other to counter old scores.

If he continued, how would he feel when his full time had run out and he had retired? Would he think his life well spent? He enormously doubted it. Wouldn't he have wasted what remained of his years and his talent with no inner satisfaction to show for it?

His soliloquy had exposed an abiding truth obvious to moralists down the age but prohibited to those, like himself, so deep in the secrets world – that a cornerstone of a contented life, in any of its aspects, is freedom from deceit. By the time he reached the checkpoint at Langley he had made up his mind to take up an offer from a girl friend's father to join an insurance business back in New Orleans where he had relatives and friends. It would be dull but not searing. And it would be real.

Betty Pilgrim was not really surprised at her husband's treatment, which she had always thought was inevitable. He confided that he had been fired but, still governed by 'need to know' as he always would be, he could not tell her exactly why. She felt deeply sorry for him, knowing what the breach would mean, but did not conceal her relief and even pleasure. She, more than anyone else, had noted what had been happening to Ross. His mind ever more tortuous and obsessive. Conversationally he was so buttoned up that he spoke to his dog more than he did to her, for ever making telephone calls, often late into the night, to people he rarely chose to name. He could think about nothing but the next deception and she was unutterably bored with it all. No wife had been hit harder by the side effects of secrecy.

It had not always been like that. Basically, Ross was kind and generous by nature, though mean with his time. His love for her had been steadily and inexorably usurped by his love for his work. Most well-matched couples needed to be happy in each other's silences but the awesome demands of security had put so much out of court that silence was the norm. When a man was so wrapped up in his profession and could not talk about it there was little left. She thanked God that, with her unremitting support against their father's insistence, their sons had spurned the profession and had been spared the effects of the serpent suspicion. She had not resented Al, whom she liked very much, but he had replaced her as far as confidences were concerned.

In her heart she was glad that Ross had been fired: there was no other way he would have quit. She had never really believed that he would keep his promise to retire at sixty. It would always be too easy to concoct some imperative reason for staying on just one more year. The loss of his salary was of little consequence. He would still receive an excellent pension and their investments provided more than enough anyway. Maybe things would be different when he had recovered from the shock. A mind as active as his would have to do something to fill the emptiness of not being in the know. He could not just sit in the departure lounge waiting to be called. At least they could do some travelling. There were so many places she wanted to visit, especially historic centres of religion in Italy and Spain.

For years Ross had been able to cover his hatred of holidays with the excuse of some urgent operation or other, which he could not possibly explain, and had always taken the minimum. On the few occasions when they had travelled to Rome, Vienna, Paris or wherever, he had indulged his infinite capacity for combining business with business, spending time with the CIA agents there, while she was left to sightsee on her own. He would sit up half the night talking to this and that station chief and he was ever on guard, wondering about the real identity and intention of any itinerant photographer who might approach them at an open air table in the Piazza Navona, the Prater or Boulevard des Capucines.

Now, for health reasons alone, he would need to be taken out of himself. As he had often said himself, 'If you retire out of life, life retires out of you.' She would do her best to be understanding – if he would let her. She was deeply concerned by his lack of religious faith but held out little hope of interesting him in her church work. When she had suggested that, with dangerous decades looming, he should discard his doctrine of hopelessness and begin to make peace with his Maker, his response had been, '*Gloria in extremis Deo?* If I ever did that, it would be no more than a triumph of fear over reason.'

Betty was sure that if he did come to experience such fear he would keep it to himself, like so much else, however desperate his predicament.

Pilgrim still had work to do. There were too many loose ends for him to be capable of leaving the situation alone. The chrono had raised a lot of questions to which he needed firm answers before he could close the file on Operation Turbid. He believed he knew them but, for peace of mind, he had to be certain. Al had denied telling Arnold anything and he was as straight as a gun barrel. He wouldn't lie to him. Neither would any of the other Disciples. But someone had betrayed him to Arnold. Who?

As he tickled Dallas behind the ear, staring into space, one candidate repeatedly came to mind – a man who was big, bulky, jovial and florid and answered to the name of Butch.

Chapter Thirty-seven

The contents of Pilgrim's safe had been delivered, in several boxes, to Arnold's office, as he had ordered, and the Director sifted through them with fascination and a few mild expletives. His first find of consequence was Pilgrim's birth certificate, which caused him to guffaw.

'Good Heavens! The M's for Mayflower! No wonder he wanted to hide it. Mayhem would have been more appropriate.'

A thick wad of papers told him that Pilgrim had run Brown Derby. He had seen a report on the defector but had not realized the extent to which he had been in collaboration with Pilgrim or the amount of valuable 'chicken-feed' on which he, and the GRU, had feasted. Arnold made a note to inquire further.

But it was a batch of older documents which made him whistle with astonishment and anticipation. After absorbing their contents he switched on the intercom with his secretary. 'Get Mr Charles Yates back from London immediately, for consultation.'

For almost a week, Pilgrim remained in something of a daze, fatigued to a degree which he had never experienced, even during the height of an operation involving consecutive nights with little or no sleep. With the removal of whatever it was that had fired him for so long, he felt as drained of energy as a rundown car battery. He had never contemplated dismissal, believing himself to be indispensable, for it was generally accepted that he knew more about the Soviet bloc intelligence services than anyone outside the Soviet Union. Now he faced the dreadful prospect of 'taking things easy', without any preparation for it.

Still, however he felt physically, when a devious mind had been as active as his had for so long, it had a life of its own. As he sat at home, dressed as he would have been at the office in a good suit and bow tie, the inevitable question insisted on posing itself – how could he extract some advantage from his apparently disastrous situation?

For the first time in his professional career he could see no immediate hope of any. Somehow, he needed to shoot Arnold off his perch – in the best interests of the Agency – but no course of action presented itself. The only thing to do was to keep in touch with internal events in the CIA and wait for a windfall or a banana skin. Arnold was very inexperienced, he was bound to make mistakes. But, without access, he wouldn't hear about them or be able to take any action if he did. How to get back in touch? Al was his best hope but he seemed to be set on quitting, though he would have one more go at trying to make him change his mind. There was only Butch.

If he could get back into Butch's close confidence he might still be a man of some influence – at a distance, operating with long tongs. There was no room for sentiment in the intelligence game, in which he was determined to remain, somehow. In countering Soviet gambits he had always tried to put himself in the adversary's position. So he asked himself what he would have done in Butch's situation? He, too, would have put loyalty to a friend second – a poor second. Friendship should never be allowed to bias important operations, in which anybody was expendable.

Whatever Butch had done, it would have been through a sense of duty, with much heart-searching if any friend was to be hurt. He would have to go through the motions of forgiving him. The alternative was facing the awful emptiness of being as blind to the secret events shaping history as any ordinary citizen.

Yes, when the opportunity arose he would make his resentment plain but trade it off for the greater benefit of renewed communication. The good-natured Butch would always harbour guilty feelings which would give him an on-going edge in their relationship. So he would do what he could to heighten that sense of culpability.

Pilgrim took down his large edition of *Stevenson's Book of Quotations* and looked in the index for Betrayal, seeking a telling quote which he could throw at Butch when they spoke again. Running his finger down the relevant page, all he could find was a line from Meredith, 'We are betrayed by what is false within', which he did not know quite how to interpret in view of his own behaviour, though that, of course, had been in the interest of the Agency.

He could relax for a day or two. Nobody much would be bothering him now that the media interest had been overwhelmed by new sensations. The vengeful Arnold would ensure that CIA staffers were forbidden to consort with him and those he cared about would be scared to anyway. That was the awful penalty of his peculiar position. The agent who retired honourably could, at least, keep in touch with the old world through former colleagues. Other callers were unlikely. But he had always thrived on solitude and considered himself rich in the smallness of his general emotional needs.

Restlessly, he picked up the latest travel brochure which Betty had placed conspicuously on his desk. It was about Assisi, where that guy who talked to birds had lived more than seven hundred years ago. Betty seemed to have taken a shiner to him and was always reading up on his history. Assisi looked pretty enough, with its white churches and twisting streets, but hardly meriting the effort of getting there and not worth the time. As for the birds, from what he had heard, the Italian 'sportsmen' had shot them all, so the little friar with the bat ears would be short of an audience if he ever returned. Pilgrim smiled at the thought and committed the brochure to a drawer already containing half a dozen others, all with religious connotations. He would have to give in to Betty's pressure for a trip to Europe eventually but she would have to wait until the spring; winter was no time for trips to Europe. By then he could have recovered his balance and, hopefully, re-established some kind of communication with the Agency.

He had a sound excuse for inaction which Betty would be unable to deny. It would be safer to lie low for quite a while longer for security reasons. If Chevalsky's henchmen tried to exact revenge – not directly but in a long-tongs operation through a hit-man – where better to do it than in some foreign country where terrorists were active and for hire? In Washington the FBI were on the ball and he himself could watch for anyone taking an interest in the house and make a point of looking under his automobile. Yes, it was wiser, on all counts, to stay at home.

With nothing better to do for a few minutes, Pilgrim made a rough calculation of how much tobacco he had smoked in his lifetime. He had been coughing so badly that Betty had been nagging. His calculation showed that he had consumed just short of thirty-four miles of cigarettes. He lit another one and looked at his watch. There was one old professional colleague with whom he would have to make contact as a matter of some urgency. He had tried to remember exactly what was in his safe and recalled certain papers which were sure to be drawn to Arnold's attention. And after the way he had been treated, that heartless Puritan would not be able to resist the pleasure of making use of them. The time was convenient. He telephoned Sandy Pryce.

Pilgrim did, indeed, know his Butch. Alone in his flat, and with no wife or dog for comfort, Butch felt very badly about his friend's plight. What he had done had been done for the greater good, though it had not been a pleasant choice between loyalty to a friend or to duty. 'I slept and dreamed that life was beauty. I woke and found that life was duty' was an oft-used quote when he felt he was being overworked. That was what he had found when Al had faced him with the Mockingbird predicament. Duty had won.

Initially, in his fury at the attempt to willie him so dangerously, Butch had felt that Pilgrim should leave the CIA, for his own good as well as for that of the United States, and he had found himself agreeing with the President when he had given the green light to Arnold to dismiss him. But, contrary to his nickname, he had never been a 'good butcher' with staff and eventually had done his best with both Rockwell and Arnold to save his friend from anything. more than a severe reprimand. He had even interceded with Baby Rockwell, who had done what she could, but, though the President was compassionate, he, too, had a strong sense of duty and, having presented Arnold with his reason, he could hardly countermand his action. 'Pilgrim's Progress' had come to a final halt.

The manner of Pilgrim's dismissal had angered Butch when he heard of it. It had been altogether too undignified and sadistic with no allowance made for years of devoted service. With his increasingly transparent zest for 'one hundred per cent honesty' with the President, Arnold had not been able to resist telling Rockwell how he had disposed of Pilgrim with extreme ignominy. The President, who also thought his behaviour had been unnecessarily brutal, had refrained from reminding Arnold that vengeance belonged to the Lord but was beginning to wonder about his Director's zeal and to what other excesses it might lead.

As the White House Chief of Staff, Butch had been advised to stay away from Pilgrim, at least until a decent interval had elapsed, to avoid giving the media cause for any comment about their friendship. But he felt driven, by guilt as much as by friendship, to commiserate

266

with him on the telephone, risking the possibility that Pilgrim had tumbled to what he would regard as his betrayal. He rationalized that those in the deception game, as they both had been, have to be prepared to deceive anyone. Pilgrim had only been doing what he had perceived to be his duty, as he had himself.

'Gee, Ross, I really am upset about what's happened,' Butch ventured.

'So am I, Butch, so am I.'

'What's it all about?'

'Don't you know, Butch?'

Butch was hesitant in his reply. 'I don't know any details.'

'Well, I won't be telling you any details on the telephone,' a remark suggesting that Butch was welcome to call round.

'Of course not,' Butch replied, declining to take up the offer. 'How are you feeling?'

'I think I'm all right. Everything is working at the moment.'

'I meant morale-wise?'

'What's important is how morale is in the Agency.'

'The Agency is sure going to miss you, Ross.'

'And I'm going to miss the Agency. It's been my whole life,'. Pilgrim added with a discernible touch of bitterness.

'Yeah, it owes you plenty.'

'I guess it was my own fault, to some extent,' Pilgrim admitted. 'Even I didn't think that the Russians would be such bastards.'

'You mean sending that thing back infected?'

'Yeah, just that.'

So Pilgrim was continuing with the fiction that he had not tried to infect it. Even with him.

Sensing that Butch was either still too embarrassed to see him or had been advised not to – probably both – Pilgrim decided to end the conversation.

'I'd like to talk about all this one day, Butch, but not just yet.'

'I understand, Ross. Pause for reflection, as you always say. Pause for reflection.'

'I don't think I need to reflect very long.'

Butch got the message. 'Well, I'll be in touch later, Ross.'

'Yeah, you do that.

The phone went dead in Butch's hand. At least he had broken the ice but the water was clearly very cold.

The more he thought about Pilgrim's plight the more he was concerned for him, physically as well as mentally. He did not think that he would last long in retirement without the 'game'. It was like having his life-support machine switched off. Without access to secrets and the secrets fraternity he would be consigned to the wilderness of ignorance, the world of ordinary knowledge and ordinary people, which would be unutterably boring for him and where his ingenuity and cunning would have no outlet. He would miss not only being in the know but also the operational power which he had come to regard as his right.

What was it that Cicero had said? 'The keystone to a happy life is freedom from care.' That was rubbish in Pilgrim's case. He needed something to care about, in the shape of clandestine action, and there was no substitute for it. 'No memory of having starred atones for later disregard' was a more fitting quotation. The withdrawal symptoms would be terrific and Pilgrim was going to have to endure the cold turkey treatment for the rest of his days. Poor Ross! Poor Betty!

Chapter Thirty-eight

Pilgrim was not the only one wondering what advantage he might make of the situation. The CIA chief was not finished. He had another burden to offload, another character whom he could not trust.

Among the effects in Pilgrim's personal safe, Arnold had found the documents relating to his entrapment of Sandy Pryce in Washington. There was the original report and supporting material, including a copy of a bugged conversation – all the material Pilgrim could have used if Pryce had ever decided to backslide. They were fifteen years old but, to Arnold's eyes, they were red hot.

He had called Al Quest into his office, ostensibly to appeal to him not to leave the Agency, and, adopting his praying mantis pose, had then questioned him about the episode. Though harrowingly embarrassed by the disclosure of his part in it, Al had no alternative. but to give him the details. He was leaving and Pilgrim had gone, so there seemed to be no point in holding back on what he knew, which was fairly comprehensive.

Arnold had been horrified. What Pilgrim had perpetrated had been close to blackmail. Anyone who had been so sinful and so disloyal to his own service, as Pryce had been over so many years, could not be trusted with American secrets, as the MI5 chief had to be. The CIA, or rather Pilgrim, had received a stream of valuable information in return but, in Arnold's view, that could never neutralize the shame of it all.

Responding briskly to the Director's command, Charlie Yates flew to Washington and was fully briefed by Arnold on the details. He, too, was astonished, not so much by what Pilgrim had done as by the way he had managed to keep it absolutely secret within the Agency, apart from Al. After being instructed to inform no one else within the CIA, Yates was dispatched back to London to accomplish his mission with all speed and to communicate his progress reports to Arnold in person on his private, scrambled telephone. As Arnold could not risk being accused of interference in British affairs, he wanted no personal involvement. Nor did he want any prurient scandal involving the CIA. So the operation which he and Yates had hatched exploited the advantage of long tongs. The coup de grâce had to be delivered quietly and 'in house' – by MI5 itself.

It did not occur to Arnold that he was beginning to operate privately and surreptitiously in the style of the man he had fired and that Yates was being made something of Disciple. But he was aware that what he was trying to do should be kept from the prying eyes and intrusive ears of the oversight committees.

On his return to London, Yates set up a seemingly routine lunch with Lesley Barrington-Fuller, who was always keen to meet him after a visit to Washington. He was certain to have picked up some useful gossip and the unexpected invitation, immediately on his return, implied that he wanted to impart. The venue was the Café Royal Grill, in Regent Street, which Charlie had chosen for a cogent reason.

They had their aperitifs in the Wilde Bar, named after Oscar and the site of his famous encounter with the Marquess of Queensberry over the playwright's relationship with his strikingly handsome young son, Lord Alfred Douglas. Charlie had done his homework. and was able to introduce his subject without appearing to contrive it.

'It was over there, in what used to be the Domino Room, that Queensberry appeared with a horse whip looking for Oscar. Fortunately he wasn't there. Or perhaps unfortunately. As you know, the matter of whether Oscar was a sodomite or not was settled in court.'

'And that was the end of a great writer,' Lesley commented, sipping her glass of cold, white wine.

'Yes. And I fear that something like it is going to be the end of someone else.'

'Meaning whom?' Lesley asked.

'Your chief.'

'You don't mean Sandy?'

Making a credible show of looking embarrassed, Charlie replied, 'What I can tell you is that relations between our two outfits will never be quite as close, now that Ross Pilgrim has gone.'

'Why ever not?

'Because there was a specially intimate relationship between Pilgrim and Pryce.'

270

'Are you suggesting that they were more than good friends?'
'Yes.'
'You don't mean like Oscar Wilde and Lord Alfred Douglas?'
Charlie smiled and shook his head. 'There's certainly never been anything queer about Ross Pilgrim.'
'And Sandy?'
Charlie shifted uneasily and adjusted his glasses. 'There's been a buzz about Sandy Pryce in the higher echelons of the CIA for years. Something about Sandy being caught in some homosexual activity in Washington when he was drunk and Pilgrim getting it hushed up – at a price. Secrets like that are supposed to be safe in an outfit like ours but you know how it is, when two know, five know, and when five know, twenty know . . . But I never checked it out with the FBI. I guess they'd know if it was true.'
'In that case wouldn't they have done something about it?' Lesley asked, her interest mounting by the second.
'Not if it was to our advantage. Not if it gave us some useful leverage on your outfit, on MI5.'
'You mean leverage as regards information you might not otherwise have got? "UK Eyes Only" stuff.'
'We certainly got it a lot quicker. At least that's what I've been told,' Charlie added, hurriedly.
'But as head of station here, Charlie, didn't all the MI5 information to Washington go through you?'
'No way! What I'm talking about was not on any official net. Just a private deal between Pryce and Pilgrim. I believe that until Pryce became Director-General they used a cut-out.'
'Let me get this clear, Charlie. What you are saying is that Pilgrim had this hold on him and – er – well, kind of blackmailed him?'
'That's the buzz, Lesley. But it was more payment of a debt than blackmail.'
'What a bastard!' Lesley commented.
'Oh, Pilgrim would easily defend it as being in the best interests of the Agency. And remember, the alternative was Pryce's total disgrace and the end of his career.'
Lesley's intuition was working overtime, as was her dedication to her ambition. 'But doesn't it follow that if the allegation is true then the DG must have repeatedly falsified his PV form over the years when asked about any homosexual problem?'

'I guess so, if it is true.'

'That's terrible, especially when he's been so tough on other homosexuals in the Service. Could you check it out for me in more detail now that Pilgrim's gone?'

Charlie pondered for a few seconds. 'What would be in it for us, Lesley?'

'Well I, for one, would be eternally grateful and you never know who might succeed the DG if he chose to depart early.'

Charlie got the message but would not commit himself. 'I'll take advice,' he promised as he prepared to pay the bar bill.

They moved into the grill room with its painted ceiling, its caryatids and array of antique mirrors which had reflected so many eminent faces in their time. Staring at the large menu, Lesley, who appreciated good food and usually made the most of Charlie's expense account which was less limiting than that allowed by MI5, made a quick choice. She could not wait to get the ball of conversation rolling again. But Charlie soon indicated that he had given all that he intended and they fell to discussing more general issues. She had budgeted for the lunch to last until 3 p.m. but at 2.30 announced that she had a meeting. Charlie was not misled.

'Have a nice day!' he said, cheerily as he saw her out of the grill room.

He recovered the racing edition of the *Evening Standard* from his overcoat in the cloakroom, returned to his table and ordered some fresh coffee and a brandy. There was time for a bet and he was feeling lucky.

Walking the short way back to Curzon Street, Lesley was almost oblivious of the crowds. She had not been taken in by Charlie's diffidence. She knew that he would never have put such an issue into her mind without being sure of it and without wanting her to do something about it. It could not be coincidence that he had been recalled hastily to Washington and had contacted her immediately on his return. He had given her prodigious information and the question she asked herself, repeatedly, as she crossed Burlington Street, Bond Street and Dover Street was 'How do I play it? How do I play it?'

Charlie had not told her all he knew. His briefing had been very thorough but he was keeping certain details in reserve in case further action was needed. Pilgrim had always been suspicious of British liaison officers after the proven cases of the Maclean–Burgess–Philby network and of Maurice Oldfield, a secret homosexual who had eventually become head of the British Secret Service. Discussing Pryce's arrival with Al who was then his young protégé, aged twenty-four, he had remarked with his occasional streak of coarseness, 'The anus of proof is on any bachelor the British send.'

Al had suggested that Pryce, who was stationed in the British Embassy under diplomatic cover, should be given the benefit of any doubt unless and until events proved otherwise but his mentor had disagreed. 'The Agency can't afford to take any more chances. With this guy we need to *know* that he's not blackmailable *before* we tell him anything of consequence. You see, Al, we have to exchange a lot of secrets with MI5. That's why this guy's been sent here. He's the conduit.'

'But now that homosexuality between consenting adults is not a criminal offence in Britain, would he be blackmailable?' Al asked.

'He most certainly would. It's still a social stigma and most of these queers need to keep their problem secret, especially in this profession. The Brits would not knowingly have sent a queer. Homosexuals are supposed to be barred from their secret services. So if Pryce is one, he must have faked his PV clearances. That alone would make him blackmailable. And if there's a hole in the dyke in MI5 there might as well be a hole in the dyke here.'

'So what's to do?'

'There's nothing I can do, Al. I'm too old and too ugly. But there's something a good-looking fellow like you could do. He could take a fancy to you.'

'Steady on, sir. That's not my scene.'

'I know that, Al,' Pilgrim said, soothingly. 'I don't want you to go through any motions. I'd just like you to see something of this guy socially and if he makes a pass at you, let me know.'

Al found the idea repulsive but was keen to oblige his master – in the interests of the Agency.

'You'd just be testing him out,' Pilgrim explained encouragingly. 'Acting as an *agent provacateur*. That's thoroughly professional in our business. The FBI use that tactic all the time with people they suspect.'

Pilgrim was a hard man to deny. 'OK. I'll see the guy, but nothing else,' Al agreed.

Pilgrim had arranged for Al and Pryce to be seated next to each other at the dinner which he and Betty always put on at their home for selected Agency people and allied colleagues on Thanksgiving Day in late November. Betty was a splendid cook, and being limited to the occasional entertaining her husband would allow, made the most of the opportunity.

They never slavishly segregated the sexes at the dining table, preferring to seat guests on the basis of likely mutual interest; there had, in fact, been more men there than women. The special significance of the date hardly seemed appropriate to Al but Pilgrim had swept aside any objection with 'The better the day, the better the deed!'

As a first-time guest at such a festivity, Pryce had been induced to drink too much, and had then been advised not to drive back to his apartment but to be driven there by Al who, as something of a fitness buff, took only soft drink. On arrival there, Pryce had asked him in for coffee and Al had put his arm round his shoulder to steady him and help him to the escalator. Once in the apartment Pryce had taken the first opportunity to put his hand, gropingly, on Al's crotch in such a provocative way that there could be no mistaking its message.

It was the kind of pass that Al had made at a score of girls in his time but he found it so distasteful that he experienced difficulty in refraining from 'punching the slob', as he had reported to Pilgrim next morning. After voicing his disgust he had stormed out in genuine anger, ignoring Pryce's confused apologies.

'You were dead right, sir. We need to get that feller out of contact with the Agency, out of the United States and out of intelligence, soonest,' he told his chief next morning.

Pilgrim expressed dismay. 'So, the goddamn Brits sent us another poofter! Don't they ever learn? What evidence have you got for me.'

Feeling in his pocket, Al produced a mini-tape which had been connected to the microphone in his heavy right cufflink.

The proper practice, as Al had expected, would have been for Pilgrim to have reported his complaint to the FBI which, after inquiries, would have reported to the State Department. Instead – as he had always intended should happen – Pilgrim asked Pryce to see him. Sheepishly, Pryce did so to hear that Pilgrim had received a complaint from Mr Quest.

'I greatly regret it, Mr Pryce, especially when you are so new here, but I have no option but to report it to the FBI. I fear that your Ambassador is then bound to hear about it.'

'But your colleague mistook a harmless gesture,' Pryce protested.

'Well, he is sure he didn't. Here's his report and he's pressing for action.'

Pryce read it and handed it back with despair. 'I must have been drunk. In fact I know I was drunk. I can't really remember anything about the episode. I will be ruined if the Ambassador hears of it. I'll do anything to prevent that . . .'

Pilgrim rubbed his chin. 'I might be able to calm Mr Quest down but I would be taking quite a personal risk in not reporting your conduct.'

'I repeat, I'll do anything if you could bring yourself to avoid that.'

'I wouldn't want any favours myself, Mr Pryce, but there might be ways you could help the Agency in the future . . .'

Pryce had been a pushover and did everything he could to keep Pilgrim fully informed of MI5 matters. Over the years he had more than kept his word and, as each had achieved promotion, he and Pilgrim had become firm friends.

At first Al could not understand why Pryce had been allowed to remain, so Pilgrim had explained. 'You see, Al, the situation suddenly changed and one has to be flexible in this game. To keep all the options open. Thanks to you, this guy is going to be grateful, very grateful. I don't set much store by gratitude as a rule but, in the circumstances, he could be a fine asset for the Agency.'

'What if the KGB gets at him, like you said?'

'I'm confident they won't. I've got this guy under control.'

Al had appreciated that he had been willied. It would not be the last time.

In spite of Pilgrim's general admonition that there was no room for emotion in the intelligence game and that shame was a particularly cramping emotional attitude, Al had felt ashamed at the time. Pilgrim noticed it but did no more than put his arm round Al's shoulder and remark, 'Every operation exacts some price – no pun intended.'

Sitting at her desk in the Curzon Street headquarters and mulling over her lunch with Yates, Lesley deduced that Pryce must have told Pilgrim about the silicon business as soon as he had heard of it. So that had been the origin of the leak on which she and others had spent so much time and effort! She also realized that she had been

275

willied by Pryce when he had sent her to Porton to induce Adrian Allen to leak the story to Fort Detrick. He had been covering his own indiscretion. 'The devious old sod!' she muttered. 'Yes, sod is right.'

She could not get home to Devonshire Street quickly enough to discuss the day's events with her husband.

'I've got news for you, darling, You've missed out on Sandy Pryce.'
'In what way?'
'He's a homosexual.'
'What makes you say that?' Paul asked.
'Charlie Yates told me. The CIA has cast-iron evidence going back a long long way.'
'Maybe so, but he's not practising now.'
'That's academic,' Lesley said, forcefully. 'He could never have admitted it on his PV form so he must have falsified it. He secured the DG-ship by fraud. It's another Oldfield case.'
Paul looked serious but said nothing.
'You don't seem surprised,' Lesley said.
'I suppose I'm not, really, now you've said it. All the predisposing factors are there − a bachelor, the distress of mental loneliness, a mother complex, an uncaring father who died young. And he has prodromal symptoms − a drink problem indicating an unstable temperament, some kind of chip on his shoulder. It all fits. I overlooked the basic tenet of diagnosis − common symptoms have common causes. Perhaps it has just been something that I never wanted to face.'
'Do you think you ought to see him now, dear? He's been looking unduly harassed recently and is very irritable. I would guess he's hitting the bottle again − hard.'
'Why do you think he's doing that?' Paul asked.
'It's just a guess but he may have heard that the CIA has discovered his secret and intends to do something about it. If so, he needs help.'
'Oh God, it's going to be terribly embarrassing but I suppose I had better see him. If he was just an ordinary patient I wouldn't be the slightest bit fussed. I sometimes wonder if this MI5 job is worth the candle. If the authorities knew half of what I hear they'd do their nuts.'

His wife refrained from reminding him that he enjoyed being in the know as much as the next man – or woman.

Paul telephoned Pryce from his office at the Maudsley Hospital. 'Good morning, Sandy. How are you?'

'A bit weary,' a sepulchral voice replied. 'I'm sleeping badly. What can I do for you?'

'Nothing. It's a question of what can I do for you. Lesley told me you're not looking too well. The diary tells me it's time we had another chat. After this week I'm pretty full for the next month or two. Can you manage this week?'

'Sure. Things are reasonably quiet – or as quiet as they ever are.'

They fixed a date at Paul's consulting rooms. Sandy enjoyed his sessions there. He got things off his chest. With a doctor of such eminence and especially one who had been positively vetted, all secrets were safe. Pilgrim had been the only other person in whom he had been able to confide in safety. And it looked as though he had been deprived of him.

Chapter Thirty-nine

Paul's consulting rooms in Wimpole Street were austere, with nothing extraneous that could divert a patient's concentration from his own thoughts. The patient relaxed on an upholstered leather couch with an adjustable headrest. A carafe of water and a glass were conveniently positioned, for confession tended to dry the roof of the mouth. Paul preferred to interview sitting in an upholstered leather armchair with a small swivel table for note-taking. A desk would have been more convenient but he needed an atmosphere of informality. The only other concession to comfort was a plain, thick-pile, wall-to-wall carpet. There were no flowers, to which some patients might be allergic. The cream-painted walls were pictureless. The only other furniture was a rather fine break-front bookcase stuffed with medical volumes.

Since M15 personnel regularly opened their hearts there, the rooms were 'swept' frequently. With all his MI5 patients Paul was required to operate in absolute confidence because none of the officers wanted their colleagues to know that they were having recourse to the 'shrinker'.

With his tape-recorder, notepad and fountain pen at the ready – he had a distaste for ballpoints – Paul watched Sandy as he settled his ample frame on the couch. He was shocked by the deterioration in his appearance. With his eyes closed, his skin ashen and his hands crossed over his protuberant paunch, he could have been a corpse.

'Well, Sandy. Anything special worrying you?'

'I'm very worried about my old friend, Ross Pilgrim. You know he was sacked from the CIA in the most appalling manner. He was a great man. The best counter-intelligence officer of his generation – possibly of any other.'

'Yes. Lesley told me about him and I saw something in the newspapers. A sorry business. I wonder what was behind it.'

The patient remained silent but Paul sensed that there was more to his obvious anxiety than concern about a distant friend.

'You'd better tell me everything you know, Sandy. Everything that's worrying you.'

'I understand that the Director of Central Intelligence, Stanley Arnold, has got his hands on some papers of Pilgrim's which could compromise me.'

Pryce then told him a fraction of the story, saying only that he had been compromised over a drunken incident.

'Are you really telling me, Sandy, after all this time, that you have a homosexual problem?'

Pryce was staggered by Paul's insight, which he attributed to his psychological skills.

'I did have. But, thanks to you, I don't have it now.'

'Why thanks to me, Sandy?'

'Because you helped with my drink problem and when I don't have that I don't have the other.'

'Well, tell me about your past problem.'

With complete trust in the doctor-patient relationship, Pryce unburdened himself about the episode with Al Quest, though not all about its consequences.

'Tell me about those papers you mentioned, Sandy.'

'I gather that they record the incident I've just described. Nothing happened. Nothing whatever. But it could be made to look bad.'

'How did this man, Arnold, get them?'

'They were in Pilgrim's safe.'

'And why do you think that Pilgrim kept them, Sandy?'

'I don't know. It was a great shock to me to hear that he had.'

'How did you hear it?'

'He very kindly telephoned me the other day to apologize for failing to destroy them and to warn me what might happen.'

'And what do you think that will be?'

'Pilgrim says that this man, Arnold, is very vengeful. He might make the papers public to show that Pilgrim was derelict in his duty. You see, he should have reported me to the FBI and he didn't.'

'And you would be disgraced in the process?'

'I would be finished, Paul. Completely finished. I would have to admit that for years I have made false statements on my positive vetting form. When I have been asked about homosexual experiences I have always denied any, as they were all so long ago. But it would look bad in a report to the Prime Minister. As it did with poor old

Maurice Oldfield. They took his positive vetting clearance away, you know.'

'So that's why you've been looking so worried lately and not sleeping.'

Pryce opened his eyes and gave him a pathetic look. 'It's enough, isn't it? I can't sleep for worrying what might be in next morning's newspapers. What can I do, Paul? I would greatly welcome your advice.'

'I'll have to think about it. How much longer do you want to stay as DG?'

'Only a couple of years at the most. Why?'

'Well, if your departure meant that this fellow Arnold would be satisfied, it might be in your medical interest, as well as your professional interest, to take early retirement on health grounds.'

Pryce sighed dejectedly. 'I have thought about that as an option, in the darkest hours of the night.'

Paul smiled, appreciatively. 'Odd about the dark, isn't it. Anxieties do not obey the laws of optics – it is the absence of light that magnifies them.'

He stood up to indicate that the session was at an end. 'All I can suggest, Sandy, is that you give that option some thought, as I will, and we can get together later. I'll make time available, somehow. By the way, how are you off for sleeping tablets? I'll give you another prescription anyway.'

He dashed off a near-indecipherable prescription. Pryce collected his Homburg and was about to hold out his hand when Paul asked, 'There is just one more thing I should know, Sandy, because it affects the medical situation. Has the KGB ever suspected that you might have this, er, tendency?'

'Not as far as I am aware. Are you asking me if I have ever been importuned by the Soviet intelligence service?'

'I suppose I am.'

'Well, the answer is emphatically no! I don't think they ever tumbled to my problem. Pilgrim would never have told anyone. He's been a marvellous friend. He's extremely upset about my predicament.'

Paul was chagrined by the interview. He was supposed to be a master psychiatrist and the acknowledged expert on prodromal symptoms yet he had missed his patient's major problem. Why? Was it because it was unthinkable? He was reminded of the classic case of King George VI. The symptoms of lung cancer had been staring his doctors in the face but they had not been able to bring themselves to believe it possible because he was the King. What else was he missing? Was Sandy telling the whole truth? Or was he behaving like so many patients and hoping to get medical salvation by revealing only part of it?

He motioned Sandy to sit down on the couch while he remained standing. 'You know, Sandy, as I have always told you, it's best to make a completely clean breast of everything. You've asked me to advise you on a crucial decision. Is there any other aspect of your homosexual tendency that I should know?'

Sandy half-smiled. 'You don't believe I've had no recent experience?'

'I wouldn't say that. I just want to give you the opportunity of telling me if you have. It will do you good.'

Paul had chosen the right moment. His patient's darkest secret tumbled out. It was a common enough combination in psychiatric practice, as it was in the interrogation of traitors – the right trigger and someone who, deep down, desperately needed to unburden and confide.

'I'd learned to live with the fact that I'd falsified my PV form,' Sandy confided. 'That was just a matter for me and my conscience. But something else happened recently for which I can't forgive myself. I suppose I've been drinking to escape from it.'

'What was that, Sandy?'

'The Home Secretary sought my advice about two homosexual civil servants in the Home Office who had access to important official secrets. He made it clear that he wanted to take a "liberal" and sympathetic attitude, indicating that if I took a similar view, he would take no action against the two men. What could I do? I was in a cleft stick. I had to set aside my own problem and advise in the best interest of the Department. They had to go.'

'And they were removed?' Paul asked, affecting not to be shocked.

'Yes. Transferred to non-secret work.' Pryce looked wretched. 'One of them was a close friend of mine,' he added tearfully. 'Indeed, more than just a friend.'

'You mean that you had a relationship?'

Though Pryce did not reply, his face answered the question. He had been lying.

'It was a terrible thing to have to do but I was torn between my loyalty to this man and to the Service. He had regular access to some very sensitive material to do with warrants for surveillance. He knew the names of all the people we were watching. And they are always of the greatest interest to our adversaries.'

Paul said nothing.

'In my position I had to be seen to be taking a tough line,' Pryce continued, rotating the old Homburg in his hands. 'Not to protect myself, you understand . . .'

'Did your friend ever know?'

'About my part? No, thank God. But I know. That's my burden.'

'Do you still see him?'

Pryce paused, then answered, 'Occasionally.'

Paul was finding it hard not to despise his patient who was still being dishonest with himself.

'Now you know everything. What should I do?' Pryce asked, miserably.

'I still need time to think before I advise you,' Paul replied. 'But. I'm now in a better position to do so.' He was in no doubt where his duty lay, both medically and professionally. But he would withhold advice for a few days. There were aspects he needed to discuss with Lesley. That would not be an ethical breach. She already knew the basic facts.

'You'll keep it all secret?' Pryce asked plaintively, as he prepared to leave.

'Need you ask?'

'Even from Lesley?'

'Especially from Lesley. Have you got transport?'

'Yes, my driver is picking me up.'

Paul did not relish the possibility that the Director-General of MI5 might throw himself under a bus after visiting his consulting rooms.

282

Chapter Forty

It was unusual for Paul to discuss a patient's most secret admissions with anyone, including Lesley, but he convinced himself that the circumstances had put him into such an invidious position, affecting the national interest, that he needed her professional, insider guidance to resolve his conflict of loyalties.

'Sandy is not just a homosexual,' he told her that evening at home. 'He is a disturbed homosexual.'

'Meaning what?' she asked.

'The kind of homosexual who continually deceives himself that he has no responsibility whatever for his problem, which is the result of an unfair and uncaring society, on which he could easily take some kind of revenge.'

'You mean like that awful man, Guy Burgess, did?'

'He was the classic case.'

Lesley affected to be sorry for Pryce when Paul confirmed the danger that he faced from exposure. 'But he'll have to go, Paul,' she said. 'You must advise him to go. It would be catastrophic for MI5's morale if this thing blew. And it will if he hangs on. Charlie Yates didn't tell me all that for nothing. He'll be watching for results. Anyway, Sandy ought to go for falsifying his PV form. He's disqualified himself.'

Paul salved his professional conscience by withholding the story of Pryce's traumatic incident with the Home Secretary but Lesley was astute enough to sense that her husband had been unusually upset by the interview.

'He can't leave immediately,' she said. 'There's the question of his successor. I hope he doesn't recommend his deputy. He's a wet blanket. Do you think he might recommend me?'

'I suppose he might, my dear. He thinks very highly of you. But that's not a matter for me. Sandy is my patient. I must advise what is best in his interests.'

'Of course, darling. I wouldn't expect anything else but in this case your patient's interests and mine happen to be the same.'

Because of his ethical sensitivity Paul needed gentle handling but there was one further question Lesley felt compelled to ask in the interests of the Service. 'Did you raise the possibility that he might have been got at by the Russians?'

'Yes. He denied it and I believe him. He just hasn't got it in him to be a spy.'

'I agree. I can think of at least three operations which could not have succeeded if he had been bent but he should still be properly interrogated, like Oldfield was.'

'That's none of my business,' Paul replied, curtly. 'I am not going to be the means of subjecting a patient, who is already a weak reed, to an ordeal which could break him.'

Wasting no time in recontacting Pryce, Paul told him, 'I have looked at your situation from all angles and, in view of what I've been told by another source, I have to advise you as a friend, as well as your psychiatrist, that you should take early retirement with minimum delay.'

Pryce looked deeply concerned. 'What have you heard?'

'It's Lesley, of course, and she wouldn't mind my telling you. She has been given the whole story by a CIA contact for onward passage to you but she's been too embarrassed to tell you.'

Pryce's aspect was even more grave. 'Tell me. I can bear it.'

'This CIA man, Arnold, will definitely move against you unless you retire. It's you he's after. He's finished with Pilgrim.'

'And if I go, can I be guaranteed that there will be no publicity?'

'It would look that way.'

'I've been thinking it over, Paul, and I've already decided to go. I'm at the end of my tether. I can't take any more of the uncertainty. And, frankly, I'll do anything to avoid publicity. You remember those tabloid headlines about poor old Maurice — "Tinker, Tailor, Poofter, Spy" and all that?'

Paul nodded. 'I think you are very wise, Sandy.'

'I know I am. If it became public, there would always be doubt about whether I had been suborned by the other side. It will take a little time, of course,' he added. 'There's the question of my successor.'

'Have you given any thought to that, Sandy?' Paul asked, as casually as he could.

'I suppose I should recommend my deputy. I don't think he's very good. He's a natural Number 2. But it would be the normal practice to recommend him.'

'Buggins' turn?' Paul observed.

'That's the usual Whitehall drill. A younger person with longer to run would be better. But who is there? There's only one who's really up to it and that's Lesley.'

'Oh! She would be flattered! I didn't realize that she was that good. But that's the familiarity syndrome, I suppose.'

'Well, frankly, Paul, the competition is not all that severe. The other directors are a pretty pedestrian lot. But Lesley has all the professional qualities and she's admired and liked by her colleagues – which I never have been. If she stays in the Service she will probably be recommended for the job next time round anyway.'

'Oh, she's going to stay . . .'

'Would you ask Lesley to do me a favour?' Pryce said. 'I can hardly ask her myself.'

'Of course.'

'Ask her to let her CIA source know, confidentially of course, that I shall be retiring very soon. That should take any heat off in the intervening period.'

'That's good thinking, Sandy. I'm sure she'll do that for you.'

His patient was looking better already.

'Don't tell Lesley that I said so but I'll remember the favour,' Pryce said, with deliberation, as he prepared to leave.

He put on his Homburg, pulling it firmly on his head with both hands. 'My badge of servitude,' he said, forcing a smile. 'I always said that this would see me out and I wouldn't need another.'

Not wishing to raise hopes which might be dashed if the Prime Minister decided to appoint someone else, Paul told Lesley no more than Pryce's message. While she was excited, he was patently forlorn about the whole affair.

'It was literally like passing a death sentence,' he explained.

'How literally?'

'Once he has nothing to do, I wouldn't give him more than two years. He'll hit the bottle and hit it hard. I know he's hitting it now.'

'Poor Sandy,' Lesley said with feeling. 'It must be a terrible compulsion.'

'Homosexuality, you mean?'

'Yes.'

'It's beyond the ken of most men and all women. I never felt so sorry for a patient. When you have a memory as good as his, all the bad things in it come to haunt you, especially when you are alone in bed at night. Total recall exacts tough penalties. He won't know much peace.'

'Are there bad things you haven't told me?'

'There are always bad things I don't tell you about our friends if they also happen to be my patients.'

'We'll have to do all we can for him,' Lesley said. 'Have him in for bridge and dinner occasionally. But you did the right thing, darling. It was in the best interests of the Service. People with guilty secrets shouldn't enter the secrets world.'

'Who is without them?' Paul asked.

There was no reply.

Lesley lost no time in passing Pryce's message to Charlie Yates who quickly relayed his success to Arnold. She had no difficulty in convincing herself that her part in the ousting of Sandy had been correct and fully justified. She was aware that Charlie had willied her to some extent. But she did not mind that if the result was to her advantage – and of course to the Service's.

Paul was unable to delude himself so expediently. Lesley's behaviour, and his own, had been too remindful of his prime premise – all power corrupts and secret power corrupts particularly.

Chapter Forty-one

The summons to Number 10 Downing Street for what had become known among the mandarins as 'kissing hands', in view of the long-serving Prime Minister's almost regal status, was sudden but Lesley managed a rushed appointment with the hairdresser to match the PM's continuing band-box freshness.

She entered the holy of holies, as she always would, via the Cabinet Office building but her meeting with 'She of the We' was much less formal than she had anticipated. They talked over tea, leisurely in the study, and it was a good deal more than 'kissing hands'. The Prime Minister had not yet made up her mind. It was a look-see meeting.

From her first glance, the Prime Minister liked the cut of Lesley's jib as well as the cut of her black suit; and the professional air about her, so much in contrast with Pryce's shabbiness which she had deplored. In her experience, external appearances often betrayed the state of the mind. This Barrington-Fuller lady looked as though she would stand no nonsense and would be tough enough to take the right decisions with terrorists, who occupied much of MI5's resources. As for security, had there ever been any women traitors? If so, she hadn't heard of them. Nor could she imagine a female Peter Wright. Women weren't made that way. Blunt, Long, Hollis, Oldfield – all the security officials who had caused her so much trouble in the past had been men. She would feel safer with a woman and she made up her mind before pouring the second cups from the Georgian silver teapot.

After a succession of born-loser leaders of the Labour Party, the Prime Minister had become an international institution but Lesley was not as overawed as she had expected to be.

'We take a close personal interest in the Security Service and know its work to be of the greatest importance,' the Prime Minister said. 'We are particularly concerned about our intelligence relations with the United States. We get so much from them. So please look after them.'

The Prime Minister had particular reason for being grateful to the CIA. In deep secrecy, the slow deciphering of a mass of KGB messages intercepted during the Second World War had been continued, using advanced computer techniques. As a result, a former Director of the CIA, William Casey, had died convinced that Sir Roger Hollis, once head of MI5, had been a long-term Soviet agent. More recent breaks in the code had identified several wartime traitors who had been known only by their code-names. Some of them had been British and better known than Sir Roger. Publication of the details could be highly embarrassing to the Government, which had repeatedly denied the Hollis charges, but, to date, they were being tightly held secret by the CIA and other American intelligence agencies involved in the decrypting.

'You have right of access to me at any time,' the Prime Minister assured Lesley. 'Don't hesitate to use it if you feel you need to in the interest of the Service or if you think there is something special I need to know. Otherwise, of course, you will work with the Home Secretary. You have quite a task in front of you. I am told that morale in the Security Service is not very good and no enterprise can work effectively without high staff morale. I am relying on you to restore it.'

Lesley did not make any promises but gave the Prime Minister a reassuring look indicating her awareness of the problem and some confidence that she knew what to do about it.

'And we do hope that there will be no leaks,' the Prime Minister added. 'They are so damaging and waste so much time. As I'm sure you appreciate, secrecy is essential to good government, always has been and always will be. Open government is like saying to farmers that nothing may be grown unless the roots are visible at all times. It's simply an impossibility. The media claim that the public is with them on the secrets issue in wanting more of them revealed. I know that it is not. The public wants the nation's secrets kept.'

The Prime Minister could see that Lesley was in full agreement that secrets were sacrosanct, which was just as well. Anyone who wasn't did not last long with her and one or two of her Ministers who had departed, ostensibly for other reasons, had been removed because they were blabber-mouths.

As soon as Lesley had left, the Prime Minister took off her hand-made shoes and permitted herself a few moments' relaxation and gratification. It was an imaginative appointment for which she could take the credit among those who knew about it, for, as was customary, there would be no formal announcement. She would let it be known that she had not appointed Lesley because she was a woman but entirely on merit. It was self-evident that if a woman could deal with the Soviet state, a woman could deal with the KGB.

Lesley was walking on air as she left the Cabinet Office after being congratulated by the Cabinet Secretary.

'It's a bit of a poisoned chalice, you know,' he told her. 'Your mistakes will be obvious, your victories unseen. Don't hesitate to ask if I can help you in any way.'

Her driver took her round Parliament Square, St James's Park and down the Mall to St James's Street. She was impatient with every hold-up and could not wait to get back to Curzon Street, though nobody there could be told of her appointment until it filtered through, officially, from the Cabinet Office. She could telephone her father, though. He would be absolutely delighted and so proud. Only one thing worried her. What would happen if the PM ever found out that she had known about Pryce's homosexuality and had not instigated an interrogation?

She consoled herself that Pryce was now safely away and that nobody inside MI5, save for Paul and herself, knew the secret reason for his departure. There was that man Arnold, of course, but, having achieved his objective, he had most probably lost further interest. In her exalted position she could hardly consult Charlie Yates again about it. Others, whom she would appoint, would have to take over the cosy chats with the likes of him. She would be operating at more rarefied levels.

Yes, on all counts, Pryce was best left in peace. He could do no more damage. And she could not instigate an interrogation without breaching Paul's confidence. 'From now on I know nothing whatever about it,' she told herself.

With the traffic into Piccadilly jam-packed, she let trivialities intrude into her mind. Among the first things she would do would be to change those dull old carpets and curtains in the DG's office. How would the authorities deal with the situation in two years' time when, if tradition was followed, as surely it must be if a charge of sexism was to be avoided, she would be due for a knighthood? Would they make her a dame? And if her identity had not been publicized by then, how would they camouflage the award?

Stanley Arnold was among the first to be officially told of Pryce's retirement and Lesley's succession, and congratulated himself on an operation superbly executed. He was enjoying the game.

Charlie Yates, too, had reason to be delighted. His congratulatory note from Arnold surely implied that he would be remaining in London for at least another year, probably longer, hopefully to take advantage of his former connection with the new DG. He loved London – and Ascot and Epsom.

TOP SPYCATCHER A WOMAN was the headline on 'Wolf' Gordon's scoop. As if to ensure that there could be no back-tracking on Pryce's departure, Arnold had instructed Yates to require Joe Malinowski to tip off Gordon. The story ran:

> Britain's spy-catching organization, MI5, is to have its first woman chief. A senior woman MI5 officer, whose name I have been asked to withhold for security reasons, has been appointed to succeed Sir Alexander Pryce, who has retired two years early for health reasons.
>
> As usual, no announcement will be made. Downing Street would neither confirm nor deny the appointment last night.
>
> I understand that the new Director-General, who was appointed by the Prime Minister, has been in charge of Protective Security, but has some overseas experience, including a spell in Washington.
>
> The appointment – the first time a woman has been put in charge of any major security or intelligence organization – is a further breakthrough for women's lib and will be popular in Parliament . . .

Gordon had not been told the name but it made good copy to suggest he had and gave the impression that he was being responsible.

It was a bad start and Lesley feared that it would not be long before her identity became public knowledge. Though MI5 had been legitimized in a cosmetic Parliamentary procedure, its staff and its operations were supposed to remain as secret as they used to be before the Wright debacle. So far as she knew, no agency photographs of her existed and she would have to keep it that way. She was now a prime intelligence target for terrorists, and the IRA were no respecters of women.

Chapter Forty-two

Like any other senior civil servant, Adrian Allen put his lines out when the not unexpected news of his Director's death was announced. Though there was no need for haste in the appointment of a successor as long as he remained in temporary command, he quickly learned that he had been passed over for the post. The mandarins had decided that the Chemical Defence Establishment needed another professional administrator, as the previous Director had been, rather than a scientist, however distinguished.

Adrian had not realized how disappointed he would be, perhaps having not entertained the possibility of being passed over sufficiently. He was nearer to tears than his public-school upbringing permitted him to admit. On receiving the news by telephone he drove home in mid-afternoon, oblivious to the wheeling flocks of plovers which usually gladdened his journey and arriving churned up by his introspection.

'I'll bet it was that freckle-faced bitch!' he told himself. 'If MI5 was asked for a report on me she'd make sure I got a bad one. Poking her nose into my private life! What the hell had it got to do with my ability to do the job?'

In fact, Lesley had not been asked for a view about him. She had too many new areas of responsibility to be bothered by such detail and working herself into the top job was taking more time than she had imagined. Her desk was never clear by evening, as it had been in Pryce's day.

The appointment had been resolved without any reference to MI5. Sir William Brook had proposed Adrian as Director, but had been overruled by the Treasury. Needing Treasury support for another matter closer to his heart, he had not been prepared to make a fight of it.

The December day, with mist and lowering sky, was as grey as Adrian's news. Gillian was indoors, sitting in the lounge in front of a log fire, her legs curled up on a couch. She could sense by his expression and the way he ignored the welcoming cat that something was wrong and she was half sure what it must be.

She rose to switch off a compact disc of a John Field piano concerto but Adrian asked her to leave it on. He particularly liked the spirited joyousness of the Irish composer who was little known only because he had been overshadowed by Mozart. 'It will cheer me up,' he said.

'Why? What's happened, darling? You look very down.'

'It's what hasn't happened,' he replied bitterly. 'I'm not getting the Directorship. You know what the bloody Whitehall mandarins are like. They've never wanted scientists. They are using the job as a slot for some redundant administrator.'

Knowing how much he hated losing, Gillian rose and put her arms round him. 'Oh dear, you must be terribly disappointed. Let me make some tea and then tell me all about it.'

He followed her into the kitchen. 'I'm afraid it's the end of the K. At least for the foreseeable future. I only wanted it for you.'

'You are sweet. But it doesn't matter a twopenny damn. We don't need any of those trimmings. You'll get your recognition in other ways.'

He said nothing and followed her into the sitting room as she took in the tray. She was smiling but was almost as disappointed as he was. She would very much have liked to be Lady Allen.

'We have to be constructive about it, darling,' she said as they sat together in the firelight, the licking flames reflected from her collection of copper jugs and the dark, polished furniture. 'I didn't like to say it but I think you should get away from Porton. Get back to academic work. It would be a much fuller life for both of us.'

The combined traumata of the silicon business, the demos, the publicity, the spooks and Wendy's death were foremost in both their minds but neither cared to mention them. They had gorged so much of Adrian's time and energy that his research, already eroded by the demands of routine administration, had almost come to a halt. Wendy's funeral, which Adrian had been required to attend, had been particularly harrowing. It had been covered by the television news agencies and he had been shown consoling her parents, simple souls who fortunately knew nothing of his affair with their dead daughter.

'Porton was only ever just a stepping stone,' he said, staring over his cup.

'I know and it's served its purpose. What would it matter if you

293

took a chair at a red-brick university for a while? You'll get to Cambridge eventually. We both know that. There's America, or even Australia . . .'

Adrian smiled. 'It's odd you should say that. I've had two feelers about chairs abroad in the past month but there was no point in considering them when I thought I might get the Directorship. I had earned it, though, hadn't I?'

'Of course you had, darling. Ten times over. But that's in the past now. It's the future that matters and it's going to be bright. Remember, I'm your lucky black cat.'

She refilled his teacup. 'Now tell me about those two chairs.'

'I don't think either is for me,' Adrian told her. 'Too pedestrian. I have a more exciting idea. If a bacterium can be genetically engineered to metabolize silicon, why not other forms of inorganic material? Why not a whole new subject of inorganic bacteriology? God knows where it could lead. It could have enormous potential for technology and industry.'

'And with your name on the first silicon papers, when they are published, you could become the acknowledged leader in the field, darling.'

'If they ever are published.'

'Oh, they will be, eventually.'

'I suppose so. I can see some of the universities being very interested,' Adrian enthused. 'In the not too distant future there could even be chairs in inorganic bacteriology.'

'Including Cambridge?' Gillian asked, excitedly.

'Why not? It was in the forefront of molecular biology.'

'The world's first chair in inorganic bacteriology! Perhaps you will fill it.'

Adrian laughed. 'I'm afraid science doesn't move that fast but I'll do my best to push it along. It's odd how ideas come to mind at the most unexpected moments.'

'Well, you always said that I was your sounding board.'

Feeling quite elated, Adrian told himself that he would have been mad to stay at Porton even as Director in what was, essentially, an administrative post when such an exciting research prospect beckoned. Any fool could do administration. He would use the Porton job until it suited him to leave. Then balls to the Civil Service and to hell with anything to do with secrecy. Wendy had been absolutely right on that score. It was degrading for a scientist of his stature to have to submit his work for vetting by bureaucrats.

It was wonderful what a supportive wife, a cup of tea and some looking on the bright side self-delusion could do.

Chapter Forty-three

The method of alerting the Chinese to the silicon discovery and its implications chosen by the National Security Council was the simplest and the least likely to provide an opportunity for reprisals from Moscow or raised eyebrows in London. The discoveries made by the late Dr Payne and Dr Julian Flickinger's medical developments would be published in the normal scientific periodicals. This would make the information available to everyone but that trade-off was considered worthwhile to balance the defence equation. There would, of course, be no publication of any purely military developments, such as the dry biological form of the clone.

The State Department expressed some political reservations. 'The Soviet Foreign Ministry is not going to like it,' the Secretary of State observed. 'Neither will General Secretary Primarkov.'

'But isn't that the political value of the exercise if we go ahead with it?' Rockwell asked. 'We don't want them to like it. Primarkov has shown us, in the most positive way that he could think of, that we can expect no favours. I can't see any objection to paying him the same compliment. Let's publish and be damned. It's all going to come out one day.'

Arnold, who invariably followed the President's line, agreed. 'If it's all published in the scientific press I don't see how the Soviets can object. It will be a good lesson for them in the *glasnost* they keep making such a song about.'

As Chief of Staff, Butch Blanchard was able to add his support. 'Look at the score box. The President can't go to the summit one down. I say play the China card.'

Finally, nobody had disagreed but as a courtesy and a sop to the State Department, the President undertook to explain what was going to happen in advance to Primarkov when next they spoke on the telephone.

The first that Adrian knew was a call from Flickinger saying that he had been given the all clear to publish his research results to date and proposed to do so with a preliminary research letter in the American journal, *Science*. Adrian was asked if he would prepare a letter covering Wendy's work and giving her the credit for the discovery in the British journal *Nature* and follow this with a full paper in one of the microbiology journals. He agreed in principle but first consulted Brook.

'We have no objection now,' Brook told him. 'It's all been agreed with the Pentagon.'

'I'm delighted, of course, but why the sudden change after all the secrecy?' Adrian asked, in some bewilderment.

'I guess that reason has finally taken over,' Brook lied. 'It was impossible to hold it against all the pressure from the American academics.' He had been briefed on the 'China card' but only in absolute secrecy.

'Good God,' Adrian thought. 'What would poor Wendy have made of it all?'

Adrian recovered Wendy's working notes from his security safe. All stamped Top Secret but now to be revealed to everybody, they showed, step by step, exactly what she had done.

He telephoned her parents in Darlington with the news. They were deeply gratified that credit was finally to be given to their daughter but confused. If it was all so secret that it might have caused her death, how could it not be secret now? He had no answer understandable to them or, indeed, to himself beyond the generalization that, for reasons unknown to him, the official situation had changed.

By arrangement with the Editor of *Nature*, Adrian's letter was published in the next weekly issue. It recorded the late Dr Wendy Payne's discovery of the clone which attacked glass and their joint finding that it would also attack elemental silicon, giving some details of the genetic manipulation which produced it. The implications for the electronics industry and for defence were mentioned but not developed. The publication of the full technical details in further papers was promised as soon as possible.

Flickinger's letter in *Science* dealing with the medical implications gave full credit to Wendy for the initial discovery and for the realization that it could be applicable to the treatment of silicosis. To date, the bacterium had proved to be non-pathological and exerted some effect on silicon spicules embedded in animal lung tissue.

As agreed, Rockwell telephoned Primarkov to explain his position.

'We have been under insupportable pressure from the scientific and technical communities, both here in the United States and in the United Kingdom. Because of the overriding commercial and medical considerations – people's lives are at stake – there was no way that we could hold out any longer. We did our best. I'm sure that you will face this kind of problem yourself when your democratization is further along the line.'

There was little that Primarkov could say. His defence scientists were rather more voluble when they heard what was about to happen.

The Times led its front page with the main story revealed by *Nature* and there was a major feature inside discussing the far-reaching technical implications.

'Wolf' Gordon took a different and much more sensational line – the 'human' angle, as his news editor called it. He deduced that the silicon aspects were the reason for all the secrecy at Porton and assumed that this was why Wendy Payne had been unwilling to discuss her work when they had dined together. He then speculated about the cause of her mysterious death, on which the inquest had brought in an open verdict.

'Was Wendy Payne murdered?' he asked in bold type. 'If so, who was responsible? Until now no motive has been clear. Now the situation is different.'

It had been disclosed that she had discovered a secret of supreme defence interest. To Gordon, there seemed to be only three possible culprits – MI5, the CIA or the KGB. It seemed hard to understand why the KGB would have wanted to kill her. Both MI5 and the CIA had motives – to silence her when she was known to be so opposed to secrecy while the British and American authorities wanted the secret kept. Gordon reported that he knew that she had been chafing to publish and that the Defence Ministry had gagged her. With the publication of the silicon secrets it followed that Dr Payne had been killed in vain, whoever had done it. Had Sir Alexander Pryce's premature retirement been just a coincidence or could there have been some connection? Gordon asked. MPs would be wanting to know. Scotland Yard detectives were said to be reopening the Payne case. In fact, they were not.

At Lesley's behest, the legal adviser to MI5 carefully examined the story for a possible breach of the new Official Secrets Act but decided that nobody could be prosecuted just for asking questions. He strenuously advised against bringing any action because it could not be sustained without making damaging admissions in court. The MI5 management was looking for an opportunity to prove to media nuisances like Gordon that the new Official Secrets Act had sharp teeth but it had to be absolutely certain of legal victory. An acquittal would undermine the Act in which the secrets world had lodged such hope. Patience had always been an MI5 virtue and the management would wait for a softer target than Gordon.

Parliament's 'Band of No Hopers', those who could never tackle problems but were always keen to cackle them, wasted no time in questioning the Prime Minister. She described the allegation against MI5 as monstrous but was not in a position to answer for the CIA. To jeers from the Opposition, she fell back, thankfully, on the Parliamentary tradition of not commenting on security matters regarding Pryce's retirement. Her trouble was that nobody could explain Wendy's death and Gordon and the Labour backbenchers would be able to capitalize on it until they became bored and transferred their attention to something else.

In sorrow's obsession, Joe Malinowski had not been able to believe that Wendy had killed herself, least of all as a result of their tiff, but neither had he been able to dismiss from his conscience his perfidy in serving as what she had accurately described as a 'CIA stooge'. Gratefully, he latched on to the possibility that she had been murdered and Gordon's story gave him an excuse to question Charlie Yates about any possible CIA involvement in it. Charlie's reaction was robust. 'What the hell do you think we are, Joe? Are you crazy? The Agency doesn't go in for killing people, least of all innocent young women!'

Joe did not seem entirely convinced.

'Snap out of it, Joe! You're not responsible for Dr Payne's death in any way. And neither am I.'

But Joe was not so sure. He certainly felt guilt, and shame, for his part in the CIA's involvement in Wendy's pitiful distress.

Charlie had still been toying with the idea of inviting Joe to join the Agency, to transfer from white diplomacy to the black. But seeing his dejection he realized that he would not have the fibre for the job. Charlie would have been wasting his time, anyway. Joe was aware that he was no flier. He would never achieve high rank in Government service but he wanted no further truck with dirty tricks, whatever patriotic appeals might be made to him by Charlie or anyone else.

While immune to any feelings of guilt, Charlie entertained some private doubt about Wendy's death. Within the Agency, Pilgrim and his Disciples had a reputation for ruthlessness.

The resurrection of the silicon story did not help Lesley in her drive to uplift MI5 morale. She wondered how much Gordon knew, especially about Sandy Pryce's departure, but decided that if he had any inkling he would have found some way of blowing it. Without need of her advice, Pryce, who had retired to a Berkshire village, was keeping his head down. He had gone there to be near his aged mother who was in a high-quality old people's home. Though she could not recognize him much of the time, he visited her most days. The area, by the River Kennet, rich in reed beds, was also excellent for bird-watching, especially of marsh species in which he specialized.

The response of the scientific community to the technical publications was extremely brisk with various authorities, excluding Adrian, who declined appearing on television in explanatory programmes. Working parties were set up to examine all the implications and to make recommendations and prepare reports. Porton was deluged with requests from various laboratories for cultures of the clone, the Chinese being among the first from abroad to stake a claim. The Ministry of Defence advice was to fob everybody off until various working parties had reported. The issues dominated the technical press for weeks.

At the height of the American publicity, Rockwell remarked to Butch, as they sat alone in the Oval Office, 'I guess that evens the score.'

'Yes, Mr President, but I wonder what the little man will do in response. His team will be in a huddle and his offensive line will do something.'

Chapter Forty-four

Brown Derby had been showing signs of restiveness and frustration just jogging round the safe house grounds and playing chess with his CIA minders, who were no match for him in either activity. The daily debriefing sessions, in which his interrogators tried to extract every fact he could recall about his days as an electronics intelligence officer and his service with the *Spetsnaz* forces, had become boringly repetitive. He seemed increasingly disinclined to provide any new information that mattered.

His only other contact with the outside world was television and listening to the radio, especially Moscow radio, which he was encouraged to do to alleviate the inevitable 'defector blues'. On occasion he had deliberately outrun his accompanying minder, who was not in good shape, and had gone through the motions of preparing to escape over the wooden perimeter fence, which offered no serious obstacle to such a fit man. These efforts had been passed over as a joke, though the minder, surprised at his charge's physique when stripped, was in little doubt that he could be overpowered in any serious encounter. As a *Spetsnaz* officer, Peter Ivashutin, as his minders now knew him, had been trained to kill, but having seen so much of the defector with his family, they were satisfied that there was no way he would desert Mrs Ivashutin and the children, and they certainly could not escape.

The CIA had fitted him up with an exercise bicycle and other gadgets in a makeshift gymnasium to absorb his energy. He worked hard with them but as the days passed, with little prospect of change, the signs of irritation intensified and, as the chief minder had been half-expecting, he exploded to the extent of throwing a barbell through a window pane.

'I'm not prepared to go on skulking here like some caged animal any longer,' he cried. 'I must get out into the open, like Shevchenko did.'

'In due course,' the minder counselled. 'It would be dangerous for you to take that risk now, Peter. The GRU won't have given up looking for you.'

'I'll take that chance. At least I would die like a soldier. Don't forget, that's what I am. I'm not afraid of them and I want to show them I'm not afraid. I demand an end to all this living like a recluse. I want a press conference so that I can explain my position. Once I've let the world know why I defected they wouldn't dare to kill me. If I stay here like a rat in a stink-hole they well might.'

'You're crazy to suggest such a thing.'

'It's you who's crazy if you think that I am going to go on like this. My wife agrees with me. We want out! I insist that you let your chiefs know that I demand a press conference – in Washington, with all the media there, *Pravda* included.'

The minder sighed. 'OK but we're wasting our time. They'll never agree to it, not at this stage.'

He was wrong. There were minds in the CIA, including Arnold's, who saw a press conference with Brown Derby, properly briefed and fully rehearsed, as a dramatic way to score off the Russians, publicly, after the infection of the Mockingbird. Arnold was also determined that he was not going to have the CIA accused of keeping a defector imprisoned against his will, as it had done in the past.

He consulted with Butch and the President and they saw some advantage in putting up such a high-level defector to get another goal in the score box before the summit. Baby Rockwell was again exerting her influence. The 'little two-timer' was not going to be allowed to 'get away with it'.

To ensure the defector's security, the conference was arranged in the largest interview room at the State Department. The first the media knew of it was an invitation to an important occasion which would be certain to provide dramatic copy, at 11 a.m. on the following morning. As befitted any enlightenment organized by the CIA, the building was surrounded in thick mist as the corps of correspondents, TV camera men and still photographers bore down on Foggy Bottom.

The Washington correspondents of scores of foreign newspapers were there in force, the Soviet representatives being from *Novosti, Pravda, Izvestia*, the Soviet Embassy and, clandestinely, the KGB and the GRU. There were the usual precautions against infiltration by terrorists, and armed plain-clothed guards paid special attention to all the Russians.

Brown Derby entered, theatrically, from behind a curtain, sat himself in front of the battery of microphones, darting glances at his audience. He was introduced by a State Department spokesman as Colonel Peter Ivashutin, a descendant of a famous former head of the GRU with the same name. With some drama in his voice, the spokesman announced that the Colonel was going to tell the world how the Soviet techno-bandits operated to steal American secrets, having been in charge of them in the United States.

Ivashutin began, dynamically, by thanking everyone for coming, in English and Russian, and confirmed that, indeed, he had been a soldier and intelligence officer for twenty years until some two months previously. Reading from a prepared text, he said, 'Earlier this year I decided, entirely of my own volition, to seek political asylum in the United States. I did not betray my country, I betrayed a regime which is oppressing my country. For some time I — '

With a gesture of defiance, as the still cameras flashed and the TV cameras scanned, he threw down the statement, shouting, 'I cannot continue with these abominable lies. I did *not* seek political asylum.. I did *not* defect of my own volition. My wife and I and our children were kidnapped by the CIA while on a family visit to Disney World. We were set upon while we were in the Haunted Mansion there. My children were drugged. The experience will haunt them for the rest of their lives. We have been held prisoners ever since . . .'

There was a wild rush of news agency reporters to telephones as Ivashutin continued to the rest of his spellbound audience.

'I was forced into coming here to make a false speech by threats to my family. The CIA told me that if I refused I would be held in solitary confinement. But I saw it as a way to reveal my plight to the American people, secure my freedom and return to the Soviet Union.

'I have always been a loyal citizen of my country and a loyal member of the Soviet military forces. I detest the capitalist jungle.

'I demand my immediate release so that I and my family can return to our own country.'

The pandemonium was unprecedented. State Department officials moved in to try to end the conference but the media men prevented them. The Colonel, who refused to move from the microphones,

303

was prepared to answer questions and the representatives from *Pravda* and *Novosti* began to bombard him in Russian. The media had never had such a field day, not even with Yurchenko.

The event, witnessed live by millions, dominated the free world headlines in all the media, with Ivashutin inevitably being called the 'Mickey Mouse spy'. While the CIA denied the kidnapping, they could not deny the events in the Haunted Mansion, including the 'drugging' of the children. The Colonel's version was widely believed.

By the time the media conference ended, a senior Soviet diplomat had arrived from the Soviet Embassy to demand the handover of Colonel Ivashutin, who went readily and was soon joined by his family. His wife spoke little English but was put up for interview by the Soviet Embassy with an interpreter and confirmed her husband's story. The Embassy declined to show the children or allow them to be questioned but issued some appealing photographs which were widely reproduced.

'The bastard's done a Yurchenko on us!' the CIA chief minder exclaimed. 'Serve him right if he ends up in the crematorium.'

Acting on long-term instructions, the defector had listened to Moscow radio during a certain period every evening. When he had heard a rousing performance of the GRU military march he had known what to do.

Had the press conference gambit failed, there had been a fallback plan to jog on a certain afternoon, to outrun the CIA officer, overpowering him if necessary, and rendezvous with a waiting car.

An immediate 'post mortem' was held at Langley to determine if Ivashutin had been a plant or had suffered a change of mind and heart. The obvious move was to question Pilgrim but Arnold forbade it with a curt, 'Whatever that man told us, we couldn't trust it.' What was really in his mind was the fear that, if pressed, and in a vengeful mood, Pilgrim might tell too much. If anything about Turbid-Skinsaver leaked, it could lead to a Congressional inquiry which could involve Butch Blanchard and, through him, the President. So the onus fell largely on Al Quest. All he could honestly say was that as far as he knew, Brown Derby, as he had known him, had been genuine.

Ivashutin and his family were quickly flown back to Moscow from

304

Kennedy International Airport. He gave no further interview but was photographed waving happily to the press and television cameras from the steps of the Aeroflot airliner. He did not look like a man going back to a crematorium.

Newspaper and magazine comparisons with the Yurchenko case were inevitable but the more perceptive saw a more telling likeness – to that of the long-term FBI false defector who had been called 'Fedora'.

Investigative writers asked if Colonel Ivashutin had been another agent-in-place, feeding false information to the CIA while being manipulated by Soviet Intelligence. Had this manipulation included his apparent defection and re-defection at a crucially sensitive time politically? Was the case the real cause for the sacking of Ross Pilgrim? Had Pilgrim, the Great Deceiver himself, been tricked into 'doing a Hoover'?

On Arnold's instructions, the questions went unanswered and, as Director, he took the brunt of the wrath from the journalists and the Agency's inveterate critics, who made the convenient assumption that silence implied guilt. The CIA's response was ineffective because it simply did not know the answers to the major questions. Un-officially, in nod-and-wink leaks, it took the line that the defector had been genuine but had suffered so severely from post-defection trauma that he had become temporarily irrational and deranged, as had happened to others in the past. Regrettably, he would probably be executed for treason, *glasnost* or no *glasnost*, 'confidential sources' maintained. The CIA specifically did not deny that it had been fooled. It did not know what new evidence might be revealed if Ivashutin was put up for further questioning by the media in Moscow. Mean-while, its analysts were working overtime on the slogging backtrack to deduce how much of Brown Derby's information had been disin-formation.

In fact, no further publicity materialized and Yakushkin saw to it that the case was barely mentioned by the Soviet media, in spite of their heavy representation at the Washington conference. *Glasnost* still had its limits. Instead, Ivashutin's many decorations were privately increased by the Order of the Red Banner. He had earned it. By carrying out his orders, at extreme personal sacrifice, he had enabled Yakushkin, then his chief, to make a *peshka* out of Chevalsky and fool him into making his fatal strike.

President Rockwell was as shaken as anyone else by the turn of events but resilient, as usual. 'We didn't have to wait long for the little man's response to the China card did we?' he said to Butch.

'How do we respond, sir?'

'We don't. The summit's too close now. Enough's enough.'

Chapter Forty-five

It was Arnold's first experience of the abuse which the media can heap on an individual when balked of copy. As head of the CIA he took the hammering for the Brown Derby fiasco, being widely accused of gross incompetence, though it was obvious that the main responsibility for accepting Ivashutin as genuine lay elsewhere, before he had been appointed. He had, however, been in command when Ivashutin had defected and could not dodge his responsibility for agreeing to the media conference.

When he complained in the President's presence, Rockwell simply shrugged and said, 'You'll have to learn that unfair criticism goes with the job. It will be a nine days wonder.'

In Arnold's narrow eyes it had all been Pilgrim's fault and no doubt he was deriving some amusement at being free of the flak. It was all so unfair. Until the fiasco he had felt that he was shaping the Agency the way it should be and had even begun to enjoy the cult of conspiracy. His conscious purpose was to acquire merit and impress the President, with a view to promotion to a political position. Chiefs of Staff tended not to last long and Butch Blanchard's association with Pilgrim might be a black mark – or could be made to look like one. Now his own judgement was being questioned and his public and Congressional image blackened by events which had never been under his control. He hankered after public recognition and his main objection to the CIA job was that he could not tell people much, or anything, about his successes. In his legal career he had been adept at backing into the limelight, which was how he had come to public notice, and it was not in his nature to hug achievement to himself.

He was seething with frustration. He could not wreak further vengeance on Pilgrim but there was still that fellow Pryce, who continued to interest him. With Lesley's sudden translation to the MI5 leadership, Charlie Yates had been unable to secure the details of Pryce's confession but, to have gone the way he did, he must have admitted his guilt to someone in the organization. How far had this guilt extended? The KGB and the GRU were sharp. Look how they had latched on to that fellow, Vassall, when all the other Brits had missed his obvious propensity. No, they didn't usually miss sodomites. Sodomites – the very word aroused Arnold's fire and brimstone fervour. Sodomy was the foulest sin of the flesh; an abomination, as the Lord had decreed to Moses. Nobody should be saved from censure for it!

The fact that sodomy had ceased to be a criminal offence, through the legal permissiveness which he deplored, did not reduce the risk of blackmail in the case of those high in the intelligence world, like Pryce. The fear of public exposure, dismissal and disgrace remained powerful enough. And if Soviet Intelligence had a grip on Pryce, then what about all the CIA secrets which Pilgrim must have fed him over the years of their relationship? Had they gone any further East?

Arnold asked one of Pilgrim's old Disciples for a brief rundown and analysis on Pryce. It highlighted his hobby of photography as worthy of note. Most Soviet spies were required to photograph documents, and bird photography was an excellent cover for clandestine activities. All that time spent in hides! What opportunities for meetings in remote places and the location of dead-drops!

It all fitted. The more that Arnold thought about it, the more he became convinced that Pryce should be interrogated, preferably under the polygraph, if the Brits could bring themselves to go that far, to find out if he had been suborned. According to a report from Charlie Yates, the new MI5 Director-General seemed to have no intention of interrogating her old chief. Well, that might be convenient for her and MI5 but it would not do for him and the CIA. It was typical of the Brits to avoid cleaning house for fear of what they might find.

Again, he could not suggest an interrogation without being accused of interference in a domestic British matter, but it could be done through his cut-out, Yates, who so far had handled the situation most competently.

As Charlie sat in his office in Grosvenor Square overlooking the garden and the bronze statue of Eisenhower, he gave his new assignment deep thought. Who could serve as his willie on this occasion? Like any good intelligence officer, he was a student of character and he soon decided on his man – the Air Marshal who was Deputy

Chief of the Defence Staff, whom he met socially as well as through his daily liaison work. He had sized him up as being anxious to avoid having to go into retirement from that post, which was a likely event, so he would be keen to acquire merit with those who might extend his career. He had heard the Air Marshal comment on Pryce in the past, with little good to say for him. And he was senior enough to have direct access to those who might be induced to take some action.

If that avenue failed there was a fall-back situation – Joe Malinowski's link with the journalist, Gordon, but in view of Joe's state of mind, he would prefer not to use it.

'What do you make of Pryce's departure?' Yates inquired, casually, of his elected willie at the first adequate opportunity.

'I approve of it,' the Air Marshal replied. 'That suet pudding didn't go a day too early for my money.'

'But do you know why he went?'

'Health problems, I gather. He's been looking terrible lately.'

Charlie had been trained on the principle that it was stupid to guard the tongue and let the face say it all but there were occasions when to do exactly that paid dividends. The Air Marshal could not miss the half-smiling, quizzical look.

'Do you question the health grounds?' he asked. 'Have you heard something?'

'Well, for God's sake don't tell anyone I told you but our information is that he had been found out falsifying his PV.'

'In what way?'

'The usual way, I'm afraid.'

'You don't mean another Oldfield case?'

'That's the buzz with us.'

'Jesus! What gets into these bloody spooks? You can't lift a corner of their over-blanket without releasing a stench. Does the PM know?'

'I doubt it. No need to know and all that.'

'Well, she damn well ought to know,' the Air Marshal said with sufficient conviction to assure Charlie that he would not be needing Gordon's services – for the moment.

The Air Marshal was genuinely shocked. Yates was too professional to retail malicious gossip; he must have had good reason for his tip, which had obviously been deliberate. Walking briskly across St James's Park towards his club, he ruminated on possible willies, quickly dismissing the obvious choice – his immediate superior, the

Chief of the Defence Staff. He was stuffy and would probably regard the information as muck-raking rumour with which he would rather not soil his mind. Instead, he would mark the card of Sir Richard Carlton, the Chairman of the Joint Intelligence Committee, about what was being thought and talked about in the CIA.

'Thank you, I'll take a look at it,' Carlton said, thoughtfully, when appraised.

Carlton's first move was to consult the new Director-General of MI5, who had joined his committee in place of Pryce. Lesley stalled. 'All I have been told officially is that Sandy resigned on medical grounds. Ill health, nothing more.'

'What do you think the medical grounds were?'

Unwilling to lie verbally, she made a gesture indicating total ignorance.

'Was he examined by your husband in his capacity as the senior MI5 psychiatrist?'

'Yes, but he is the last person who would tell anyone anything about his patients. He's a stickler for medical ethics. Medical reports remain completely confidential in a case where an officer has re-signed.'

'No doubt,' Carlton commented but Lesley could sense that he was far from convinced that, on such an important issue, Paul Barrington-Fuller would continue to withhold any details about Pryce now that she was his successor.

His suspicion fortified by Lesley's fencing, he sought out the Cabinet Secretary at Brooks's, the club they shared, that same day. Since the cock-up over the *Spycatcher* affair, the Cabinet Secretary was not prepared to countenance another situation in which the Prime Minister had not been kept fully informed. So he, too, took early action.

'I have a gut feeling, Prime Minister, that we might be facing another Oldfield situation,' he said after imparting what he had heard. 'It could explode in our faces if the CIA are openly talking about it.'

'Then we must take the same action that we did in that case,' the Prime Minister said decisively and without much apparent concern. 'I leave it to you to arrange things with the new Director-General.'

Privately, she was horrified at the prospect of what the investigation might reveal but, fulfilling the requirement that to be successful, politicians need acting ability, she managed to conceal her emotions.

As Accounting Officer for the Secret Services, the Cabinet Secretary had frequent reason for consulting the Director-General of MI5 and Lesley was not perturbed at being asked to attend his office.

'How are you settling in?' he asked affably. 'Any problems?'

'None that I know of.'

Lesley had made it easy for him. 'I think there may be one that you don't know of. The PM is very concerned about your predecessor.'

'In what way?'

'Remember the Maurice Oldfield case?'

'Very well.'

'The PM thinks that Sandy Pryce may be another one.'

Lesley did her best to look surprised but could not avoid a revealing pause while she marshalled her thoughts. 'What makes her think that?' she asked.

'Something she's heard on the Washington grapevine. I gather the CIA are talking about it. It's not for me to tell you how to run your department but, if I were you, I wouldn't risk offending the Lady. She doesn't like being caught out by fast ball Parliamentary questions.'

'What do you think I should do?'

'Do what we did with Oldfield. Have Pryce in for interrogation.'

Lesley winced at the prospect. 'But how can I do that? There were police reports against Oldfield and a requirement from the Home Secretary. All I know officially about Sandy is that he is ill.'

'That's your problem, DG. Suppose the CIA is right and it leaks? Then, if we haven't taken the necessary action and the PM is caught on the hop, there will be the usual clamour for heads to roll. I wouldn't like one of them to be yours – or mine.'

Lesley felt that he was exaggerating concerning his own decapitation but needed no more prodding.

There was little doubt in Pryce's mind concerning the reason why he was being recalled to Curzon Street for urgent consultations, though Lesley could not give it on the telephone when she made her personal call. 'I think you should be prepared to spend the whole day here,' was all she was prepared to say. 'I'll send a car for you.'

The car arrived at Pryce's cottage early in the morning and drove into the rear entrance of MI5's headquarters in a stone-bricked alley at the back of Curzon Street. Lesley treated him as gently as possible

311

as she explained the Prime Minister's requirement, making it clear that she had not talked.

'In my opinion – and I have my reasons for saying this – the leak originated across the water. I know that any interrogation is unnecessary but you must understand the PM's position. There may be questions in the House. She must be able to say that all the necessary steps were taken.'

Pryce, who seemed dazed, nodded.

'You will know what to do, Sandy. Just tell the truth.'

He looked so forlorn and broken that she wanted to give him a reassuring hug. But it would have been unprofessional.

The former Director-General was taken by car from the rear entrance to an MI5 flat in Clarges Street, no more than two hundred yards away. It had been suitably wired for recording and a specialist interrogator, well known to Pryce, was waiting. In view of the suspect's medical condition, the interrogator had been told to avoid being hostile.

Usually, in such circumstances, another officer would be listening in from a distance to detect hesitations and nuances but this refinement had been eliminated on Lesley's orders. In the interests of internal morale it was essential that the minimum number of officers should know about Pryce's predicament and the reason for it.

Without hesitation, Pryce admitted his homosexuality and to falsifying his positive vetting form but strenuously denied ever having been approached by anyone representing the Soviet bloc.

He was asked about his association with Pilgrim and dismissed it as no more than a close professional relationship between two allied intelligence officers.

He insisted that he had always been loyal and had never had any motivation to be anything else. His memory remained remarkable and he had no lapses to arouse suspicion. To the interrogator's surprise and relief, he did not become emotional.

Lesley's report to the Cabinet Secretary assured the Prime Minister that, while the negative could not be proved, it was as certain as it could be that Pryce had never been approached by an adversary intelligence organization. Had he been suborned, at least three operations against the Soviet Union could never have succeeded. These were so secret that they could not be described in the report. It did reveal, however, that a recent high-level defector from the KGB had

312

been questioned about Pryce and had stated that, as far as he knew, no attempt had been made to recruit him.

The feedback to Lesley from the Cabinet Secretary indicated that the Prime Minister was satisfied but it had been a close run thing. If the Second Lady had known that Lesley had been aware of Pryce's homosexuality and had done nothing about it, the reign of the first female Director-General might also have been unique in its brevity. Lesley realized the nature of her error. She had put the interest of an individual before the interest of the Service and she would never do that again.

When Pryce was delivered back to his cottage, in the evening, he was devastated by the experience. To have his loyalty questioned and his most private life probed by someone whom he had seen come up from junior rank, and not necessarily to be believed, was the ultimate shame. He would not be able to face the embarrassment of meeting any of the few who knew about his ordeal. For that reason he would be resigning from his beloved Travellers' Club, his one remaining point of contact, where his interrogator happened to be a member.

There would always be doubt in the minds of those who knew the facts – even in Lesley's. And in the Prime Minister's. A brief on his ordeal and its results would be going to the Second Lady, for whom he had high regard in spite of her dislike of him, which she had taken no pains to hide. So still more in Whitehall would know why he had resigned and certain people in the CIA would have been informed of the interrogation and its results. How long before the story would blow through some wretched 'investigative writer'? If only Ross Pilgrim had destroyed those papers! But then he himself had always been adverse to destroying records of any kind. One never knew when they might suddenly be useful.

Normally he would have cooked himself some fast food from one of the packets produced by his daily help. But he did not feel like eating anything. Instead he poured a large whisky, keeping the bottle handy.

From the moment Lesley had told her husband that Pryce's interrogation was unavoidable, Barrington-Fuller remained deeply concerned about him. 'He really will cane his liver now,' he remarked. 'I wonder if I should ask him to see me? Or should I go down and

313

see him? I feel terribly responsible for what has happened. I must look after him if I can.'

'It's not your fault, dear,' Lesley assured him. 'He did bring it on himself. He's his own executioner.'

Paul stopped himself from remarking, 'I fear that is exactly what he may be.'

With some difficulty, he also avoided voicing his private acceptance that they shared some culpability for Pryce's plight. He had tried arguing that, without his advice, the CIA chief, Arnold, would have exposed him but being made of less stern stuff than Lesley, he knew that, at the very least, he had been ultimately responsible for doing what no good doctor should ever do – deprive a patient of hope.

The only person to derive pleasure from the process was Stanley Arnold who received a brief official account of the events from Lesley, together with the assurance that, while Pryce had been a security risk, there was no evidence whatever that he had breached security. The CIA chief's professional fear was assuaged but not his pious fervour. In the interests of his duty to the Lord's draconian decrees in Leviticus, which he knew by heart, he wanted the sodomite exposed.

Before setting any action in train he persuaded himself that Pryce's disgrace would also be in the interests of the Agency and Western intelligence in general – as an admonition to others of deviant persuasion.

Chapter Forty-six

When Charlie Yates received the instruction to leak the story of the interrogation, he began to think that his chief was becoming as weird in his way as Pilgrim was, though the vengeful motivation was something which had been in Arnold's nature long before his entry into the world of intelligence. Sickened by the requirement, Charlie went so far as to suggest to Arnold that any further action could sour the CIA's relations with MI5 and particularly with its new Director-General. But the only response was an instruction to ensure that the leak was organized in a way which would be deniable.

Charlie contrived to see Joe Malinowski for an evening drink in a quiet corner of the bar at the Connaught Hotel, close to the Embassy. Joe anticipated another patriotic requirement when the venue was not the Embassy staff bar.

'I'd like you to do me another small service,' he said, after the opening pleasantries.

'In what way?'

'Another brief for your friend, Gordon.'

Joe looked anything but enthusiastic. 'I'm out of touch with him.'

'Then give him a buzz.'

'Would anyone suffer as a result?' Joe asked.

Charlie did not answer the question. 'If you feel that badly about it, Joe, forget it. Far be it from me ever to pressure anybody. I'd go easy on the cashew nuts, they're very fattening,' he added to change the subject; his guest looked like he wanted to empty the little dish in front of them.

'I always take it out on the food when I'm dispirited,' Joe responded.

Charlie declined Joe's offer of a return drink on the grounds of having to work late, which he had hoped to avoid but which had suddenly become necessary.

Using his secretary's word-processor he dated a piece of blank paper, inserted the address as Wimbledon and using the minimum number of words typed the message he needed to impart. He addressed the envelope to Gordon at his home in the fashionable part of Docklands then took the Underground to Wimbledon to push it into the nearest letterbox there.

Gordon was wary of anonymous letters but from the address, the Wimbledon postmark and the nature of the contents, he had no doubt that it was another reliable tip-off from Joe. Within hours of receiving it he was down at Pryce's cottage 'door-stepping' his victim, who refused to talk to him on the grounds of routine security. The visit was not entirely fruitless. As Pryce peered round his half-open front door a photographer flashed a picture of him. He had just returned from pursuing a pair of short-eared owls, passage migrants from the north feeding on the rats on a dump site, and looked even more crumpled than usual.

Gordon had already written his story but the office lawyer would not let him run it. 'I know your sources are good but if they are wrong about this one we could be in court for a million. Homosexual and possibly a spy? No proof! It's a great story but this is a risk I am not prepared to take.'

Vehement argument by Gordon that Pryce could never sue because the Government would not allow him to appear in a witness box cut no ice with either the lawyer or the editor.

'There always has to be a first time for everything,' the editor said.

'The Government just might allow him to appear to see you, me and this newspaper well and truly in the shit, which we would be without proof.'

The two words 'Found Dead' in the police report said everything about the solitary circumstances. In the evening following Gordon's visit, Pryce had become progressively more drunk and more morose. Public disgrace was now almost a certainty. Why should he live through it?

Pryce had not even enjoyed the comfort of his bed. The daily help had found him slumped at a table, fully dressed, even to his Homburg hat, the empty whisky bottle, glass and sleeping tablets in front of him. He had left no note. There was nobody to leave one to and perhaps his decision to put an end to his misery had come to him when he was already drunk and incapable of writing. His will ensured that his mother would be cared for in some luxury until the end of her days. She was incapable of understanding what had happened and no effort was made to inform her.

The event was reported in every newspaper with the inevitable speculation as to its cause. From their police contacts, the crime reporters learned that 'foul play was not suspected' and that Pryce had almost certainly committed suicide.

As the only journalist to know about the homosexual aspects of the case, Gordon's reaction to the news flash delivered to his desk was to rush upstairs to see the office lawyer with his original story in his hand. The lawyer looked up from his work on the latest libel action being brought against the paper's gossip columnist and shrugged. 'Now he's dead you can say what you like about him.'

Gordon did just that, extending his story, removing all the safety qualifications, 'hardening' the question of Pryce's possible suborn-ment by the KGB and even his possible involvement in Wendy Payne's death. His story, which led the paper, was accompanied by a photograph of Pryce looking like a hunted and guilty figure peering fearfully through a half-open door.

It was Gordon's story which Charlie Yates faxed to Arnold's private office, having read it with the professional satisfaction of a modest operation successfully achieved. It was a pity about Joe but he was a busted flush. No asset lasted for ever and any betting man took his losses philosophically. Needing to find another conduit, he would have to arrange a posting for him. It would be in Joe's interests, he assured himself. After the Wendy Payne tragedy he would always have bad memories of England.

Joe read Gordon's story with extreme disgust. He had no doubt how he had come by it and that Charlie had tried to target him as the means to that disgraceful end. A 'small service'! Thank God he had kept himself out of it. He already had his involvement in one death on his conscience. Wendy had been right. The secrets game was a cesspool.

There had never been a faster race of the Band of No Hopers to table private notice questions to the Prime Minister. Thanks to her advice from the Cabinet Secretary and her own determination, she was able to answer them. When told of Pryce's admission to homo-sexual practices by the Attorney General she had leaned forward and put her head in her hands, despairingly, as she had done when

317

similarly appraised of the news about Oldfield. But, as usual, any emotion was quickly repressed. Speaking with confidence in answer to a crude supplementary question she told the House that it was at her behest that Pryce had been interrogated. Her prepared statement satisfied the Members, save for the few who claimed that they were not disposed to believe anything she said.

Far from feeling his responsibility for Pryce's death, Arnold took the first opportunity to tell Rockwell, at a National Security Council meeting, 'I am not at liberty to explain how, Mr President, but it was my Agency which was responsible for exposing that dreadful man and ensuring that he was interrogated.'

Rockwell did not express his distaste but wondered whether his choice of Arnold had been wise. As the fat, sleek-headed Butch had remarked to him afterwards when they were alone, 'Yond Arnold hath a lean and hungry look.' The President had understood the implication and noted it.

The obituary notices on Pryce were brief because so little was known about him and, in the circumstances, none of his former colleagues was prepared to write an assessment. More was said at the high-security Memorial Thanksgiving Service for his life, held in the confines of the Chapel of the Naval College in Greenwich. There was a fair gathering of 'spooks', present and past, many of them coming out of long retirement for the social opportunity of meeting old colleagues, especially those still serving. It offered an occasion to relive old conspiracies and, perhaps, retrieve the peculiar joy, however transiently, of learning a little about new ones.

Lesley and her husband sang away at the hymns. While saddened, she felt no guilt for her part in Pryce's demise. It had been his own fault. Burdened by such a private secret he should never have gone into the secrets world.

Though defended, to some extent, by the detachment to suffering which all doctors must develop, Paul could not dismiss his deep sense of guilt. There was no denying it. He, too, had trimmed on his ethical principles. He, too, had been corrupted by secret knowledge. There was no excuse whatever for a person in his professional position; what he had done to promote his wife's ambition would haunt him. As he recalled remarking to Sandy in defence of some hapless MI5 junior who had been dismissed for disreputable behaviour, the key, unrelenting witness to a shameful act, whom one

318

cannot escape or outlive, is oneself. The simple service confirmed his determination to resign from his MI5 consultancy.

More thickly armoured by his training and experience, Charlie Yates, representing the CIA, stood silently with his thoughts, which were centred on the contacts whom he should seek out when the service was over.

Few of those present had really liked Sandy and none had admired him. Most were there for the appearances and the gossip on the steps afterwards.

Chapter Forty-seven

'I know a bank whereon the wild thyme blows,
Where oxlips and the nodding violet grows
Quite over-canopied with luscious woodbine,
With sweet musk-roses and with eglantine:
There sleeps Titania . . .

Butch was reading aloud from his Boydell Shakespeare, rather well, as he had done so often to his dear wife, when the bell to his apartment rang. He closed his treasured volume and pressed the button which allowed his caller to enter the block. In a final bid to induce Al Quest to remain with the Agency, Arnold had asked Butch to intercede. He was glad to oblige. The loss of contact with Pilgrim had compounded his loneliness.

'I know Quest has a high regard for you,' Arnold had explained. 'He's a valuable man and, beyond that, he knows too much about certain matters affecting both of us to be out on the loose.'

'You can say that again!' Butch had replied. 'I'll do what I can.'

There was another matter which was nagging him and on which Al might throw some light.

'I hear you are thinking of quitting the Agency, Al,' he said when he had settled his visitor and offered him a drink, which had been declined.

'Yes, sir.'

'You would be a great loss. There are not many officers of your calibre, or, if I might say so, of your integrity.'

'How did you hear I was leaving? From Mr Pilgrim?'

'No. Stanley Arnold told me. He asked me to try to get you to change your mind. He very much wants you to stay. So do I. Your future would be assured. What's eating you, Al? Is it the way Arnold fired Mr Pilgrim?'

'Not really, though it wasn't very pretty, was it?'

'Is it because of your involvement in Mr Pilgrim's departure? Are you feeling a bit guilty about it, as I confess I am myself?'

'A little.'

'Well, you shouldn't. You did you proper duty and it wasn't you who took the decisions. That was my burden. We all have to make a choice some time. And events have proved that you made the right one.'

'Actually, sir, my problem is purely personal. I don't like what the Agency work is doing to me as a person. In fact, I'm very concerned about it.'

Butch raised his eyebrows in surprise. That was a different matter; and he understood it. He could see that Al was on his way.

'Well, I still hope you'll stay, in the interest of the Agency.'

Al shook his head decisively. 'I've looked at it all ends up, General. When I joined the Agency I left the real world. Now I need to get back to it. I know I will regret it if I don't.'

'Well, you know your own mind best. On another matter that bothers me, what do you make of this Ivashutin defection? Did you know anything about him?'

Al's silence answered the question.

'You can confide in me, Al. After all, I am the Chief of Staff. I see everything.'

'I serviced Ivashutin, though for most of the time I didn't know him by that name. He had a code-name. But you know what Mr Pilgrim was like. I was never allowed to know much about him.'

'For how long did you service him?'

'About three years.'

'And all that time he was an agent-in-place, a GRU traitor working for the CIA?'

'That's what we thought.'

'Could he have been a double, working for both sides for money and with the GRU aware of it?'

'I often wondered. It's possible, I suppose. Mr Pilgrim set great store by having a conduit to the GRU, on the basis you can't fight an enemy you don't know.'

Butch nodded. 'I've heard him say that many times. Did he have a conduit to the KGB?'

'Not to my knowledge, sir. At least not to the same extent. He had no trust whatever in the KGB so long as that Chevalsky was in charge.'

'Are you saying that he trusted the GRU?' Butch asked in some astonishment.

Al fiddled with his cufflink. 'I wouldn't say he trusted them. They were still the enemy but he seemed to think there were occasions when they could do business together if their interests were the same.'

'Did Ivashutin get much chicken-feed as a result, genuine stuff to keep Moscow sweet?'

'I never knew what it was but I delivered a lot of material to dead-drops.'

'Provided by Mr Pilgrim?'

'Yes, sir. Always provided personally by Mr Pilgrim. He regarded Ivashutin as his special baby.'

'Did he get anything else, Al?'

'Well, I know of one or two easy runs of high-tech equipment.'

'Can you cite me an example?'

Al was reluctant to oblige but, under pressure, he outlined the Dealer episode in San Francisco.

'Do you mean to say that Mr Pilgrim made a willie out of the. FBI?' Butch asked.

'I'm afraid he did, sir, but only to protect his asset.'

'Didn't that worry you, Al?'

'Not really, sir. I thought it was in the best interest of the Agency. The FBI wasted some time but that was all. They had to be involved because the whole idea was to make the Soviets believe that the acquisition of the equipment had been a genuine coup. Ivashutin had sent a distress signal saying that unless he managed to get something good in a hurry he was likely to be recalled to Moscow.'

'But shouldn't Mr Pilgrim have secured the willing collaboration of the FBI for such a venture?'

'That's not his style, sir. He couldn't be sure that the FBI would agree to look foolish. And it would have put more people in the know and prejudiced security.'

'You mean, Al, that Mr Pilgrim didn't trust the FBI?'

'Mr Pilgrim never entirely trusted anything or anybody.'

Shaking his head in disbelief, Butch said, 'But he trusted this Russian, Ivashutin, and now it looks like he was a plant.'

'Sure does, sir.'

'It wasn't like Mr Pilgrim to be taken in so easily, was it?' Butch asked.

'No. But with a defector you can never be sure. He might genuinely have had second thoughts.'

'What do you think, Al, in all honesty? Do you think Ivashutin was another Fedora?'

'I guess he could have been.'

'It bothers me, Al. It bothers me. It's so out of character for Mr Pilgrim to have been fooled that way. He's the sharpest man I ever met.'

'Well, we fooled him, sir.'

'I'm beginning to wonder if we did, Al.'

Al was genuinely puzzled. 'What do you mean, sir?'

'Nothing really. Forget it.'

Butch stood up and held out his hand. 'Let me know if I can ever help you in any way. Any way at all. I am in your debt. We all are.'

After Al had left, Butch sat back in his chair. The disclosure about the fooling of the FBI had intensified the concern which had been nagging him ever since the shock of the Ivashutin defection. Ross had willied the FBI. He had tried to willy him. Who else had he fooled? Everybody?

Had Ross, of all people, really been willied by Ivashutin? It didn't make much sense. And why had he gone so quietly, and maintained his silence when he must be consumed with indignation? Was Ross afraid of a thorough investigation?

Why had Ross been so sure that the Russians would intercept the Mockingbird? Had he *known* that they would? Had Ivashutin been in on the act?

Why had Ross been so confident that the simulator would end up at Sary Shagan?

How had he known that the Mockingbird would come back infected?

There were many worrying aspects of his behaviour, now that he came to think about them.

Why had Ross never been caught when he was running agents in Moscow for all of three years? Nobody else had been so successful over so long a period. Was it just his cleverness or had he been permitted these successes for an ulterior purpose?

In short, monstrous as the question seemed, had Ross been a deep

323

Soviet mole? Had Ivashutin really been his controller, with Al as the chief willie, innocently servicing the two of them? Had Al tumbled to it and was that the real reason why he was so determined to quit in mid-career?

It was all unthinkable, but in the intelligence world the unthinkable had to be thought. Things were never what they seemed.

At first, Butch rejected the suspicion, with shame and disgust, when it insisted on intruding into his thoughts, but Pryce's suicide forced it firmly back to consciousness. Pryce had been 'cleared' but only on the basis of probabilities. As for those MI5 operations which would have been bound to go wrong if he had been under Soviet control, it might well have paid the Russians to let them ride to protect such an irreplaceable asset as a Pryce-Pilgrim espionage collaboration. When faced with the absurdly improbable, Butch always remembered how, during the Second World War, the KGB had once sacrificed a whole shipload of soldiers to protect one agent who was exceptionally placed. The agent had warned them that the boat was to be blown up and the Soviet intelligence chiefs let it happen rather than risk putting him under suspicion. He was an on-going source with irreplaceable access.

The possibility that Pryce had been suborned by the Russians through his proven homosexuality must always have been present yet Ross had not appeared to be bothered by it. Why not? Was it because the Russians knew that they had no need to suborn him?

Arnold had been absolutely right, professionally, in forcing Pryce's interrogation, however reprehensible his methods may have been. From what he had heard, Pryce had been an introverted loner, brooding, much of the time, in solitude – the classic type for recruitment. Might not his suicide have been conditioned by his guilt? As for all the information from Pryce which Pilgrim had chosen to feed into the CIA system, had most of it been monitored by Moscow – bullshitsky? And what of the occasional information that Ross must have fed to Pryce in return? Had Pryce been the conduit for CIA secrets to Moscow? Christ, what a fantastic cut-out! The possibilities for the CIA were horrendous. Had they both been bent?

'My man's as true as steel,' Butch had assured the President. He was beginning to wonder, seriously.

Lost in Pilgrim's own Great Domain of Doubt, Butch did what his old friend had always recommended his staff to do: on lined paper he began to draw up a balance sheet of what would seem to be the debits and the credits of Pilgrim's career in the CIA, as far as he knew them.

First, under Debits, he listed some of the successful operations which they had achieved together and which seemed, in retrospect, to have been too facile. There was that planting of sneakies at the Tyuratam Missile-Space Complex. A Russian worker in a Kiev factory had been bribed to implant micro-sneakies into a consignment of replacement telephones destined for Tyuratam and they had worked for several weeks. Another corrupted Soviet worker, on a production line, had been induced to insert sneakies into dashboard instruments which would be fitted to several types of military vehicles. Some of these had ended up, productively for US intelligence it had seemed, in sensitive places like the nuclear missile base at Kozelsk and the military port at Nikolayev, on the Black Sea. One had even found its way into a Red Army general's staff car.

In retrospect, the KGB and GRU were not likely to have been such pushovers as he and Ross had gleefully assumed in the euphoria of triumph. How much of the 'productive' intelligence the sneakies had provided had been bullshitsky? The Soviets were masters of it. When the Americans and the British had tapped into Red Army telephone cables in Berlin, the KGB had learned about it immediately from a mole inside the British Secret Service and fed in a mixture of chicken-feed and disinformation, so perfectly contrived that it had fooled the eavesdroppers for years – until the Soviets decided to end the game. Could Ross be a counterpart of that mole?

Then there was his obsessive feud against Arnold which was calculated to damage the CIA, though of course he claimed that his purpose was to improve it by getting rid of a bad Director. It had certainly been excessive. So, perhaps, had Ross's insatiable appetite for action against the Soviets, looking back on it all. Had it been part of the build-up of his legend – the man who was so competent, so zealous and so dedicated to his country that he could never possibly be suspect?

There was also that British girl who had died so mysteriously, according to the newspaper reports. Had that been another of Ross's 'long tongs' operations? Did he have a motive? Yes, he could have been fearful of a leak until what he thought was a successful operation had been exhausted. The CIA was supposed to be out of the assassination business, but perhaps not, if the tongs were long enough.

Top of the list under Credits were Pilgrim's many undoubted operational successes over the years but, if he had been a GRU agent, his Moscow masters would have allowed him a reasonable share, some even spectacular, to permit him to maintain his position. So they were discardable.

The dismissal of Chevalsky had been a major plus for the CIA but this had not really been Pilgrim's success. It had been due to the willieing of Pilgrim by himself and Al. Ross had exulted over the dismissal of Chevalsky but that could have been genuine if he had been a GRU agent, especially since the GRU chief had taken over the KGB. There had always been bitter animosity between the two Soviet services. Yes, Ross as a GRU agent fitted a lot of facts, including Ivashutin's membership of that organization.

It was difficult to count the intrusion of the Mockingbird into Sary Shagan as a credit because, unknown to Ross, the purpose of the operation had been completely changed.

The possible permutations of the few certain facts seemed endless but the return of the Mockingbird, 'dripping with germs', surely put Ross in the clear because, had he not thought his way out of it so ingeniously, it threatened his whole position, which the Soviets would have been anxious to preserve.

High among the Credits was Butch's own intimate friendship with Ross. Could he have been fooled by him all that time? He didn't think so. Ross was exceptional but he was still human. Surely, in all their time together, he would have made some slip which would have aroused his suspicion before now. Could he possibly have been so competent an actor when permanently on stage? It seemed most unlikely. On the other hand, there had been that awful Philby, who had deluded all his friends for years.

If Ross had been a spy, things had gone horribly wrong for him, but then things did go horribly wrong for spies, however clever they were, as had happened, eventually, to Philby, Blunt and a host of others.

There were other items Butch would have to add to the list of Debits and Credits when he thought of them but, assuming that Ross had been a Soviet agent, what could his motive have been? It could have been something that had happened during his service in Moscow or in Vienna, when he might have become entangled in the coils of the GRU. Who would ever know the motives of a man as secretive as Pilgrim? Butch's many years in intelligence had made him conscious of the arrogance of ignorance, which had so often clouded the judgement of counter-espionage officers when investigating suspects – 'I cannot see a motive, therefore he could not have been a spy'. One thing was certain. If Ross had somehow been forced into treachery he would have come to enjoy it – the biggest and most dangerous deception exercise he could possibly have conceived.

That could be the answer. For anyone who loved the deception game as much as Pilgrim did, playing it in a double role would double the scope, the danger and the excitement. Perhaps for him the means had become more important than the end.

'Oh, to hell with it!' Butch threw down his pen. It was all a waste of time. In the intelligence game any interpretation of events was possible. There were so many possibilities that he could make them fit any theory. What about the President's part in saving Primarkov? Was he a Soviet agent? No, there were too many straws and not enough wind. There was no hard evidence and there could be none. He was becoming too introspective through loneliness. And introspection was bound to breed suspicions that were no more than apparitions of his imagination. He would put the whole damn nonsense out of his mind before he, too, became a sceptomaniac as mistrusting as Ross himself. Let the historians sort out the goddamn 'preponderance of probabilities'!

He tore his balance sheet to small fragments and returned to the more credible world of *Midsummer Night's Dream*.

That evening, while soaking in the solitude of his bath, and thinking about nothing in particular, inspiration flashed upon his inward eye. There *was* some hard evidence that might help to resolve his doubt, in the form of a sealed capsule which was still in his icebox. If it contained a culture of Clone Fe 113 then almost certainly Ross could not have been a Soviet agent. But if it did not . . .

With his hands clasped behind his head and his chin almost touching the water, Butch thought through the movements which Pilgrim must have made when Al had left him at his house in P Street, after delivering the clone and before he himself had arrived. If Operation Turbid had really been designed to inflict damage at Sary Shagan, Ross would have inserted the capsule with the bacterial powder still

327

inside it, as both he and Al believed that he had. But supposing that he had not wanted to inflict damage but simply to present the Soviets with the valuable Mockingbird? What would he have done? He could simply have failed to insert the capsule. But Butch was sure that, if Pilgrim had been a Soviet agent, he would have been too wily and farsighted to have taken such a simple course, which could have threatened the whole operation. There was always a possibility, however remote, that Al might somehow get access to the module again – as indeed he had – and if he had found that the capsule had not been inserted, Al would have drawn the only possible conclusion: Turbid was simply a device to make a present of the Mockingbird to the Soviets. And the whole purpose of securing the culture and pretending to insert it would have been to willie Al and the rest of the Disciples. No, Butch told himself, Pilgrim would certainly not have taken that risk. Instead he would have emptied the capsule before inserting it into the module. From what Al had told him, it would have been a simple operation – just the removal of a sealed phial.

It followed, then, that if the capsule in his icebox was empty then Ross was almost certainly a Soviet agent. But if it still contained the clone, which Al had assured him would survive indefinitely in a refrigerator, then Ross was surely in the clear.

Butch considered one further possibility but dismissed it. If Ross had been a Soviet agent he might have been using Turbid to provide his masters with both the Mockingbird and the clone. If he had informed Moscow that the capsule contained live culture, and exactly where it was, it could have been removed when the crates containing the Mockingbird had arrived at the Soviet Embassy in Vienna. But Ross had already known that the Soviets were going to be given the clone with official blessing, so it was not conceivable, to Butch's mind, that he would have taken an unnecessary risk in supplying it surreptitiously in such a way. The culture was highly dangerous material and in intricate operations, so prone to human error, things could, and often did, go wrong.

As he towelled himself, Butch felt rather pleased with his ingenuity and made a decision. He would take the capsule to his office next day and get Al to have it examined secretly, professionally, and under totally safe circumstances.

His first telephone call from his office in the West Wing of the White House early next morning, before his staff had arrived, was to Al at his home but he was told that he had left the Service, working out his notice in the form of accumulated vacation which he had rarely taken in the past. He was already on his way to Hawaii. Offhand, Butch could not think of anybody else whom he could involve in such a supremely confidential business, which involved his own integrity as well as Pilgrim's.

Whatever Al might say, loyalty to Pilgrim must have been a potent factor in his decision to quit his career. Loyalty and his feeling of guilt. Butch opened his briefcase and took out the bulging padded envelope into which he had thrust the little cash box containing the capsule and which he had marked Top Secret with a thick felt pen. What about his own loyalty to Ross? And his own guilt? And what did he face himself if the result of an examination indicated that Ross had been a traitor?

The whole of his own career would be in the discard because it had been so intertwined with Pilgrim's. All the operations they had done together would have been blown in advance, their results hopelessly adulterated with bullshitsky. If Ross had been a mole then Butch had been the biggest willie of all time. As he weighed the envelope in his hand, his faith in himself as well as in Pilgrim was in the balance.

What was he in danger of doing? If analysis of the capsule indicated that Pilgrim had been a Soviet agent, should he report his suspicions? He wouldn't be thanked for transmitting his doubts to the President, to Arnold, or to anybody else. Bearers of bad news never were. It would create too many problems. Wouldn't he be playing the KGB's game by starting a massive mole-hunt for officers whom Pilgrim might have recruited or favoured? The wholly admirable Al would, automatically, be the biggest suspect of all! He would be recalled and subjected to polygraph tests and every other indignity. The damage to morale would be enormous – not least to his own. If the doubts became public he would have to resign as Chief of Staff because his judgement would be so devalued. That would seriously damage the President. The chain reaction would rumble on for years.

On all counts, ignorance was the lesser of the evils. In any case, in the light of morning and the work-a-day ambience of his office, the idea that Ross could be a traitor seemed utterly ridiculous. He needed to snap out of 'foul contagion's spread', his own sceptomania. It was dreadful to entertain such doubts about his old friend. What was it Belloc had written? 'There's nothing worth the wear of winning save laughter and the love of friends.' That was the real, the worthwhile world.

Ross had over-reached himself through being too long in the game and he had paid the price. There was nothing more to it than that. He had sometimes made common cause with the 'opposition' but diplomats and politicians did that too when it suited. Collaboration was a slippery slope which could so easily avalanche into conspiracy. It was possible that he had got himself so involved with the GRU that he didn't know who the hell he was working for half the time, his mind fogged by self-deluding deceptions. But whatever he had done would only have been in line of duty. His problem had been an excess of loyalty, not treachery.

Arnold had been altogether too impetuous in discarding such an irreplaceable fount of experience as Ross. He had put his personal prejudice before the interest of the Agency. Ross should, at least, have been retained as a consultant – for advice – and he would do what he could to see that such a unique asset was not just left to rot.

Butch rose in a determined way, picked up the envelope and took it down to the White House incinerator, which he switched on. There was no one about as he took out the cash box, which still felt cold and had rusted slightly. He unlocked it and tipped the plastic capsule into his palm, holding it rather gingerly. Wasting no time, he opened the incinerator and dropped the capsule into its roaring flames, closing it immediately.

He experienced no regrets, only relief, as he strolled back to his office, where he consulted his diary. Christmas was not far away and would provide him with a good excuse to telephone Ross. But, what the hell, why wait? Why not ring the poor old devil now, instead of leaving him to stew in his grievance?

'Ross, this is Butch. I'd like to come round to take a glass of Macallan off you some time soon. I've got some quail shooting for us in Georgia. We need to fix dates.'

Chapter Forty-eight

The conversation had been cordial, with no rancour raised on either side, as the two old friends arranged a meeting and noted it in their diaries. Pilgrim smiled for the first time that day as he put the telephone down. He had been depressed enough by the news of Pryce's death before Al's early morning call from the airport, confirming his final departure from Langley and from his life. Now, he was not finished after all, he told himself, as he twisted his wedding ring. On the contrary, Butch must need him, for advice if for nothing else.

Most excellent access was about to be restored. And feedback. He might not work for the Agency but he could still be an agent of influence – in the highest places. That way, he could still have some hand in channelling the course of history.

'We're back in business, boy,' he said to Dallas quietly, but with deliberation and a note of triumph.

Had Butch opened the clone capsule he would have found it empty but would have drawn the wrong conclusion about Pilgrim's motives. He had been near the truth: Pilgrim had been in dangerously intimate collaboration with the GRU, to the point of frank conspiracy, but was not and never had been a traitor or, in his mind, anything remotely like one. And the whole sequence of events had been more bizarre than Butch could ever have surmised.

Vladimir Primarkov had never been one to 'sit on his fanny'. Far from it. Realizing that he was being cornered for the kill before the forthcoming summit by a clique headed by Chevalsky, with his whole position, and possibly his life, in danger, he was faced with only one course of action. If he could strike first and eliminate Chevalsky in circumstances which disgraced him, then all support for him would also vanish.

In discussions with Tamara, the only person in whom he dared confide at that stage, he had quickly concluded that any attempts to use his political power to dismiss Chevalsky without manifest reason would fail because, in such a showdown, the military chiefs, with only one exception, would be ranged firmly on the KGB Chairman's side.

He knew he was too isolated to achieve anything on his own. He desperately needed at least one powerful ally by his side. So he had looked for someone who could have the same urgent interest – the elimination of Chevalsky. There was only one, the military exception, who happened to be someone he admired and liked: General Yuri Yakushkin, the head of the GRU, with whom he had deliberately made friends to protect himself from the KGB and its chief.

He had observed Yakushkin's personal distaste for Chevalsky and his appreciation that if the KGB Chairman ever became General Secretary he would be summarily dismissed from the GRU. Primarkov was not close enough to the GRU chief to know his real view about radical reform of the Soviet system but he sensed that he would support his bid for greater freedom and reduction in the KGB's power within the Soviet Union.

It could be dangerous to approach him but there was no alternative and Primarkov considered Yakushkin to be an honourable man, with a strong traditional sense of duty and love of his country. Further, and this was crucial, he was not politically ambitious.

The immediate problem was how could he meet Yakushkin in private without arousing suspicions which could alert his enemy? Being all-powerful had its disadvantages. He was guarded at all times. Every minute was monitored one way or another. Moscow was in winter's grip so secret trysts in open country were impracticable anyway. Tamara supplied the answer. She would rope in Yakushkin's wife to assist with one of her more prominent charitable organizations, ensure that her recruitment was given publicity and then invite her to dinner at the Moscow residence, with Yakushkin accompanying her.

'Do you play chess, General?' Primarkov asked when the foursome meal had been concluded.

'I do indeed.'

'Then let us leave the ladies to their talk of children's hospitals and crèches and see what we can do with our wits.'

The game had moved slowly, being more in the nature of a fencing match as Primarkov sounded out Yakushkin and proceeded to a gambit he had conceived before his guest's arrival. Picking up the black knight he had won, he remarked, 'I understand, General, that in your world of code-names you refer to Comrade Chevalsky as the "Horseman".'

Yakushkin nodded with a bleak smile. 'I think it's more of a jibe than a code-name. If that man has ever had close contact with a horse it could only have been some mangy cart-horse on the farm at Chelyabinsk.'

With deliberation, the smiling Primarkov then moved one of his own knights into a position where Yakushkin could take it with a pawn. He looked at his opponent fixedly before removing his finger from the piece. The message was not lost on the General. 'Eliminated!' Yakushkin declared with obvious glee as he removed the 'Horseman' with a flourish.

'Tell me, General, entirely between us and these four walls, what do you think of Chevalsky? I admit to you that I dislike him.'

'That makes two of us. My professional priority is the same as yours and if he ever secured full power it could never be achieved.'

'To what are you referring, General?'

'The elimination of the American military forces from Europe. Thanks to your policies they are virtually on the way home. If Chevalsky and the other hardliners took over they would never go.'

'That's certain. And what do you think would happen to you if, by some mischance, he succeeded to my position?'

'I wouldn't last a day. He has made that very clear.'

'So it is rather important to you that I remain,' Primarkov said rhetorically.

'Not just important, General Secretary. Essential. And not only for my sake. For the nation's.'

'You approve of what I am trying to do?'

'Totally. And it follows that I disapprove of those who are trying to undermine you. I have my sources and lately I have been very close to warning you about what is being prepared by people I can only call conspirators but I had no safe means of access.'

'Well, you have now, General.'

From then on it had been plainer talking, with the chess abandoned in the interest of a starker challenge – the disgracing of the KGB chief so thoroughly that even his friends would have to agree to his removal.

They had quickly agreed that in any kind of straightforward showdown they could find themselves with no military support when it might be guns and tanks that mattered. So any effective assistance could only come from outside the Soviet Union. Where in the world was there a potential ally with the same interests?

There was only one answer – in the White House. Rockwell's friendship was a ready-made asset and they cast around for some way to capitalize on it.

'Obviously I cannot make any direct request to Rockwell for assistance,' Primarkov said. 'Trying to involve the President officially in any such operation would force him to veto it. And, however critical the circumstances, there is no way that I could put myself into a position which would allow Rockwell to think I am beholden to him.'

If he remained in office the whole future was going to depend on relations with America and he could not negotiate from such an inferior position – at the summit or at any other time.

'However, I can prepare the ground by making one or two judicious telephone calls to the President,' he continued. 'I think that I understand his mind well enough to stimulate his concern, and maybe his connivance, without appearing to.'

The little man had appreciated that Rockwell would have to be willied into playing his part so effectively that he would believe it was his own idea.

'As for the precise arrangements for discrediting the "knight", which is how we had better refer to our quarry in any future communications, you are the professional, General, and I leave them to you. We should communicate as little as possible and, when we have to, it had better be through our wives. I take it that your wife is thoroughly trustworthy.'

'One hundred per cent, General Secretary.'

'Then *Derzanie cheloveka – Zalog uspekha*,' he said as they shook hands prior to joining the ladies. He felt confident that the mutual interdependence of all four of them guaranteed the absolute secrecy essential to their survival.

'Achievement through individual initiative.' Some achievement!

Some initiative! And it would certainly have to be individual. With one exception, there was nobody in the GRU whom Yakushkin could completely trust with such explosive information. The GRU was always infiltrated at various levels by KGB spies reporting to Chevalsky. And any leak in that direction could impel the conspirators to swift and ruthless action.

As soon as he was in his car, Yakushkin lit the cigarette he had been pining for all evening and wasted no time in putting his mind to the task he had accepted so willingly. His wife appreciated the need for silence in front of the driver, even though the glass partition had been closed. There would be time enough for sharing their exhilaration at becoming close to the Soviet Union's First Couple. Madame Yakushkina spent the drive home looking out at the day's snow which had been piled on the roadsides, mainly by female labour, and was freezing in the moonlight. Her husband stared ahead, his cigarette glowing occasionally, as he realized that any conceivable operation would, somehow, have to involve the CIA. Again, there was no way that such assistance could be forthcoming with official CIA approval. For that, the CIA chief, Arnold, would have to be involved and would inevitably reject the whole concept as a gross interference in the internal politics of another country. By the time the limousine pulled alongside the entrance to his Moscow apartment, Yakushkin had decided that the only route lay through Ross Pilgrim. He would have to look for some significant circumstance in which their interests were the same.

Fortunately, and by chance, there was a completely reliable conduit in place – Colonel Peter Ivashutin, whom Pilgrim called Brown Derby. He also happened to be the one GRU officer whom Yakushkin could take into his confidence with absolute safety, one of very few with the privilege of reporting directly to him in the GRU chief's personal code.

When he awoke next morning the full measure of the mandate seemed even more alarming but he had slept well and his mental agility displayed itself in his message to Ivashutin. It was a report of an assassination attempt on the General Secretary and his wife during a visit to Volgograd with the instruction that it be transmitted to Pilgrim with all speed. It was total disinformation, fabricated by the GRU chief while being driven to his office. It was planted to prepare the ground with Rockwell and his Chief of Staff for what was to

335

come and was supported by contrived collateral evidence, including the disappearance of the Primarkovs from the public scene for several weeks. Tamara had feigned intermittent migraine while her husband had busied himself with desk work and meetings in ways which did not excite comment in Moscow.

Pilgrim had perused it with his customary caution and passed it to Arnold who had lost no time in transmitting it to the President's desk.

Alone at his own desk in the Aquarium, Yakushkin had not had to look far for a common interest with Pilgrim. He knew of Pilgrim's personal hatred of Chevalsky, who had often boasted about the episode in Salzburg when the CIA man had been forced into retreat to the sound of ironic KGB laughter. So collaboration in getting rid of him could appeal and might be hard to resist. The idea of Chevalsky achieving such a triumph as to assume command of the Soviet Union would surely be anathema to Pilgrim.

To establish the principle of co-operation in the venture, Brown Derby had then approached Pilgrim indirectly through the dead-drops emptied by Al.

The first of the brief messages excited Pilgrim as he deciphered it: 'Chevalsky and certain other Politburo members are plotting to oust Primarkov within the next few weeks with the intention of wrecking the projected summit.' There was no mention of Yakushkin, which the GRU chief had strictly forbidden.

Yakushkin's appreciation of Pilgrim's reaction had been correct. The political convulsion of a successful coup, with all the internal upheavals it would cause, had immediate appeal as he pondered on it while sitting at home, where Brown Derby's messages were always delivered by Al. But the prospect of the detested Chevalsky as head of the Soviet state had outweighed all other considerations. But was Brown Derby's information correct? Or was it disinformation which had been planted on him for an ulterior purpose?

Always fearful of such a trap, Pilgrim had skilfully pumped Butch who, without revealing his Presidential source, had confirmed that Primarkov was indeed on the slide and that Chevalsky seemed likely to replace him.

In his next coded message, Brown Derby had then dangled in front of Pilgrim the concept of a joint operation making use of GRU facilities which could oust Chevalsky. At that stage there was no indication what the operation might be but, in principle, Pilgrim found it highly attractive.

It had not escaped him that the more positive purpose must be the saving of Primarkov. He had ambivalent views about that – unable to make up his mind whether it was in the US interest for the little man to succeed or fail, for he greatly feared the growing pressure, not only in Germany, but among the American people themselves, for the withdrawal of all American troops from Europe. The alternative, however, of seeing Chevalksy reach the pinnacle of power and doing nothing to stop him, had proved totally unacceptable. Surely, he told himself, seeking resolution, it was his duty to seize any opportunity to disgrace the head of the KGB, with all the disruption that would cause!

He had not been misled by Brown Derby's efforts to give the impression that the proposal was his own. He had sensed that such an ambitious venture could only have emanated from the top and that he would, effectively, be collaborating with the GRU chief but it would be at a decent distance – with long tongs, using 'not–quite speak' for communication. While each would know what the other was saying, neither could be accused of collusion, or at least it would be deniable.

He had never collaborated so deeply before but it was a possibly unique opportunity really to influence the course of world events. If it succeeded it could be his greatest Pilgrimage. But it would have to be to his specifications and he would have to be in command, as he made clear in his quick coded response to Brown Derby.

As Yakushkin deciphered it, he had no objections to Pilgrim believing he was in command of events as long as it served his interests. He had already worked out the bare-bone parameters for success. Somehow Chevalsky had to be induced to call Rockwell's honesty and integrity into question to such a degree that Primarkov's trust in him could be challenged in the Politburo. Clearly, this would have to involve some new incident which would have to be manufactured. President Rockwell would somehow have to be involved in it and Pilgrim was told no more than that the ground had been prepared in that direction.

With Pilgrim's tension mounting as each new message was brought in by the indefatigable Al, the challenge alone became irresistible, apart from the prize if the operation succeeded. Pilgrim cast around.

Time was short. Whatever he did had to be done without delay, with 'tools' readily to hand. What 'tools' were available?

Operation Turbid, the infiltration of some electronic equipment infected with the clone somewhere into the Soviet Union, was already early in train. As then conceived, its main objective had been to inflict damage on the Soviet defences in some area not yet decided. Sary Shagan was the target of choice but getting it there was something of a pipedream. Since it would be the GRU that would 'buy' the deception, the discrediting of its chief, Yakushkin, had been an important secondary bonus. Always flexible, Pilgrim had asked himself, 'Can Turbid be modified to fit the new requirement – getting rid of Chevalsky?'

By that time he knew, from Butch, that the Russians were going to be given the clone so, in his next reply, he had felt able to tell Brown Derby about it and his intention of using it in Turbid, knowing that he would immediately report back to Yakushkin. His purpose was to sound out the GRU leader concerning any specific ideas he might have for using the situation to undermine Chevalsky.

Yakushkin could not have been more delighted or relieved. He had already been at work preparing several possible scenarios in which, with GRU assistance, the CIA would be permitted to inflict such damage on the KGB and Soviet interests generally that Chevalsky could be disgraced in front of his colleagues.

He had not been happy about any of them. They would all have severely damaged Soviet intelligence assets though, in the critical circumstances, that could be regarded as an acceptable trade-off. Then, when Brown Derby's information about the silicon-eating clone and Operation Turbid had reached his desk, Yakushkin had quickly spotted how it might be utilized in a scenario which should cause no real damage at all. On the contrary, Soviet Intelligence would benefit. He had consigned his previous scenarios to the flames and, stretching out his legs, had fiddled with his moustache feeling that he had fair cause to be more than pleased with himself. At that stage he was not sufficiently sure of success to report to Primarkov, from whom he was keeping himself remote. Hopefully that would be accomplished later, through their wives.

So it had fallen to Brown Derby to be the first to suggest the Mockingbird to Pilgrim as the medium for the clone and he had come to the same choice, which happened to be the obvious one.

338

One of Brown Derby's messages had contained the electrifying information: 'When the Soviet government was trying to purchase the Mockingbird it was required for Sary Shagan and that is where it will go if it can be obtained by other means.' Momentarily, Pilgrim had regretted that Operation Turbid would not be going ahead as planned. As jointly conceived with Brown Derby, there would have to be a major change to it. It would be essential that the Mockingbird should *not* be contaminated though it had to be fitted with a sneaky. This meant presenting the Russians with the forbidden equipment but that was a small trade-off in view of the magnitude of the goal, and the President had wanted them to have it anyway. The new deception – Skinsaver – was to be focused on making Chevalsky and his KGB henchmen believe that it *was* contaminated.

The challenge extended all Pilgrim's ability and experience. He weighed up the elements. If Chevalsky took the bait it could be the perfect dangle, his long-sought 'grand-daddy'.

It had to be another Pilgrimage with need-to-know kept to the limit. He had never been prepared to let anyone know the extent of his collaboration with the GRU and, this time, it was on a scale that could be dangerously misinterpreted. Those who had to be involved in the operation would have to be willied into playing their part, believing it was something quite different. Al had already organized the preparation of the sneaky and the capsule so it had to appear to him to be going ahead as planned. Pilgrim could not be seen by Al to be making a present of the Mockingbird to the Soviets, as he would be if the capsule was not inserted. That could raise all manner of suspicions in Al's mind. So he had inserted it after removing the phial containing the clone.

Far from being fogged, Pilgrim's brain was functioning with the clarity of desert air.

With the GRU's connivance, it all seemed to be plain sailing except for the involvement of the President. How could that be achieved with certainty? Before he could be entwined in the plot, even tacitly, he would have to be convinced that the source of the infection had been removed from the Mockingbird. Pilgrim could do nothing directly. It could only be done through an intermediary and that had to be Butch.

He had already decided that Butch would have to be brought in anyway because, to further Chevalsky's belief that the Mockingbird was infected, there had to be a sneaky for the KGB to find. And Pilgrim could not get access to the Mockingbird at Vandenberg Air Base without Butch's co-operation.

Pilgrim had thought long and hard about the dangerously deeper involvement of his old friend. He could not tell him the real purpose of the operation without putting the White House Chief of Staff in an impossible position and exposing the extent of his own conspiracy with Yakushkin to a dangerous degree. It would have to be done indirectly, through a willie, and the only one to hand was Al.

So how could Al be induced to tell Butch the truth? For that purpose, Pilgrim had exploited the doubts which Al was displaying, if silently, about the whole operation of insinuating the clone. His wild talk of pushing Primarkov off his perch had been deliberate. So had his cynical remarks about the surreptitious involvement of the Chief of Staff. He had not been 'over the top', as Al and Butch had imagined. Far from it. He had read both their minds accurately and had functioned like a conjurer forcing the cards which they had both taken.

As though at his command, Al and Butch had removed the clone capsule purely to prevent him from wrecking the summit. He had been confident that they had done so, for on his drive to take Dallas for a walk in the nearby park, he had deliberately passed Butch's apartment and seen Al's car parked by the lobby. That observation had assured him that Butch would inform the President, a requirement which was essential to the final ousting of Chevalsky. That could only come from the President's personal assurance to Primarkov that the Mockingbird was not infected.

Rockwell had risen to the situation like a trout to a fly, sensing an opportunity and asking Butch to work something out to save Primarkov. Though Butch had mentioned the need for Skinsaver, half jokingly, to Pilgrim, he could not possibly involve him in the peculiar circumstances which had arisen. Pilgrim had always wanted to fill Primarkov full of buckshot, anyway. So Butch had turned to Al.

Leaving the irreducible minimum to chance, Pilgrim had drafted a letter ready to send to the KGB Resident and set in motion Chevalsky's fatal doubts about the Mockingbird. But he had the forethought to realize that, if Al's mind and Butch's functioned as he believed they would, Al might also be required to send such a letter.

And if two such letters were received by the Resident it would ruin the whole exercise because the KGB would then, undoubtedly, smell a deception.

When appraised of the arrival of Al's letter by Brown Derby, his source of feedback, Pilgrim had smiled appreciatively not only at his own foresight but at the polished professionalism of his protégé. Presented with the parameters, Al had followed the established Pilgrimage guidelines and, with no knowledge of what Pilgrim was really doing, had come to the same conclusion as to how they should be used to discredit Chevalsky. When, eventually, he learned the exact contents of Al's letter, he found it was almost identical to his own. He had certainly fashioned his chief Disciple in his own image and his behaviour had given him immense satisfaction.

Between them, Pilgrim and Yakushkin had organized all the collateral which had fooled Chevalsky, including Brown Derby's defection. Yakushkin had been involved in organizing the bullshitsky fed to the sneaky at Sary Shagan and Pilgrim had known what to expect. In Al's presence, he had needed to go through the motions of accepting the sneaky reports as genuine but, to him, all they provided was proof that Chevalsky had taken the bait.

It had indeed been a grand–daddy dangle. Yakushkin had dangled it in front of Pilgrim. Pilgrim had dangled it in front of Al, Al had dangled it in front of Butch, and Butch had dangled it in front of the President. Finally, it had all been dangled in front of Chevalsky. Between them all, as Pilgrim put it, 'they had torn Chevalsky up for ass paper'.

Pilgrim had achieved his place in history and did not care that nobody else would ever know it. It could be helpful to the Agency if the details could be recorded as the perfect example of how a complex and highly successful operation could be constructed out of existing elements – the 'tools' to hand. But he would not be writing any memoirs. All his secrets would die with him. That was the way it should be.

From the start he had know that, like all operations, Turbid would exact a price. It would lay his friendship with Butch on the line. He would look a willie in the eyes of both Butch and Al. He would even have been seen to have committed the professional crime of having 'done a Hoover' regarding Brown Derby, who had, indeed, been a 'Fedora'. They were sacrifices he was prepared to make for the

341

glittering prize which had given him such personal satisfaction. Then the much bigger penalty, which he had not foreseen, had been imposed – his dismissal.

From the beginning, Primarkov had been greatly concerned about his position in being beholden to Rockwell, who would always believe that the operation had been his idea. 'Somehow,' he had instructed Yakushkin, 'the Americans must be made to understand that no favours are to be expected for services rendered. I don't mind how you do it but it must be done.'

In fulfilling that tall order Yakushkin was completely on his own. He had cast around without success until the windfall of the official handover of the silicon-eating clone to the Soviets fell into his lap.

His suggestion of sending back the Mockingbird duly infected had appealed to Primarkov at once, even though it had meant sacrificing the equipment. 'I must have my message made loud and plain and that's a way of doing it that they cannot fail to understand,' the General Secretary had pronounced, with jubilation.

As the originator of the concept of the White House intervention, Primarkov believed that he had really engineered his own salvation, the rest being mere mechanics. What Rockwell had done had been in his own and America's interests. So he felt no gratitude.

Relaxed at Chevalsky's old desk in KGB headquarters, it had not escaped Yakushkin that sending back the infected Mockingbird would be highly dangerous for Pilgrim. But that was a bonus. Now that Skinsaver had been accomplished, it was back to battle stations with the CIA. In their collaborative effort Pilgrim had displayed such admirable skill that the sooner he could be eliminated from the intelligence scene the better for the KGB. Getting rid of him could be his first major success in his new position, Yakushkin told himself. One that Primarkov would surely applaud.

There was nothing personal in his animosity towards Pilgrim, as there had been on Chevalsky's part. But he had known, from Brown Derby, that part of Pilgrim's original purpose with Operation Turbid had been to discredit and probably unseat him. So he owed him nothing, in spite of his recent role. In the deception game there were no debts of honour.

When the disaster of his dismissal had followed, Pilgrim had felt no hard feelings against Yakushkin. It was what he would have done himself. It was the way of the secrets world, the way things had to be done. As he had always told his recruits, he was as expendable as anyone else in the cut and thrust of intelligence operations and he had meant it. Nor, true to his principles, had he permitted himself the indulgence of any regrets.

Though Chevalsky had gone and Primarkov was firmly in the saddle, at least until the next attempt to unseat him, Pilgrim's satisfaction with his truly historic achievement was not nearly as lasting as he had expected. A stickler for self-discipline, when necessary, he had always derided addicts of any kind, being convinced that they could resolve their problems by sufficient effort of will. Now he himself was suffering from severe withdrawal symptoms, near to gnawing his knuckles and frankly in need of a 'fix'.

With Butch back in regular contact, a 'fix' which would give him particular satisfaction had come to mind. All the elements for another exciting deception operation could soon be to hand, with The Nephews readily available to break the publicity which would be essential to its success. He had figured out a sophisticated scenario, aimed at the adversary, which should work, provided he could obtain further assistance from the GRU. And he felt confident that he would get it because, again, their interests would be the same.

'We shall have to leave you for a while,' he said, stroking Dallas's handsome head. 'And you won't like that, will you, with no Al to take you out?'

Betty would be getting her way, after all, earlier in the spring than she had hoped. With no conduit with the GRU in place, now that Brown Derby had gone, it would be necessary to re-establish contact. Vienna would be the most convenient venue but Assisi would be much less likely to raise any suspicion. A trip to Assisi could be a pilgrimage for both of them.

He settled down, with paper, pen, a stiff Scotch and a cigarette, to inject some detail into Operation Benedict.